D0951882

First Edition

This is a work of fiction. Names, places, characters, and incidents are either the products of the author's imagination or are used fictitiously.

Arcade Publishing books may be purchased in bulk at special discounts for sales promotion, corporate gifts, fund-raising, or educational purposes. Special editions can also be created to specifications. For details, contact the Special Sales Department, Arcade Publishing, 307 West 36th Street, 11th Floor, New York, NY 10018 or arcade@skyhorsepublishing.com.

Arcade Publishing® is a registered trademark of Skyhorse Publishing, Inc.®, a Delaware corporation.

Visit our website at www.arcadepub.com.
Visit the author's website at www.jamescharlesworthauthor.com.

10 9 8 7 6 5 4 3 2 1

Library of Congress Cataloging-in-Publication Data

Names: Charlesworth, James, 1977–
    author.
Title: The patricide of George Benjamin Hill : a novel / James Charlesworth.
Description: First edition. | New York, NY : Skyhorse Publishing, [2019]
Identifiers: LCCN 2018035876 (print) | LCCN 2018050368 (ebook) | ISBN
    9781510731820 (ebook) | ISBN 9781510731790 (hardcover : alk. paper)
Classification: LCC PS3603.H37659 (ebook) | LCC PS3603.H37659 P38 2019
    (print) | DDC 813/.6—dc23
LC record available at https://lccn.loc.gov/2018035876

Cover design by Erin Seaward-Hiatt
Cover illustration: iStockphoto

Printed in the United States of America

Fathers are teachers of the true and not-true, and no father ever knowingly teaches what is not true. In a cloud of unknowing, then, the father proceeds with his instruction.

—Donald Barthelme, *The Dead Father*

Alaska

Sunday, September 9, 2001

FOUR HOURS IN, HIS PLAN nearly dies. A storm whites out the sky above Icy Bay, obscuring the 18,000-foot glacial dump of Mt. St. Elias. He has piloted his secondhand DHC Beaver down from Fairbanks on a day that dawned brilliant with autumn, the wilderness a thousand-hued carpet. Now the system has stormed in from the southwest, roiling off the Pacific and blooming silver on the ridgeline of the Wrangell Mountains, the corridor of light from the retrofitted headlamps illuminating the precipitation that rattles the airframe and freezes on impact.

He is a veteran of this weather, has nearly twenty years of bush experience—has piloted this battered vessel as far north as Nome, as far south as Kodiak Island, has guided it through storms like the end of the world to set it down on strips of fireweed the size of city driveways, has logged more hours than half the so-called pilots flying commercial jets in the Lower 48. But today was the one day he had wished for calm weather, had hoped for clear skies to give him time to think.

From Juneau, he will catch a flight south to Seattle, from there on to Las Vegas and then by car east to Omaha via Denver. But first there is the process of selling his plane. A potential buyer has responded to his advertisements in the equipment trader and is meeting him today at the airport. He has already sold his pickup truck, his guns, his hunting and trapping equipment, has already foregone every possession, including the cabin and parcel of land straddling the Canadian border where he'd thought he would spend the remainder of his life. Why has he done this? He has done it at the behest of the calling that has tormented him for the past three years. He has done it for the money that will help him to procure the object that has become his preoccupation, the motive that has led him to track down and send letters to the three siblings he has not seen in over twenty years, that has led him now—in the year of his forty-first birthday—to be on his way to Omaha, Nebraska, to find and confront the man he now refuses to call Father.

It almost dies up here, in the turbulent solitude of fifteen thousand feet, impact ice in the air intake causing the engine to run rough, a drop in manifold pressure. The tachometer flickers as ice begins to form in the carburetor. The engine coughs and then is silent. He lowers the nose into the whine of wind and procession of cloud, flaps at cruise to maintain air speed, opens the throttle and primes with the wobble pump. Up ahead, invisible, is the face of a mountain, a cliff side, a spectacular death. If the restart fails, a dead engine landing is impossible. He closes his eyes and waits for it, and then, against every lesson life has taught him up to this point, the engine crackles and returns. The lights of the instrument panel dazzle. He reengages the controls and imagines he can hear the landing gear scraping the frozen peaks of the foothills.

The system passes and he is aloft in the blue dome over Glacier Bay, the archipelago speckling the golden ocean, an obscured face behind the grimy glass of this prop plane that has served him for two decades. The sun is at his back and showing purple on the snow-covered mountainside, assuring him. *Yes, you were saved today. You were saved from certain destruction in order to finish what you have started.* As he radios in his descent, he watches the light prism on the water and the tin rooftops of a salmon town and the icy ridge above and whispers something inaudible. Not a prayer—he doesn't believe in God—but a pledge. To his twin sister, to his half brothers, to his estranged mother. And finally, to the man he refuses to call Father, the man whose far-off mansion on the plains marks the X-spot of this three-thousand-mile journey, the man whose life story will always serve as preamble to his own.

Sons and Wives
of
Fast Food and
Oil

It begins half a century earlier.

On a sun-dried day in January 1956—seventy-five degrees in mid-winter, for there were no seasons here in San Berdoo, in the arid valley that separated the city of the stars from the desert—a twenty-four-year-old delivery boy named George Hill (though he went by Georgie in those days) arrived in his four-axle delivery truck in the sandlot out back of the burger stand that was the last on his route every Friday. He was sweating. He'd worked fifty hours this week. He and his wife had had an argument the night before, an argument centered around several small things and one not-small thing. When the raised voices had proven inadequate for conveying her feelings, she'd thrown a pot at him and struck him in the face, which was why he had a Band-Aid on his forehead, the skin beneath which was itching and driving him crazy. Yet another thing that was driving him crazy. His young son, GB, was turning five in two weeks, and he was afraid he'd stopped loving him. Or maybe he'd simply stopped loving his wife, the woman who only six years previously had advanced to the final round of the country's most prestigious beauty pageant, whose graceful promenades across the stage and runways at Boardwalk Hall could not have predicted her proficiency in pot throwing, and who'd told him, just months before, that what he'd been dreading was true. She was pregnant again.

The first time he'd heard these words from Mary it had been confirmation of his arrival. Until then, he'd been a silent, restless boy, a directionless, insecure adolescent. He had avoided mirrors throughout his youth, originally because there were none to be found in the drafty ramshackle homestead on the Oklahoma panhandle whose 160 acres of dying fields had formed the bleak backdrop of his earliest years. Later because he couldn't bear to look at himself: despised his lank greasy hair and olive skin and heavy brow. Hated his long arms and the unavoidable slouch that was his father's slouch, the slouch of an overworked Okie raised up in spartan conditions on the great plains, on plows and in sweltering stables, endless days of sweat and sore muscles. In his siblings he had always detected inheritances from their mother, her stern but gentle eyes, her coarse but lively hair, her soft-spoken wisdom. But not in Georgie. He was his father's utterly graceless offspring.

He'd met Mary at a place just like this one—just like the burger joints at which he now arrived every day with his truck full of vats of grease, delivering the liquid fuel that kept this industry going. He'd been a hood in those days—or at least had tried to fashion himself as one—drove with a manufactured confidence and aggressiveness the T-bird he'd purchased from a shady friend of a friend, cash only and a stain on the passenger seat he liked to imagine was blood, the pedal to the floor as he blazed along California freeways willing the world to believe he belonged. It was an illusion he'd worked hard to craft, an illusion in whose grasp he could almost forget Oklahoma, except when he saw himself in the rearview. San

Berdoo was fifty miles east of the epicenter where lived the stars and starlets he'd once watched on the big screen at the Omni in Bakersfield before he'd moved down here. He'd gone every day the summer he'd turned six, enough that he'd memorized every line of some of his favorites, *Dodge City* and *Stagecoach*, begging dimes on street corners to gain admittance to the dark, shady theater on hot days because his father never had a dime to spare, never would. A philosophy rather than an economic decision.

When they'd moved down here the summer the war ended, his father had one message for Georgie: "Never be afraid," he'd told his young son, "to take a risk in life. You look at all the successful people in the world, I'll tell you one thing they all have in common. They all had a chance to take a risk or sit on their ass. And not a one of them chose to sit on his ass. What do you think we did when we saw that dust bowl rising up around us? Did we sit back on our ass? No sir. We picked up and we moved on. And look at us now."

This in his used Packard on the way south from Bakersfield, just the two of them, the rest of what had been a family of seven eradicated on the trip west over Route 66 and in the war in Europe. His father had heard of work in the newly thriving city of San Bernardino, a dusty valley in the center of a bowl at the foot of the mountains sharing the name of the same saint. He'd heard there were all sorts of jobs springing up for men willing to get up off their duff and do it. Good, honest work for a solid wage. Not this shady business on the grape farms, working like a slave for wages little better than the Mexicans'. He'd come down a week earlier and gotten them a place, had found a job cleaning swimming pools. Came home and told Georgie it wasn't easy in this heat, wasn't back breaking, though. Wasn't nothing he couldn't handle. Went back the next day and fell in the pool and drowned. Couldn't swim. Was an

Okie through and through. Nobody had been around to hear his splashing. The folks who owned the house had arrived home the next day to find a figure in a starched white uniform floating face down in their swimming pool. Had called the cleaning company, who'd come over to pick out the body.

Georgie hadn't heard the news for two days. He'd been locked away in the new apartment by himself, thinking that his father was probably trying to impress his new employer by working a straight forty-eight-hour shift. When the knock came at the door, he didn't open it, so they broke in, Children's Services finding him sitting cross-legged on the floor in the still-empty two-room apartment— they'd never owned any furniture in California, Georgie and his dad, hadn't had the chance or the dimes to spare—a dark-eyed boy eating peanut butter out of the jar with a vacant expression, the windows closed though it was another scorcher.

They'd turned him over to orphan support, operated out of a mission-style building near the Rancho Cucamonga line. Two years spent prowling those crowded hallways, waiting in line for stale food and lying in hard cots staring up at a dark ceiling, four to a room, Georgie's bunkmates constantly changing though they were all basically the same: boisterous, scared boys full of implausible tales of one-upmanship and outrageous plans for redemption. On his fifteenth birthday, Georgie and a group of kids he'd met inside had formed a solemn pact to escape and set up on the outside, make some fast cash robbing jewelry stores and maybe some trains, then get into the sort of business that would make them some real money, the business making its way over the border from Mexico. They'd planned and executed a late-night liberation under cover of the smog-laden LA stars, had climbed into the foothills of the San Gabriel Mountains, living in the wilderness for all of seventeen hours before one of their number was attacked by a coyote and had to be taken back down to the city, had to practically have his arm stitched back on, to hear him talk. Their plans for escape fizzled. The boy who'd nearly had his arm chewed off by the coyote was adopted within a month, which touched off a brief smattering of self-injury. It didn't work. Georgie climbed up to the roof of the orphanage and stood looking down at the pavement six stories below, pictured himself executing a graceful dive to splatter on the blacktop, saw his blood, brown and dust-colored like the world he'd come from, the world he knew he belonged to though he couldn't stand even to imagine the worthless, middle-of-nowhere people they'd been back then, working like dogs on 160 acres, twelve hours a day—even him! A four-year-old kid!—and for what? An uncertain existence that could turn like a tornado and did just that the year the rain stopped and the blowing dust swept across the plain, enveloping them all and setting in motion the events that had led to their perilous hike to the Pacific, leaving his mother and little brother and little sister dead of pneumonia and two older brothers shot to pieces on French beaches by bullets the size of bookends. What good was life if these were the sort of decisions it left you with? Whether or not to jump off the roof of a six-story orphanage, the last surviving member of your family? And what about those folks with the swimming pool? Those folks who could afford to have a tub of however-many gallons of water in their backyard—enough water for some schmoe to drown in (for this was how Georgie would ever after think of his father: a schmoe who'd drowned in a swimming pool he was supposed to be cleaning because he was nothing more than a stupid Okie trying to fit in out West). What was it that made one person like they were and another person like Georgie's father? It sure wasn't his father's way. It wasn't following a string of flyers a thousand miles west to grape country to find you were at the end of a long row of ants at an already-dry popsicle stick. It wasn't packing your bags and moving south to some upstart city outside LA just because some Mexican told you there was honest work. But if it wasn't any of these things, then what was it? Georgie saw the haze drift off the desert breeze and thought he caught a glimpse of the same stars he'd once seen so clearly back on the farm, sitting on the back porch with his mama or off in the fields on a retired plow with his older brother Carl and little sister Debbie. He looked at the stars so long and with such fervency that he forgot entirely what he'd come up here to do, and when he remembered where he was and why and had crept over to the edge of the roof and looked down, it filled him with such fear that he had to fold his legs up against his chest, had to wrap his arms around his knees to stop trembling.

One week after he climbed down from the roof and snuck back into his bed just hours before wakeup, he was adopted. A family from San Berdoo who'd filled out an application and waited with their fingers crossed while it was processed and reviewed and eventually approved (they'd suffered through heartache before, had lost three of their own to miscarriage and twice been denied adoptive rights by the state of California) was at last granted the right to bring a child into their home. They were called the Ambersons, Jack and Molly, and they lived in one of the long rows of houses that lined one of the identical streets that had been built along the hillsides during the past ten years—stucco in benign pastel, ranch style with a low-pitched roof and a lawn exactly the size of everyone else's. Jack was a salesman; he sold hand soap to restaurants and businesses, soap in a mechanical dispenser, brand new and all the rage that year. Molly was a former reference librarian who was between jobs. She'd found herself so disturbed by the loss of the first child that she'd quit her job, devoting herself entirely to a new pregnancy and remaining a stay-at-home mom. Two more horrifying rounds of despondency and shock had followed. By the time Georgie arrived at their home, having ridden with them along the new freeway to park along the quiet street in Jack's Buick, she'd been a childless stay-at-home mom for nearly six years.

They led him down the hallway at the back of the house, told him to open the door at the far end and look inside. They'd read his file, knew that he'd never once in his life had his own bedroom, had shared a room at the farmhouse in Oklahoma with three brothers, had roomed at the orphanage with a total of fifteen different bunk-mates (each of them successfully placed with foster families or adopted). They'd expected him to be thrilled about the idea of his own space, his own nine-by-eleven corner of the world in which they vowed to allow him whatever privacy he needed. But Georgie had lost all sentiment for such a gift. Over the years, he'd been moved from room to room as necessity demanded, and so he'd come to consider a bed as merely a bed, a bedroom just the walls that sheltered one while one slept. He had no notion of what they meant when they said he could decorate it as he pleased, could set things up however he wished.

They'd been warned and had steeled themselves against the possibility of his being stalwart. They'd heard tales of newly adopted children who locked themselves in their new bedroom—or, worse yet, the bathroom—for hours, unwilling to accept a new landscape as their own. But what they hadn't anticipated was the response they received from Georgie, who rolled his lower lip in a way that said, "Not bad," then walked directly past them and over to the television—they'd had one at the orphanage, in the lobby—and turned it on and watched *The Lone Ranger* until it was time for lights out.

━━━━

By THE TIME HE WAS eighteen, the television was in his room. He watched it in the darkness of an early summer evening, his eyes black beneath blacker eyebrows, lying on his bed, his upper half propped against a stack of pillows with his head resting on the headboard, the black-and-white image throwing its eerie light over the room and his feet, which were clad in boots at the foot of the bed.

The house was silent, had been silent for hours now while he watched the shows he'd watched so many times he could mouth the cryptic dialogue along with the actors. Jack Amberson had left them, had come home one night to confess to Molly of his indiscretions involving a waitress at one of the restaurants he serviced, had apologized and wept and sought forgiveness from Jesus for his tormented and hell-bound soul. He'd never meant for it to happen, he'd said, but now the poor young girl was pregnant and what could he do? He couldn't do anything but go off with her, for the child she would bear would be his—truly his—and so in the eyes of the Lord would be owed a greater portion of Jack's love and support. Molly had come at him with her ironing board. Jack had barely made it out the door and roared off in his Buick, leaving her collapsed in the painted-green front lawn with her folded-up domestic contraption while Georgie sat watching from the window, feeling something like relief to watch him leave, something like esteem at his willingness to go.

He sat up, swung his legs off the bed, let his heavy boots plunk down on the floor, switched off the television, and stepped out into the warm, breeze-blown evening that smelled of smog and jacaranda. He opened the door of the T-bird he loved so well, started the noisy engine, and drove off along the wide, glinting streets of the valley. Friday nights were for cruising up and down the boulevards, stopping at the drive-in for a burger and a shake, smoking butts in the parking lots before driving into the hills at the foot of the San Bernardino Mountains, taking the 18 up to Panorama Point and beyond, up to Crestline and Moon Lake for long nights with ladies just as wayward as the boys. They all wore white dresses or skirts, as if in contrast to the dark colors of the boys' leather and denim, hair done up stiff with gel, everybody acting like they'd just stepped off the silver screen. He saw her first through a crowd of people, his friends and their girls all gathered at the burger joint while the newest Brando film played on the immense board at the base of the bare brown mountains in the distance, a pale image squared off in the foreground of a landscape so devoid of vegetation they might've been on the moon. He noticed her eyes at first, looking directly at him and then turning away, then back again. A vibrant, intense blue, as if she'd been drawn here, striking and in technicolor at the drive-in theater.

Arrogance was his armor. He pursued girls with an intensity close to hate. He was an Okie. He could never forget this, no matter how hard he tried. He saw himself always from an outsider's per-spective, looked not at the girls he was attempting to woo but instead at himself attempting to woo them, wondered not what the girl was thinking but how the whole ceremony came off to the idly observant bystanders who witnessed his approach. This one looked like Grace Kelly, only sweeter. When she smiled, her lips pursed in a girlish way; she looked at him as she slurped up the last of her milkshake through a pink-and-white striped straw.

They drove out to the lake at midnight, his T-bird hurtling along the ridgeline that overlooked San Berdoo all the way to the Santa Anas and, far beyond, through the haze, the skyline of Los Angeles, obscure and eager.

"I bet you bring a lot of girls up here," she said, the two of them looking out over the valley and the city. She'd already told him all about herself, had talked throughout the car ride because she couldn't get anything out of him, had told him that her mother was a movie actress—"No one you would've heard of"—and her father a director. She'd smiled that puckered smile when he'd told her she should be in movies herself, had explained that she'd been in a few roles as a young girl, had gotten tired of it. The drama and the pressure. It was so shallow, the whole industry. Full of thugs and vapid starlets with reefer madness. Nobody cared about talent. All they cared about was money and favors. When she'd lost out on a role to the daughter of a known mobster, she'd vowed she'd never again act in a movie.

"Now I do beauty contests."

This was one month before she'd learn she'd been selected as a finalist in the Miss California pageant, three months before she'd board a plane bound for Atlantic City, so confident in her victory that when she didn't win it—when she finished third behind Miss North Carolina and, of all people, Miss Oklahoma—it would throw her into a shiftless state of mind in which she considered herself already washed up at the age of eighteen, already having missed out on her dream, a state of mind that would make her give up her aspirations of marrying James Dean and settle for this odd-job-working former farm boy with olive skin and a unibrow. On the night she first met him, however, she was just being playful. She knew his type, was forcibly approached by three or four of them every time she stepped out her front door, had already divided the world into two types of men: those that desired her in silence and those that had the guts to come up and talk to her. She wasn't even attracted to him at first—though he'd grown on her by the time they'd arrived at the lake and looked out over the valley. At first she'd responded just to his manner, his confrontational arrogance. He wasn't from here, she knew. Too uptight. Even when he was driving his fancy shmancy car, he still somehow managed to look uptight. "We should get out," she said. "It's such a gorgeous night."

They walked to the picnic bench that looked out over the string of lights. Freeways and runways and a glistening rim she knew was the Pacific Ocean blending with the sky. "Now you know everything about me," she said. "But what about you?"

She wasn't afraid of him. She knew that whatever success he must've had in the past—whatever history had given him the courage to approach her—was a product of the unease his silence would evoke. But she was a soon-to-be Miss California. She ate boys like him for breakfast. Chewed them up and spit them out. Most women might have worried at the way he clenched his fists all the time, the way his brow became an angry bracket over his eyes. But she touched his leg and encouraged him to confide in her, gave her best smile and waited.

He was growing impatient with anticipation, too. Couldn't wait to crush her small body against this picnic bench, to raise a flush on her cheeks with his urgent movement against her, to hear her making soft noises as he fought his way toward satisfaction. Now she wanted to hear his whole life story, for crying out loud! He didn't mean to tell it to her. He started off by lying, trying to take on the identity of one of those heroes in his Westerns. He said he'd robbed a bank in Van Nuys and gotten away with it, but she laughed, which made him angry enough to tell the truth.

"Fine!" he said. "You wanna hear it? My father drowned in a swimming pool he was getting paid thirty cents an hour to clean. My mother and two of my siblings died on Route 66 and are buried somewhere in the middle of New Mexico. My two older brothers got mowed down on Omaha Beach, and I ended up in a back bedroom in a house in the middle of the worst city in the world with a job cleaning the high school. I've learned one thing, though. I've learned how you can get out. I've learned to watch and wait for your one chance. And that's what I'm doing now. I'm watching and waiting for my one chance."

She leaned toward him for the first time, causing him to part his lips and close his eyes. *Finally, I'm gonna get to bang this broad!* But she only gave him that puckered smile, touched his gelled but somehow still lank hair, and said through ambiguous laughter, "Oh, darling. You're the one who oughta be in pictures!"

He drove her home, unsatisfied, taking backroads into West Hollywood. He hadn't even kissed her, had been unable even to talk to her after he'd spilled his guts as a last-ditch effort, only to have her laugh and think him melodramatic, or flat-out lying, or whatever her comment was meant to say. She didn't let him drop her off at her house, but instead made him stop two blocks away, between Sunset and Santa Monica, saying she'd walk the rest of the way, which made him so angry he wanted to punch the steering wheel, wanted to reach up into the sky and pull down the gray sun that was just rising over the heights, to scorch this whole city out of existence.

But he'd misunderstood her silence. He'd made an impression with his outburst, though she wasn't yet ready to admit it. She'd never tasted defeat, and perhaps it was not until her failure at the competition in Atlantic City that she was able to understand the reality of what he'd told her that night by the white lake in the mountains high above the city of her birth. She must've felt something though, even then, when he dropped her off and she marched along the street, ready to disappear from him forever. Likewise, he must've been struggling with his simultaneous desires to kiss and kill her, for he realized only then the strangest thing about this night. His voice came to her, a cool sound out of the still-dark morning, an edge of laughter.

"Hey! By the way!" she heard him shouting. "What the hell's your name?"

And she stopped, puckered her lips—involuntarily, for the first time that night—and even almost half turned toward him as she called back softly in the quiet, six-in-the-morning street.

"Mary," she said. And stood for a moment, as if considering walking back to his car, which she could barely see now in the miasma of sunrise that grew glazed in the east. "My name is Mary."

———

Now she was fat. Her belly looked like a big barrel of worms. Georgie knew it was his offspring that made her look this way, but he wanted his slim-waisted wife back, wanted to be able to wrap his large hands around her waist and touch his fingers and thumbs together as he'd once been able to. Mary had been his mother's name also. And in those early days he'd seen something of his mother in her, something of the pale-eyed strength of the woman who'd perished on Route 66 and been buried before he'd even known she was gone. But even his wife's eyes had lost their luster. Her eyes were always red. She was always crying. And she'd said things lately that had made him come as close as he ever had to just walking out on her, the way Jack Amberson had walked out on Molly.

The fight last night, for instance. GB had witnessed it and had run off rubbing his eyes. So sensitive, that boy. "Try coming west on Route 66 once!" he wanted to shout to his five-year-old son who had the benefits of a roof over his head, food on the table with unfailing frequency, and a mother who babied him all day long—all of this because Georgie had taken this horrendous job as a truck driver for a grease company.

When they'd discovered she was pregnant the first time, they'd moved in with his adoptive mother. Her own parents had separated not long after she'd lost the pageant, as if they'd been hanging on for that decision before making theirs, hoping the money or the celebrity might bring a new sense of purpose to a marriage long since lacking. Her mother had moved back to New Jersey, abandoning her dreams of success, and her father had rented a cabin in the woods in the mountains of Washington state to resolve the series of missteps that had led from such promise as a young director to such resounding disappointment in middle age.

Mary had chosen to stay on. She'd always lived in California, had never understood a place the way she did these wide valleys embraced by the mountains of the Spanish saints. She'd been to Florida, where her father was from, and had no desire to go back. Nor did she wish to check out Jersey with her mother, where she'd visited once and could remember only a handful of overweight aunts cooking pasta and silent, stern-eyed uncles playing bocce on the dead lawn. So she'd taken a room, against everyone's wishes, in Silver Lake, with three other girls trying to make their names, had run into Georgie again at the drive-in and agreed—after some flirtatious negotiation—to another drive up into the hills, and six months later she was pregnant and living with Georgie at his adoptive mother's house in San Berdoo.

From there it had taken only another five months for Molly Amberson to realize that she had no business being there anymore, that even the idea of a grandson or granddaughter would be hollow. She and Mary simply could not get along. There was an obvious resentment that Molly carried with her, evident from the way she looked at Mary's pregnant belly, and Mary resented Molly's resentment. Plus, it was creepy, and so she would unwittingly instigate arguments with her comments. "I'm sorry, Molly, but is there something especially fascinating about me? Then why, I must ask, will you not stop *staring* at me?" It came as no surprise when Georgie had approached Molly one night just two months after the baby had been born and told her that the house was no longer big enough for all of them, that somebody had to move and that she knew as well as he did that he and Mary and young GB could not afford their own place. And did she really need all this space? Wouldn't it be better put to use by him and his young family?

In the end, Molly had martyred herself to it, as he'd known she would, and so that was how they'd ended up just the three of them living in the ranch-style house they never could've afforded unless it was handed over to them, the house where they'd hoped they'd settle in and be happy, a roof over their heads and a future worth imagining.

These were the words Georgie always used; they were the words his father had used when Georgie was a young boy and they'd just arrived in California, and though he'd nodded at his father's austere notions—and would even pass them along throughout his own sporadic career as a father, as if trying to convince himself—the simple idea of a roof over his family's head and food on the table had always struck Georgie as pedestrian. Even on the trip out here, traveling west from Oklahoma to the coast, even when he'd watched his mother shivering beneath a frayed blanket, his father telling her that Buster and Debbie were getting better though they'd secretly buried them the day before, he'd felt not a sense of loss but the heightening of his own significance. Each tragedy that had befallen him, each rotten break and hard-fought victory had only served to reinforce the idea that he'd always harbored and kept hidden from others: that he was meant to be someone important, that he'd been endowed by his creator with certain unalienable etc., but that he'd also been granted an extra proficiency that would allow him, force him, to rise above his peers. And to make a pile of cash in the meantime.

Therefore he'd never been satisfied with any of the manual labor jobs he'd bounced around in, though some of them had earned him decent money, all the best things for GB, some nice gifts for Mary. (The marriage, incidentally, had taken place in Las Vegas, the desert outpost they'd gone to visit the summer after GB was born when Mary had stumbled into a spot on a new television program billed to be the next great comedy. But it was canceled and the most tremendous depression of her life up to that point had settled in, and they'd been left only with memories of a few dull nights in Vegas and a wedding band on her finger that, without the income from Mary's spot on the comedy, Georgie knew he could never have afforded.) This grease job was the worst of them all, though it paid the best. Every day at five in the morning, Georgie woke and drove his car—a regular green Ford now; the T-Bird had long since blown a transmission and been totaled—out into the desert beyond Victorville, where he'd punch a time clock and take the keys to the truck off the hook, find the clipboard with his name on it containing the paperwork assembled the night before by the dispatch manager.

He was not just a deliveryman; he was also a salesman. When he arrived at the restaurants he would unload the vats of grease while the managers watched him sweating to beat hell. Then they'd lead him into their offices, sometimes air conditioned, sometimes not, occasionally ordering someone to go get Georgie a milkshake or a cola, and they'd sit and look over the figures from the previous month and last year and determine how much grease would be needed on the following week's delivery. It was these visits with the restaurant employees that tired out Georgie the most: the condescending attitude the managers would take with him, the rotten owners who wouldn't even offer him a drink, who'd ask him—when he requested a glass of water—if he had his own cup.

Georgie would glean their condescension from the most innocuous comments. And then, because he knew he was smarter than six of them put together, because his wife had been Miss California, because he'd known since he was eight years old that the world had something special in store for him, he would take it home and take it out on poor depressed Mary, who'd wanted nothing more than to become a movie star and had instead become housewife to a grease salesman.

"You should just hear them, Mary. The way they say my name when I arrive. 'Well, hello there, Mr. Hill, sir! How's the daily grind treating you today? Is it hot enough for you?' It makes me want to punch them in the face, Mares. Why can't anyone see it? Why can't anyone understand that this isn't who I am? I'm not a truck driver! There's . . . there's something good waiting out there for me . . . Down the road, I mean. Don't you think? Can you see it, Mary? Please tell me you haven't lost your faith in me!"

Had she ever *had* faith in him? It was something else that had brought them together. Never was there an agreement made between them that one day Georgie would pay the bills with some as-yet-unappreciated talent. Mary sat listening to his rants. Or not listening, her mind shutting down. And it was to these silences of hers that Georgie was most vulnerable. He'd watch her picking at a plate of food and infer all sorts of tales of woe. She didn't love him anymore. Never had. Was having an affair with a movie star, was acting in blue movies, was hiding from her stupid husband the fact that their son was not his but Marlon Brando's. He'd yell at her to speak to him and watch her fold up on herself, walk over to the sink, pick up a dish and—howling suddenly—turn and hurl it at him, always missing by a huge, anticlimactic distance, always scoring a direct hit on the adjacent object capable of creating the greatest disturbance. She'd knocked over vases and stand-alone liquor cabinets, had broken a glass table-clock and several centerpieces. But worst of all was the howl that made little GB sitting at his chair eating his peas cover his ears and kick his bare feet. She'd spin with her face toward the ceiling fan, open her mouth wide, and let loose with a sound that penetrated the core of his insecurities.

It was the memory of that sound—as much as the itching of his flesh beneath the Band-Aid on his forehead—that was driving Georgie nuts on this day in January when he stepped off his delivery truck and crossed the sandy back parking lot of the burger joint that was his most successful account. Usually he'd ring the bell for fifteen minutes, but this evening the two owners were already out back, around a corner and obscured from him, sounding like teenagers on a smoke break until Georgie went to investigate. The two owners, one fat and one slim, one clean-shaven and one with a moustache, were speaking with a man who'd come not just to deliver some milkshake machines, but also to make a sales pitch.

"It takes a special kind of individual," the man was saying as Georgie stepped over to them, "to recognize beauty in a hamburger."

Those were the first words he heard him say, but somehow they erased immediately the memory of Mary's shouts. They were like something his father might have said if he'd been a little more ironic, a little more American. In that first instant, Georgie felt the same magnetism as when he'd seen Mary across the parking lot of the drive-in all those years before, felt the same sense of the spinning world slowing down, allowing him to see directly down a previously obscured corridor. The milkshake man kept talking, wouldn't stop, though the owners—whom Georgie knew to be brothers—seemed ready to be done with him.

"Couldn't believe it when I got the order. *Eight* milkshake machines! Wanted to write you all a note to make you understand that each of these babies is capable of cranking out five milkshakes at once. And you want *eight* of 'em? That's forty simultaneous milkshakes! I just had to come and take a look at this place. I came all the way from Chicago because I didn't believe it. But now I do. Didn't believe it before but now I do. I can see through the window yonder what kind of operation this is. Hard-line efficiency. You've got that part down. A dozen workers all pumping out the same product. Everything measured and kept to standard. Look at that fella in there! Trying to keep up with all the shakes he's gotta make! And here it is five o'clock in the evening. Can you imagine what this place looks like at eight? 'Course you can, you're the owners. Can *you* imagine what this place looks like at eight o'clock at night? All the young fellas like yourself and their girls?"

Georgie was surprised to discover that the milkshake man was talking to him. Their eyes met for the first time. Georgie tried to speak. Failed. Cleared his throat. Glanced at his clipboard. Nodded.

"You talk about an efficient engine. You know how much energy a car engine wastes?" The man looked back and forth from Georgie to the two brothers, as if ready to field guesses. "A whole bunch," he said at last. "A whole darn bunch. A whole heck of a lot. But you know what I see when I look in that window right there? I see no wasted energy. I see a group of workers functioning to optimum capability. I see income being generated from a minimal amount of capital. I see a reason why somebody might need eight of my milkshake machines."

Georgie had listened to all of this with an acceleration in his heart, his mouth drying up, had felt the energy humming off this encounter and understood that there was a better life contained in it. He was amazed to discover that the milkshake man looked at him in a way he'd never been looked at in such company, that the man seemed to include him in the conversation in a way none of the restaurant owners ever had. He looked at Georgie, a slim boy in his early twenties, holding a clipboard and dressed in a sweat-stained uniform, a Band-Aid on his forehead and his hair still gelled in a style reminiscent of three years ago. But a face as rugged as you'd ever hope to see around here. A midwestern-looking boy. The milkshake salesman looked at the twenty-four-year-old grease truck driver and asked him, "What do *you* see?"

And Georgie knew that this was his moment. He looked at the owners, the brothers who were one type of business person, then beyond the windows to the efficient small-scale success they'd created. He looked at the middle-aged midwestern milkshake machine salesman, who'd come all the way from Chicago just to see what sort of place needed to make forty milkshakes at once. Another kind of businessman altogether.

Georgie fixed his gaze on the milkshake man and said, "I see a lot of beautiful hamburgers."

———

WE HEARD THE STORY A thousand times, each of us, even those who weren't born yet—*especially* us. It was a rally cry, our creation myth; the one thing we knew for sure about our mysterious father was that he'd stood up at the correct time, had made the right first impression on the right man, had provided for the future of us all on that hot January evening in a parking lot in San Berdoo, had sealed our success and our fates with one clever line spoken through exhausted hope with a dry mouth and aching head. It put his authority beyond question, made him our hero on the strength of one arbitrary and largely accidental instant. Our early lives were touched by that moment, blessed in a way that made us feel different. Even later, when the lying mirror that reflected only happiness and perfection had long since been shattered, we retained this marbleized view. We never had friends outside the family, only each other. The disdain our father had for other kids—their behavior, their ready assumption of their parents' lazy habits—infiltrated our own minds. The world was a place that existed outside our own experiences; we didn't control it (who would want to?) but we weren't tied to it either. And it was any- thing but an example to us. At the center of the world was our father, the provider and patriarch, never satisfied, never relaxed, pacing on a Sunday afternoon, always caught up in some mind- consuming activity—washing his car, vacuuming the house top to bottom—always up on a ladder or occupied with some noisy lawn- maintenance machine, inaccessible. We'd watch from the edge of the yard or from a second-floor window. We existed for him in the way the neighbors' kids existed for us. We were satellites. Our mothers included. Our mothers especially. Bound by tradition. Only two things a woman could do to get rid of her husband in those days. And we witnessed them both.

NOVEMBER 1963. ON THE DATE of the first attempt on their father's life, the ballplayer and his bodyguard were walking along the ravine of the dried-up Arrowhead Creek, north of Highland Avenue in San Bernardino, behind the long row of houses lined up like dominoes, one of which—the pastel yellow one over there at the end, with the swimming pool and the single maple tree rising over the fence—was theirs. They'd moved five years ago and still the boys had never gotten used to it. Five years since they'd uprooted from the house on Van Sunderland, sold it off for, in the words of their father—whom they both worshipped—more money than you could shake a stick at. Had come out here to the neighborhoods north of Highland, where the long streets held row after spiraling row of houses filled with young families like themselves, housed dozens upon dozens of kids GB's and Jamie's age for them to play with and plenty of young adults for their parents to invite over for cookouts, though they never did. This afternoon, in fact, was the first time either of the boys had ever witnessed any kind of community activity, and it was hardly the sort of thing you could feel good about.

GB was twelve, already built like an athlete, bearer of his mother's extravagant eyes and heart-shaped face, her dusty blonde hair, dressed always head to toe in a pinstriped New York Yankees baseball uniform procured via mail order in response to his persistent pleas. It was the only thing he'd worn for over a year despite his father's protests—though his mother was the one who had to wash it three times a week and she didn't seem to mind—the uniform having become his every day attire since they'd gone to Dodger Stadium to see the team recently emigrated from Brooklyn and GB had vowed that he would one day be the greatest ballplayer ever, had stood out in the yard for the remainder of the evening, tossing a Wiffle ball in the air and cracking it toward the fence with a thin yellow bat, counting off homeruns as he hit them, approaching records like his hero Roger Maris. Jamie was seven and carried with him a toy M-16 assault rifle like the kind they'd soon be using in Vietnam, occasionally aiming it toward the woods at the sounds of invisible attacks. The dutiful younger brother, always willing to carry on the role of sidekick in someone else's elaborate fantasy, he'd taken on the character of armed attendant to his brother. That day in the backyard, he'd played a frustrated outfielder to GB's home run king, had chased the tailing balls until he'd run out of room, then watched them drift over the fence toward the ravine. He was a softened version of their father, with olive complexion and boyish frame, skinnier and more frail than his brother, forced by severe myopia to wear thick black-rimmed glasses that somewhat obscured his dark eyes and long lashes and the serious look that their mother adored, that made her reach forward and touch his face while he ducked away, that made her run her hands through his thick movie star hair.

They'd been let out of school early, had been informed over the intercom of what had happened. The staticky voice of Principal Cruz, whom everyone called Principal Khrushchev, informing them that the president of the United States of America had been shot as he rode in a motorcade with his wife in a convertible down a crowded street. They'd been ushered in groups past weeping adults, past tall female teachers they'd thought heartless for the punishments meted out for incomplete homework, past grim men in suits and ties, faces covered with handkerchiefs, out to the busses, which they were told to board and go home early to be with their parents.

Among the children, a festive atmosphere had ensued. GB and Jamie had watched it, sitting together in the back of the bus as always, watching the boisterous kids in the rows ahead of them.

Theirs was the last stop. Far out beyond the cleared land that would soon be a freeway, the bus slowed at the entrance of their subdivision, paused at the gate that read Canyon View Estates on a sign over a yellow brick entryway, and they emerged from the bus, a string of a dozen kids aged five through twelve, and came through the entrance into the main street of their neighborhood to an amazing sight.

Everyone was outside, standing on their lawns. Not just the parents, but all the adults, all of them having been sent home from work, too, having now come out together onto the lawns and streets to await the arrival of the children, as if to derive some sense of hope from the vision of the kids coming off the bus, or perhaps uncertain that there was anything they could take for granted— that on a day like this one, gray and overcast even in California, the president shot in plain sight, anyone could disappear.

They'd watched him take the oath of office on a January day two years ago in Washington, DC, Robert Frost on hand and the forty-three-year-old man with the funny accent urging them to ask not what their country could do for them, GB and Jamie on the floor playing Monopoly while their mom and dad sat on the couch, whispering, teasing, their father imitating the accent, the long drawn-out vowels and the dropped R's, their mother having nothing to do with it, unwilling to submit the inaugurated president to such ridicule, even on a private scale. "Who do you think you are?" she'd said to her husband. "Who are you to make fun of the president?" Their father looking reproached for a moment before letting his expression settle. "Why don't you just admit it then, Mary? Admit that you're in love with him. Tell the boys that you're in love with the new president. That if you could you'd go to bed with him in a heartbeat and the hell with me and the boys."

The evening had descended into one of their unanticipated arguments, the game of Monopoly never finished, the television soon broadcasting to an empty living room, the boys in their rooms crying, their mother in the kitchen, their father out back by the pool, chain-smoking.

For the boys it was nearly impossible to recognize these pivots in their parents' conversations, these moments when it went from all's well to awful in a heartbeat. It seemed to them that something fundamental had changed in the way they communicated, a change that had come when they'd uprooted from the house on Van Sunderland and moved out here to the hills north of the city as a result of their father's hard work at the restaurant, the labor that had led him from a lowly West Coast liaison to the milkshake machine man all the way up to assistant quality supervisor for the fastest growing restaurant company in the history of the United States, a company that had begun as a single asphalt hamburger stand in San Berdoo and had been turned—through the sweat and vision and relentlessness of the milkshake man and his associates—into a multimillion-dollar business, two hundred locations in nearly half the states in the union, famous throughout the country for its already iconic symbol, its golden trademark beckoning motorists on their long trips across the country on Eisenhower's fast-developing interstate system.

The boys still remembered the day their father had come through the door of the old house on Van Sunderland, the day he'd lifted them into his arms in the foyer and told them that it was done, that they'd finally succeeded, after endless negotiations, in buying out the two brothers, that for only 2.7 million dollars they'd secured the revenue of what he promised them would be the greatest company in the world. They'd watched him kiss their mother on the lips—the first time either of them could remember, they'd later agree in the tiny room they shared in the house on Van Sunderland—had been lured into believing that this moment really would change things, had been awestruck at the sight of their new house, their new bedrooms at the back corners, with three windows apiece and plush carpeting and a view of the ravine and the foothills, stunned by the backyard and the swimming pool, the new neighborhood that rose and dove among the dry hills and dales. And yet still, even in this new location, even surrounded by a beauty that made their old habitat seem all the more dismal, they'd found their parents to be more distant, always thinking of something else. That day he'd taken them to Dodger Stadium, had led them up the hill from the Pasadena Freeway to the new complex among palm and olive trees, they'd sought and not received some new connection with him, had hoped that today—the three of them attending a ballgame together—they might get to feel a certain warmth from their father that had been missing. Instead he'd been disinterested, unable to answer their questions about the rules, had called out to the passing vendor and urged them to be satisfied with this gesture while he turned inward, turned to contemplate the great bowl of seating, the boys sharing their box of Cracker Jacks each with one eye on the game, one eye on their silent father.

George Benjamin Hill didn't know the rules of baseball. Didn't care. It was a pointless game, one he would come to resent even more over the years as his oldest son became devoted to it. He had never so much as watched an inning on television, didn't know a strike from a ball nor a Dodger from a Yankee, had reluctantly agreed to take the boys only when the milkshake machine man had all but forced the complimentary tickets upon him in the aftermath of one of their heated meetings at the office that afternoon, the latest Friday meeting in which they'd gotten together with the board to attempt to figure out a way to resolve what was so clearly wrong with their company. It was the milkshake machine man's franchising model. From the beginning, he'd been a handshaker and a backslapper, always quick with a line like those he'd thrown out that day Georgie had met him. His mantra had been growth: expand as much as possible and get their restaurants in as many states as they could. They'd offered franchises at outrageously low start-up fees of less than a thousand dollars, had advertised enormously low kickback agreements—agreements that had helped them expand but had done nothing for the long-term well-being of the company. In his old-fashioned style, the milkshake machine man had insisted they treat all their franchisers with respect, had insisted that they think of them as business partners rather than customers. A nice gesture, certainly, but one that, it was becoming clearer every day, was driving the company toward insolvency. They were drowning in overhead, had brought in $75 million dollars in sales the previous year but had only turned $160,000 in corporate profits. The franchisees were getting rich while the franchisors were barely keeping their heads above water. There'd been conversations—at the water cooler in the corporate office, over drinks in dark bars with the air conditioners running—George Benjamin Hill and the other board members getting drunk and commiserating over the wealth they'd imagined and the disaster that seemed inevitable, the company headed straight for bankruptcy within a year or eighteen months. Two hundred restaurants packed with customers one day and closed down the next. Two hundred franchisers ruined, the milkshake man defaulted on dozens of loans, pursued by creditors, foiled by his own inability to work the numbers.

It was on that summer day in 1962, seated in the baby blue pit of Dodger Stadium with his two sons, that George Benjamin Hill had seen the answer to the company's problem. The day he sat looking out over forty thousand people—like franchisers, really, in their cramped seats on loan from the Los Angeles Dodgers—the boys pulling on his sleeve with questions whose answers he didn't know, their father always with bigger fish to fry. By the time forty thousand stood to sing "Take Me out to the Ballgame," he'd ironed out most of the details, was already picturing himself not here at the ballgame with his boys but in the board room on Monday, presenting his new idea to the men with whom he'd shared late-night roundtables of gloom and desperation, watching their expressions change as he pitched it to their boss, a new plan that would use real estate as a money-making device, the same way the Los Angeles Dodgers used this bright bowl of a stadium, a plan that would eliminate the risk of day-to-day business by making them first and foremost landlords to their franchisers. First—he would tell the board members—we scout out potential sites for future restaurants. We buy or rent the land with fixed interest rates, sublet the buildings at a significant markup, force the franchisers to contribute a minimum fee or percentage of sales (whichever is greater). As sales and prices rise, the company will collect more rent and revenue, while our costs remain constant . . .

It was a once in a lifetime idea (he knew it immediately, as soon as it had begun to form in his brain), one he'd tried to explain to his boys in the car on their way back from the stadium, only to find them uninterested—GB already talking of his baseball dreams, asking his father for a uniform that he could wear at all times—had tried to explain it to Mary throughout the remainder of the weekend while they sat together at the pool, the annoying sound of the

Wiffle ball bat and the ball occasionally drifting up to the deck, bouncing around, floating in the pool, his younger son getting in the water with his shoes on, which drove Georgie nuts. He'd tried to explain it to them and found that he couldn't, that this life could already not hold him. That an upper-class home on a hillside was far too mundane. That contentment could never be found in this immaculate yard with a former Miss California and two bright, healthy boys.

THEY WALKED ALL THE WAY out to the trestle bridge—a mile one way—and then turned and headed back, two brothers shielded from the world by the high brown flanks of the ravine and the chain-link fence that stood atop the ridge at the rear of the mall on San Manuel Avenue, each of them old enough, in his own way, to understand what this day meant. The president had been shot! "Do you think it hit him in the head?" Jamie asked. "Do you think his brains splattered all over the place?"

But GB would not answer. He could feel the heaviness in the air, could hear the cries coming from the open windows in the backside of the long row of houses above the fence that separated the ravine from the backyards, could sense a building anger in the world and in the clouds that curled across the normally sun-bleached hills. Jamie looked up at his older brother, trying to gauge him for a reaction, trying to copy the calm and steady expression that Jamie admired but could never emulate. Too impulsive was he, too quick to seize on whatever thought came into his mind. On the bus, he'd laughed at some of the antics of the kids in the rows of seats ahead of them, only to have GB give him a look and then train his serious face forward, as he did now, late in the afternoon, as they returned to their house to find a kitchen light on, their father's car—it was a BMW now—parked out front, the engine still clicking as it settled, their parents' voices already beginning to rise as the boys crouched at the window and listened with their little faces peering in from just above the window sill.

Their mother was in a rage like they'd never seen before. She'd spent all day watching the footage from the tragedy in Dallas, thinking this is what television had brought them. She'd watched this take place and had felt the emptiness of her life filling up the room in which she sat, on the couch she'd never found comfortable in the house that was drafty in the winter and stuffy in the late summer when the Santa Anas came across the valley, long days waiting at home for the two boys she barely felt were hers and the husband she hadn't loved in years, had never loved perhaps, had simply ended up with because he was the most convenient option to settle upon when she'd needed the reassurance a husband would bring. He'd never been faithful to her; she knew this. He'd stopped loving her the instant she'd bore him a child, the instant she'd struggled to lose the weight. She'd stopped eating—one last effort to salvage the marriage, though she had no idea, even at the time, why she was doing it—yet still he was always boarding some plane, flying off to some unknown city where there were restaurants to open and hands to shake and, she knew, young women to meet.

Where else could all the money be going? Where else could he be spending all his time? He was never home. Even when he was in California, he was always claiming some important meeting to attend, was always darting off and not returning for days, looking as if he didn't know her, spending only an obligatory afternoon or evening with the children before going to bed, sleeping eleven hours and back to the airport. But his lies were lazy. He'd tell her he'd be back in a week and return in two days with a vague smile, Mary relieved in spite of herself—for what would she tell the neighbors if he ever just left? He'd sit on the couch and put his feet up on the coffee table, would linger like that for a moment, maintaining the pose until he thought she was back in the kitchen. And then she'd watch him—watch his reflection, in fact, in the open French door that separated the kitchen from the foyer—as he swung his feet back to the carpet, leaned forward with chin on fists in an expression of indecision, of instability, angled strangely in the warped glass, his features drawn out like an image in a knife blade.

It was upon the advice of the television that she'd done what she'd done next. She'd hired a private detective. Too much television, too much Hollywood had led her to conceive the idea with embarrassment and then embrace it. She'd hired a man whose name she'd found in a half-inch ad in the classified section of the *Times*, had paid him an outrageous sum of money to tell her what her husband was doing on those long trips away from home. The phone had rung only six weeks ago. The raspy voice of a stranger telling her she'd better come into his office. What he had to show her—he didn't want to do it over the phone.

That had been six weeks ago—the day that the truth about her husband's other life had come crashing in through the windows. She'd had no idea what to do, and so she'd taken comfort in the presence of her one true friend. The man with the kind eyes whose face looked out on her almost nightly from the television set. The man whose words and smile she'd come to think of as being intended just for her, the sort of man with whom she'd been meant to end up, a Miss America for a president of the United States. Instead of lashing out in response to her new knowledge, she'd basked in it, had

used it as an excuse to descend completely into her imagined life—
had embraced entirely the fantasy that she was Mrs. President
John F. Kennedy, had spent not an instant of the previous six weeks
in the house in California but rather in the White House, imagining conversations not only with him but with everyone else she
might run into, imagined herself in robe and slippers, gracing the
carpeted corridors of the executive mansion, whose interior she'd
fancied as a medieval castle updated for modern times, had pictured herself eating dinner with him, discussing the day's events
during the warm afternoons while her sons were at school—she'd
been thrilled when it had started up again in the fall, thankful for
the hours of privacy it afforded her. In those long hours with just
herself and the voice of the president in her ear, she'd dreamed all
sorts of dramas, had planned vacations with him, had met his
family and spent weekends in the sand. Alone on her couch, she'd
created a world so real that on the day it collapsed—on the day
she, riding along in the cavalcade with him, the top down on a
Texas afternoon, had heard gunshots in the sky and felt the blood
on her face—she'd found herself so fully alone that she'd been frozen in place, had lay motionless on the couch until she heard the
noise at the front door and knew it was him, heard him step into
the room and stand behind her, looking at the television, taking in
the scene.

"Mary—" he said, but that was all he got out before she rose up.

"I know," she said. "I know all about where you go when you
leave me."

He stood looking down at her, a man just turned thirty-two,
refined by success and confident in his evasions. He gave her a look
meant to display confusion, meant to convince without words that
he had no idea what she was talking about.

"I know about them. There's nothing you can say. There's no explanation you could possibly give me—"

He turned on a lamp. She snapped it off. He came over to the television and she blocked his way, wouldn't allow him to turn off the never-ending coverage that was taking place on all the channels.

"Tell me!" she said. "Tell me about them! Tell me their names!"

He'd turned from her, had gone out to the kitchen and picked up the telephone. She followed him, her eyes red with awful circles beneath them, lips chapped, hair astray. She watched him flipping through the phone book. "This isn't natural, Mary. You've had this problem for years. I've watched it take control of your life. It's time we got you some help."

"Help?" she said, and felt her hand on the drawer, felt it tighten around the handle of the knife, held it hidden next to her hip and then raced across the kitchen toward him, watched his eyes widen as he saw the knife being revealed, lifted into the air for an over handed swipe, saw him raise the phone book just in time to receive the blow, the knife they'd bought for five dollars after watching it cut through aluminum and then an apple carving through the yellow pages and skidding across the floor when he shoved her away, knocking her against the cabinet so she was woozy for just a second, still seeing him through the haze of her hate, the shredded phone book, the knife toward which she crawled across the floor and picked up.

He turned as if to flee, and that was when it occurred to her that it wasn't worth it—that it could not change her life for the better, wouldn't bring back Jack, would send her off to prison with no television and no recompense for the tragedy that had taken place.

She stood up straight, watched him fall over a dining room chair as he scrambled to escape, saw him turn fully while she raised the carving knife and—thinking of the imagined life that now lay on a gurney in Dallas—brought it powerfully across her throat. And it was in that very moment, her head turning to the side to receive the blade, that she saw two wide-eyed boys looking in at her over the dining room window sill.

THE AMBULANCE ARRIVED IN TIME to save her. She'd done severe damage to her larynx, had nearly severed her jugular vein. It was so serious that they'd thought there was no way she could survive; yet she'd disappeared in the ambulance and he'd received a phone call just hours later saying it looked like she would live. To which he responded: "Where do you recommend we send her?"

He hadn't ridden in the ambulance with her, had told the men who'd arrived at the scene that he couldn't bear to, that she'd done it in front of her own children, that it wasn't enough for her to destroy her own life, she'd needed to destroy theirs as well. From the medical team, there'd been sympathy. But also a look passing over their faces that said they didn't want to get mixed up in this: a mother attempting suicide in her own kitchen, two boys too stunned to cry being comforted by a father already telling them they'd get through this, they'd find a way, he already had a plan, already knew where they could go, where they'd never have to live in tension and fear again, where they could find out what a true family was like. That night, he took them out for burgers, sat them down in the uncomfortable dining room of one of the restaurants he'd helped open—the idea, he'd told them once, was to get people in and out as quickly as possible; when maximum turnover was your goal, comfort was not a priority—and while they picked at their food, still sniveling, eyes watery, he explained to them that he was taking them somewhere they could all start over. He knew a place where they could come to live with him and a very special lady who would treat them like her own, where they could have two little siblings— twin siblings, a boy and a girl only three years old. Out toward the foothills at the edge of the city, where they could begin to decide what their next step might be, decide as a *family*—all six of them. They'd be able to see their mother, of course—"Of course!" he answered his younger son's concerned look, his hamburger half eaten in its paper wrapper. She'd be nearby in a place where she could be taken care of, where they could visit any time. Though not *too* often, he hoped, for he was convinced this was something they needed to move on from. "Your mother needs time and space to work things out," he told his boys at the table in the restaurant only blocks from the hospital. "She'll always be your mother," he reassured them, cleaning up the wrappers, stuffing them in the bag and carrying it all over to the garbage. "But this place I'm taking you tonight," he said on their way out to the car, which he started up and directed along the streets of San Berdoo, "this is going to be your new *home*."

And for six years, it was. For six years, we spent a temporary existence in the house where he brought us together that night of the first attempt on his life, the low-roofed bungalow on a quarter acre of pavement off Wildwood he'd rented in secret for his second family while the failure of his first became complete. For six years, while his first wife languished alone in the desert to the east, we his children lived huddled up amidst a desolate grid of city streets, between a halfhearted dog park and a dozen acres of excavation perpetually on its way to becoming another shopping mall, blinds pulled to keep out the light or the spying world, a narrow hallway of shag carpeting and peeling wallpaper and strangers we learned to call family, awkward gatherings at the dining room table—a scarred leave-behind from previous tenants—with all eyes downcast but his. The breadwinner, the provider, the patriarch, privileging us with the stories of his next big idea sprouted illogically from the remnants of the previous. I'm telling you, kids. This time next year, we'll be on our way. Alaska. Just the sound of it a terror in the ears of four California kids, a word whispered reverently and with disbelief and implicit danger throughout those six years—years he spent largely on the road. Long stints away for weeks and months at a time, making preparations, plotting career moves, telling us abridged tales of an oil field discovered on something called the North Slope and then charging off in pursuit, returning late on a Friday night or early on a Saturday afternoon, coming through the front door of that somber house in a suit to find us gathered on the living room floor, cross-legged in pajamas and huddled around a pointless board game called Life—and pausing, surprised, as if he'd forgotten we existed. Or maybe we simply aged too fast in those rapid-moving days, the twins walking and talking, rolling dice and making a ruckus, the boys' voices changing, bodies taking on that hungry look of adolescence and beyond, the first inkling of a life racing off without him, years accumulating too swiftly to keep up.

For just a moment, before heading down the hallway to where his second wife waits—where she always waits, or so it seems—he pauses as if prepared to speak, as if ready to address the four of us looking up at him from the carpeting that screams late sixties. Instead, another chance passes awkwardly; another scene concludes prematurely. Shuffling down the hallway with his briefcase and barely a smile, long arms swinging: the breadwinner, the provider, the patriarch. Too preoccupied or busy to begin the labors that might start to lift that silence, too ill-equipped or scared to confront what might return to haunt him when this little brood of his grows old enough to look back on these years as something other than what he has trained us to see.

Monday

GB HILL FELT LIKE A ghost.

Four in the morning in the pouring rain on the New Jersey Turnpike and the old ballplayer was driving with the top down, dressed in a pinstriped Yankees uniform and shouting along with the radio to the classic Gloria Gaynor hit, "I Will Survive."

He was giving it everything he had, really belting out the words though he didn't know half of them and it wasn't making him feel any better, a shining dampness having collected upon his face though the pulled-down brim of his ball cap had mostly kept the rain off that part of him.

He was drunk, had been sipping Comfort and Coke for some twelve hundred miles through the plastic lid of a convenience store coffee cup situated at his crotch, steering with his knees when necessary to mix up stiff refills from containers concealed beneath the seats of this antique '73 Stingray that had long been his most prized possession. Now it was his roofless home, his worldly accumulations reduced to a knapsack and a baseball bat bag in the trunk and an eleven-year-old chocolate lab scrunched down on the passenger side floorboards trying to stay dry, looking up at him like a picture hung not quite straight as his tone-deaf chanting rose over the storm and the engine and the stereo: *I will survive . . . I will survive!* Words even he didn't believe.

For what seemed weeks they'd been shackled to these interstates, pursuing white numerals on blue and red shields at speeds upwards of eighty, tracking with a tattered road atlas their progress along the mostly monotonous landscapes of the I-95 corridor. It had been unfathomable at first, impossible to imagine when they'd set out from Miami just eighteen hours ago that this pondered-over and then impromptu departure perpetrated in the calm of a Sunday morning could lead them so far in so short a period of time, that this tar-patched path of asphalt strung out lazily along the suburban tracts of Fort Lauderdale and West Palm Beach could deliver them in a seamless push across seven state lines and countless states of mind.

The plan, if it could be dignified as such, had called for him to leave Friday morning, to reach his destination by Saturday afternoon, to accomplish what he meant to accomplish and be on the road west by Sunday. And yet anything resembling intelligent design had long since disintegrated, the decisiveness born of desperation with which he'd achieved a sort of escape velocity those first hours having degraded by degrees throughout the late morning, a hazy pall settling gradually over the cloying glaze of four hundred miles of Florida coastline. It was not just the alcohol. There had been other things, images speckled across his eyelids every time he blinked, things he'd seen that Sunday morning in a cold sterile capsule of white walls and stainless steel that he could now not *un*see, confused intentions that had blazed white hot at his departure only to burn themselves out, little more than smoking embers by the time he'd made the Georgia border just past two,

mixed up another drink and comforted himself with the manufactured reassurance that the worst of it was over, that it would now
officially be easier to keep going than it would be to turn back.

Four decades had done a not uncommon thing to the ten-year-old
boy who'd once cracked Wiffle balls over his backyard fence and
called himself the next Roger Maris. A lifetime of nonachievement
had taken his once animal-lean frame and turned it flabby, the face
once striking and heart-shaped like his mother's gone amorphous
and livid with middle age. In February, he'd turned fifty, had hon-
ored the occasion behind a single-storied row of numbered door-
ways, a budget motel in Hialeah across whose shadowy lot—beneath
a faded signboard promising free HBO and Cinemax—he had
smuggled the dog with a series of well-practiced movements, had
placed the key and watched the door slide open to reveal the disappointment beyond.

Since the separation, this had become his existence. Days spent
alone but for the old dog who was like a souvenir he couldn't get
rid of, afternoons filled by circuitous excursions across the city of
Miami and its outskirts in the top-down Stingray, not exactly
searching for anything but not exactly *not* searching, continuing
south sometimes toward the Everglades or along the intracoastal
waterway, all the way to Key West and back once. In a sort of manic
daze they would drive all day, stopping only to fill up on gas or to
answer the call of his nagging prostate or the dog's watery bowels,
and when the sun set he would allow the neon signs to lure him off
the interstate, would settle onto a bed smelling of sanitizer in the
blue light of the television for distracting marathons of former
blockbusters and B movies, big budget flops and soft core porn at
whose conclusion—toward dawn, with the dismal light of another
perfect Florida morning foiled by the heavy curtains drawn tight,

the room turned frigid by the rattling air conditioner—he would step into the bathroom and stare down this dour countenance he barely recognized, would confront again the persistent mystery of just what he was supposed to do with himself now.

Just months before, he'd had a life. He'd had a wife and a daughter, a cushy job crisscrossing Broward and Dade counties scouting high school baseball players that had allowed him to linger on old triumphs (also to dwell on old regrets)—a house at the end of a quiet cul-de-sac to come home to, a pillared wrap-around porch behind bougainvillea in the suburbs, in Coral Gables. His former father-in-law, the real estate baron, had found it for them some sixteen years ago now, had shown them the photos and dubbed it their dream home, had led them through the doors and stepped back while they'd stood—GB and Tammy—beneath the glass chandelier that hovered in the two-story entry flanked by formal living and dining rooms, their hopes leading them along the polished hardwood to a kitchen of granite countertops while their young daughter raced up and down the carpeted staircase. They had stood together looking out the bay window on half an acre of oleander and had both gotten caught up in the moment, Tammy hugging and thanking her father while *he* had fought back emotions he hadn't felt in he couldn't say how long, had found himself nodding his head—making it unanimous—that this ostentatious pre-fab was the perfect place for the three of them to make a life. The perfect place to raise Emma.

That was all gone now. The so-called dream home that had made them stand in awe of their own fortune and future together had been up for sale for nearly six months on that night he'd turned fifty in the motel room in Hialeah, well over a year now on this weekend he'd aborted even its memory and set out on this frantic odyssey toward a city to which he'd once vowed he'd never return. It had gone on the market and then off and then back on again at the advising of Tammy's friend and co-worker Marc (an underling of her father's who'd told them, separately, that it was the best way for them to "move on," the best way for them to "pick up the pieces")— the FOR SALE sign crooked on the unkempt front lawn, the dark windows and all that lay beyond having become like cold ash in his mind as this Sunday afternoon, so bright his eyes hurt from squinting, had given way to the lavender decay of dusk along the coastal plain of the Carolinas.

At times, he had overcompensated, had attempted to outpace his misgivings, the radio blasting while he yelled along to old favorites—"Jumpin' Jack Flash" and "Magic Carpet Ride," "Smoke on the Water" and "When the Levee Breaks"—floorings of the pedal beneath his baseball spikes turning them into a white streak in the passing lane while the hours and the big valleys of Virginia rolled on, the nation's capital a luminous blur at midnight. Other times the car and the interstate had dissolved around them and these false assurances had vanished also, time and space stretching out and constricting and swinging back to catch up again, so that by the time the rain had arrived as they'd crossed the Delaware, by the time he'd peeled his ticket from the automated booth at Deepwater and waded out into the black boiling pool of the turnpike, wipers on high from Trenton to Brunswick, the tires of the eighteen wheelers creeping along in the right-most lanes stirring up a second storm more blinding than the first . . . by the time the intimate loneliness of the interstate at night had given way to the false dawn of city glow blooming a brown shade of pink beyond the backsides of night-slumbering strip malls, he had become little more than a presence looking down on himself from a point located high above the arc lamps. He'd become something like the uncertain hero of the previous summer's most-talked-about blockbuster (which he had watched on that lonely night of his fiftieth birthday with an unwarranted interest, a desperate identification), two hours of superfluous plot suffered through in sympathy with the somber creature at its center only to discover—at the end, while *he* had lay on that bed smelling of sanitizer near dawn, trembling with cold while the dog looked up warily—that he'd been dead all along.

He switched off the radio. The song had ended, had been replaced by a less redemptive tune of a more recent vintage. The rain had abated, and in the vaporous stillness of its absence he paid his toll with one of his last twenties, ascended a steel viaduct in a vague arc toward the Holland Tunnel until another stronger impulse made him swerve hard and exit, a procession of blinking yellow stoplights splayed out across Jersey City's bright landfill.

That morning—standing for the final time next to the For Sale sign on the front lawn at the dead end of their cul-de-sac in Coral Gables, listening to Marc talk about moving on and picking up the pieces—this flight toward far-off diversion had seemed inevitable, the required step to help him assemble some sort of salvation. Now, as he killed the engine where the asphalt ended and staggered out toward the worksite debris of a waterfront skyscraper on the make, as he stood beneath the weekend-silent tower cranes and the fifty-foot-tall Colgate clock looking out across the dark field of the Hudson toward the clustered gray totems of lower Manhattan, GB Hill found himself seized again by a fate he'd fought hard to escape, the recognition of a familiar curse in this rain-soaked pre-dawn portrait: that of all the days he might have finally allowed it to come to this—of all the Monday mornings he might have shown up here in search of a stranger he hadn't heard from in twenty years at the urging of another he hadn't seen in thirty—it was in perfect keeping with this life of his, and this plan of theirs, that he had happened upon this one.

HE'D WARNED THEM.

For sixty missions and more the Snake had been warning them, had filed reports with the appropriate superiors. Had anyone listened? When the ground beneath the city had shaken eight years ago with the half-ton payload in the delivery truck, had anyone looked back upon his report of the previous summer? Just twenty-one months ago (watching a new millennium dawn with the descent of a colored ball in Times Square from the shadows of the rocks in Central Park), the Snake had intuited that the moment was approaching, and yet had anyone bothered to follow up on the conspiratorial artifacts he had unearthed? It was like shouting into a long tunnel, urging the darkness and receiving no response but for the dull reverb of his own voice, his heartbeat a pounding that morphed in his ears, acquired an echo and a purpose, became the distant imminent footsteps of those he'd always known would one day come for him.

At seven o'clock on the morning of the eve of his vindication, the twenty-year veteran of the secret wars known only as the Snake was escorted from Rikers Island Penitentiary wearing sweatpants and a sweatshirt and a long trench coat, was taken by taxi across the unmarked bridge into Queens. There he stood at the bus stop in sunlight prismed by drying rain puddles while a class of kindergarten students scurried around him. He'd been collared again on a disturbing the peace charge, though he hadn't been disturbing a thing, certainly not whatever it was they called peace in this city—it was just his former bosses with the agency checking up on him, letting him know they still had him in their sights. They'd done it a dozen times in the lifetime that had passed since he'd gotten out of intel and straight into special ops, these quick collars to shake him up. You knew they were hard up if they were even giving the ground troops a rough time of it, if they were infiltrating the ranks of the silent army they themselves had set up on the hectic floor of the city. These last few weeks it had felt like Moskva, like Area 51 or nights in Hue, the tension like a bottle rocket set to go off, the whispers just out of reach but rising toward a cacophony that could only mean one thing.

The bus driver was a foreigner with an earnest expression, quick to look away when the Snake leveled his eyes and stood rigid against the wall next to the handicapped platform. He took the busses because they weren't as expensive as taxis, weren't as personal as trains, which were like riding through a labyrinth with a piece of string trailed behind you. The Snake knew these roads and bridges and overpasses like nobody's business, the city a crazy man's diorama, steel and one-way glass and rust, steam off the stale rivers and a sun turned gold and gray. Some days he rode for hours, sat in stations all day long, lay down in moonlit parks just to hear the crunch of last autumn's leaves. He'd wear his black trench coat, his hair sometimes long and sometimes short because of the wigs he carried in his pockets. Sometimes he took off his glasses and sported facial hair. Other days his eyes were blue like his mother's. The coat itself could be turned inside out, straps pulled out of Velcro enclosures and—presto!—he was a backpacker in sneakers and striped ankle socks. But usually such theatrics weren't necessary. This was NYC—which most of the time stood for Not Your Concern. Nobody paid attention except for those who were paid to do so. The bus growled along a pot-holed access road, mounted a ramp, and merged into airport traffic on the parkway. The Snake kept his face forward while monitoring, by use of the driver's three mirrors, the crowd behind him, looking for familiar faces among the suits holding folded newspapers while, beyond the tinted windows of the bus, six lanes merged chaotically down to four.

In the short-term view, all of this, the collar on Central Park South, the night's stay in Rikers, smelling shit and come in the holding cell of a hundred and twenty, even this Monday morning bus ride with the GCP backed up from the B-Q Expressway halfway to the Triborough, all of it had begun six months ago, when, contacted in the traditional way (an abandoned duffel bag on the marble wall behind the Maine Monument at Merchant's Gate) the Snake had met his contact with the agency at a pizza parlor on 46th and Ninth. A slice of sausage pizza had been sitting on two paper plates in the booth in the corner; the Snake had sat down, folded the wide slice in half lengthwise, and taken a bite. He'd seen a man watching him from the phone booth beyond the counter. When the Snake pulled a napkin from the dispenser and placed it unfolded on his lap, the man had emerged from the shadows and come over to take a seat.

It had always begun like this. A meeting at some innocuous location in the heart of the city, a briefing as they marched uptown to the park, which was where the agency's business was always conducted. Got something for you, Snake, the man in the suit coat had said that evening, a cold one in February, the snow still piled in heaps around the sidewalks and wrought iron, the wide swath of sky dull with the faint luster of the city. He'd reached into the pocket of his coat and retrieved a photograph taken from the corner of 31st and Seventh, a crowd of humanity emerging from Penn Station and filtering along the streets, a thousand headshots coming and going, though the Snake immediately picked out the face he'd been intended to pick out. She'd dyed her hair—it was bright red now—but the Snake could've recognized that face anywhere despite the overcoat with collar turned up and sunglasses. The Snake nodded. You want me to keep an eye on her, he'd said.

The man in the suit coat never paused, his voice a cool whisper. We need to find out what they're up to, whom they're working for this time. No one's closer to her than you are. On the wide mall beneath the skeletal elms, he stopped walking and turned to face the Snake. If you get something, you know where to bring it. And he'd pulled on his fedora and stepped along the puddled paths of the Dene, headed east toward the gate at E. 72nd.

He hadn't seen the man in the suit coat since, had done his homework and put his ear to the wall. In his room with a single window on the fifth floor of the brownstone walkup in the middle of Hell's Kitchen (arranged and paid for by the Feds, a cover for his real operations), he'd pored through the dozen file cabinets full of notes taken over his ten years of service in this city—the file cabinets having come from the Columbus Branch of the New York Public Library, "donated" to him as a "token of good will." (Strings had been pulled, in other words.) He'd frequented all the spots one could go if one wanted to get information, had kept his own meticulous notes in pocket-sized stenographer's pads, had begun by scrutinizing the photo in early daylight of the station, had noted the time on the marquee and determined this to be the massive exodus of the Northeast Corridor train from Jersey.

He'd rode out one late May afternoon, donned a suit left over from his days with the agency, and took a train across the river to Newark, a bus out through the gritty suburbia to West Orange, where

he made his way up the hill along Prospect Avenue to the seventies-
style bi-level that sat above a suburban ravine. He'd stepped right up
the cracked sidewalk intending to knock on the front door, intending to assume some innocuous persona, as he'd done a thousand
times in similar situations, had heard instead as he approached the
sound of voices murmuring from the rear of the house. Through the
low branches of a Jersey pine in the side yard he observed them: a
small crowd of perhaps two dozen standing on the back lawn, picnic
tables and paper plates and plastic cups, low-voiced discussions centered around baseball and local politics, two liters of soda half emptied and growing warm on tablecloths and coolers with beer cans on
ice in the grass. In the near corner was a grill from which the smell
of meat and charcoal lifted lazily, hot dogs and hamburgers, potato
chips and pretzels, casseroles and pasta dishes in great serving
bowls with a few insects buzzing around them, a handful of children racing here and there while the adults stood in awkward
crowds or sat on benches, picking away at their food and nodding at
what a nearby person was saying.

He'd waited in the ramble alongside the ravine until only a few
stragglers remained, drinking beers on lawn chairs in the shade.
He snuck around to the front door, picked the lock, and stepped
through the shadowy gloom of the unlit house at dusk, the kitchen
with its outdated cabinetry, the dining room unused though exten-
sively decorated, the living room embraced by an old couch and love
seat of green-and-yellow paisley, a coffee table with knickknacks
and photographs he dared not touch. He went upstairs, felt his way
along the claustrophobic hallway, and searched the cramped rooms
for some sign of her, dark bedrooms with small windows slightly
open and looking down on the neighborhood, on the backyard where
a few voices still lingered, on the brown ravine that revealed itself

now as a disused railroad bed six tracks wide, a far-off view across the lowlands of Newark and beyond. At the end of the hall, in a particularly dismal sitting room with a daybed and bookcases, he watched the last daylight disappear from the wall and lifted the dusty triptych in its old-fashioned frame from the cloth-draped end table next to a decrepit recliner, carved a finger through the dust and looked at her, all sepia-toned and smiling from the cradle of a maple tree, wearing a striped sweater on a boardwalk with the sea breeze blowing her hair across her face, seated candidly on a couch staring intently away from the camera, a look of inscrutable intensity.

So the reports were false after all: she was not dead.

On the cold bench at Penn Station in Newark, waiting for the train to take him back across the river, the Snake had tried to put it together, had leafed back through the materials he'd assembled in the manila folder that he'd brought along, intending to show the family. Instead he had only become more convinced that they'd gotten to them, had no doubt filled their heads with lies that had made of her a villain, a pariah. Riding through the barren landscape as the train approached the tunnel, the Snake wondered what lies they'd told *his* family, wondered what had happened to the letters he'd long ago sent, lengthy epistles he'd taken weeks to compose, poring over every word in his room and in the back stacks of the library, logging on to the donated computers looking over both shoulders as he sought addresses, only to wait and hear nothing, responses not forthcoming and memory slowly fading until he was barely able to recall their faces, barely able to remember their names. It was at times like this, lonely moments riding endless pathways across this city that had long ago become something more than his home, something almost like his prison, that the Snake came as close as he ever did to getting beyond it. This veil that had folded over him and clouded his thoughts, altered his observations—moments when the chaos took on familiar patterns, when the chiming components of the city seemed to rise into a clattering harmony, moments when the world's reflections seemed to merge and double and find meaning on a larger plane—it was at these moments that he always seemed to come as close as he ever did to reaching out and grasping it, whatever *it* was.

The train had long since descended into the tunnel beneath the river, turning the glass next to his face into a ruddy mirror that he peered into, watching the distorted bodies of his fellow passengers as they turned the pages of newspapers, rested weary heads against rattling windows. Now, as the train emerged into the station, the light filtering down from the platform lamps killed his reflection and replaced it with another face. Just ten feet away from him, separated by the span between railcars, sunglasses and a beret and the same plaid overcoat he'd seen in the photograph, her hair dyed again. Peroxide blonde.

She was a working girl. Stalked the area around the Plaza Hotel, along 59th and Central Park South to Sixth Avenue and 58th, approached parked cars and leaned through the windows, tossed her beret onto the man's lap and trotted around to the passenger side, the car disappearing around a corner while the Snake observed. He'd waited until last night, when the light rain had driven her under the awnings, had snuck up close enough to hear the Midwestern accent she'd perfected, the face still recognizable despite what appeared to be some carefully done plastic surgery—a raising of the cheekbones, a drawing-up of the heart-shaped face—her expression as he approached assuring him of all he'd suspected all along. She knew that he knew, and she knew that he knew that she knew that he knew. She'd pulled out a can of mace and aimed it wildly in his direction, calling him a freak and a perv. He'd stumbled blindly toward her and lifted her on his shoulder, groping in the dark tunnel of her screams, the fists that beat down upon him—the screams and fists of a Midwest girl trapped in an eastern city, in over her head, kicking with stiletto heels that broke against his forehead, loose change and little plastic-wrapped candy canes falling from the pockets of her imitation leopard-skin coat, all of it resulting in a black eye he wore this Monday morning in early September. He'd tried to reassure her, had tried to whisper that he just wanted to talk, to tell her that the Feds knew she was back in town and had recruited him to watch over her, to see what she was up to, whom she was working for, and that he had no intentions of bringing her in, of making her face the nightmare they'd faced together all those years ago.

To this end he'd lugged her across the street toward the entrance to the park, though he heard the sounds of the police siren approaching, heard them calling at him to put her down, to let the girl go and put his hands over his head and spread his legs, had heard their approach over the damp pavement, felt the shock of a gun butt against the back of his neck, the cold metal of the handcuffs on his wrists while the girl—clearly not the one he was looking for, he saw now, not even a lookalike—got to her feet and spit in his face, the police (Police? Then why were they wearing headsets?) pushing him onto his belly on the sidewalk and reading him his rights and carting him off to Rikers for a night of piss-and-shit smell because this was the *new* New York City, where everyone was safe, even working girls out walking the streets through a steady rain after midnight, even these folks riding the bus through a bright Monday morning, everybody in the whole wide city except for the few that really knew what was going on, the few that comprehended what all of it meant.

It was in the midst of the traffic jam on the Grand Central Parkway—the Middle Eastern bus driver with the sad eyes continually watching his movements in the rearview, the group of kindergarten students growing restless, their singing having ceased in favor of complaints of *Are we there yet?*—that the Snake first understood they were being followed. He watched the man behind the wheel of a black Lincoln and felt his certainty grow until it was pulsing inside his head. It was a trap. All along it had been. They'd been using him to track her down, and now that the job was done . . .

"Let me off here," the Snake said, moving toward the door, the driver regarding him nonchalantly until the Snake pulled out his weapon, the shank he'd planted months ago near the unmarked bridge to Rikers, just in case. "Now!"

Horns blared as he raced across four lanes of traffic toward the exit ramp to 111th Street, dove over the concrete wall and the angled footers to street level, a Sunoco station in the shadows of the overpass and, beyond, a dozen blocks leading down to the flats above Flushing Bay, where he crouched breathless an hour later in the swamp grass beneath the sulfur trails of LaGuardia Airport, listening to his own heart beating and thinking it sounded like gunshots, or footsteps—the steady approach of those he'd always known would come for him eventually.

———

GB HILL POPPED THE TRUNK, scratched the dog's scabby neck and stood looking in at the knapsack and the baseball bat bag.

It was rush hour again, and high up on the silver platforms of the GW Bridge the traffic crept west, away from the city. It felt good to be out of the car. For so much of this day they'd been surrounded by the deafening rush of expressways that the quiet crunch of his spikes on asphalt seemed hallucinatory. He had found this place by accident. His confused intentions had taken him down detours, had led him eventually, inevitably, to Yankee Stadium . . . and it was afterwards, as he'd crept along the growling trench of the Cross Bronx with the vague notion of going back, of climbing the crumbling ramps and heading back the way he'd come—that he had seen instead an unmarked exit ramp, had descended steeply through shade and emerged onto this forgotten shelf of land twenty feet above the river, a dilapidated lot for some long-ago razed building, an oasis of macadam heaving with cracks and neglect. No one would notice him here. He'd flipped the ignition, had dug the leash from beneath the passenger seat and stalked the relative calm while the dog squatted, wandered some more, squatted again.

The city had changed, had acquired in the interval of his absence the excess clutter of twenty years of bright ideas, the memory of the last time he'd been here—the *only* time—so distorted by scrutiny that he could now barely summon it. He had blacked out. He had no memory of the previous night's arrival save a damp discomfort, no recollection of the transition from rain and mist to sun and high skies but for the funk and chafe of the soaked leather, the drowned look of the dog, and his own hypothermic tremble. The day had begun amnesically amidst a procession of taillights, a mechanically ventilated purgatory far beneath the bedrock of the Hudson River, coming above ground then into shine and chaos and a complex rotary clogged by orange-and-white detour barrels. Stop-and-go traffic. Had he slept? Or had those hours simply vanished? The parched and burning feeling in his throat and chest told him he'd been sick, though he didn't know where or when—a quick check of the sodden floorboards had revealed no evidence—the pain of his hangover unrelenting in the slow go of the financial district, turning debilitating against the lattice-work of light and shadow slung from the three bridges to Brooklyn.

He was killing time. He had decided that he could not do it, that he could not go through with this plan of theirs. It had been crazy of them to ever think that he could, insane to believe that in his current condition this trek of the previous day could ever result in anything other than what it had resulted in. So when the pounding behind his eyes had at last forced him off East River Drive in search of gas and aspirin (only to end up gridlocked at First and 59th), when he'd broken his fast and the dog's with a pretzel in a wax paper sleeve and then meandered back out into the early morning traffic, which had relented just enough to make it possible, somewhat, to maneuver along the crowded narrow streets of double-parked garbage trucks and taxis—he had gone and done something he seldom did.

He found a bar.

He'd always been one to drink alone, holed up in the darkest, most sorrow-intensifying settings he could find, his own cruel form of self-punishment. Yet something about the morning spent circumnavigating the city had made him desperate to speak. Something about the dim light coming through the frosted front windows of the neighborhood dive on the Upper East Side where he'd killed an hour and then two more at a tall stool drinking kamikazes and southern blues had made him feel the need to hear the sound of his own voice—scratchy and deep after months of rare use, months of talking only to himself or to the dog. The barkeep was in his seventies: white hair and gin blossoms, flannel sleeves rolled up past his elbows, a slightly outdated prototype who'd seemed reluctant at first, a pause and a sigh before he'd ambled over, polishing a glass and playing a role. "What'll it be, fella?" A half hour and three drinks later he'd ventured to ask what was with the uniform, and from there it had been easy for GB to wade out into it like a confessional, easy enough to begin with how he'd driven up here from Florida the previous day, twelve hundred miles in just under eighteen hours, alone but for an eleven-year-old chocolate lab in the passenger seat of his '73 Stingray convertible whose roof he'd left back in Miami, the dog now leashed to a fire hydrant out front while he sat here beneath this stained-glass billiard lamp trying to figure out what was next.

And why had he done all this? Well, that was the complicated part. That was the part that would take some explaining. Was there any way (GB had wondered, his voice already slurred, eyes glossing over as he gazed up through the empty glass tumbler)—was there any way he could make the next drink *just a tad bit stronger*?

It was difficult to recall, later, just when or how the idea had come to him. He was not even sure it could be called an idea or if it was little more than the momentum of desperation, the muddled distress that had trailed him throughout the remainder of the afternoon after he'd stumbled back out into the sun-drunk street, already going on one o'clock when he found the dog and located the Stingray (he'd forgotten, at first, which street he'd parked on), removed the bright ticket from beneath the wiper, and, falling into the same semi-catatonic state that had sustained him these last months (the dog looking up from the floorboards, his own haggard reflection looming red-eyed in the rearview) had improvised the side trip over the Willis Avenue Bridge into the Bronx.

A hazy intermittent layering of clouds had drifted in from the mainland through the lunch hour, a translucent quality infiltrating the light as he continued north along the Deegan past the tenement towers of Mott Haven, through a motley gray and brown landscape until at last the low-slung light standards had emerged above the rooftops, signs guiding him off the expressway. And there it was, precisely where he'd left it: blue block letters emblazoned upon the façade, a nondescript signboard right out front.

YANKEE STADIUM

BOX OFFICE HRS. 9–5

TOURS DAILY!

It no longer shamed him to see it. He was no longer bitter. Despite what Tammy might have said—what she *had* said during countless arguments over the years, accusations and recriminations that had threatened to shake the foundation of the so-called dream home in Coral Gables—the truth was that he *had* done exactly what he'd promised back when they'd gotten together, that getting married and having a daughter *had* changed him, that a decade or more truly *had* passed since he'd spent a single sleepless night agonizing over the years he'd pissed away in pursuit of the promise this place had once seemed to hold for him. And yet as he'd found and then paid for his parking, as he'd made his way on foot back across the neighborhood, quiet on this Monday off-day (the Yanks just off a weekend sweep of the Red Sox, the owners of the delis along 161st Street out smoking butts on stoops while the 4 train rattled by on its elevated track), he had been powerless against the awakening of a part of his mind he'd previously been too preoccupied to focus on, nostalgia breeding a somber possibility as he'd stood looking up at that famous white frieze, handed over a ten and followed the brash tour guide and a crowd of milling Midwesterners beneath the entrance at Gate 4.

It was baseball, after all, that had proven his savior on previous occasions, had provided a void-filling fascination for the angry, confused kid who'd lost his mother at eleven and felt his world turn twenty degrees colder, yet also more focused and purposeful. Out the clattering back screen door of adolescence it had led, a tattered ball and a borrowed glove toted up the block to an abandoned warehouse in the foothills of the San Gabriels, a billion fastballs hurled against a cinder block back wall until the seams had given way, until the scuffed cowhide had peeled back to reveal the wrapped wool underskin. By high school, he'd more than gotten noticed. Letters had arrived by the dozens the summer of his senior year— the summer they walked on the moon and anything had seemed possible, even a kid from San Berdoo making it big. Pro scouts flocking into LAX, driving rental cars east along the 10 to huddle in the hard bleachers at Perris Hill Park to get a good look at him, the fireballing lefty with signature blond curls pouring from the back of his cap, cheese that topped out mid-nineties and a curve that fell off the table, his perfect game in regionals followed up by another in the city finals (which he'd also single-handedly won with a late-inning homerun) making the typically enthusiastic post-game discussions that flared up like wildfire in the dusty cut behind the dugout turn downright worshipful. ("The kid's *filthy*! He's ready for rookie ball right now. What are his plans? And where are his *parents*?") A commotion of praise that had chased him home along cracked sidewalks, his shadow slung out a hundred yards ahead of him like something to be lived up to, the voices of the scouts like oracles' in his ears making him pull the brim of his crimson-and-black San Bernardino High ball cap down low over his eyes as if it would make him invisible, as if it could give him strength.

He'd known for some time he would have to do something. Had
listened all summer to the way those voices turned solemn when
the truth was given in whispers, the story of his not-so-secret "family issues" dragged out and stared at like a dog run over and bleed-
ing in the street. Had listened also in the cramped discomfort of the
house off Wildwood as his old man—who'd never come to a single of
his games, had never even asked about them, had more important
things to do—would regale them all around the dinner table with
the stories of his plans for them in the Great White North, an
unimaginable future discussed later in the tense silence of the
attic-like room he shared with his little brother Jamie, commiserations beneath the cover of their father's snores in which GB would
confide as to what *he'd* decided to do, how *he* planned to stay right
here in San Berdoo because you could hardly play ball in the snow.
Weren't too many baseball diamonds on glaciers last time he'd
checked. And if the old man had something to say about it, well
then, he'd just have to find other ways of convincing him, wouldn't
he? (A verbal cracking of his knuckles. A whispered plea in that
little lair beneath the eaves in the hopes of recruiting a sidekick,
only to find his kid brother too complacent or content, too scared or
brainwashed at thirteen to conspire such.)

And so as that summer had bled toward August, as the stacked
boxes signifying the imminence of their move had accumulated in
the front hall and the old cobwebby shed atop the driveway, as even
poor confused Jamie had acquiesced and begun packing up his half
of the room, GB's long walks home from Perris Hill Park in the
aftermath of his glories had become something like nervous dress
rehearsals, anxious anticipations of the final face-to-face with the
father who stood in the way of the future foretold by the baseball
scouts, the most important pitch of his life up to that point practiced

and polished and perfected until at last the time had come to deliver it: a smoldering night in late August, wild fires raging in the valleys as he ascended the driveway to find the old man stacking boxes in the boiling dark shed out back, asked for a few minutes of his time and received that rolled-lip nod for which he was famous.

He'd moved out the next day. Waved goodbye to his stepmother and the twins who'd gathered politely on the front porch, and was off, the bearer of an uncomplicated confidence incomprehensible during the half hour he'd spent roaming the lower concourses of Yankee Stadium in a solemn daze of remembrance. It had all been not nearly so simple as he'd been led to believe by the scouts and big-league representatives, by his high school coach in whose basement on a cot next to a water heater he had whiled away the remainder of that last summer of the sixties. There'd been two things a kid could do: two alternatives hashed out on the Labor Day evening he and his coach had sat in the vacant bleachers at Perris Hill, the grass infield gone brown in the hot brush of the Santa Anas. A kid could declare eligible for the pro baseball draft and, in doing so, could also make himself eligible for the *other* draft. A kid could risk having his name called, could go over and do his tour, could hope a season spent dodging defoliant and trying not to get turned inside-out by machine gun fire would not damage his poise or command. *Or*, he could go to college. And though he had said all the right things—had given his old coach a final tentative hug, had pasted a smile on his face from the moment he arrived at the party school outside Phoenix with a blonde "escort" named Pamela on his arm right up to the afternoon he'd stood on a crowded dais holding a diploma that went straight into a dumpster—those four years of delays and frustration at college had been characterized mostly by the reluctant certainty of a misstep, the underlying suspicion that he had traded some integral part of himself in return for a compromised ease.

Oh, he had enjoyed himself. The sixties had swung a corner toward the seventies and he had swung right along with them, had set conference records and reveled in the lazy dominance of the big man on campus, the gifted athlete given a free ride and a deferral in return for having his left arm on loan for as long as the war dragged on. And yet beneath all the glory and the acclaim, beneath the mastered pretentious coolness of the small-time superstar always looking disinterestedly at his nails while others raved of his achievements, there had been also the reality of something lost in the transformation, a dilution of the desire that had once driven him each time he summited a mound and stared down a sixty-foot, six-inch tunnel at a tight window of hope, a loss of the desperation that had compelled him on those long walks home in the solemn dusks of San Berdoo. So that by the time the war *had* at last ended, by the time he'd stood shell-shocked in his revelry-wrecked off-campus apartment listening to a voice on the phone telling him that none other than the New York Yankees had secured his services with their top pick in the draft, all trace of that brave, earnest boy who'd shown up for college four years before had been replaced by a vainglorious imposter with little left to lean on but arrogance, an incorrigible caricature he had wished, ever since, he could go back and talk some sense into.

How many times had he imagined it? How often had he dreamed of returning to warn that brash insecure know-it-all with blond surfer's hair who arrived in March of '73 in the top-down Stingray for his first day of spring training in Port St. Lucie, Florida, dressed in wayfarers and a silk leisure suit, twenty-two and beyond reproach and wealthy as all get-out thanks to the signing bonus that had dropped out of the sky? How many times, in these years gone by, had he pictured himself, an aged ghost in white pinstriped rags arriving to deliver the sad truth: That these days of fame and regret were not the beginning, or the end, but the beginning of the end? That these dire, burdensome days—spent preoccupied not by the glory that seemed to await, but rather by what the old man, wherever he happened to be, might think of him now—were as close as he'd ever get to gratification?

<hr />

THE SKY ABOVE FORT LEE had deepened and cleared, the sun rupturing hugely over the tall banks across the water, and though high up in the city the light of this long day still plagued the commuters on the bridge trudging home toward Jersey, down here the world was in deep blue shadow and perfect silence. He had already unzipped the knapsack. Now, carefully, meticulously, he arranged its contents across the interior of the trunk, a dozen or so small stacks of lined notebook paper, stapled or clipped and filled to the margins with a scrawled child-like handwriting he could not make out unless he held it up to his face, studied the indecipherable marks that passed for words. The edges of the pages lifted slightly in the breeze that came off the water, the chill of the air harsh against his still-damp uniform as he reached into the baseball bat bag and retrieved the heavy item contained within, the hunting rifle procured months ago from a Miami pawn shop when he'd first felt this inevitability settling over him.

All the way back across the city he had told himself that he was ready. Yes, he had entertained those thoughts of heading back to Miami, had even retrieved the tattered road atlas and retraced his path. But it had been little more than background noise, a disguise of hope hiding the ugly truth that he just needed to find somewhere quiet, somewhere peaceful and forlorn, and if he could find such a place then the rest would be easy. He hadn't intended for the tour to end so shamefully. But what he had thought might be a remedy had turned quickly to something else. He'd been powerless against the memories and even worse had been the looks from the tour guide and the Midwesterners, their belittling gazes filling him with the same indignation that had arrived in the bar as the lunch crowd had filtered in and the barkeep's expression had drifted toward the unsympathetic impatience of the city-dweller. The same resentment he'd somehow kept at bay throughout the previous forty-eight hours—the previous thirty years—turning to a simmer as the tour had led out into the astonishing sunlight of the left field grandstands where stood the shrine of famous Yankees, the names immortalized on the stone altars beyond the bullpens bringing a bile so bitter he'd had no choice but to spit it out, to harangue the confused Midwesterners with a scene so odd it must've seemed like part of the tour at first—until this strange man in a pinstriped uniform had begun howling about how by all rights *he* should have an altar of his own, how if not for *his own fucking father* he might've ended up in the Hall of Fame. For them the scene had concluded rapidly with the arrival of the rent-a-cops. But for him it had continued as he'd rattled north along the Harlem River and then west on the Cross Bronx, the fading orange blush of afternoon finding him at last on this dead-end lot beneath the city, his entire existence boiled down to just three simple alternatives: to go back, to keep going, or to finish this once and for all, right here on this apron of asphalt where no one would notice.

He closed his eyes. The shining dampness had returned to his face and he wiped it away with the back of his hand. With the setting of this stage had come a kind of assurance. And yet something about this place—this city. Something about all those deliberate pauses and now this one, perched above the river with the dozen letters spread out like a dare in the trunk, the dog having come up to brush against his calf and looking up as if to say *Where we goin' now, boss?* Something about every moment of this long morning into afternoon and now becoming evening had transformed his guilt and his shame, had awoken the other impetus that had propelled him along all these months and miles. Not just the love he had felt for his daughter, but also the disregard his own father had shown. To think of all he'd lost, and then to recall the way the old man had looked at him. The flash of his Zippo as he ignited a Camel and stood smoking with scorn and disapproval. The creak of the floorboards beneath his feet and the sound of his own voice—strained and juvenile, willful and deluded in the cobwebbed darkness of that long-ago shed—imploring the old man to understand that this bold plan of his, this ungrateful abandonment, was in fact *his* opportunity, *his* Alaska, *his* moment with *his* milkshake machine man. And hadn't a wise man once told him there were two types of men in the world? Those who talked and dreamed and those who *did*? Hadn't a wise man once told him there came a time in every boy's life when he had the choice of sitting on his ass or getting up and *doing* something?

To remember the way his father had turned away, had dismissed and disowned him. And then to think of what *he'd* seen, what *he'd* suffered. To recall what *he'd* endured as they'd led him down a dark corridor into the cold sterile capsule of that Sunday morning. To think of all these things while the dog that was the only souvenir of the life he'd left behind in Miami looked up with such sad loyalty was enough to spin the revolving wheel of his emotions once more, enough to make what he'd almost done here seem not just a mistake. Enough to make him return the rifle to the bat bag, to reassemble the dozen letters and stuff them in the knapsack. To gather up this confused jumble and refine it into something else entirely. Something not quite like anger. Not quite like rage. But close enough.

He slammed shut the trunk, helped the dog back up into the passenger seat. The Stingray's big-block revved high in low gear as he climbed the switch-backed access road, rising up from the calm by the river. The Westside Highway had long since been dismantled, the elevated yellow steel monstrosity from his memory replaced by a street-level urban boulevard. Joggers and dog-walkers in the last amber brush of quitting time, giant faded advertisements and a series of stoplights that he followed all the way to 57th Street, made his way in zigzags along the one-ways of the west fifties while the nearby docked cruise ships waged low-pitched horn battles in anticipation of evening departures.

He had wondered, during the rare moments of the previous day when he'd allowed his mind to stray this far forward, just how he might remember it. He had never imagined that as soon as he turned onto the correct street everything would lock into place in a moment of instant and complete recall, the place where the story of his baseball career had finally come to an end still here and mostly unchanged. The shambled gargoyles still gazing down from the crumbling corniced roof, a flurry of pigeons alighting and a place to park right out front. He had never imagined he might find himself so readily standing on this rugged stoop, looking up at this building that masqueraded as just another tenement, though the signs that it was something different were there for those who knew what to look for. No air conditioners jutting from the windows. No abrupt Juliet balconies with geraniums in terra-cotta planters catching sun. No mailboxes in the lobby. Instead, a low credenza with pamphlets beneath stone paperweights to keep them from blowing away each time the heavy doors swung open, turning this dingy anteroom into a wind tunnel.

ROGERS HOUSE: A PLACE TO COME HOME TO.
WHAT TO DO WHEN YOU HAVE NOWHERE TO GO.

After this bright day circling the city in the Stingray, it took several minutes for his eyes to adjust to the dark interior of the cold lobby. Mahogany walls and marble flooring. A disused fireplace against the far wall. The sounds of the city shut out by those heavy doors that had swung closed behind him, leaving only the click of his spikes, the dog's nails, and a voice. A voice coming through the air thick with age and dust that he tracked to a far corner of the room, where the half-obscured figure of a young woman in a ski jacket had materialized behind a glassed-in booth.

"May I help you, sir?"

There was still the option of turning around, stepping through those heavy doors, and retracing his path back through the Holland Tunnel and from there along the southbound corridors of I-95. There was still the opportunity to accept his failures as his own and not the product of some concocted curse, still time to try to find some other way of coping that involved neither self-destruction nor the heaping of blame into long-abandoned corners of his life so he could douse it in his anguish and set it ablaze—still years and years to ponder and dwell and perhaps someday absolve. There was still time for all of this. But he knew also that he had come too far to turn back, that a decision had been reached and that something indistinguishable as courage or cowardice was in control now. And what would he have done with himself, anyway, if and when he ever arrived back in Miami? What do people do? he'd wanted to ask Marc on that Sunday morning they'd stood next to the FOR SALE sign on the front lawn of what had been his and Tammy's dream home. How am I supposed to *move on*? How can I ever *pick up the pieces*— he'd wanted to shout at that bright unforgiving Florida sky—when these fragments of a life, this car and this dog, this knapsack and this baseball bat bag, this pinstriped uniform and this plan if it can be called such, *are all I have left*?

"Sir? May I help you?"

The girl behind glass was Emma's age. She looked out at him with a bored contempt he knew all too well, one pierced eyebrow raised as he approached tentatively, a specter in a Yankees uniform smelling of whiskey and wet dog, his haggard mutt on a leash and his face a gray mask beneath the pulled-down brim of his ball cap as he fought to form the words he'd been silently rehearsing all day, the most pivotal pitch of his life up to this point now ready to be delivered: words that came at last, thrust through cracked dry lips.

"I'm here to find my brother."

So we went with him.

From the sunbaked streets of San Berdoo to the end of the earth, we went with him. From sunny California to night-shrouded Fairbanks, Alaska, in search of oil—in search of something that had eluded him during those years in California, something we must have known, even then, with some part of our hearts, he would never find, a goal that had transformed and would continue to do so each time he approached it.

From the westernmost edge of the continent to which he'd traveled with his own father, some thirty years previously, across desiccated fields of lost hope, we went with him even further, boarded a plane and stepped out into a land of month-long nights and days, the sun always low and striking, dime-sized as if we'd traveled outwards in the solar system. A cabin at the end of a dirt road with little furniture but a battered coal stove, a screened-in porch looking out on a field and a towering row of pines beyond which the little boom town crouched, a land of newfound wealth, and this transformed village its gateway, a place where a few months hard work—so they said—could make you set for life, or at least several years.

Make a few bucks, invest it right, take an early retirement. The American way. I'm not asking you kids to love it here. God knows I'd rather be soaking up some sun in Southern California. All I'm asking is for you to give me a year or two. Just a year or two and then we're out of here. Words spoken to those of us that remained in the large main room of the cabin huddled around the fire that first winter with the second wife he'd found to replace the first. All I'm asking for is a little bit of faith. You all know I just want what's best for you and it turns out right now that's Alaska. Is it ideal? Hell no. But is it something I've got to do? We wouldn't be here if it wasn't . . . Because in the end, it all comes down to you kids. In the end, we're here because of *you*.

So we went with him. Followed him to that isolated end of the world with some small shard of hope left, found only the other thing husbands could drive their wives to, the other form of abandonment that could take our lives and seal them off like surrendered cabins in the wild.

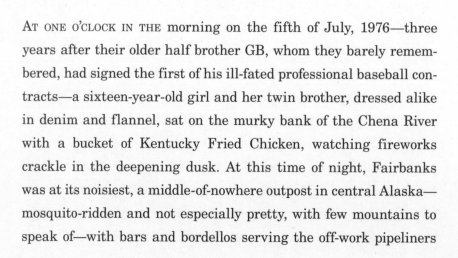

AT ONE O'CLOCK IN THE morning on the fifth of July, 1976—three years after their older half brother GB, whom they barely remembered, had signed the first of his ill-fated professional baseball contracts—a sixteen-year-old girl and her twin brother, dressed alike in denim and flannel, sat on the murky bank of the Chena River with a bucket of Kentucky Fried Chicken, watching fireworks crackle in the deepening dusk. At this time of night, Fairbanks was at its noisiest, a middle-of-nowhere outpost in central Alaska— mosquito-ridden and not especially pretty, with few mountains to speak of—with bars and bordellos serving the off-work pipeliners until five in the morning, closing down only long enough to rid the floors of the peanut shells and filth and satisfy state regulations before reopening at seven-thirty.

The pyrotechnics shattered and rained down from the sky, the two kids sitting on the concrete half wall that protected the city from the spring breakup, eating the chicken purchased from the all-night store on Second Avenue (Two Street to locals and pipeliners) with the Chugach totem pole out front. Max was working on a wing while Maddie tore into a breast, the show coming toward the grand finale and reflecting on their soft, upturned faces, the light already beginning to return to the northern sky where the sun had set only one hour before. Maddie had bought the bucket of chicken with a hundred-dollar bill. Two bucks it would have cost in California, but it was four eighty here. She'd handed over the big bill like nobody's business, and the taciturn Indian woman behind the counter had made her change without a second glance, assuming her to be the daughter of a pipeliner just paid. Maddie had found the hundred on the floor of the Flame Lounge, a bar and dance club into which they'd snuck hours earlier, ducking past the gathered men and women in the back alleys that separated it from the French Quarter, another dive. She'd had Max hoist her up and over the fence that divided the alley from the receiving area, then had gone around and let him in; they'd snuck through the kitchen and out into the main room, where the night had already been in full swing at nine o'clock, though outside the sun was still shining.

Together, they'd watched the little town—their home town, they guessed—change overnight, turning from a backward settlement of thirty thousand to a boisterous place more dangerous than LA and almost as interesting. They'd arrived in early winter of 1969 with no idea what to expect and had taken a cabin on Fireweed Hill, a ramshackle place constructed of pine board and tin that had shaken with the cold in the winter and teemed with mosquitoes in the spring. They could have purchased a more up-to-date place to live, but their father had said this would all be temporary, that there was no sense spending a bunch of money. He'd said it all throughout their first two years here, responding to the looks of the kids that ranged between confused alarm and terror, insisting that this was the place where they would truly strike it rich. "That bit with the fast food," the twins had heard him explaining to their older half brother Jamie on the cold nights of their first summers here while they'd listened from the mosquito-proofed porch where they slept (canvas blinds zipped to keep out the sun), "that stuff was all small beans. We're talking real money here, my boy. D'you know how much oil they're talking about up there on the North Slope? They're talking twenty-two billion barrels of original oil and thirty trillion feet of natural gas on top. Does that mean anything to you, boy?"

"It don't mean anything if they can't get to it," the twins heard their older half brother mumble, could see him out there sitting on the sink basin, lean and flannel-clad with a teenager's semblance of a beard, thick lenses of his glasses obscuring his eyes or revealing them in distorted magnified flashes. He'd become so sullen and contentious in the past three years, ever since his brother had stayed behind in California while they'd moved up here with Annabelle, the twins' mother, their father's second wife. Jamie's life had become one constant complaint about how he'd ever ended up in such a redneck dump in the middle of nowhere, a pack of smokes a buck and a quarter and a beer—which he drank plenty of up here, though he was not yet seventeen—fifty cents, the temperature thirty degrees in September and thirty below throughout January, ice and snow melting in the spring into slush and mud and something worse called muskeg.

Sometimes they'd go out into the back field with the rifle their father had bought when they'd moved up here and had set about teaching Jamie to shoot, though he himself was little more than an amateur. The shots would ring out in the evening after dinner, punctuating the discussions while the twins listened and watched from the windows, their father often still in his dress shirt and slacks though he'd remove his coat and tie and leave them hanging from the clothesline, Jamie slouching with the weapon, raising it suddenly and sighting across the far-off line of spruce, their father giving instructions that he never seemed to acknowledge, never seemed to obey. The sky crackled with the echo of the gunshot. Jamie glared across the field, then lowered the rifle and discharged the spent shell.

"I heard what happened to that tanker you guys sent up around the Bering Sea," he said. "Got caught up in the ice and nearly sank. In July! And it don't look like they'll ever get that pipeline built. Not with the jackoffs they've got working on it and the EPA. Too many environmentalists in the way. Can't say I blame them that much."

"Those are just delays, my boy," the twins heard their father say, watched him seize his teenaged son gently by the arm as he took the rifle, the way the twins had seen him seize any number of folks over the years, bringing them closer and lowering his voice, inserting an element of pleading into his normally even drawl. The twins had seen their father do this again and again, not only with their mother but also with state legislators and union delegates (they may not have known what these titles meant but were familiar with their father's lingo). They had listened as he dispensed his practiced charm and had watched the other party's eyes soften always, had heard the reluctant acquiescence in their voices when they at last spoke their agreement.

"I promise you, Jamie," their father said. "They're going to build that pipeline. Close to a billion dollars, they're saying it's going to cost. But once the tankers start cruising out of Valdez"—he pronounced it Val-*deez*, like a local, like he'd been born and would die here—"we're going to be raking in profits like you read about. The Arabs can twist the screws all they want then because the United States of America will be a self-supporting nation. We won't need their Middle Eastern oil. We'll have *Alaskan* oil."

"Three years," Jamie said. "Three years you've been selling me this crap. Three years since they struck oil and it's still sitting there, untapped. Three years and they haven't even so much as ordered the pipe. Haven't moved a single shovelful of land for the pump at Valdez. What makes you think I can wait for all this to get done?"

"What else are you gonna do?" asked their father, sighting with the rifle barrel over the back field. "Hunt caribou?"

But Jamie had had another plan, a plan he'd told the twins about one night in May of the following year. In the winter, the cold and the darkness made them a wild-eyed bunch; they'd stayed away from each other, had spent the long nights in separate rooms, which was difficult in the log house, kitchen and living room separating the bedrooms on the first floor, the little attic under the eaves where Jamie slept always quiet with his absence or, when he returned, his deep soundless sleep of adolescence. The twins tried to make do, tried to make snowmen, but in February the thermometer did not rise above zero for the entire month, and they'd watched the frost collect on the glass of their bedroom window, secure in the relative warmth, though they could still see their breath and wore four layers under their parkas. The breakup had come in May, and with it a new flourishing—the first arrivals at the airports and on the highways were like the circus rolling into town, freaks from Texas and California in cowboy hats and fur coats, wide sunglasses that hid half their face and long hair either parted in the middle or stacked up in afros. They waited in lines that stretched three blocks from the hiring hall, only to find that preference would be given to those who'd lived in Alaska for over a year. In November, while the twins had been steeling themselves for yet another winter, President Nixon had signed his approval to the bill. In January, when the world was locked in a bitter freeze so deep even the stars seemed frozen in place, Interior Secretary Morton had at last issued the long-awaited construction permit. Word had spread quickly and, by spring, the highways from the Yukon and north from Anchorage had brought them by the thousands. It was during these days that Max and Maddie had begun their long afternoon sojourns downtown, into the heart of the transforming city, their father off at work in one of the makeshift office buildings or down in Anchorage, where he was flown twice a week in a single-engine Cessna, the head of public relations for such a large project always on the move, always with a group of investors or union officials or with a group of Indian kids in a nowhere school house, smiling and reading picture books. The twins knew their mother had resigned herself to this existence, locked in a log cabin nine months out of the year, swatting mosquitoes the size of rats and mindful of grizzly bears when she came out to the yard full of purple wildflowers, in a bikini, to get some sun on the rare days when it was warm enough and not raining in the summer. It was on one of these days—June, the temperature in the mid-sixties, which felt tropical up here, the fireweed in bloom and the sun high over the main street of Fairbanks, with its false fronts hiding square concrete buildings, a weird assortment of freaks waiting in line for employment, smoking cigarettes on benches along Two Street, the whole place looking like the set, full of extras, of a Hollywood movie—that Maddie had leaned toward her twin brother and whispered something to him, and their dark faces, eyes like moles' after the long winter in the cabin, had peered across the street to find their older half brother, Jamie, engaging in a shady deal in one of the alleys between the hot spots.

He was selling fake ID cards. He'd explained it to them later, after he'd led them on a wild goose chase along First Avenue, toward a place where the river ducked under a narrow bridge for foot traffic. He'd leapt up just as they'd come over the bridge, where the last remnants of the snow still lingered. "A hundred bucks," he said to them. "Each. I've already sold twenty today."

That was his plan to get out. He already had the money for the bus ticket and—since he was still only seventeen—one of these picture-less state-issued IDs he was hawking (picked up on the sly from sources he didn't care to mention) would be used by none other than yours truly. "Only I'm not gonna use it at some fool employment office to get a job welding pipes in sixty-degree-below-zero weather. I'm going straight down to Anchorage and signing up for the Marines. Any luck I'll be overseas in two months."

The war in Vietnam was yet another mysterious component in their lives that the twins did not understand. "I thought it was over," said Max, while Maddie remained silent, dark eyes set, chin like a chisel.

"Hell no, it ain't over," said Jamie, stood up in the slushy land under the bridge, and handed them some cash from a thick fold concealed in his shirt pocket. "Now scram," he said. "Get yourselves something to eat. I got work to do."

Only two months later, he'd told their father of his plan, had told him while they'd stood out in the yard in the echoing reverb of a gunshot, the rifle lowered in Jamie's arms while his father told him he had to be joking, asked him what the hell he was thinking and pursued him into the house when Jamie shook his head and turned away, their father saying, "Don't you dare walk away from me, boy!" which had induced a verbal altercation of new and epic proportions in the kitchen, curses and recriminations that had brought even Annabelle out of her dark hovel in the back bedroom on the first floor where she slept half the day, coming out only long enough to take bubble baths and then stand by solemnly, barefoot and wild-haired in a sleeping gown, rubbing herself down with Neosporin while the boy and his father's voices raised in the kitchen, the boy with the bus ticket sticking out of the front pocket of his favorite flannel shirt—the same pocket where Maddie and Max knew he kept all those hundreds he'd use to get to Anchorage. It was now late June—and though the big work on the pipeline would not begin in earnest until the following spring, the work in Valdez had started, and every day in the streets and in the bars there was the murmur of anticipation, the shady dialogue of men claiming it would start any day now, the busses up to the camps in the north with the funny names—Dead Horse, Cold Foot, Old Man—for the heavy duty of laying pipe, the work that called for 7-12s (seven days a week, twelve hours a day, every third week off) but that paid as much as fifteen dollars an hour with time and a half for overtime and double time for holidays. Their father said Jamie was a fool to be giving this up. The military? The military didn't pay! Private enterprise paid! "They want that pipe done in three years and are willing to pay whatever it takes to make it happen. In three years you could make two hundred thousand dollars, which you can invest and then figure out what you really want to do with yourself." But Jamie would not hear it. The last thing he'd said, before marching out the door without even saying goodbye to the twins, who were out in their beds in the covered screened-in porch, was that he would never live in a world of his father's making. That if it drove him crazy or killed him, he'd resist it always. Then he'd slammed the door, the only person in Alaska who was heading away from Fairbanks, hell-bent on a far-off war whose end everyone had been anticipating but him.

Back in the cabin, Annabelle put her arms around her husband, but he nudged her away. She was getting Neosporin all over him. He came to the door of the room where the twins now pretended to sleep, took one step in as if contemplating soothing his loss with their proximity. Then he pirouetted and took off out the door into the yard for a cigarette, a faint red twinkling that the twins watched float in the darkness. "He'll be back," they heard their father whispering beneath a new moon and the towering woods. But he was wrong.

WHEN THE FIREWORKS WERE OVER, Maddie heaved the half-emptied bucket of chicken out into the river, and they watched it float then sink while the swans clambered over it. They watched the birds come flying in from wherever they'd been hiding, as if they'd smelled the chicken from all the way up where the hills rose to the north on either side of the river, the land rolling on in a tundra of permafrost, bog, and black spruce. "Where to now?" Max said, and Maddie, wiping her lips with a damp napkin, said, "Back to the Flame."

They smoked cigarettes on the way, flicking ashes along the filthy streets. Max didn't know why his sister was so obsessed with the Flame Lounge, why she seemed so captivated by the dancers who stalked out onto the stage naked as the day they were born and then lounged on the couches in the corners until one of the rugged men sauntered over and grabbed an arm. There was something reckless in Maddie, a constant desire to court trouble that Max did not quite understand, though he did admire it. She had not been like this in California, but then nothing had been the same in California, where they had spent their days roaming the halfhearted dog park or, at their most adventurous, sneaking into the night-shrouded construction site of the shopping mall down the street from their house. Here in Alaska, even in the endless daylight there was always a mysterious dark energy to be explored, and Maddie seemed to thrive on it, was always looking for a thrill.

It was no longer strange to the twins that they had become regular visitors to the Flame Lounge, despite the fact that they were only sixteen. It was because of Jamie that they had initially been introduced to this downtown area with its all-night bars full of racket and ruckus. He had often regaled the twins with stories of his adventures while the three of them sat in the screened-in porch, and in the months after he'd told them of his plans to leave with his money earned from the fake ID cards, he had on a few occasions let the twins walk downtown with him, where he would buy them something to eat. One night, after they'd eaten, Jamie had stood up, his eyes flashing strangely behind the thick lenses of his glasses. "I need a drink," he said. "C'mon." And then he'd led them down noisy Two Street in the ten o'clock dusk and stopped in front of the door to the Flame Lounge, beyond which the twins could hear the shouts and country western music blaring.

"What the hell do you think you're doing?" Maddie had said. "Max and I can't go in there. We're not old enough." But Jamie had scoffed, had told them no one here gave a crap how old they were. "Besides, I'm not gonna let you drink anything." It had turned out he was right. The bartender on duty had been happy to allow the kids to sit behind the bar while Jamie sat and sipped beers. They were not even the only kids in there; others could be seen crouched in the darkness, little urchins looking shocked while their pipeline fathers stood at the tables chugging beers and occasionally buying them a Coke. Jamie had taken them again the following night, and that was how Maddie and Max's presence around the downtown area had come to be accepted, first showing up with Jamie and then, later, by themselves. "Don't ever tell them who our father is," Jamie had warned the twins on several occasions. "In this town, it's better to stay anonymous." And the twins had listened, would hide in the corners and observe as the country western bands played and the drunk pipeliners boasted of their exploits while stacking shot glasses into towers, watched as the welders wiped the bars with hundred-dollar bills because they could and then carelessly stuck them back in their pockets, watched as the intoxicated men staggered off to the juke box or over to the couches lined along the far wall where the working girls sat ready to be taken upstairs.

Over time, Maddie had developed a relationship with one of the female bartenders, and when she was in charge the twins would help run drinks for a share of the take, would step around the bar taking cigarette orders for a small fee, which the arrogant quasi-rich welders would happily contribute. Maddie had also made friends with several of the working girls, some of them Athapaskan women with long black hair hanging to their hips, some of them young Texas girls dressed in boots up to their knees and little else. But the one Maddie had become closest to over the years was Jasmine, a black woman from Chicago who'd arrived in Fairbanks via

Las Vegas the same summer Jamie skipped town, who'd watched from a corner of the bar when Maddie had made a risky dash for a hundred-dollar bill that had fallen from the billfold of a careless pipeliner. Jasmine had stepped across the floor while Maddie ducked among the stools and under tables, six-foot-tall stride making up ground, and Max had watched as she'd driven the high heel of one boot into Maddie's hand just as she'd reached out to grasp the bill. He'd watched Jasmine's slender fingers pick up the hundred, hand it back to the man who'd dropped it, a sharp-featured welder named Lyle Greeley who'd been showing off his new paycheck all night, and then march off with him toward the rooms at the back. Later, outside, while Maddie counted her take from the peanut-shell-strewn floor in the shade of a dumpster, Max had heard the click of heels again, had seen the tall woman standing in front of them, wrapped in a mink coat. "Just what the hell do you think you're doin' in there, little girl?" she said.

"Fuck you," Maddie said. "Mind your own fucking business."

The money was gone from her hand. Jasmine had snatched it away. And though Maddie fought to get it back, Jasmine dodged her attempts, jerking the money away from her again and again, back and forth. "Two fifty," she said, and smirked. "Not bad. Here's the hundred that stupid cowboy dropped on the floor." She'd added the bill to Maddie's take and tossed it back down at her feet. "I gotta tell you though, you keep hangin' around a place like this, you're gonna be sorry."

Maddie smiled her sweetest smile and raised her middle finger, its nail painted a deep rich red. "C'mon, Max." And she took him by the arm and pulled him away.

Max had thought that would be the end of it, but Jasmine seemed to have seen something she liked in Maddie. She would come over to talk to the twins occasionally when she saw them doing cigarette runs, would try to get them to tell her who their father was. "Is it one of these asshole pipeliners? I already asked all the other girls and no one knows. You kids should be home getting ready for school, not hanging around a dump like this." Yet she would smile and ask Maddie how much money she'd made that night, would turn to Max and say, "What's cookin', good lookin'?"

"She's just messing with you," Maddie told him, but Max refused to believe it. He had already begun dreaming of ways he might persuade Jasmine to marry him, of ways he could purchase her a ring and convince her to settle down. He knew with some part of his mind that this was ridiculous, that she was just being nice and trying to look out for them, but he couldn't help it. He would think about her constantly, would toss restlessly in his bed while Maddie slept her deep sleep next to him, and one night, he had told Jasmine he wanted to show her something. He had asked her to follow him upstairs, and when they'd gotten to one of the private rooms, Jasmine saying, "Whatever this is, it better be good," he had showed her the money he had brought with him, had asked her if she'd do with him what she did with the other men. Jasmine had looked at him for so long, her face grown serious, that he thought maybe she didn't understand what he meant. Then she turned away and shook her head, looked back at him and smiled. "You're too young," she said.

"I'm sixteen!" Max had said, desperate. He had reached for her, but Jasmine held out her arm to stop him. "Like I said. The answer is no. You're too young." And then she had gone back downstairs, where Lyle Greeley was always waiting every third Friday with his paycheck held out in front of her and a fat cigar clenched between his teeth.

Max Hill hated Lyle Greeley. That night, he had stepped outside and sat down in the dirty alley against the brick wall of the Flame. Had heard the sounds coming from the window above and had known what they were. But that wasn't the only reason he hated Lyle Greeley. The real reason was what had happened just a couple weeks prior to the night they'd sat out on the river with the bucket of chicken, when he and his sister had exited the Flame into the eerie purple light of the summer solstice to find Lyle Greeley urinating against the concrete wall of the building, skipping the long bathroom line often a dozen deep. He'd seen them and didn't stop, just began speaking with his back still turned to them. "There they are," he'd said. "The famous twins." He'd zipped up, turned to them and stepped in a wide half circle toward the back door, and the twins had circled against him, as if revolving around the same empty point in the cracked concrete. "I heard plenty 'bout you two. I've heard you do a lot more around here than just bring drinks and go on cigarette runs. Creepin' around under the tables stealin' folks' hard-earned dollars and what not."

He paused at the back door, adjusted his wide-brimmed hat, took in each of them in turn. "I been keepin' an eye on you two. I don't like the way *you* talk to Jasmine. Make her feel like something she's not. And *you* . . . you try to hide it, but I know exactly what's going through that pretty little head of yours." Maddie flicked her cigarette at him, and he deflected it easily. "I'm more than happy to do the initiating. I'll pay you and everything. Pay you as much as I pay Jasmine. Whenever you're ready, you just let me know," he'd said, turning and making his way back inside. "I'm prepared to make you the richest little girl in Alaska."

Maddie had turned away, her face without expression, as if hiding something. "Let's go, Max." The anger that had been boiling up in her brother's blood—her older brother, for he was all of nine minutes longer to the world—the desire to see Lyle Greeley's face and that ridiculous cowboy hat smashed, had turned into an energetic pride in his sister. Even if she'd not spit in his face or called him a name, and even if he'd noticed her more pronounced silence over the weeks that had passed, the looks Lyle Greeley still angled her way and the broken, almost coy way she refused to return them—even if he could sense a new distance between them as he sat watching her watch the fireworks, watching her hurl the bucket of chicken out into the river for the half-starving Alaskan birds—even if he understood that something about his sister had changed, Max Hill chose not to accept it, chose to believe that this young woman sitting next to him was still the girl he'd always known.

FOUR IN THE MORNING IN Anchorage, and George Benjamin Hill had not slept a wink, had not witnessed any fireworks, had been up all night trying to figure out what to do about the latest train wreck. A subcontractor had been caught trying to rush the project by falsifying X-ray inspections on the welds. Some he hadn't even X-rayed at all, and others he'd certified despite deficiencies. Big Ben—as he was known by everyone on the project—had been called down to deal with the perpetrator and discuss options with a board consisting of Fred Madden, Chairman and CEO of Alyeska; Charlie Unger, Executive Vice President; and Harry Baker, a PR man. "No choice," said Madden, stern faced, his mouth always twisted in a Texas frown. "Got to dig the whole pipe up."

Faces held in hands. Much sighing.

"Do you have any idea," asked Charlie, "how much that is going to cost?"

"Fifty million was the estimate I got," said Madden. "But that's the least of our concerns. The deadline is what we need to worry about now. Only a year and a half to go. Big Ben. Baker. I've got enough shit to deal with. This faulty welds business is on you two assholes."

He'd left the building and walked down A Street to his hotel, avoiding the crowds gathered in anticipation of the fireworks. It was nine o'clock already; word of this most recent disaster in the pipeline project would no doubt hit the papers tomorrow morning, and Madden had already informed him of the press conference tentatively scheduled for three the following afternoon. There, the man they knew as Big Ben Hill would have to again do his best to patch the wounds that were always festering on the surface of this project, which was already 600 percent over budget and getting more out of control every day. If it wasn't workers buried by avalanches, it was trucks sinking in muskeg; if it wasn't people complaining about who they hired—not enough Indians, not enough Alaskans— it was people complaining they'd hired too many. And if it wasn't state officials bitching about rumors of goldbricking, then it was the teamsters headed up by Randall J. Carr, demanding the most outrageous things Big Ben had ever heard of. And getting them!

Big Ben had only ever been confronted by the legendary Randall J. Carr on one occasion, at a debate in Fairbanks two years ago regarding the clerical workers' election for a bargaining representative and a place in one of the unions. Initially, CEO Madden had been scheduled to stand podium-to-podium with Carr, but he'd balked at the last minute, had asked Big Ben to take his place. Big Ben hadn't been worried. Already in only five years of working in the oil industry, for Humble Oil, first as a refinery manager and then as PR director for the California branch of the company, he'd gone head-to-head with plenty of loudmouthed teamsters, had settled them down through the strength of his own personality. The idea of some document-waving crazy-faced Alaskan did not concern Big Ben. But this Carr was no half-assed amateur. A Los Angeleno by birth, he'd come north after the Second World War, had driven a truck and flown a plane. "I don't know," he'd said when they'd taken their positions at opposing podiums. "Seems to me like it's hard to do collective bargaining when the employer doesn't show up at the table. I know, Mr. Hill, that you consider yourself a reasonable representative. But could you, right now, even if you chose to, give these people what they want? Power's like being a lady, Mr. Hill. If you have to tell them you are, you aren't. Now all these people want is all any teamster and his family wants. They want a fair day's wage for a fair day's work and freedom from foreseeable disaster."

It had ended in frustration, Big Ben frustrated because he knew he'd been outdueled. For the first time in as long as he could remember, he'd come into a room and not succeeded in becoming the one everybody agreed with. And it was frustrating for everyone else because, though they'd clearly won the debate, they knew nothing would come of it, because this nobody that Randall J. Carr had just finished dressing down in the VFW hall—"See what I'm saying, folks! You get 'em by the balls and their hearts and minds will follow!"—this man from the Lower 48 with the stumped smile who was escorted down to a taxi afterward and driven off in silence was only a PR man. Not a decision maker.

Big Ben walked the streets of Anchorage by night, listening to the first firecrackers and alert for sounds from dark corners. It was shady business, dealing with these teamsters up here. Six times in the past ten years, the federal government had had to indict the head of the Local 959 on charges such as extortion and embezzlement; each time evidence had been thrown out or disappeared or the case had dried up when a witness wound up in the hospital. Bodies had been found along the rivers from Eagle to Fort Yukon, half eaten by fish; others had been dropped all over the state, always made to look like an accident of the wilderness, the elements. Big Ben had adopted a manner of looking in all directions, even here in Anchorage, but especially in Fairbanks, where the cold drab streets seemed capable of hiding anything.

Some of the locals, guys Big Ben had talked to when he'd first moved up here, businessmen who'd had to deal in the past with Randall J. Carr, told a story of how the famous union despot had gotten his way with just a piece of stationery. It seemed a young salesman was in town getting ready to pitch a new product at the gas refinery out Sitka way. This was back a few years ago now, maybe '71 or '72. The product was new to the market, the salesman an up-and-comer from Seattle, ready to take over the world and not afraid—or, in his naivete, not even aware—who his product might affect. He'd gotten two phone calls at his hotel in Juneau, neither of them very friendly, but it hadn't made him worried. His company had set him up on the top floor looking down through the fog at the state capitol, a room that was an actual *suite*, a living room and kitchenette with a door leading into the bedroom, which is where he kept all his presentation materials, all rolled up in a tube and ready to be unfurled, ready to convince the people at the gas refinery that they were crazy to be paying a unionized group of workers a fat wage—$11.15 an hour plus $3.00 paid directly by the employer to the union to establish a pension fund—when they could eliminate 75 percent of their workforce merely by installing the computers and software this young man was peddling. The day of the scheduled meeting, the young man felt trepidation mixing with excitement. At breakfast, he'd seen the eyes upon him, had taken the elevator back up to his room next to a man in a suit with a black tie and sunglasses, who'd stood completely still and watched him get off and joined his hands in front of him as the door slid shut, though this was the top floor, and the man in the suit had ridden all the way up with him only to ride all the way back down. The young man stepped to the door of his suite, thinking: *All I have to do is get my materials and get the hell out of here. Make my pitch, make the sale, then get a taxi to the airport and get the hell back to Seattle.* But when he arrived at the door it was slightly ajar. He walked in to find the venetian blinds pulled, the whole room in darkness, a cool rain pattering on the balcony. At the foot of the door to the bedroom was a folded piece of stationery, as if a matron of the hotel had placed it there. The young man, shaking, went over to the piece of paper, picked it up, and read it:

Open this door and you're dead.

That was the end of the sales trip. The young man had made his way back to Seattle, was fired from his job, and lived happily ever after. The folks at the gas refinery were not so pleased. They solicited another company, who recruited another salesman, whose remains were never found.

This was all rumor, of course. And Big Ben would never have believed it, might have forgotten the story completely had he not been thinking of the press conference later that day, visualizing himself at a podium with a set of crosshairs trained on his forehead, if he'd not been reminded of the story by the slow elevator ride up to the seventh floor at six o'clock in the morning, having finally returned from his long walk along the dark streets of Anchorage.

He was scared—had been scared for the last three years of his life, ever since they'd finally gotten the final clearance from Tricky Dick and set the project in motion. Before, despite all the words he'd spewed at his son, Jamie, despite all the salesmanship he'd heaped upon the boy in an attempt to get him to stick around Alaska and get rich off the largest domestic utilities project in history rather than marching off to the Far East to try to clean up the scraps of a war and maybe get killed in the process—despite all of this, Big Ben had known from the start that this was not the place for his family. Annabelle could barely bring herself to go outdoors. If it wasn't too cold then the mosquitoes feasted upon her, a visible cloud forming around her body as they swept in and attacked. Big Ben had watched her slowly lose a part of herself throughout the long, cold winters, when an almost psychotic cabin fever set in. The kids were no better. They'd been smiling, happy Californians when they'd arrived here seven years ago, nine-year-olds ready for an adventure in the wild that had turned into a dismal existence in the bleak isolation of the interior. Seven years of their lives—it was not an unendurable period, but for children their age, it was enough. He'd seen the way this place with its frontier ways and misfit ideology had affected them, and yet the long exhausting hours had left him with no time to do anything about it. He'd known from the start that he'd plunked himself down in a place that he would never understand, that was as different from California as you could get, a place more like the Oklahoma of his childhood that he barely allowed himself to remember, where the world could dawn one day intent on making a dust storm that would uproot your life. He'd felt uncomfortable with the eyes of these people, the way even the most casual conversation was always steeped in the knowledge that you were from the Lower 48, that you would without doubt try to deal with uniquely Alaskan problems in a way that didn't work up here, that you'd come in with a nice suit or a flashy outfit and soon enough be frozen solid against a tree with a black bear chewing out your innards if you didn't learn the ropes quick.

He'd felt all of this distrust, had known that it would take every ounce of his ability to make acquaintances, and that even if he were successful, there would be someone else he'd pissed off. Still, he might never have made the final connection between his own life and that young salesman's story were it not for the dim corridor leading back to his hotel room, the faint light spilling from the sparingly placed wall sconces creating pockets of nearly complete darkness amidst halos of visibility, through which he stepped to the end of the hallway, where—unbelievable! No! It couldn't be! He almost laughed when he first saw it, when he still thought it was just a trick of his eyes. Then he started trembling so hard he could barely move.

On the crimson paisley carpeting of the hallway in front of his room, on the early morning of the day he was scheduled to make a press conference regarding the future of the Alaskan pipeline operation, he found a little piece of stationery, folded in half.

He didn't read it. Couldn't bring himself to look at it. Didn't want to know what brutal message they'd crafted. Instead he marched back downstairs, found a couch in a hallway beside the emergency exit, and holed up for four hours. He awoke startled, a pay phone ringing. He thought he was back in Los Angeles, at Union Station, on the morning after he and his father had arrived at eleven at night and slept on benches with the Packard parked outside because they couldn't afford a hotel room, preparing for what his father had called a long day. *Our first in the city,* he'd said.

It was already noon, the press conference scheduled to go off in three hours. He was supposed to be there by now, so they could all meet and discuss what would be said. What angle they'd take. But instead of heading right over, Big Ben borrowed a razor from the front desk, shaved and fixed his hair in the bathroom mirror, walked two blocks up the hill to a men's shop and purchased a two-hundred-dollar suit. If I'm going to be assassinated today, he said to himself, I'm at least going to look good doing it. If they've decided I'm important enough to kill, then God damn it, I'm not going to let them down. Outside, dressed up and sweating, he looked at himself in a glass storefront, superimposed over a sign reading WE RESERVE THE RIGHT TO REFUSE SERVICE TO NON-ALASKANS! He looked good. Much younger than forty-five, which was what he would turn that fall, which was already winter here in the forty-ninth state.

At the scene of the press conference, they straightened his tie, polished his face, made him appear bright and unconcerned with this minor inconvenience regarding the faulty welds. These sorts of things happened all the time, he told the audience, looking out at flashbulbs and waiting for the one that would end his life. So certain was he of his pending execution that he grew impassioned at places he should have remained solemn, chuckled at moments of gravity. He looked out and realized that half the crowd members were pensive, the other half openmouthed. Somehow, he came across with just the right amount of savoir faire, just the right amount of reverence, his cadences and responses to the questions just measured enough that he was able to convince himself that he had saved his own life, that he had looked down the barrel of a rifle with a telescopic lens into the heart of a man being paid to kill him, and had touched some sacred place that had made him lower the weapon and join the applause. The response of his superiors was different: rolled lips and nods. Madden displayed his ever stoic nature, and it was Charlie Unger who finally took Big Ben aside, put one hand on his back. "We sure appreciate it, Ben. We sure do. Especially with what you've got goin' on back in Fairbanks."

Big Ben shook his head, dumbfounded.

"We understand you need to get going," said Madden. "We've got a Cessna ready to take you out of Merrill Field if you want. Probably be quicker anyway."

Were they firing him? Was it that bad? Had he overestimated his delivery and the reaction of the crowd? But he couldn't ask them. Big Ben had never been able to admit to a lack of understanding, had never been one to say he didn't know precisely what was going on. All the way home on the Cessna, three hours in a noisy plane flying low over the Alaska Range, he wondered what it could be that they were talking about. He tried to piece together what it might have to do with the assassination attempt. He wondered what had been written on that piece of stationery.

———

ANNABELLE SANCHEZ-HILL HAD BEEN NOT quite asleep when she heard the rustling outside the log cabin she abhorred in the town she hated like she'd never hated anything in her entire life. This was a state of consciousness she'd come to know well and practically look forward to—a state of mental exhaustion that nonetheless would never allow her to sleep, because her days were filled with such lethargy that her body was never ready to shut down. She'd stopped eating altogether, blamed it on an utter lack of activity, an inability to find anything worth spending calories on. And when she tried to actively participate in something, her state of malnutrition would leave her spent in only minutes. In California, she'd been a cheerful, energetic woman, a former college soccer player, petite but strong and thick-legged. In Alaska, she was a face behind the soiled glass of a frosted window in a cabin, so lonely she felt barely human, felt she should grow a beard and hair on her back, long claws for protection.

For seven years now she'd lived here in Fairbanks—seven years of her one and only life spent barely making it through each time-consuming day. She couldn't recall whether it was night or day when they'd first touched down at the airport in Fairbanks, because it had seemed to her that first month that it was always dark. They'd arrived in early winter, and even the vision of the aurora borealis, of which everyone back home had made her promise she'd send pictures, was not enough to startle her toward enthusiasm. She'd felt that first blast of arctic air when she got off the plane and prepared to settle in, to hole up in a protected place and not come out until he was ready to leave, or at least until spring. But spring was fleeting, summer nonexistent. She'd tried to spend an afternoon on the hammock in the back yard the first summer and ended up with more mosquito bites than the twins could keep track of— though they'd tried, flipping her over and running their little hands over her body, so bored they were ready to make a game of anything: "One hundred nine! One hundred ten!" Their ability to adapt had made her feel even worse every time she complained, or, more often, when they'd ask her what was wrong and she'd say, "Nothing," unable to describe what she was feeling and able to tell from their sad faces they knew she was lying. The only person to whom she'd been able to talk about it in the beginning was Jamie. He was obnoxious, quick to anger, and sometimes casually cruel to the twins, kind to them one moment and then aloof the next. But for some reason he'd been able to serve as an audience to her grief. She'd found it possible, on rare nights they spent alone together at the cabin, to sit down with him at the kitchen table—where they never ate as a family, only argued—to spill her guts about anything, and the teenager would listen, would do his best to make her feel better.

That was why she'd kept his secret. He'd told her his plans to leave long before he'd done so, had asked her not to let anyone know, especially his father, and though Jamie himself had spilled the beans to nearly everyone involved, Annabelle had understood the importance of keeping his father in the dark. She still remembered her husband's reaction when he'd finally learned that, despite everything Ben had told him, all the advice he'd given the boy and strings he'd pulled to assure him a lucrative position despite his utter lack of experience, Jamie was denying the opportunity and taking a bus to Anchorage to sign up for the Marines. Annabelle had seen him hurt before, had seen him devastated when GB had stayed behind, and though it had only lasted a single evening before the steadiness had returned to his eyes—an evening spent out in the field beyond the cabin in the dark, smoking and pacing—she'd in time come to believe that it had changed him. She'd waited in the kitchen for him to come back in—this man who'd ruined everything good about her life, who'd made her come up here to Alaska with him, claiming it would be only six months, maybe a year, only to have it drag on for seven—had waited for hours, only to be shrugged off as he made his way up the stairs toward the boy's bedroom, where he gathered everything to be burned. And it was then—her only confidante off to the Marines, her husband blaming her for his loss—that she'd stopped eating. When she'd sunk to a hundred and five pounds, he'd decided that something had to be done. He'd pulled her out of bed and walked with her down to the car, past the front field where the twins were digging for gold nuggets. "C'mon," he'd said to them. "Field trip. We're taking your mother to the hospital."

Since then there'd been visits to various specialists, diagnoses made and revised, medications prescribed and side effects suffered, afternoons when she'd felt almost human, almost capable of coming out into the light and sharing herself with the world again, only to be foiled by exhaustion, her own inability to form or satisfy an appetite, this dead weight inevitably dragging her back to bed, the blinds pulled against a nocturnal sun, settling into this secondary level of consciousness in which she'd become so comfortable. A place that passed the hours. A place so far from Alaska that it often took several moments to summon herself back.

It was the pounding at the door. With a baseball bat, she padded out through the kitchen, unsteady because she hadn't eaten in two days. Dehydrated to the point of hallucination, she at first didn't believe what she saw, which was a six-foot black woman, dressed in a fur coat over a dirty white corset gown and standing on the porch, grabbing Annabelle's arm and leading her down to the car parked along the dirt driveway, where Annabelle was startled to see her two children in the backset, both of them filthy and with bloody noses, Max's face swollen and Maddie's locked in an expression of shocked hatred.

She went to them, opened the car door and tried to put her arms around them, but they fought away from her, their eyes blank like stones, Max's fixed on Maddie and Maddie's on the floorboard. "What happened?" Annabelle kept asking, because she needed to hear their voices but didn't know what else to say. "Tell me what happened!" But even when the tall woman told her, she didn't understand. She sat in the passenger seat in a daze while the woman directed them down the long driveway to the road. She could hear Max whispering in the backseat, could hear Maddie telling him to shut up. Just shut up! But when she turned, they would not let their eyes meet hers. Annabelle's body began to tremble and she put her arms around her shoulders to stop it. "I have to call Ben," she said, but then kept forgetting. She couldn't remember how to get to the hospital, but the woman in the white gown seemed to know, drove them along the silent streets on the outskirts of town in the civil twilight of four in the morning and then up the road to the emergency entrance, where she parked and ran around to the back opening the doors, helping first Maddie and then Max get out, Annabelle standing next to the car that this woman Jasmine claimed to have borrowed from her friend, Jade, and whose trunk held a secret she could not confront or accept.

Jasmine. Jade. Annabelle knew what kind of names these were. "You're a—" she said, but she couldn't finish the thought.

"Not anymore," said Jasmine, already climbing back in the car. "After tonight, I'm outta here."

It was the Fairbanks she'd witnessed from afar, brought now unmistakably before her eyes, and Annabelle understood she'd been blind not to realize what her children would find themselves involved in, what sort of trouble kids growing up in this environment would inevitably encounter. It had happened downtown, on Two Street, the vile center of alcohol and prostitution Annabelle had given one sideways glance upon their arrival and then turned away from for good. It was a place of almost caricatured debauchery; in her descriptions she'd sent home to her parents—the descriptions that had led them to urge her to get the hell out of there and come back to Simi Valley—she'd pictured sex acts being performed in broad daylight, drugs changing hands in alleyways, alcohol consumed at an unfathomable pace while naked women danced on a stage and a country western band played nearby. She'd asked him a hundred times to reconsider, to please please please tell them that he couldn't do it anymore, that Fairbanks was not a place to raise a family, that it was a den for itinerant workers out to make big cash and then blow it, for hardened men willing to work fourteen days straight if it meant they got to spend the next seven in a drunken, sex-fueled haze. But he'd always been unwilling to listen, had told her how he'd known all his life he was destined for something big like this. That he'd hoped it would come by the time he was thirty. That when he'd reached that age with no extravagant achievement yet under his belt he'd been certain it would occur during the next decade. How he'd made the same bargain with himself when he'd turned forty. "This is my last chance," he'd said to her.

"Your last chance for what?" she'd asked him. "Your last chance to get us all killed?"

She could not help but think back to what Mary had said—or written, rather. The little piece of paper that his first wife had handed over on their only meeting, a slip of paper no larger than a business card that Annabelle had kept all these years in a shoebox in their bedroom. At last check, Mary still lived in the Santa Jacinta Home for the Mentally Ill, a place Annabelle had visited only once but that had been burned in her memory so indelibly that she could picture every phase of the trip, even now, nearly ten years later. It haunted her still, as she sat in the hospital waiting room while Max and Maddie were led back the hallway, the nurses having asked her what had happened but Annabelle unable to say, able only to endure their looks of disapproval. They recognized her, of course. Knew her from the times her husband had brought her here and stood pacing while the doctors opined and dispensed prescriptions, Annabelle lying on her hard hospital cot finding it difficult not to believe that she'd brought this all on herself.

She'd known early on what she was doing, that she was sleeping with a married man, though he'd told her it wasn't true. He'd told her he was divorced, then that they were *separated*, then that they were in the process of *getting* a divorce. She'd known all along that those out-of-the-way rendezvous at motels in beach towns far north of LA were evidence of a truth she'd suspected all along, a truth she'd attempted to confront and then turned away from in disgust when she'd learned that she was pregnant. Pregnant with a married man's baby. *Babies.* She'd tried to talk to him about their options—he wouldn't even have to pay for anything—and that was when he'd fallen on his knees in their shaded beachfront motel room and told her how much he wished for her to be the mother of his children. *All* his children. For he knew it was time he came clean with his wife, was long *past* time he came clean with her and told her of the life he'd been hiding, of the beautiful, amazing young woman with whom he hadn't meant to fall in love, but who'd been his only refuge these past months.

There were complications, of course. The divorce could not be finalized right away. But *God!* he hoped they could work something out. In the meantime, enough of these dingy hotel rooms! He'd rented her a small house in San Bernardino, had shown up at the hospital and held her hand while she gave birth, had held the babies—a grumpy-faced pair they named Madeleine and Max after her mother and father (a ploy, of course, to win some sort of favor)—and shook hands and unwrapped cigars and stayed with her until she fell asleep. He'd been a sporadic presence that first year, working hard to make the money that paid her rent and settling the final details of the divorce with Mary, who'd agreed to give

him everything (including the children) in return for a monthly ali-
mony stipend—so selfish was she, he'd told her, that she was willing
to sell her children if it meant not having to work. She'd fought with
him, had fought with her conscience telling her this was a bad situation. But what was she to do with two babies? And who could she
blame but herself? She'd known he was married all along, had
noticed the wedding ring the first day they'd met—the wedding
ring that was gone the next time she'd seen him. And then, one day,
when she'd thought she was almost ready to leave him—when she'd
listened to enough advice from her parents and her brother and her
college friends, when she'd finally convinced herself that the only
way was to make a clean break, to move and change her phone
number and maybe get a restraining order—he'd broken the ground
rules he'd so specifically set. She'd heard his car in the driveway,
looked out the living room window and there they were, he and his
sons, GB and Jamie, aged twelve and seven, their grief-stricken and
confused faces softening when he introduced them to the twins,
introduced them to their new *family*, the vision of the four of them
sitting then on the floor watching television together undermining
her intentions, trapping her in emotion as he led her down the hall
to the master bedroom where he told her what Mary had done.

It hadn't surprised her to discover what had happened to his first
wife—though under different circumstances, it might have made
her incapable of so much as looking at him. But because she attached
so much of the blame to herself, it became a thing she could not run
from but instead had to face. What *she'd* done to this woman, what
her sleeping with a married man had wrought. She had never
stopped thinking about that day—even in the years when their
relationship was at its best, when the twins were still infants and
GB and Jamie seemed almost grateful for her presence—she'd never

forgotten the day she'd grown so frustrated by his broken promises, so touched by the boys' constant appeals, that she'd at last agreed to drive them out to the desert to visit their mother. She had never stopped recalling that five-hour trip across California on barren roads through the featureless desert, their arrival in the parking lot, just after one in the afternoon and so hot she was sweating the instant they got out of the car. Coming through the front door of the building to find it freezing, the sweat drying on her neck and shoulders and turning to little daggers of ice, the air conditioning keeping the rooms at a constant 55 degrees, the patients and nurses and doctors bundled in long-sleeved clothing, the two young girls at reception wearing coats and scarves and directing them down a long hallway toward a makeshift elevator.

She'd thought it her place to stay outside in the hall, unwilling to face the scene she imagined taking place behind the closed door, the two young boys crawling up to their mother whom they hadn't seen in nearly a year, the woman she'd heard could not speak—would never again speak after what she'd done to herself—a woman sentenced to live the rest of her life out here in this lost corner of the California desert. In all the years that had passed, Annabelle Sanchez-Hill had never forgotten the way she'd waited out in the hallway for nearly half an hour, sitting in an uncomfortable chair next to a padlocked and barred window; the way the door drifted open and she'd breathed a sigh of relief, watching the boys step toward her, thinking it was finally time to leave; the way she'd seen it on GB's confused face even before he'd jerked his thumb back toward the slightly ajar door of his mother's room. "She wants to see you."

In the car, on the way home, with the boys sitting expectantly around her—GB in the passenger seat, Jamie leaning forward from the back despite her efforts to get him to buckle up—they'd begged and pleaded with her to tell them what their mother had said, only to have her tell them she couldn't, that it was a secret. She'd driven on through the blazing evening, hotter now at five than it had been at noon, not even feeling the heat anymore. She hadn't felt the cold in Mary's tiny room either, whose door she'd pushed open and whose corners she'd scanned until locating the woman, seated in a plastic chair and looking hollowly out at her, her expression not of anger or resentment but more like pity, the long, frail arms reaching out and around her, the embrace cut short and the woman holding her now at arm's length. Those eyes, more pronounced than young GB's, looking through her as she took up a slip of paper and a crayon— she was not allowed pens or pencils—and carefully scripted the message that she then held up into the space between them, Annabelle's eyes playing tricks, making her see the note and the face behind it as the same object:

Get away from him!

It was in the car that afternoon—on the ride home through the desert, with GB and Jamie finally drifting off to sleep—that she'd first determined she was going to leave him, only to talk herself out of it by the time they'd arrived back at the city, the knowledge of her compromise a sad weight when she at last turned in at the house. Since then, she'd spent more time during their dozen years together convinced that she should leave him than she had content with their lives together, but then she'd wonder if it was only her guilt talking, if it was only Alaska talking. He'd keep convincing her, continually altering his timelines to make her happy, though his promises never translated into reality. Only nine more months, he'd say, and then the pipeline will be finished and we can move back to California, or wherever you want to live. We can finally settle down and relax. But Annabelle no longer wanted to relax. The last seven years had made the idea of relaxing worse than anything else. And by now she didn't care whether he said it would be six years or six months, because either one was too long to wait.

She wanted out. Now.

At the hospital, she sat cross-legged on a table in the middle of the waiting room, watching a television positioned high up on the wall in the corner, while two nurses looked on from the registration booth. At first they'd taken her for a junkie—a specter new to the area and brought by the pipeliners—but she'd tested negative, and though she was severely undernourished, she was alert. For two hours she'd been watching the breaking news story, which had pre-empted—to the nurses' chagrin—*The Price is Right*, and which had been the only thing you could find on any of the networks ever since nine that morning. Something about the pipeline. Another billion bucks down the tube seemed to be the general gist.

Annabelle Sanchez-Hill was watching the television and seeing through it to her future and the future of her children. Faulty welds. It meant nothing to her from a construction standpoint. It meant only that whatever hopes she'd had that she'd seen her last Alaskan winter were crushed. The news reporters kept talking about a press conference in Anchorage, scheduled tentatively for three o'clock, the main speaker at which was expected to be Head of PR Operations G. Benjamin Hill. The network flashed a picture of her husband on the screen, a smiling head-on shot of the man whose hotel she'd called that morning at five, whose room had been empty, and at the foot of whose door she'd asked the hotel management to leave a note asking him to call his wife at the hospital in Fairbanks. "It's urgent," she'd told them. "Tell him something awful has happened to the children."

And yet she hadn't heard a thing. Not one word. Rather than facing up to it and calling her and telling her the truth—that this business with the pipeline was flat out more important to him than either she or the children or all three put together—he'd done the very thing she'd expected and dreaded he'd do. He'd ignored it entirely. Would arrive up here sometime in the late afternoon, out of breath as if he'd run all the way from Anchorage, saying, "What is it? What's wrong?"

The newscast had completed its loop. She looked at her husband's photo and felt herself beginning to rock back and forth. A handful of new patients had arrived, and their family members sat in the chairs along the walls, not wanting to get too close. Annabelle resisted the urge to throw something at the TV. She waited while her children were inspected by emergency room doctors, while the network prepared for the televised press conference to begin, and she thought about what she would do. She considered the possibilities and decided that the best way would be to register each and every one of the reactions he'd hope to find on her face: the reactions a father arriving twelve hours late to a tragedy might pray for but never think possible. She would throw herself into his arms, showing a side so unlike her that he'd be forced to believe it, forced to lower his defenses and accept that—against all odds—he was somehow still in her good graces.

But it would all be a distraction. In her heart, she was already gone. She was already planning the things she would have to do to finally heed the warning of her predecessor, to finally do the thing Mary had urged her to do all those years ago.

———

MAX HILL COULDN'T BREATHE. HE had broken ribs from when the cowboy Lyle Greeley—who was dead, his head bashed in with a piece of rebar—had picked him up and hurled him across one of the upstairs rooms at the French Quarter. His body had collided awkwardly against the edge of a dresser, knocking the wind out of him and making his vision double as he sat paralyzed while the cowboy pushed his sister back onto the bed where she'd been lying, propped on an elbow, looking stunned.

Max had been pleading with Jasmine to come upstairs with him. She had resisted, telling him nothing had changed, that he was still too young, but when he'd told her he just wanted to talk, she had relented with a sigh. It was when they'd arrived at the top of the stairs that they had heard the voices coming from somewhere down the hall, soft at first but then increasing in volume, the woman's voice as it became more argumentative revealing itself unmistakably as Maddie's. They'd found them in the last room on the left, the room Lyle sometimes rented when he didn't feel like returning to the welder's village, Maddie lying on her back and squirming, fighting on the bed while the cowboy leaned over her and held her down, pants around his thighs, a sight that had made Max hurl himself in a strange feet-first kickboxing attack that the cowboy had easily defended, grabbing Max by a shoulder and a shirttail and heaving him across the room.

He hadn't seen Jasmine's arrival. But he had heard what the cowboy called her, heard her cry as her body was sent reeling backwards into the hallway while Max rose onto his hands and knees, crouched in the corner, recovering his breath.

That was when he'd seen the piece of rebar. Someone had used it as a prop to keep the window open, to let the cool night air into this stuffy moldy room. Max didn't remember picking it up, but he remembered the moment of contact, the sound that had sent a shockwave along his spine and made the world mute. He remembered watching the body as it crumpled to the floor covered with dirty magazines and cigarette butts, its pockets still full of hundreds, face upturned with an expression so cryptic Max had to look away, the rebar settling on the bed and falling to the floor in slow motion. Turning then to find Jasmine helping Maddie up as the sound returned to the world, his sister already fighting and swearing and pushing. He remembered the colors and the pattern of the blanket they wrapped him in, the blood on the back steps as Jasmine tried to drag him out toward the dumpster in the deep blue light of morning, their eyelids crusty and their awareness dulled by the four o'clock dawn of a nightless evening. He remembered the car parked along the cindery street around the corner and down the block by the river, remembered Jasmine dragging the body in that rowdy hour before the bars closed, her struggle to lift it up and shove it into the trunk, which she then slammed shut. And now, years later, seated in a window seat in a 747 on a rainy runway in Juneau, with his DHC Beaver sold and a suitcase of cash on the floor between his feet, Max Hill remembered himself writhing in his hospital bed that night, desperate for more medicine to make the pain go away. He didn't know where his mother was. But he knew where Maddie was. He'd seen the nurses coming down the hallway and watched them turn into the room across from his, had heard one of them mention the words that had hurt even more than his ribs, words that had told him his sister would never be the same again. With his body screaming, he'd rolled over and gotten out of bed. They'd told him not to move, had informed him that the jagged edges of his ribs were dangerously close to several vital organs. That if he wasn't careful, he could stab himself to death with his own bones. But he didn't care. He snuck across the hall and saw the shadow of his sister behind a veil, turned away, though when she saw him she rolled over and sat up, her black eyes flecked with light, her hair wild.

"You shouldn't be here," she said. But only because she knew he wouldn't go back, just as he knew she didn't want him to go. And as he crawled into bed with her, he knew already that this was one moment they'd be stuck with forever. That this morning—the fifth of July, 1976—would be with them no matter where they went or what they did. Even after his mother and Maddie had deserted him, even after his father had at last seen the conclusion of the Alaska Pipeline portion of his life and settled into a holding pattern, waiting for what would come next . . . even after all this, Max Hill—who would be the only one of them to remain in Alaska, a place he hated to leave (even now, as the 747 lifted off into the night)—after all this, Max Hill would still look back on that morning in the hospital, the pallid sunlight seeping through the window blind and the veil, his sister's bruised face against his shoulder, his own jagged ribs nudging at his vital organs, ready to puncture them at the slightest wrong move. Any move.

Monday Evening

THE SNAKE WAS IN HIS element.

He was crisscrossing the five boroughs in his endless labors, trains and busses and a cab whose back door he'd pushed open at Broadway and the Avenue of the Americas, leaving the dark-skinned driver of ambiguous origin shouting at his back in a guttural language. He hid behind bushes at the park near the library, watched two NYPD cars meet next to a taxi stand, found the brown satchel he'd hidden in a hedgerow some months ago and threw on the sunglasses inside, the fake beard, a walking stick he'd adhered to a tree trunk with brown packing tape, limped along the concrete with the stick wavering in front of him. *Excuse me, please, sir. Thank you.*

It was the only life he could imagine, this life that—in the long-term view—had begun nearly thirty years ago, when he'd abandoned the existence their father had attempted to carve for them out of the Alaskan wilderness and taken the bus to Anchorage, walked the dismal streets until he came to the recruitment office and, from there, within weeks, had been on a plane to Houston, Texas. The Snake could still recall—on days like this one, taking public transportation across the city that had grown to encompass

his whole world, the city it had been his duty for so long to protect—
that bus ride through the northern summer, could still remember
the anxiety of a young man striking out on his own, something akin
to hatred for his father though not precisely, something not quite
like sympathy for the ones he'd left behind.

They'd manipulated his impatience. The Snake didn't regret it,
was as acclimated to his existence as he imagined the lawyers and
the stock brokers he saw walking in their suits along Wall Street to
be. But that didn't mean there hadn't once been a time when he
might have pictured something different for himself. If the Snake
could've gone back in time—an impossibility, though the US government was working on it, had been for the last forty years—if he
could've gone back and talked to his seventeen-year-old self, stood
on the banks of the Chena with that young man selling work cards
to new pipeliners outside the French Quarter, he would've told
him . . . Well, he didn't know what he would've told him. Talking
wouldn't have worked. The seventeen-year-old boy who climbed the
walls of an Anchorage motel for a week waiting for his paperwork to
come through distrusted conversation. In their fractured family,
the talking had always been done by their father, who was always
trying to salvage some hare-brained idea about moving to the middle of nowhere to become billionaires. His seventeen-year-old self
equated dialogue with lies. You couldn't trust a word anyone said in
this world; the more they talked, the bigger liars they were, the
extent of their vocabulary directly proportional to their level of bull-
shitting. The seventeen-year-old boy hated speeches, found them
fucking boring. Same with politics. Same with the people who were
out protesting the war. The seventeen-year-old boy had known
nothing about the history of the campaign in Vietnam, had known
only that it had been going on since seemingly before he was born,

that for as long as he could remember, young men had been mentioning it as an option. Not a great option, mind you, but for boys of a certain age like the Snake had been—he wasn't going to college, had no interest—for boys of a certain age in 1973 it had seemed viable, a way of beginning a life if you could only manage to keep from getting killed.

Basic in Texas was a slave camp on the sun. He'd thrived in a setting so impersonal, avoided eye contact and sat at tables in the mess halls with others whose blank stares told him they'd never bother him with an attempted conversation. He'd taken masochistic pleasure from a world so parched by hundred-degree days that his skin grew hard like a reptile's, had shaved his head and all his body hair to let the sweat run its course and take away the itch, vomited more than he ate, slept every night like a corpse and woke without a thought in his head except casual dread for the day to come. The verbal berating did nothing to him. He was immune, obedient but aggressive and looking forward only to his commission, couldn't wait for them to ship him overseas so he could leave behind this insulated world of formalities and inconsequence and be thrust into the beating heart of whatever violent upheaval was taking place. Not because of patriotism—that was all just verbiage he'd heard elsewhere, macho ventriloquism adopted to make him seem more with it (he didn't even really know what a *gook* was, or where exactly Vietnam was located on a map)—but because of what it offered him, which was a way of placing himself on some dramatic stage where he could succeed or die trying with everyone watching. It had nothing to do with saving the world; it was about the world saving him through its severe power of adulation. It was why, when he found out about the end of the war—the peace pacts all signed, the armies on their way back home—he'd gone directly to his superior officers,

had scheduled a sit-down and come barging into the low-roofed
Quonset hut on the edge of camp five minutes early, talking about
"these recent events" with such vehemence that the corporal and
his aide at last had to give up their façade of omniscience and ask
exactly what recent events he was referring to.

Why, the end of the war!

The corporal had sat back in his chair, asked the aide to give
them a few minutes alone, had crossed his legs and threaded his
fingers together in his lap. This was the spring of 1973. The official
treaty had been signed only months ago, but for all intents and purposes as far as the media had been concerned, the domestic and
international media, the war had been over for years. It had been
some time since they had seen boys like this PFC James Hudson
Hill, though once upon a time, they'd been plentiful. They all seemed
to come from out-of-the-way places, from hard childhoods without
many friends in nowhere towns out in the country, one narrow
street carved into a gulley between two mountainsides, the earth
always wet from the runoff and the storefronts battered by the wind
sweeping down through the pass, a gravel road for a young boy to
walk up and down day after day and ponder a future that would
blow a hole in the universe. They were always quiet, these lonely
boys, didn't talk about themselves so much as the others because
they were always *thinking*, always dreaming, already living in their
minds the life that rested at the far end of destiny. Yes sir, it had
been some time since they'd seen this PFC James Hudson Hill's
type: boys barging into offices and asking what they could do, what
role they could play, how they could get themselves shipped off
someplace where they could perform the duties of a soldier. It had
been a damn long time, and most of them were dead now. They'd
been replaced by a hodgepodge of misfits, college dropouts, unlucky

draftees, none of whom wanted to be here, all of whom were coming around to the military as a last resort. For these types of soldiers (and for the rest of the world, always ready to criticize when it was other people's hands on the table; the same people who'd sure enough come running the instant they found themselves at the heart of some crisis) for all of them this war might have been over. For the idealists and the peaceniks burning flags in the heartland it might have been over. For the politicians and their delegates it might have been over. But for the real soldiers, the true warriors, it wasn't over yet and never would be. Sure, we pulled out of Vietnam. January 27, 1973. Didn't you see it, PFC Hill? Hell, the whole world was watching. We pulled right the fuck out and came hightailing it back to the US of A with our tails between our legs. Yessir, we pulled out and let them have their goddamn fucked-up bullshit country back.

Only, you know what?

In the frigidly air-conditioned office at the back of the nondescript Quonset hut in a far corner of the base outside San Antonio, Texas, PFC James Hudson Hill shook his head.

"It's not true," the corporal said. "The war's not over."

It was all a lie. Everything you read in the newspapers. Everything you saw on the TV. The troops hadn't *all* come back. Most of them, that much was true. They'd come home to a country surreal with indecision. But not all of them. The corporal was pacing the room now, not nervously but dramatically, kept turning his gaze to form his thoughts, then seizing the boy with a stare of immense intensity.

"Don't believe it, PFC Hill. There's still a war going on. And just because you can't hear about it on the radio doesn't make it less real. Fact is, that makes it even more of a war. No more of this honor and polite crap. No prisoners and no stories to bring home to Mom.

What happens in Vietnam stays in Vietnam. You hear what I'm saying, PFC Hill? What I'm saying is this: while the world was watching all those troops coming home—those slackers who spent their whole tours drunk or stoned and catching VD—while the whole world was eating up that Kumbaya bullshit, the people who really know what's going on were getting together on a new plan, a plan that would not be televised, that would do its work by night-fall, that would save the world in spite of itself with nobody the wiser. We're halfway to Hanoi, PFC Hill. This war is still burning hotter than ever. And if you're ready to go, we're looking for a few good men. Sometimes, you know, it's quality, not quantity, that gets it done. So what I'm asking, PFC Hill, is this.

"Are you ready?"

THAT WAS HOW IT HAD begun. A quarter century in the darkest annals of the unwritten history of the world had begun with the easy con-vincing of a not yet eighteen-year-old boy that his destiny lay with the United States government, with a secret base in the middle of the desert where only the best of the best got invited, a place that only the cream of the crop even *knew* about. So had begun a quarter century so guided by the whims of his superiors that looking back he couldn't differentiate which of it was real and which of it he'd imagined. Had he really marched north from Da Nang along a scorched path across the earth, shooting at everything in sight, a thousand men armed to the teeth and nourished only by little red pills they received every morning that made their minds fortresses of conviction and the world a blood-red atmosphere of smoke and sightlines, crosshairs directed at any movement, the corpses of the fallen cut into pieces and worn as fatigues, *No sleep till Hanoi!* their battle-cry, coming across the fields and rice paddies with mortars screaming, a wave of destruction that left the whole sky and earth trembling, a corridor of evil stomped out by the most aggressive offensive since Alexander the Great, planes spreading napalm across the path of the infantry, PFC James Hudson Hill lugging a mortar on his back that had already scorched his skin and twisted it with scars, burning out foxholes and shredding the enemy with M60 fire, Hanoi a wreck of an outpost whose outskirts they came marching through, waiting for the battle to arrive, though there were no soldiers and hardly any citizens, charging like demons on command toward the capitol, PFC James Hudson Hill from San Bernardino, California, via Fairbanks, Alaska, pulling up a hundred yards away, ducking to set up his weapon, arranging his tripod atop a parked car whose driver had been shot at close range in the face with an automatic rifle, pulling a shell from his sack and dropping it in the tube, ducking away and covering his ears at the echo, opening his eyes to watch the projectile descend toward the building ahead of his fellow soldiers, his brothers, watching the mortar shell strike a direct hit through one of the top floor windows—then turning away from the heat, a great cloud of flame that encompassed the entire building and sent pieces of rubble soaring through the air as he dove through the window of the car, abandoning his mortar on the roof and curling up on the floor next to the executed civilian, hearing the approach of a great snarling destructive breath preparing to crash down upon him, a high-pitched whistle slicing beneath the roar before the world went black.

Had that really happened? Or was it just more of the reality cooked up in the silver bunker in which he'd awake periodically, his head always aching, his mouth always dry, specialists in extensive outfits appearing to administer more pills, record his pupil size, test his urine, take hair samples, inspect his testicles, stick tongue depressors down his throat and cold steel tubes up his asshole. They'd told him he was five hundred feet below the surface of the Earth, in the largest bunker on the planet, a place where even the Soviet satellites couldn't keep an eye on us, the loneliest corner of the country and tailor-made for such experiments, a place where some of the most amazing and unprecedented testing in the history of the human race was being done, where new technology was being proven every day, where the future was now. The year up there didn't matter, was not his concern, because down here was a place outside time. It was a military base—a training facility, long pale corridors, slots on the doors into which cards were swiped to gain admittance, every word spoken in a code he was never able to fully crack. The exits were guarded. All movement, he learned quickly, was monitored by the little cards scanned every thirty feet. Color coding spoke of clearance. His was blue, which meant he had none. He was allowed to go only where he was taken. Sometimes he was blindfolded; sometimes he was forced to wear headphones playing white noise. At the end of his strange excursions along the stark corridors he was placed alone in sanitized rooms with beds or pool tables and told to act normal. Take a nap. Shoot some stick. He'd sense something being pumped in through grates high up on the wall. Then he was lying on his back in his room, unable to determine how much time had passed because there were no clocks. He had no appetite, ate only when they led him through a line and heaped nourishment upon a tray and guided him to a table. With no sun, the order of days became confused. This was his life and everything beyond had ceased to exist. He was always tired. Always had a headache. The hours in between the moments when men in military uniform would appear at his door he'd spend lying in his bed in his room without a window, writing long letters to his older brother, to his half sister, letters he didn't know where to send and wasn't sure he would've wanted to even if they'd allowed him. When he'd first arrived, he'd attempted to get some news of them, had asked for newspapers, and though the nurses had told him they'd see what they could do, the MPs, when he'd mentioned it to them, said it wasn't part of the agreement.

He couldn't recall making any such agreement. He couldn't recall his arrival, except for the spotty imagery of a green military jeep, a desert landscape with cyclone fencing and guards holding M-16s, a sign reading Deadly Force Authorized. And yet from the beginning there had been an overarching sense of something cloistering, something protective and womb-like, a presence manifested occasionally by a familiar face seen from afar, a figure moving along the corridors at a distance. He had never found out her name. Names were guarded, identities sacred. Taboo. But it seemed to him that he already knew it, that it had become for him a word like hope, evocative of a freedom he could barely imagine anymore as the years revolved in this Moebius strip of an existence, in this tent of his own fears where he sometimes wondered if anything he witnessed was true. There she was, recognizable through the crowd when they'd line up for quarterly physicals, or peering through the glass pane in his door, which she'd unlock and enter, cloaked in a crimson robe that she removed as she crossed the room, letting it fall around her on the metal floor. And months or years later, when they'd at last set him free from that place, when they'd at last deemed him ready and sent him out on transcontinental flights on the vague missions for which he'd been training, she had continued to appear to him. At airports as he'd moved through customs, a

slender figure beyond revolving doors, beneath signs in other lan-
guages, her face in adjacent taxis as he'd made his way through the
old capitals of foreign countries the only thing that had strung the
episodes of his life together.

It was during his time in Russia—(the Union of Soviet Socialist
Republics, as it had been called back then) living as a journalist in a
featureless apartment block surrounded by wire fencing, a soldier
standing guard at a sentry box with a Kalashnikov day and night—
that her presence had become haunting and continuous. He had seen
her or thought he'd seen her during his monitored trips outdoors,
smoking Turkish cigarettes in the plaza outside Lenin Stadium
beneath the colorful mural of the old leader, a red sun setting over
the Kremlin; had thought he'd seen her during digressive tours of the
city in the backseats of cars designated with yellow license plates to
distinguish him as a foreigner, coded messages allowing the guards
along the highways he was permitted to travel (a forty-kilometer
radius from the Kremlin only) to know who he was, GAI posts radio-
ing dispatches if he took too long between checkpoints.

He wasn't a journalist.

The KGB knew, had to know, for in the world of international
espionage there were no real secrets, only ambiguous agreements.
The age of foreign ambassadors and diplomatic immunity made it
folly to keep the enemy out of your backyard—the trick was in con-
trolling which windows of your house the enemy could see through.
He was treated like *vlasti*. The United States government was paying ten times the rent a Russian citizen would have paid for his
two-room apartment, but that was imaginary money anyway, laun-
dered through so many foreign accounts that it never could have
gone to domestic affairs. Instead it treated him to the best services
the Soviet government could provide. He'd been picked up and

driven to entertainment spots around the city, taken through the most luxurious neighborhoods, shown the streets whose fronts hid the darker side that hunkered down in the off-limit quadrants. They kept him under their thumb, the Snake filing stories and sending them back to the *Post*, his secret messages to the Pentagon encrypted amidst the news stories, which were dry and lifeless, his true mission remaining a secret until, on a balmy late spring day, taking a tip from a coded communiqué slipped under his door, he took the crowded train across town, skirting observation, crossed a stone courtyard to the columned entrance of the bathhouse, the *banya*.

Inside, veils of steam collected along the green algae-stained walls and marble floors, men walking naked along the dark halls, military men and common workers, students and elderly, undressing and hanging their clothing on hooks in a dressing room decorated like an Orthodox church. On marble benches beneath a hazy light filtered through frosted windows the men lay nude, sudsy water from oak buckets applied to their backs and heads and legs by more naked men, the city dust running off their bodies and onto the benches and from there to the floor, spreading in silty rivulets along the cracks between the tiles. Two naked men with buckets and a sponge descended upon the Snake, gave him a pedicure and a manicure, a shave and a haircut. The Snake rose from the bench an hour later and made his way through the corridor to the next room, where already he heard the sound of whips being slapped against wet skin, heard the hissing and shouting.

"Potepleye!" Just a bit hotter!

It was a steam room, the walls lined with wood like a winter cottage, men reclining on terraced benches while others circled with flails of birch twigs, slapping the recliners on the back, generating a soft aroma of the woods. Across the room, next to the open furnace whose soaked heat was a physical presence, two men lifted buckets, shouted their repetitive cry, and tossed the water onto the red-hot stones, a hiss filling the room. The Snake selected a space in the corner and lay on his belly, eyes barely open so it appeared he was asleep while he observed the comings and goings of the naked, pink-fleshed men. When not in use, the birch twigs were always being rattled, a rustling undertone the Snake was surprised to hear approaching. Before he could turn, the twigs had been brought down painfully upon him, the Snake rising up on elbows to watch the man who'd done it stepping off through the far door, taking a single look back over his shoulder through the haze that obscured the dim light of the room.

It was his father.

Through the door and along the tile hallway then, another room even more murky than the last, the only light from lamps situated at corners and clouded by the steam of hot bodies and cold water colliding. A swimming pool, thirty meters by ten, rimmed with faded ionic columns worn by dampness, mosaic tile floors stained by age. Daylight radiated through a roof of paneled glass, the water tinted green as if it hadn't been changed in decades, though it didn't discourage the score of men who dove headfirst, glided beneath the surface, emerged gasping from the cold to climb the sides and sit on the tile with water streaming from their hair.

He stepped over to the water and dove in.

It was so cold it made his body turn inward. It made him hold his breath, filled him with a rush of adrenaline that carried him the entire length of the pool and out the other side, water pouring off him as he stepped through the columned door and back into the ornate dressing room, where he turned a corner amidst the classic

Orthodox décor and came face-to-face with his father, his hair dried but still uncombed, a towel draped over one arm but otherwise naked, the Snake speechless and shivering, his eyes as he accepted the towel trained not on his father's nakedness but the snub-nosed revolver aimed at his belly.

An overweight man who otherwise looked like his brother GB drove. The Snake rode shotgun, watching the low hillsides as they headed southwest from the city toward Dachaville, where his father, verbose in the backseat, pistol still trained on his passenger, had told the Snake what he had in store for him. "I have a certain room in my dacha," he said, the paling scenery outside the car making the Snake's head feel dizzy, "which I think you will like very much. I call it the death room."

It was a two-story affair of brick and glass, embedded in the hillside with outbuildings stretching toward the road, a path leading down to the lake. The driver was dispatched to the garage, which his father pronounced in the British way, while the Snake was led up the hill to the main house.

"That building," said his father, "belongs to Annabelle and the twins. They do my laundry, tend my garden, fix me meals when I wish. It's a good life. One you might've considered for yourself."

The glass-lined living room was two stories tall. "A drink before dying?" said his father, but as he made his way across the room to the wet bar, the sound of exploding glass echoed from behind the Snake's back. His father dropped his glass and his drink, one hand moving up to his throat, where a rhythmic spurt of blood erupted. He dropped his pistol and had time for one frantic glance at the Snake before the second gunshot rang out—audible now through the shattered glass—and his head disappeared, brains sprayed across the bar. His body stayed crouched on both knees, then lay forward against a stool, and in the silence that remained, the Snake looked out the disintegrated window to the far-off balcony of the outbuilding and saw, rappelling along the rooftops, a single figure dressed in black.

Annabelle and the twins lay dead in their kitchen, throats cut, the door to the second-floor balcony open with drapes billowing, looking out on the empty porch from which the figure in black had sighted and killed the Snake's father. The garage lay empty, the scene of a recent escape, the keys left beneath the driver's side floor mat. The Snake got in the Volga and started it up, not knowing how to get back to his apartment, not knowing what he was going to say to the guards at the checkpoints along the way, knowing only that he'd been saved, and that he'd seen her. In the graceful movements of the shape scurrying along the rooftop, he'd witnessed the same assurance that had saved him years ago in the tunnels beneath the desert. He knew he was not mistaken, could have recognized her anywhere. The heart-shaped face, the slender build of her youth returned now. It was she: the person who had rescued his brother GB, who'd mercy-killed Annabelle and the twins, who'd sighted along the rifle barrel on his father's head, was none other than the nameless woman whose night visits to his cold, steel room in the underground bunker had been the only thing that kept him going, whose occasional presence had been just enough (he knew, and he knew that she knew that he knew that she knew) to reassure him that she'd always be there, that she'd always watch over him no matter how dangerous and disgraceful the rest of the world became, the woman who'd once held his serious face in her hands and showed him a love that had covered him in the encompassing restless sleep of decades, the woman whose memory haunted and adorned his life, the shining memory of his beautiful mother named Mary.

"*JAMIE! JAMIE?*"—EVEN THE MEMORY of the voice gave the Snake pause, made him stop and listen for footsteps at his back.

"Hey, it's your big brother, GB! How you holdin' up, buddy? Everything straight there in the Big Apple? Everything still hunky dory with my main man? Yeah? Good! That's real good! Hey, listen. There's a reason for this call, as you might've guessed. I've got some great news as a matter of fact. Some real great news. You ready?"

It was night, the sky coming to life with the city lights. Slowly, deliberately, circuitously, the Snake had made his way across and up Manhattan Island, had watched the early September sun descending among bridges and the faded pink townhouses of Chelsea, avoiding the trains because they'd be the first place they'd look for him. He did not know why he could not stop thinking about his brother GB, did not know why he was remembering this conversation from so many years ago as he exited another bus at the park at Twelfth and 52nd, walking faster now, the other pedestrians maintaining a wide berth—did not know why he was recalling this phone call from so long ago it seemed barely real, a phone call that had seemed convenient at the time and had come to seem even more so in the years that had passed, the voice on the other end a bit too excited, a bit too friendly.

"You ready? Well, your big brother GB is goin' to the show! You hear that? It's true! I'm gettin' called up! I'm comin' to goddamn New York City to play for the goddamn New York Yankees! Just got the news last night. Took me long enough, huh? Buddy, you don't even know the half of it. Damn near ten years I been traipsing the minors on overnight busses, playin' poker for per diems and luggin' my own suitcases up ramps to crash headfirst into motel beds. I ended up a journeyman. Didn't have what it took to be the big-time number-one-draft-pick starting pitcher so I ended up an outfielder, a roster filler, a babysitter for the younger players. Long story short, it just didn't work out, I guess you could say. And so instead of a half dozen Cy Youngs and maybe a few World Series rings, I spent ten years wastin' away in sunflower-seed-strewn dugouts in every half-rate town between here and El Paso. Ten years spent fightin' mosquitoes beneath the flood lamps on heartland nights too hot and hopeless to dream. But I still dreamed, kiddo. Went through the motions cuz I'd already spent so much faith on that fantasy I couldn't imagine what my life might look like without it. Guess it's true what they say, huh? 'Bout you're never too old to dream? Isn't that right, old buddy? Old J-Bird?"

The Snake remembered the cold feeling of the phone in his hands, the immediate uncertainty when they'd told him—at the halfway house where the federal government had set him up, masquerading as a homeless man to hide his identity, to hide his true mission— that he had received a phone call, that someone claiming to be his brother was holding the line on the phone in the office, waiting to speak to him. It was a feeling he had been unable to shake all day as he'd made his way across the city, cloaked in the shadows slung from skyscrapers, marching north now along Ninth Avenue with the river barely visible to the west.

"Anyway, last night. I'm standin' out in left field in some backwater town along the Mississippi, two on and two outs in the bottom of the fourteenth when a weakly hit flare that woulda been a can of corn if I hadn't been playing shallow to take away the play at the plate sends me reelin' in pursuit, spikes tearin' at the turf while that tailing ball outpaces me, touches down just inside the foul line while the winning run races home and you know what I did? I just kept goin'. Trotted right off the field and up the clubhouse tunnel to the showers with my mind made up. Knocked on the skipper's office door and sat in only my towel with my forearms resting on the back of a plastic chair turned backwards and spilled my guts out. A thirty-three-year-old man spillin' his guts out to the skip about how I was finished, how I was finally ready to hang 'em up, finally ready to call it quits in this game that was damn near the only thing that sustained me all these years. Looked up to see the skip all grinnin' at me like *you done yet*? And that's when he told me he'd just gotten off the phone with the big club earlier that evening. That's when he told me I had a plane to catch this morning. So long story short I'm gonna be there in three days, this weekend, in fact. Come Friday night I'll be suited up in pinstripes shaggin' flies at Yankee Stadium. And you know what I'd like? You know what I'd really love, bro? I'd love for you to be there. For you to be sitting in the front row above the dugout when I come running onto the field for the first time. That's why I'm calling, see? I got a ticket for you and everything. *Two* tickets, in fact, so you can bring along any special lady you might have."

And the next day, there they were, contained in a thick, unmarked envelope that he had paused before opening in the front room of the post office where he maintained a box, weighing the possibility that this would be the inconspicuous act that would end his life, the opening of the flap serving as a trigger that would cause the iodine crystals and liquid ammonium hydroxide to mix with and ignite the powdered aluminum and iron and magnesium that would plaster him all over the walls of the post office. Instead he had found two sets of tickets in continuous perforated strips, a pair of seats reserved by his brother for him to attend each of the games on this final homestand to end the season, ten evenings in a relatively unfamiliar part of the city, beyond his jurisdiction, trapped amidst thousands of unknown civilians, the very thought of which had filled him with such misgivings that he'd had to sit down and curl up beneath the water fountain, rocking back and forth until a postal employee had come over to throw him out.

He'd had no one to invite, so he invited the desk lady from his building. But she had backed out at the last minute, perhaps had been informed of who he really was or had been threatened. Perhaps her file had been pulled and come back with a hit and the Feds had gotten to her. At any rate he had gone himself, had taken the train through parts of the city he'd seldom ventured, the words of his brother still singing in his brain as they'd rattled over the Harlem River into the Bronx. "So what do you say, Big J? We can go out afterwards, just the two of us, get a bite to eat together. Just the two of us out on the town with nothing between us, nothing to keep us from being completely honest with one another. Just like all those years ago in that stuffy attic bedroom off Wildwood in old San Berdoo. How does that sound to you? Does that sound good? Because to me it sounds just about perfect."

It had sounded too easy. It had sounded like another of the agency's ploys. Perhaps they'd been wagering he'd invite *her*. Still, he had marveled at the size of the stadium, had looked up the high façade at the lines extending toward the deepening sky. The beginnings of autumn had arrived, the air cooling and most people in sweatshirts and blue jeans, the vendors hawking hot chocolate and booze. He'd wanted to buy something, just to look normal, but at the souvenir stand the two workers had shared a whisper while looking in his direction. He had eventually made his way through a shifting line to a concession stand, had descended the steps along the first base line moments later with a red paper Coke cup and a hot dog wrapped hastily in wax paper.

The seats were even more exposed than he'd expected, directly above the dugouts so you could set your drink on top of the Yankees symbol, though the Snake placed his at his feet, the grounds crew making the final adjustments and preparations, the sandy dirt of the infield receiving a final soaking to make it a lush brown, the scoreboard showing the lineups in a series of uniform numbers in a vertical column along the sides. Batting ninth for the Yankees, playing left field in place of the injured stolen base king, was an unfamiliar number 54, though the crowd along the first base side was introduced to him now: an older-looking fellow with a sharp face standing at the railing of the dugout and turning to scan the crowd. A smile. "Jamie!" he shouted, and then was rattling along the dugout beneath them. "Jamie! You made it! Did you see?" He raised his right hand, which bore his big outfielder's mitt. "They're starting me! I'm the starting left fielder for the New York Yankees!" A hand reaching up and pulling him back to the dugout, and then there they all were, jogging onto the field in a pinstriped phalanx, Frank Sinatra crooning that he wanted to be a part of it. GB Hill at the front, racing across the infield dirt and onto the outfield grass to his place in left, catching a ball on the short hop from the bullpen and warming up his arm while, back in the stands, his brother's foot began tapping, he began looking over one shoulder and then the other, began whispering in a voice so low those sitting next to him could not make out the words.

Now the Snake saw the light in the window of his room and stopped in his tracks. He had arrived at his building in the center of Hell's Kitchen and thought at first it was a trick, a mistake.

Thought he could discern movement through the colored cloth he'd placed over the window months or years ago to keep his activities off display, to keep anyone with binoculars on a rooftop from spying. But who would leave the light on? An assassin would wait in darkness; an operative come to give him the latest news would likewise not give any indication of his being there. Which left only one option: the one rare and brilliant possibility that had pulled him along all these years doing whatever he could to help the cause, for it was the only way of keeping her memory alive. He was whispering to himself as he buzzed and came through the lobby, past the empty desk where the girl with the bone in her eyelid sometimes sat. The stairs were dark and located at the back of the building, emergency exits locked and alarmed to keep them in or the rest of the world out. He reached the fifth floor and let his eyes scan the corridor that stretched to his room, feeling the cold steel of the shank in his coat. The door was ajar, light seeping through the crack and falling across the hallway, and it reminded him, briefly, of a similar upper-story corridor in a cold building deep in the California desert, a memory that he pushed away.

He waited. Listening. Said something almost like a prayer. Holding the knife level, he stepped through the narrow crack of the doorway and saw, in the corner where the file cabinets formed a shadow, a figure seated cross-legged on the floor.

It was not her.

It was a man he didn't recognize. The Snake readied his knife, but then he saw what he was wearing and recognized the number 54 on the back, remembered that night at the stadium in that unknown part of the city beneath the yellow halo of floodlights, the moment he had stood atop the dugout and hopped onto the warning track, had dodged a security guard at the pitcher's mound and raced

past a terrified shortstop on his way out to left field. He remembered his arrival, screaming—"I knew it! It's a trap! I knew it! My
own brother!"—throwing punches the man in the baseball suit had
easily parried, putting him in a headlock long enough for security
to arrive, a group of rent-a-cops dragging him away while "The Star
Spangled Banner" rang down from the rafters (for this was New
York City, and it took a whole lot more than some crazy field char-
ger to delay a Yankees game), a face looking down at his as he
twisted in the grasp of the rent-a-cops: the face of his brother GB,
now sitting with his back to the Snake on the floor, turning his
head at Jamie's exhalation, standing and coming tentatively forward, ignoring the weapon the Snake still clutched. Then his arms
were around him, the shank clattering upon the floor.

"Oh, brother," he was saying. "It's so good to see you. My life's
been a mess, brother. A true mess. Oh God, it's been too long, Jamie."

THEY HAD ALWAYS WARNED HIM it would arrive like this: masked in
friendship. The agency had always told him to watch the hand that
wasn't hugging you, to make sure it didn't hold a blade. But no one
had ever told him it might look so haggard, so worthy of pity, so prepared to be dissuaded. Just as no one had ever told any of us that
reunions are inevitably the victims of our visualizations, that years
are hard things that cannot be reshaped and molded like memory,
that the trajectories of our centrifugal lives had taken us to such
remote desolate landscapes that a safe return was impossible, that
pieces of each of us had been sacrificed along the way. No one had
prepared any of us for how those first moments of arrival—moments
we had each maybe dared to fathom in darkest solitudes, our arms

around a stranger we once knew—might bring nothing but an unde-sired recognition, a flash in a mirror better off missed, a time capsule unsealed to reveal only the hard evidence of our prevarications.

Throughout the days to come, on interstates and in the dreary vistas of our minds, we all must have recognized it, we all must have confronted it in some irrevocable cellar of our souls, the futile submission of our explanations and scars to the only other person who could confirm or challenge them, the only other living creature who could validate or villainize or vindicate.

Had we really traveled so far merely with the hope of encounter-ing some portal to the past that would finally allow us to forget? To forgive? Had GB really come all this way seeking only someone to talk him out of it?

If so, the Snake perceived in the suspicious ease of his brother's embrace, he had come to the wrong place. For the peace or whatever passed for it in this city was about to be disturbed once and for all. And twenty years had taught the Snake that this halfway house in Hell's Kitchen was not the place for happy endings.

Heartland

Wednesday

MAX HILL COULDN'T STOP LOOKING at his twin sister.

She hadn't aged. Not according to his memory. Seated in the passenger seat of the blue Buick he'd procured via his own vague Vegas connections, dozing now as the flat, featureless country of pink rocks and purple dusk spread before them—all curled up with her face toward the door, the flat blade of her cheek outlined by shadow—she was the same girl she'd been twenty-four years ago when she'd packed up and left him for a life in Las Vegas that had forced him to forget her. They were in eastern Utah, a hundred miles outside Grand Junction, where he'd planned to spend the first night of this trip east, the brief swatches of forest and national park land that had colored this afternoon spent on a clogged interstate having given way to a nocturnal landscape with nothing to catch the eye, no trees and no color. The next stage of his plan would not begin to go into effect until they reached Denver, and he'd hoped to use this long drag across Utah to explain to her exactly what he meant to do.

Instead, he'd become her caretaker. He'd been amazed, paralyzed by how different it was. Setting foot in this foreign world he'd disdainfully called the Lower 48 for the past thirty years had been like climbing a ramp from a potholed two-lane road through a tunnel of trees onto a futuristic highway of lights and levitation. This was not his America. He felt no connection to the people who lived like this, surrounded by concrete and steel and tinted glass, their hopes for the future nesting in the lap of a government as random and irresponsible as a slot machine. He had never owned a credit card, never had a car payment or a gas bill. His first pickup he'd bought in return for chum salmon from a river Indian named Sam Chainsaw. In the cabin where he'd lived with Alice and Lynk—the cabin in the country, which was what they called the interior portion of Alaska between the Yukon and Charley Rivers—he'd had no television, no electricity, had carved out a living minus these mind-numbing influences. The result was a body built for heavy work, a tight barrel of a body that looked out of place here, dressed in a flannel shirt and old jeans, a suitcase full of cash on the seat next to him in the taxi he'd taken from the airport to the south end of the Strip, where he'd stepped out into this atmosphere that felt unreal, stood under catwalks pulsing with pedestrians with the handle of the suitcase gripped in his fist, the traffic trudging ahead in a river of lights.

His discovery of her most recent place of employment had been lucky. Or inevitable. For though the never-ending torrents of tourists made it seem like a global capital, Las Vegas was not a big town—not by *their* standards. Starting at the southern end of the Strip and working his way north, the Excalibur was only the second resort on the left, and it was in its tawdry main game room that he had spoken with a man who'd told him sure, he knew her, hadn't seen her in three days though, hadn't seen her since she'd left her shift on Friday night, a shift that had ended, according to some, with her saying she wouldn't be coming back. So who could say?

She'd been working as a serving wench, after all. A what? A serving wench. In the Tournament of Kings show. Not so much a joust as a rock concert. Say, this your first time in Vegas, pal? Where you staying? Oughta check it out if you're gonna be around a few days . . .

He had stepped outside into the early morning light, had stood on the sidewalk beneath the catwalks and looked up at the fabricated New York skyline clustered across the street and tried not to imagine what this last quarter century of her life must have been like. He had heard all the stories. There were a surprising number of people who lived in Alaska who'd once lived in Vegas, but his vision of it all had been distorted by the staleness of Fairbanks, as if two places so different could not possibly exist on the same planet. And if Vegas were so much more extravagant then, well, perhaps it couldn't be so miserable. Perhaps with all the lights and action there could be no corners shadowy enough to hide anything so terrible as what she had already gone through.

It was impossible for him to stand here amidst this glitter and not think of it again. Impossible not to recall those days in the aftermath of that night at the hospital, the anger and betrayal Max had felt when he'd understood that he would never see Jasmine again, that she had made off with the hundreds in the cowboy's pockets, her fee for cleaning up their mess, or at least the part of it she could. It was impossible not to dwell on those days they'd returned home sore and damaged and medicated to find their entire lives changed, a new silence full of avoidance and denial pervading the cabin as the summer gave way to autumn, as their mother grew even more cold and distant beneath the weight of their secret. Max had sought refuge in Maddie but had found her sullen, a hard shell of independence developing over the course of the claustrophobic winter with its endless nights and the unbearable cold. By spring their conflict had crumbled like the breakup and spilled down upon them, the arguments in the main room of the cabin becoming more and more irrevocable, harsh, and vicious in a way that had, on a few occasions, made their father drag Max out into the yard and shove the rifle into his hands, made him smoke cigarettes and drink beers and commiserate as they took turns firing at invisible targets in the distant woods. An obvious attempt to win some sort of favor though the conversations were stilted, forced.

In the end, it had come down to a choice. Their mother was leaving. Her mind was made up and so was Maddie's. They were leaving Alaska as soon as Maddie finished school, and though they said they hoped he would come with them, Max could also see the reluctance in their eyes, the way his mother now seemed to look at him the same way she looked at their father.

Standing alone in the uncertain light of Vegas dawn, rolling himself a cigarette and wondering how he'd ever thought he'd be able to track down his sister in this hellhole, Max Hill recalled the night they'd left. And he recalled the day only a week before that when he'd told them his plans to stay, just less than a year since the night at the hospital, his ribs healed though he would always feel a dull ache in his chest when the rain came, the four of them at the cabin that by this point was in a state of disarray, Maddie and Annabelle's belongings half packed and lying around in a discreet clutter, an emblem of the confusion that had become the routine of their daily lives, which should have been colored by a new sense of completion—for the pipeline had at last been finished and all the checks approved, the pumps scheduled to be turned on in June and the first oil tanker set to embark from Valdez port as early as August. Their father had never spoken to them about what had happened— Max didn't even know for sure how much he knew. He had been standing out in the back field with the rifle when they'd at last arrived home from the hospital in a taxicab, had charged over to ask Annabelle where the hell they'd been and then had followed her into the bedroom, where they had stayed with the door closed for hours. Max knew it was easier for him to hide whatever he was feeling behind his new greatest triumph, and so while Annabelle and Maddie inconspicuously packed and cleaned he would smoke and pace, by turns glum and indignant, indifferent and boastful, espousing guilt trips disguised in swagger regarding the pipeline and the profits it was raking in, as if any of them cared.

It was not until after the spring thaw that Maddie had informed Max of the plans that had eventually led her here, to this runway of glitz amidst a moonscape. She'd done it all on the sly, had applied without his knowledge, had taken the SATs in the near-vacant lunch room of the high school one Saturday morning while he slept, had sent off her successful scores and applied for early enrollment and filled out the financial aid forms, checking the box that said *Check here if no one else can claim you as a dependent*, just as the guidance counselor had told her to. Max had not done any of that, had become as a result of those confusing years the sort of boy who allows all talk of college and the future to drift off in the breeze. Their mother had been the one who'd had big plans for her little boy and girl, but now that she was leaving it seemed she'd given up on encouragement. His father had never been one to supplement her message of self-improvement, had labored obliviously under the supposed assumption that if either of them needed anything, they'd just ask. So when he'd heard of Maddie's plans to go to Las Vegas, spoken to him on that night they were packed and ready to go, their father had rolled his lower lip and nodded. "Not bad!" Skinny and seventeen with a wispy excuse for a mustache, Max had watched his father in the main room of the cabin and suddenly understood. That despite all the posturing, deep down it was a relief. That beneath the arrogance and the antics, he was just pleased at the prospect of having them out of his hair.

"And you, Max?" he'd said. "What are you thinking you'll do?"

Truth was, Max hadn't been thinking about it at all. But he'd felt the need to answer, to be the sort of independent and on-his-toes son who would continue to have surprises up his sleeve. To seem unfazed and defiant against the looks he received from his mother and Maddie. "Me?" he'd said, in a voice that approached reproof, as if disappointed his father had to ask him in the first place. "I'm not going anywhere. I'm staying right here in Alaska. I'm never leaving."

Now he was over forty, still unable to grow a mustache and walking aimlessly north from the famous WELCOME TO FABULOUS LAS VEGAS sign back toward the Excalibur. What a thing to have said. He hadn't meant it, of course; or rather, hadn't known he'd meant it. Would never have guessed it might actually come true, couldn't have imagined he would be standing here some twenty-four years later searching for the sister he hadn't seen since a cold spring day in Alaska, wandering this alien strip like a lost tourist, men coming over to hand him pamphlets advertising sex shows, looking up at the towering glamorous temples of greed clustered at the intersection of Tropicana and the boulevard.

He had not noticed it at first, how the background hum of voices— ever-present, even at this early hour—had begun to change during his walk to the southern end of the Strip and back, had gradually taken on a quality of panic underlying the typical laughter and shouting, the boisterous intoxication. Max Hill had not noticed at first the taxis pulling over at the curbs, drivers' eyes locked forward on their dashboards, on their radios, pedestrians approaching to knock on the windows when their raised arms were not acknowledged, people suddenly emerging from the casinos, from the ATM booths, from the monorail platform beyond the towers with distracted expressions, cell phones pressed to one ear with a palm covering the other. He had not understood what was happening until after he'd come back through the door of the Excalibur—having finished his cigarette and stubbed it out in the stainless-steel cylinder situated next to the entrance, a revolving door he'd shared with a hustling group who'd come bursting out into the street to stare up at the adjacent miniature replica skyline, as if to take comfort from its still being there. He had thought it was more of the twenty-four-hour mania that seemed an irreversible part of these neon lights and populous sidewalks, more of the symptoms of this America that was not his until he'd arrived again at the main ball room of the Excalibur to find the evidence right there on the big-screen television that typically played advertisements and self-promotional videos, places abandoned at gaming tables and slot machines, patrons huddling, whispering, gasping, even the waitresses in their skimpy medieval costumes with drinks balanced on their wagon-wheel trays having paused, the man who had only moments before told him what he knew of Max's sister now distracted, turning away from Max's approach, everyone's eyes locked on the spectacle that passed for entertainment, leaving Max so baffled that he had almost turned and stepped right back out the revolving door to hail a taxi back to the airport—or to call up his acquaintance and see if they could speed things up. He had almost determined that this side trip had been silly to begin with when he saw out of the corner of his vision a disturbance in the crowd, people resituating their feet to accommodate the passage of some crouched creature moving along the floor, a scene Max recalled from those days long ago in the Flame Lounge, watching from the darkness as his sister—at thirteen—crawled around the feet of the pipeliners, searched on the peanut-strewn floor for their dropped hundreds.

———

SHE WAS DELIRIOUS. BOMBED OUT of her mind on something stronger than anything Max Hill had ever put in his long, thin cigarettes that burned for twice the time. He had found her at the foot of a slot machine and helped her to her feet, guided her with hands under armpits to the empty ladies' room when she'd gotten sick on herself. The last forty hours she had drifted in and out of sleep, had awakened restless and shouting out names Max had not bothered to attempt to understand, names Max had ignored as they'd made their way off the Strip by way of a noisy taxi ride through mounting confusion—voices on the radio confirming that there was a second plane, then a third and a fourth, the remote hope that it was just an accident shattered, their Mexican driver watching them like crazy people in the rearview. She had asked him a dozen times what he was doing here, squinting when she looked at him as if she had to peer through a fog. Max eventually managed to encourage her to supply something resembling an address that the cabbie was able to translate into a successful delivery out to the edge of the desert, the cab coming off the interstate onto a barren road carved into a world of creosote brush and alkali wash, mountains in the distance. Here they'd stood for ten minutes while she dug in her purse, searching for keys, at the base of a six-story steel rectangle that had once been a warehouse, that now featured a dingy lobby with a wall of mailboxes, a stark corridor leading to a bank of elevators and, beyond, a steel double door into whose key pad she punched a code as if she'd been doing it for decades, the one totally coherent moment she had before leading him into the hangar-like living space beyond, five stories of concrete and air, open aluminum staircases ascending at frightening angles without handrails, floating decks of grated fire-escape metal, rooms hovering on rooms and all of them empty, Max having to help her up a series of treacherous landings to her hanging tower of a bedroom beneath the tin roof, where he'd attempted, over the course of that Tuesday, to nurse her back to health. Her kitchen, near ground level, on a raised dais above a bathroom, was in shambles, as poorly stocked as any he might've expected from someone who lived like this. He'd watched a scorpion skitter across the metal floor as he rooted through the metal cabinets in search of anything palatable—in his cabin he would've given her beans and fresh moose and coffee brewed in a stained tin can— but finally settled on Honey Nut Cheerios he suspected were stale. No milk. In a bottom counter beneath the rusted sink he found a box of Tetley tea and brewed her a cup, exploring the flights of stairs while it steeped, in search of roommates, in search of anyone or anything that might reconcile the life of this unknown woman with her knotted hair and bruised arms to the girl he'd known, looking for the letters he'd sent, for anything that might confirm it was truly her, that he'd not stumbled upon some delusional lookalike, finding only spare rooms on platforms with dead cable wires snaking from the walls.

They'd moved out. Some of them all at once and then the rest one at a time, while she'd been searching for anyone to fill the place of the first group. How long ago had this been? Weeks? Months? It had been twelve years ago. She was too tired to do it, too exhausted to show the place, paying the entire rent and drying up her meager savings, hawking her possessions to supplement a nonexistent income and making ends meet through other means left unsaid. Life had become something worse than a chore, a tedious bout with demons more powerful than she could have imagined years ago when this city had been nothing if not fun, when Michaela had come into her life just after their mother had left for the final time, when she had ruled the world or at least their little stage at The Pal, all of it having come to a head on this weekend past in a series of lousy deals so unbelievable that she hadn't been at all surprised to see her brother approaching across the casino floor, like the last shocking hit in the craziest hand of hold 'em ever dealt. She'd informed him of all this while drinking the tea, her words slurred though she seemed to have come around a bit, eyes red and miserable, body running down quickly with the confused energy of the telling, Max watching from across the room, seated on a wooden stool he'd brought up from the kitchen.

When he was satisfied that she was asleep, Max Hill stepped back out into the evening heat, walked along the gritty road on the edge of town to a closed-down auto shop where he found a pay phone, unfolded a slip of paper he'd been carrying in his pocket, and dialed the number, letting it ring until a voice at the other end finally responded, alarmed or just surprised. "Who's this?" He'd assumed the deal was off. "Haven't you seen what the hell's goin' on, guy?" But he'd given Max the directions, had told him the car would be out past Henderson in the foothills of Lake Mead, keys behind the left front tire. And there it was, the taxi driving past the spot where the blue Buick sat inconspicuously parked on the shoulder, Max telling the driver to stop a mile down the road and then walking back, climbing into the driver's seat and pausing for a moment, listening to the quiet rush of the desert.

He was preparing. Rewinding and replaying again the stories he'd been telling himself for years, searching for encouragement, finding justification in the details. If their father had been a different man—a man who had wanted to help his children along rather than giving thanks when their own muddled decisions swept them out from under his feet, if he'd actually listened to and attempted to empathize with them rather than making hasty assumptions based on what little they were willing to tell him—he might not have charged off (the day after his son had told him of his teenage intentions) to the admissions office at the university at Fairbanks; he probably would have held off before pulling strings with his network of connections to come up with the free ride for his lukewarm son; and he certainly might've at least told the boy that he himself was planning to leave Alaska as well. He'd already by that point told Annabelle. He'd already told Maddie. But he had been unable or unwilling to tell Max. So it was Max's sister who had told him that wet day in June, just days before she was scheduled to go away, her bags all packed. They'd walked out into the nine o'clock sun and along the dirt road into town, down to the banks of the river and the same concrete structure they'd sat on years before, watching the pyrotechnics of the national holiday cascade from the sky. The Kentucky Fried Chicken was closed down. Everything in Fairbanks was closed down, including half the bars the twins had once frequented when they were younger. What remained was a ghost town just like in the movies: storefronts empty, the breeze blowing a rickety tune along Two Street, where the French Quarter still operated out of its unremarkable spot between the closed-down check cashing store and the alley.

That late winter and early spring—their last together—Max Hill had spent mostly away from the tense scenes at the cabin on

Fireweed Hill, trying to unearth his own sense of identity. When he'd reached the legal drinking age he'd begun heading out to the bars—not the ones downtown that had become notorious during the seven-year stretch of the pipeliners—but the smaller places where the real denizens of Alaska dwelled, the haunts of those after whom he had chosen to fashion himself. Long before he'd delivered his spontaneous and irrevocable decision—irrevocable because he knew his father would equate indecisiveness with cowardice—he'd been working on a plan, one that would take him in a direction so much the opposite of his father's and his sister's that he would be able to purge them from his life entirely. It had been not even a year since the disappearance of the Texas pipeliner had made rumors swirl in the raucous rooms of the Flame Lounge and the French Quarter, the talk that had driven Max away from the crowds on Two Street to confront and come to terms with what he'd done. It had been less than a year since that night that had nearly destroyed them all, but it had been a period full of change. People didn't necessarily remember Max Hill because they didn't necessarily remember his father, and so he was able that spring to create entirely new histories for himself. He was a widower prospecting for gold, a young man looking to earn his pilot's license, hoping to learn how to run a trapline. There'd been all sorts of strange looks. There'd been laughter. Yet by Memorial Day, he'd found someone willing to take him on as a trapping assistant, to take him up in his mail plane and teach him to fly the Alaskan way, willing to lay the groundwork for the life Max Hill had somehow signed himself up for.

His name was Jed Winters, and he was from Ohio, but he'd lived up here for nearly fifteen years. In Ohio, Jed Winters had sold insurance, had gotten fed up with that life right quick, had said goodbye to his mom and pop and sis and come north with little more than the money in his pocket, had arrived in 1964, plenty of time to log the residency quota and get a job on the pipeline. But he'd refused.

"I'd gotten wise," Jed Winters told Max Hill that first night they'd spoken in one of the outskirt bars where Max had pulled up a chair, already drunk. "I hadn't come up here in search of money. If it was money I'd wanted, could've stayed down in Ohio, could've kept selling insurance." He'd leaned forward, toward Max, in a way that first made the boy back up—but then, sensing something inviting about it, he'd crouched forward, put a hand on his beer glass, stared through it while Jed Winters spoke. "I knew I could've made big bucks on the pipeline. But I'd made a promise to myself when I left the Lower 48. I said I was only going to make as much as I needed. When I first got here, gold mining was the thing. Everyone and his pa had spent a thousand dollars on a sluice box. Alaska's always been the land of misfits, a hundred lazy men for every one worth a grain of salt, like you and me. Instead of trying to find gold or oil, I learned how to make an honest living, learned how to get by on my own. That's what this country was all about, you know. Once upon a time. Before it became saturated with commerce, the playground of corporations. Who wants to live in such a place? Once upon a time this country was started as a land where a guy could live the way he wanted to live. Now we've been coerced into a mainstream lifestyle. Most people have. Not yours truly. Punched my ticket and came out here. Haven't spoken to anyone back in Ohio for years." Jed Winters had been going on like this for nearly an hour while Max Hill had sat staring at and through his amber glass of beer. What he was saying had made sense to the boy, but anything would have made sense as long as it was contrary to what he'd been hearing all his life: that America was the land of the entrepreneur, that it all came down to money, that freedom was nothing without capital, and that *that* was how it should be, how it always had been and always would be.

"You're not *really* going to stay here, are you?" his sister had asked him, the day they'd walked down to the Chena River and stood along the concrete barrier, balancing above the riverside in the twilight. But Max Hill had decided that he would. That if his father was a man who lived on bank loans and credit and wouldn't face a problem unless it had a dollar sign attached to it, then Max would be the sort who lived on three hundred dollars a year. That if Fairbanks was what could be called a city—with its weathered store-fronts and great drifts of snow heaped along the empty streets— then he'd venture into the city only once a year on a snow machine to buy seventy-five pounds of flour, sugar, and ammunition. That if his sister insisted upon living in a place where the lights glared a thousand hues of neon, where great flamingoes and sphinxes stared down like extinct gods, and where every hotel room held a secret—if his sister insisted on turning such an about-face in her life, then he would turn himself even more fully to the wild haunted surround-ings of his childhood, would come into the country as they said, would learn how to live with and against this half-million-square-mile monster. Still, the only way he could deal with the loss of her was to conjure up resentment—to put his sister in the category he'd long ago placed his father. He'd reimagined that moment on the murky banks of the Chena a million times in the quarter century that had followed, had altered his sister's expression until he was able to make her turn vicious. In order to properly hate her—which was what he'd needed, all those years ago, to survive without her— he'd given her a moment of pure fury, a moment in which she'd

shouted to him the words that had made him capable of banish-
ing her.

"Fine then!" Maddie had said to him on their final meaningful
night together. "Stay here! You deserve to be alone anyway! You try
so hard not to be, but you're exactly like him!" He'd heard these
lines like religion in his ears, had come to believe them so fully,
with such dependency, that it was still difficult—even now, halfway to Denver, the sun collapsing on her turned-away face in the
front seat of the Buick procured from an acquaintance of an
acquaintance—to convince himself that it was not true, that it was
the collision of a quarter century of loneliness with the one person
who might have made a difference, that it was nothing more than
the well-honed product of his intense imagination.

<hr />

THE CAR WAS A HEARSE, and she was the corpse, her brother the
shrouded ferryman guiding her across the River Styx. A fitting end
to the shittiest weekend ever.

The story of what Maddie Hill had been doing out in the desert
since Saturday—the story that had led her to be in that disoriented state of mind in which he'd found her, high on so many sub-
stances even she couldn't keep them straight—had in fact begun on
the previous Friday night, when she'd stood among the palms outside the back entrance of the Excalibur after her four-to-ten shift,
waiting for a taxi, and had seen a man dressed in a pink suit coat
and fedora approaching across the sand-strewn lot. His name had
been Prince Dexter—a nom de plume certainly, just like everyone
else out here. He was tall and angular, a conspiracy theorist and
tabloid reporter who'd made his name authoring exposés on the

indiscretions of lesser-known Kennedys and a bludgeoned and strangled six-year-old beauty queen. More recently he'd focused on scandalous activities involving White House interns and had stumbled upon something else that was going to be big—something that was going to blow the lid off corporate America, something in which Maddie held a personal stake, hence here he was. These details he'd related in the moments after he'd avoided the fate most creeps who approached her suffered—avoided it by showing her, before she could speak, before she could reach into her purse, a photograph he presented like an amulet in the palm of his hand.

At that moment in her life, Maddie Hill had been clean and sober for six months, the longest she'd gone since freshman year of college, enrolled in an NA group that met at the Salvation Army shelter, headed up by a man named Henry Q who possessed some of the deepest, darkest war stories she'd ever heard, stories involving weeklong blackouts and hospitalized children later marched off into the resentful oblivion of foster care. Stories that made her own seem casual by comparison. In Vegas there was no way to be both clean and social. Once upon a time, Maddie had stalked long blocks of the Strip with strangers on a nightly basis; now for six months she had lived in a cocoon of self-preservation, had suffered the sad lonely freedom of recovery, going to meetings, going to work, talking to as few people as possible, absconding when she detected the movement of a chance conversation toward a potential social invitation, often calling for a cab from inside the Excalibur—not even certain she could endure the five minutes it would take to hail one from the curb—going directly home to punch her code into the double doors of her loft where she could hide until the next meeting.

With the simplicity of a photograph in the palm of an extended hand, Prince Dexter had coaxed her out of it, had walked with her along the Strip, brightened by the moon like a ripe orange above the black Luxor, her footsteps on the sidewalk cautious, eyes avoiding the faces of those passing her, wondering if they knew. Could they tell what a fine line she was walking? With the bait of a blurry picture of an old friend, Prince Dexter had sat her down in a moldy booth in the Denny's across the street from the Stardust—a Denny's (silly as it sounded) ripe with memories, whose old management and once-veteran waitstaff were long gone, replaced by teenage girls with pierced lips and a young busboy with two sleeves of tattoos and a spiked hairdo, who kept glaring at Maddie while Prince Dexter ordered them coffee and Grand Slams and, removing from a pocket of his pink suit coat a small tape recorder, asked Maddie to tell him everything she could remember about her friend Michelle Jones (a.k.a. Michaela of the once-famous M&M duo). Her friend whose body, after twelve years missing, it was his sad duty to inform her, had been found at the bottom of the lake where they'd once spent summer afternoons sunning, the excavation of a dredging project funded by the federal government and various ecological organizations, a mystery brought up from the blues and greens of that lake where you'd least expect to find one. Tahoe: whose depths caused anything dumped to sink to such a level that it never came back up, not without help. Michaela: a skeleton in a dredging sling, skull fractured by two gunshots twelve years ago.

At first, she'd been unable to speak, had sat with her head down, eyes focusing and unfocusing on the bottomless cup of coffee that she used to drink with two creams and four sugars, black and scalding now. Over the course of those twelve years since it had happened, Maddie had found ways of coping. She'd told herself lies. Had spent great amounts of time convincing herself that Michaela hadn't "gone missing" or "disappeared" but had in fact left of her own accord, had gone back to Seattle maybe. Vegas in the eighties and nineties was no longer the Vegas of the fifties, with wise guys and hit men; it was no longer even the Vegas of the late seventies, to which she'd been introduced by the gruesome newscasts in the lounge of her dorm freshman year, stories of steel-shattering car bombs in parking garages, bodies found half-petrified out in the desert, shot three times in the heart and once in each eye and buried beneath mounds of rocks, the MGM catching fire one night and burning nearly to the ground. These days, if somebody disappeared in Vegas, you didn't immediately assume they'd gotten themselves garroted and outfitted for cement shoes. Chances were they'd gotten married and gone off on a honeymoon; the next time you saw them they'd be fifty pounds heavier and pushing a stroller. Perhaps Michaela had simply met someone. Perhaps she'd simply abandoned Maddie, just like everyone else she'd ever made the mistake of loving.

They'd met at a party in the basement of the now-demolished 86 Club. 1979. The Strip still a gleam in a madman's eyes, Maddie a middling and bored sophomore who'd gotten a job waiting tables at the Palm Room, Michaela a twenty-four-year-old dancer in town auditioning for the vacancy for the Lido de Paris show that ran every night of the week and twice on Saturdays. The 86 Club was located just down the street from the Stardust, the largest casino in the world and still under renovation, four restaurants and a convention center and a half dozen swimming pools in the shapes of constellations. The sparkling sign hovering over the Strip had caught Maddie's eye during one of the long weekday walks after classes that had become her only antidote for the restlessness this city caused, west from her residence complex along the scorching blacktop between the library and the acres of desert that would soon be a basketball arena, north along Paradise Road with its string of gas stations and hotels and fast food restaurants. The sparkling sign of the Stardust had risen out of the low darkness and pulled her in, had dressed her in a white outfit and sent her around to take the orders of the gentlemanly dinner patrons who returned without fail in the evenings transformed into flamboyant patriarchs flashing twenties, leaning over to ask when are *you* going to get a dancing gig, sweetheart?

Michaela was dark-haired and dark-eyed, her face hard and stern with a smile that was like a frown. She hadn't gotten the dancing gig. Nearly fifty girls had shown up for the audition not knowing only one spot was available. But the entertainment director had approached her afterward and asked where she was from. "He told me I ought to stick around, if I had nothing better going on back home in Seattle. Which I don't. He said he'd talk to some people for me. See if anyone else has any openings. Probably just wants to fuck me. But hey, you never know when a dancer's going to break a leg, right? As for the time being? Who knows. I'll just strip, I guess."

There was something about the way she said it. Something about her shrewd intelligence. They'd left the 86 Club with the remnants of an eight ball and walked north along the boulevard, past the new colonnade of Caesar's Palace into the lights of the northern strip where the high-rise addition of the Sahara towered over Circus Circus, chain-link fences around freshly dug craters in the earth and the omnipresent cranes bearing the steel girders of more half-finished towers, Michaela telling how she'd come here directly out of Berkeley, had been accepted at a few law schools but was still trying to sort things out after what had happened to her that spring. A boy she'd known from school—this dickwad whose pleas she'd finally given into, finally agreed to go out with him though she'd known all along there was something strange about it—had drugged her and left her in Golden Gate Park, and Michaela had still not figured out what to do about it, whom to blame, for she didn't blame him, though she didn't know why, and didn't exactly blame herself, at least—she said to Maddie, forcing a smile that was like a frown—not all the time.

"But why am I boring you with all this? We're supposed to be having fun, right?"

In those days, the brightest lights were still downtown, to the north in Glitter Gulch, past the wedding chapels offering drive-thru service, left on Fremont and up past the Golden Nugget and the Pioneer Club with its gesturing cowpoke. It was in the main bar of the latter—the two of them ordering tequilas and turning away the looks of the men—that Maddie had first begun to feel that sense of something she'd never felt before, a comfort that had allowed her, for the first time in years, to turn inward. Sometimes when she looked at Michaela that first night, she'd seen a potential better version of herself, more adapted and cunning and capable of dealing with what had happened. It was not just Michaela's ability to speak matter-of-factly while nibbling on goldfish-shaped crackers about an event that Maddie could not help but compare to her own experience (an experience about which she had never told a soul, not even her mother, despite Annabelle's efforts). It was not just Michaela's apparent grace that made Maddie feel she could tell her anything. It was also her admission that, beneath it all, she was still uncertain, just as Maddie was uncertain about exactly what had happened that night in the upstairs room at the French Quarter, an unsettled scene that she had tried to replay in her mind only to find the frames disjointed and sparse: a moment when the cowboy was approaching her, a moment when she knew what was going to happen and then another when it was happening. (And yet it was not fear that she had felt, nor anger. It was certainly not love or even anxious lust but rather an almost relieved sense of resignation, as if she was finally getting something she had long anticipated, but not necessarily looked forward to, over with.) Still, the memories and those that followed chiseled themselves carefully from the denial that surrounded them, and when Michaela had at last run herself dry—"Jesus! Can I dominate a conversation, or what? What about you? What the hell are you doing here?"—when the last of the eight ball was gone and they'd marched back out into the street in search of fun (in search of another eight ball) Maddie had found herself unable to begin chiseling, had found herself telling not the story of that night in the summer of her sixteenth year—but instead the story of the phone call she'd received earlier that same day (coincidence? or cause and effect?), the phone call that had led her to that wild party at the on-its-last-legs 86 Club in the first place, the phone call that had come in just after she'd arrived for work, gotten changed into her white outfit and come out onto the floor at just after two in the afternoon, which in Vegas meant breakfast.

At first, she'd thought it was some sort of joke, had thought some cruel co-worker had set it up, or perhaps the floor manager, whom she knew disliked her for denying his sexual advances, who had reminded her that personal phone calls were not allowed, though some of the girls received no less than five a night. Would he be capable of such a thing? All day, Maddie had walked around in a daze, trying to come up with ways of explaining it away. Though she had recognized the voice immediately—not that it had stopped her from playing dumb, from adopting the tough girl act that had become second nature (Yeah, this is Maddie. Who the fuck is this?)—though she'd known at once who it was, she could not accept it as true: that after they'd so awkwardly gone their separate ways in the aftermath of their uncoordinated flight from Alaska, the woman she'd once known as Mother would be coming back into her life with a phone call, would be attempting to reconcile the last two years with an impromptu visit.

Annabelle had married some grad student, a Vietnamese guy fifteen years her junior, had moved first to Boston and now to Michigan where the new husband had taken a teaching job. Maddie had listened, mouth open, as the familiar but somehow changed voice on the other end of the phone detailed the haphazard sequence by which she, a forty-one-year-old divorcee, had fallen deeply in love with, and had that love reciprocated by, a twenty-six-year-old Vietnamese man who'd graduated summa cum laude from MIT in a branch of artificial intelligence research of which ninety-nine percent of the world was ignorant; had continued listening, still stunned, as the voice claiming to belong to her mother, that depressed sponge of a woman she'd known in Fairbanks, detailed her "reemergence" and "new appreciation of life" and gave her the full itinerary of their "extended honeymoon," which, after a week on St. Martin, was now going to take them—and here she'd even had the nerve to pause dramatically—to Fabulous Las Vegas! Maddie had been too dumbfounded to disagree or question any of it, had been startled into something like paralysis to hear Annabelle's confession that she had contacted *him* (through a lawyer, of course), had demanded that he arrange and pay for the divorce, and that if he didn't . . . well, then she might just have to publicly disclose certain unflattering details from his past—this disembodied voice from Maddie's childhood leaving her unable to speak, only to nod, incapable of cohesive thought, still sitting in the little folding chair next to the phone when the manager had come over, long after her mother had hung up, and read her the riot act.

She picked them up at the airport a week later with the same sense of disconnection, having borrowed a car from one of her room-mates. The young husband who climbed into the backseat while her mother got up front looked much older than the twenty-six years he claimed, dressed up in a suit and tie, just the type of sucker this city feasted upon, his hair (so out of fashion for someone only a few years older than she) almost making her laugh. She had driven them up and down the Strip, giving them the PG-rated tour, had led them out on to the floor at the Stardust and, while the young husband vanished amidst the maze of tables, had sat her mother down on a high bar stool in an out of the way corner and leaned in.

It was still strange to look at that face and to see herself in it. Annabelle seemed not to have aged but gotten younger. Certainly she looked healthier—healthier than Maddie—and yet there was a frenzy behind her smiles, her forced conversations that seemed intent on saying nothing. It was Maddie who had eventually tried to bring up Max, and she had watched her mother's face fall immedi-ately, watched it take on the lost expression she remembered from her brother, whom she had tried to stay in touch with only to have him stop returning her calls. She understood his anger, of course—but that did not mean she was ready to confront it. "Yes, yes," Anna-belle said, stammering and staring down at the floor, lying or concealing something. "Yes, I've spoken to Max. I spoke to him on the phone and—" But her voice had trailed off. And then a pained smile had stretched across her face. "Oh look! Here comes Dat!"

The whole week had been like that, Annabelle's talent for avoidance remarkable, her affected desire—for the new husband's benefit?—that they appear to have a boisterous, sisterly relationship pairing awkwardly with Maddie's fear of her own secrets being revealed. They didn't discuss the two years that had passed; her mother didn't ask how Maddie liked school, what she was studying, if she needed any money, what her plans were—which was a relief, actually, because Maddie couldn't have told her anyway. After two days, the new husband seemed to convince Annabelle that they ought to do their own thing, and Maddie had stressed her way through the next three days at work, waiting for a phone call that never came. It was not until their final day in town that a dinner date was arranged. They met at the MGM Grand, where Dat had offered to pay. (Remarkably, it seemed he'd come out nearly eleven hundred dollars in the black.) Maddie mumbled her way through it, indignant and perhaps jealous. At the end of it Annabelle stood and pronounced it the best meal and best trip ever, though she'd barely touched her food and her eyes were watery.

Maddie had seen them off at the airport, hungover and grumpy and sad but unwilling to admit it, Annabelle wiping her eyes and throwing her arms around her. "Thank you, honey!" she'd said, which Maddie at first had taken as gratitude for whatever fragment of forgiveness she'd managed to portion off for her mother. But Annabelle's eyes lingered, her expression one of expectation. She'd stepped back and stood before her daughter, inviting an appraisal, and it was then that Maddie realized just how *big* her mother was— that what had appeared to her the natural accumulation of weight for a Midwestern woman turning the corner toward middle age was something more, something that for some reason shocked her. "Since you didn't ask," Annabelle had said to her in the airport, "I'll just tell you. It's going to be a *girl*! Oh, Madeleine! I'm going to be a mother again!"

Later, it was Michaela—to whom Maddie had retreated in the aftermath of her mother's departure—who'd consoled her. They were still new friends then, and yet Michaela had come over on Maddie's day off with a twelve-pack of High Life and sat with her on the balcony of her apartment near campus, had clunked bottles with her and made her laugh through her tears and done everything Maddie thought a real mother should do, had talked her through that line of her mother's that had bothered her so—*I'm going to be a mother again!* As if admitting that she'd somehow *stopped* being a mother to Maddie. Michaela had dragged Maddie through her anger and helped her accept that she was a sacrifice her mother had been forced to make, a role that she'd come to embrace during the next few months, the next few years, Annabelle becoming like some forgotten aunt who'd paid a visit and could be quickly dismissed, her new husband no more memorable than the customers who came in and out of the churches of fantasy where she lived and worked. It was on that night, somewhere toward dawn, that Maddie at last told Michaela—at last told *somebody*— the story of that night at the French Quarter. How it had begun not as a seduction—she'd been way too young for anything like that— but not an accident either. And how perhaps, maybe just for a moment, she had thought it was what she wanted. Maybe she had changed her mind. Maybe it was not what she'd expected. And yet that didn't give Lyle the right to do what he'd done, it did not give him the right to keep doing it even after she'd told him to stop. And so if he'd just listened, maybe it would not have sounded bad enough for Max and Jasmine to hear, would not have looked so awful at the instant they came rushing through the door. And what had *they* been doing anyway? What had Max been doing in that room down the hall? And so who was *he* to judge *her*? Who was *he* to think that what she'd almost done was so incredibly wrong? Who was he to leave her with the guilty illusion that this was all her fault?

Maddie chiseled the last piece of it free and then lay there on her bed, reaching for this dark-eyed lover-and-mother figure that at that very moment Michaela became, the surrogate whom she somehow knew already would be there for good—would be right there next to her, looking into her eyes every time Maddie, momentarily soothed, drifted off to sleep.

———

FOR SIX YEARS, THEY RULED Vegas.

Michaela sizzled, had danced in Berkeley all throughout her years there. In blue light Maddie would wait, just offstage but still visible, dressed in a plaid school-girl skirt, a ballerina outfit, a field hockey uniform, looking reluctant. Michaela would beckon her forward through the haze, a silhouette in smoke and green lighting. Still Maddie would wait in the wings, drawing it out as long as possible.

This was at the legendary Palomino Club—The Pal—the only all-nude club in town that also had a liquor license. The site had been grandfathered in when the county had decided that beer and bare weren't a good mix and had adopted its crass trademark line: You can have booze or cooze but not both. The place had the benefit of name recognition and that vintage Vegas feel. Muted lighting and maroon upholstery, a bar upstairs with a stage and a stainless steel pole running to the ceiling that Maddie always studied for a second every time she arrived—at six o'clock, hours before the shows began—surprised not by how grimy and barren it looked now but

by the transformation when the lights went out, when the place
filled up and the anticipation began to twist in her belly. By the
time Maddie had been coaxed out onto the stage, the shed components of whatever preposterous outfit she'd been wearing tossed
among the crowd, money was being thrown at them. By the mid-
eighties, management had taken the unheard-of step of building a
special VIP room just for them, the price set at double the going
rate. Still, the line on some nights had stretched all the way down
the maroon staircase with its gold-plated banister, winding around
the perimeter of the first floor and out to the sidewalk, where a set
of stanchions were set up to accommodate the snaking line. Management doubled the price again. It didn't matter. The line still
went all the way down the block to the dumpsters in an adjacent
alley, where industrious homeless men had begun hawking stolen
wares, a new branch of staff hired simply to manage the outdoor
crowd.

In their dressing room, on these nights, preparing to venture out
onto the stage again to perform the act that had begun with an
honest energy but had transformed into something else over the
years, Maddie and Michaela would argue, would not quite fight. For
six years they had reigned like this as the most famous duo in
Vegas—more famous, even, than the two Germans with the white
tigers—had achieved guest spots at Caesar's Palace and the Flamingo Hilton, had been treated like celebrities anywhere they went,
lounging in the pleasures of what the locals called *juice*, had visited
all the parties and mansions, Jacuzzis and private jets to Tahoe for
sunbathing. It was just when the owners had doubled the price for
the second time and hired the new staff and remodeled the VIP
wing that another position had opened up at the Lido de Paris. The
director had called Michaela, had left a message while they'd been

onstage performing their first show of the night, a message she had retrieved upon returning to the dressing room, where they'd meant to towel off, get changed, powder their noses a bit as the saying went, and then head back out to the floor. Instead it had turned into this scene. This argument. The director had not even bothered to advertise the job; he knew who he wanted. They'd sat half-clothed in the dressing room, Michaela explaining the reasons why she had to at least show up for the audition tomorrow morning, Maddie holding in her hands the pink tutu she'd been in the process of putting on, unable to put into words the anger she felt, the sense of being cheated by time, of having arrived at a place in her life where she had finally wrested some sort of control from the situation that had taken over her life at sixteen and had defined her ever since.

Because for her this had not been about the money. For Michaela, it had been an easy way to make some dough, the men a necessary evil. But for Maddie it provided something she'd been lacking ever since that day she'd fought to purge from her memory. These moments on the stage, when she possessed the power to turn the revolving faces of the men into nothing more than vacant images, to rob them of their lives and their importance, had been the one thing she'd done that had made her feel better about her conception that she had been tainted for good. And it was because of this thing she and Michaela had made—this creature that emerged out of this dressing room three times a night, six nights a week—that she had begun whatever tentative steps she'd taken toward a recovery. She couldn't say anything, responded to her cue and stood reluctant in the wings while Michaela rode the pole, beckoned her, helicoptered a satin negligee and flung it at her, their eyes meeting when they came together on either side of the stainless steel rod connecting stage and ceiling, the crowd around them gone, the two of them arguing out their positions on where to go and what to do with this crossroads, each attempting to win, with the deep focus of her eyes, a victory that would either move them beyond this stage or keep them firmly attached to it, a victory that Maddie was ultimately able to secure not because of any stronger sense of purpose or inherent rightness but because hers was the avenue of less resistance. While Michaela had to win the favor of her friend, Maddie had only to poke holes in Michaela's confidence in order to ensure that the director would see what they both knew all along he'd see, what he took great pains to explain to poor Michaela the following week when she'd come in for her second audition—that six years had passed, that it had been irresponsible of him to get her hopes up, but that he had fallen so in love with the woman he remembered that it had made him forget that Michaela was now almost thirty years old, had made him forget how difficult it was to maintain the body of an elite athlete, which was what he needed for a professional show like this one.

They'd gone back to the Pal after a two-week hiatus only to discover that it had been too long. Two of the girls who'd been dancing downstairs had seen their act enough, had stepped right in and not missed a beat, a blonde and a redhead replacing two brunettes. They'd been relegated to the first floor, pleasing a few pathetic old reliables who seemed to think their loyalty might earn them something more than a lap dance. If they could do this for a few more months, maybe they could revive their act somewhere on Fremont St., maybe even somewhere on the Strip. But Michaela's heart was no longer in it. The regulars stopped coming two nights a week, then stopped coming entirely. The new customers were too jammed up in the line that stretched two blocks down the Strip. And then there had been the accidents. The backstage antics that Maddie and Michaela had gotten away with before—for what was anyone going to say to the top revenue generators in the entire city? Michaela would move in slow motion, dazed. Maddie once missed an entire scheduled dance and a substitute had to be urged on stage without preparation while one of the bouncers fought to resuscitate her. In the end, they'd quit before they could get fired, had gone home to the warehouse apartment on the outskirts and had a knockdown drag-out fight that had caused ambulances to arrive and three of the stewardesses with whom they'd been sharing the place to move out the very next day, hospital rooms on different floors, detoxing, a month apart, an opportunity, perhaps, for each to find her own solid ground and a way to move on. Yet it hadn't happened. They'd moved back in together, had developed a perilous sort of dependency, had worked out a certain "deal" with the sleazy landlord to temporarily lower the rent while they looked for new roommates, for new jobs, new alternatives. There had been long nights and discussions, Michaela contemplating a new direction, ordering books to help her study for the LSAT, books that she'd carry around for a week before letting them settle into neglected nests of dust on the floor. Trying to come up with something. She was almost thirty, after all. She was *over* thirty, for God's sake. Well past time to figure out exactly what she was going to do with her life. You too, Maddie. You could go back to school, too. But Maddie could not allow these conversations to take place, would grow indignant any time Michaela came to her with some new terrible concession for them to make a few measly bucks. A waitressing job? Was she fucking kidding? But Michaela had taken it anyway, just to spite her, had dressed up in the pastel outfit the Tropicana had provided and ridden the monorail into town with Maddie, who'd come along for reasons she couldn't explain, the two of them going their separate ways from the train stop in silence, a silence that still rang in Maddie's brain as she'd sat, later that same evening, in one of the raucous sports bars in one of the lesser-known and lesser-regarded grand resorts, the bar and main dining area packed due to some obnoxious sports game taking place on the forty-inch televisions—March Madness, the UNLV Runnin' Rebels, whatever—long-legged swerving waitresses bearing overloaded trays, Maddie sipping a margarita at a tall stool in the corner, waiting for halftime or for the game to end, for one of the hundreds of men in attendance to notice her sitting by herself.

It took less than an hour for one of them to approach, to lean against the elbow-high table and engage her in the sort of small talk she knew was typical, a coy smile with one side of her mouth sufficient proof to make him lower his voice and get down to business, speaking into the table, asking how much for a half and half? How much for an around the world?

For years, she had been contemplating this moment, its simplicity inviting her every time she'd happened to see one of the countless girls who made it their job to sit alone in bars, skinny white girls going it on their own—for who needed a pimp when you could do it this way? Outlaw style, a commission to the bartender, just watch out for the floor managers. For years, she had watched the men who approached these girls with propositions, had learned the lingo of the trade. Ever since they'd lost their gig at The Pal—and, in truth, long before that—she had spent many an evening explaining her plan to Michaela, trying to convince her that there was nothing immoral about it, that even if there were, it was not the girls to blame but rather these men out shopping for whores during company conferences or, even worse, on family vacations. Married men coming to Vegas for bachelor parties or weekends with the boys and deciding the gambling floors and showrooms weren't enough, that they needed a *real* taste of Vegas.

It was from watching it all take place a hundred times—not exactly taking notes but certainly keeping her eyes open—that Maddie had known what was meant and what to do when the man had lowered his voice and spoken the magic words, and though she had responded like a veteran—her drink abandoned half-finished, the two of them in an elevator and out on the hallway of the twenty-third floor, negotiating a price on the way, the electronic room key gaining them admittance to the mauve and yellow room where Maddie had gone over to the refrigerator in the corner in search of the "complimentary" bottle of wine—though she had acted immediately like a pro, she had trembled uncontrollably later, the following afternoon into evening, in the warehouse apartment, while relaying the story to Michaela, whom Maddie could tell had been able to detect it in her demeanor, had known something was wrong during the monorail and taxi ride back home, where Maddie had shown her the money, let her hold it in her hands, a bundle of cash large enough to make anything seem tempting. And how easy it had been! She had not been out there soliciting, Maddie told Michaela—and, in a way, this was true, for when Maddie thought of soliciting she thought of the less-popular girls from their days at the Pal, who had to wander around snapping the straps on their bikinis. *She* had not been soliciting. A man had simply come up to her and asked for it, and he had gotten it. Damn right, he had gotten it. "*I* don't feel a single ounce of shame or guilt," Maddie said. "And neither should *you. He* was the scumbag who was slinking around looking for a whore. *He* was the one who came up to me and started talking about blowjobs and fucking my ass. I just took him up on a business proposition."

Michaela had smiled—that tense, cautionary smile of hers that was like a frown—had fought against her friend until Maddie had poked and cajoled and finally reached that place deep inside her where Michaela could not resist, had never been able to resist, the afternoon wasted thinking of ways they would blow their new fortune, for if one of them could make a stack of money like that for only a half hour's work—Maddie had theorized—then imagine how much *both* of them could make. In just a month or two they could pay off all the money they owed their sleazy landlord in back rent, they could get on their feet and figure out what their next step was, they could do all the things they'd been planning on one day doing, could maybe get the hell out of Vegas and move somewhere a bit . . . well, a bit more suitable for two women hovering around the age of thirty.

It was with these images of the future that Maddie had soothed Michaela's wavering confidence as they'd come into town that evening, dressed to kill but not *too* obvious, a Saturday night not unlike the one on which they'd first met some ten years ago, convening by the slot machines a final time, Michaela's mascara running while Maddie pulled her into the bathroom and told her to get it together, bought her a shot while Michaela sat on the toilet behind a locked stall door, telling her she wasn't sure she could go through with it. It was with these promises of a life Michaela had always, Maddie knew, secretly craved—a quiet life as just another suburban woman sitting at home watching television—that Maddie had gotten her, after three shots, to stop crying, to agree again to give it a try. It was with these half-formed visions of a vague future together still on her lips that Maddie had left Michaela at the bar, sitting alone on a high stool in the corner, watching long enough to see a certain gentleman in a pinstriped suit intermittently glancing Michaela's way. It was armed with the victory of having convinced at last her closest friend (her only friend) of the benefits of her dangerous plan that Maddie had gone across the street, had settled down to wait for her own trick—and how she suddenly appreciated the meaning behind that word! The weird obvious charade of the whole ceremony felt a little like fishing, which she'd done a few times with her twin brother and their older half brother Jamie in the wilderness north of Fairbanks a hundred years ago. Nothing happened until you started to get bored, until you started to wonder if you should pick up and move a few hundred yards downstream (if you should order another margarita or try another bar) . . . and then you had to be ready.

This one was a doctor. He'd been quick to point out this fact to her when he'd brought over the drinks and settled down, his shoulder propped against the wall. Like the man from the previous night, he was wearing a wedding ring, had not bothered to take it off or even hide it from her, a trivial detail not to be mentioned—not by a man like him and certainly not to some whore like her. With her back to him, facing out the window of his room and over the southern extension of the dark Strip while he lay on the bed and watched her, she thought of Michaela, looked across the boulevard of sky trying to pick out which darkened window on the high towers of the adjacent resort was hers, wondered how she was making out with the man in the pinstripes, hoping she had not flubbed this most important moment, this most crucial step. As for the doctor, she hadn't asked him if he wanted a drink, for what if he'd said no? What if he'd been the type who just wanted to get it done as quickly as possible? He was distracted enough just watching her, having undressed as soon as they'd arrived in the room, having gone over to the bed in his underwear and asked her to strip for him, slowly. She'd originally guessed him to be thirty-five; now she figured he might be as old as fifty. A fifty-year-old man paying for sex on his vacation, pulling himself out of his briefs while she had postponed the dance—against his pleas, down to her bra and panties now—and stepped over to the refrigerator.

"Don't you get it?" she had said to Michaela that afternoon, and wanted to whisper now, her face inches from the one-way glass window, wishing she could walk her through this trickiest part, which consisted of retrieving from your purse a tiny bottle of Visine and squirting a few drops in his drink, wishing she could remind her friend—at this scariest and best part of the transaction—that it was fail-proof. "That's the brilliance of it," she wanted to remind her. "They all think it's legal. None of them know that prostitution is legal and monitored in every county in Nevada *except* for Clark. *Except* for Vegas. Who in the world would ever know that? Who in the world would ever *believe* it? Unless you live here?"

The Visine acted faster with the doctor than it had the previous night's victim. The Tetrahydrozoline lowered his body temperature and constricted his airways; within thirty seconds of swallowing the drink in one gulp—tossing the plastic glass and pulling her by the hips into bed—he was shoving her aside, flailing his way toward the bathroom, throwing open the door and letting loose with a sound Maddie had to turn away from. Though he was a doctor, the suddenness of it all had confused him, had made him lightheaded and disoriented, and so, like the man from last night, he'd tried at first to encourage her to stay, had tried to protect his investment. "Gimme just a moment. Must've been something I ate . . ."

It was while he was uttering these phrases, punctuated by groans and more vomiting, that Maddie had removed the three twenties from his wallet and ransacked his belongings, scattered among a couple duffle bags by the window, looking for socks. Jackpot. A thick bundle of fifties and hundreds. Threw it in her purse and scanned the room. Forget anything? At the door, she paused. She couldn't help it, couldn't help but delay for an instant to see the vomit splattered on the shower curtain and on the white porcelain, on the tile floor and even on his legs. For somehow it was this moment she most treasured. Even more than the money, it was this moment when the doctor had begun to understand—when his pleas had changed from requests for her to stay to more urgent matters (Take what you want! Just tell me what you've given me! I'm a doctor and I need to know!)—it was this moment that was the one thing she'd wanted to remember to tell Michaela, the one detail she knew could make her friend smile, a scene whose glory had slowly dissipated while she'd waited at their agreed meeting place—a half mile north and a couple blocks off the Strip, the sort of third-rate place no outsiders knew about—for a half hour, an hour, had paced up and down the worn-carpeted avenues of the casino floor, cursing the hands of the clock as they revolved. Later, she couldn't say when exactly it had gone from Michaela was late to Michaela was missing to Michaela was gone, didn't know at what point she'd accepted that their meeting at the bar would not take place; she could never tell Prince Dexter or anyone at what point she'd finally given in and hailed a taxi back to the apartment with the money stolen from the doctor, entertaining a brief hope that Michaela would be there, in her pajamas, red-eyed, saying, "Sorry Maddie, I just couldn't go through with it."

Twelve years later, sitting at Denny's with the man who'd come to tell her Michaela had at last been found, Maddie had remembered the words she'd used to convince her friend, the story she'd told of the first trick she'd rolled, the amusing tale of his morning as she imagined it: his waking up in his darkened motel room, finally capable of looking at a glass of water without going queasy, his pompous journey down to the front desk to complain, still thinking himself a reputable man done a disservice in a routine business transaction. Excuse me, sirs, but I attempted to hire a lady of the night from your bar there and was disappointed to discover that she had *fucking poisoned me*! And what did the staff do? They politely explained for the thousandth time to the thousandth presumptuous tourist that, contrary to popular belief, prostitution is not in fact legal in Las Vegas, and that he just might want to keep his mouth shut about this rather than revealing it to the authorities, unless of course he was interested in extending his stay by a mandatory thirty days. Anything else they could help him with? Well, they certainly hoped he'd enjoyed his visit! Have a safe trip home, sir! And do come again!

Yup, Maddie Hill had thought, sitting in the cramped booth at Denny's, telling all of this to a man in a pink suit whom she'd known all of two hours: that was Vegas. That was the reality of this place she'd chosen to live the last twenty-four years of her life, the last twelve alone, because of course Michaela had not been at the apartment when she'd arrived—nor throughout the entire decade of the nineties, during which Maddie had been plagued by memories of that night, returning home to find herself alone for the first time in their vast apartment, sitting down on the couch to find herself unable to get comfortable, going into the kitchen to find nothing worth eating, stepping out onto the fire escape to watch the stars circling over the desert only to find them shielded by cityglow. A decade during which she would contemplate and succeed, off and on, in going clean and sober, would think often about leaving Vegas and all of its vices and disregard behind; a decade she had ultimately spent—despite her best efforts—becoming that strangest sort of hermit, mistress of the casinos, old maid of the Strip, barely able, most nights, to make it back home before dawn. You would see them every night when the lights went on, these tired women coming out from wherever they spent their days. You'd see them at bars, drinking tequila alone, you'd see them at the video poker machines or in the back corners of the rooms at NA meetings, you'd see them in booths in run-down dingy restaurants, drinking coffee, sharing secrets with men who might be wearing pink suits, who might be holding battered tape recorders, who might be passing themselves off as something they clearly weren't.

THE BUICK NEEDED GAS.

Somewhere just short of the Colorado border—the flat stretch of Interstate 70 rising into the high plains west of the Continental Divide—he pulled off the highway at the beckoning of a bright sign on a hundred-foot tower, found himself on a narrow dusty road, a single halogen lamp illuminating a roadside gas station with a pair of ancient pumps out front.

She was still asleep in the passenger seat. Or feigning sleep. Impossible to tell. At any moment during this long trek across the fluorescent desert he had expected to look over and catch her staring at him, eyes bloodshot and wide with uncertainty. It had unnerved him. He was uncomfortable with the idea of being watched, resisted scrutiny on instinct. If she would just wake up and start talking again that would be fine—would be something like those endless flights over Alaskan wilderness he'd used to make, not the postal runs but the other independently contracted trips, running tourists out into the wilderness on moose hunting

excursions or taking twenty-somethings up into the Brooks Range
and dropping them off for week-long wilderness camping. Those
trips had often required him simply to listen, and he had always
been a good listener, ever since old Jed Winters. That was the tem-
plate he had applied to this trip in his imagination. He had pictured
his sister as one of those clients on their way to a life-changing
weekend in the country, when just his presence in the pilot's seat
made even his most laconic contributions noteworthy. Now he felt
an uncertainty that translated strangely in his mind, his face a
frustrated mask in the pale gas station light where he'd removed
the old-fashioned nozzle from its cradle and kept watch on her, waiting to see if she would move, if she'd been playing possum the entire
time—his attention so focused that he didn't realize the pump was
not working until the voice came over the intercom.

"Sir. You have to use a credit card. Or else come inside and
prepay."

He opened the driver's side rear door, set the combination on his
suitcase, and removed one of the stacks of money, then stepped
across the gravel lot to the front door that chimed as he entered.
Two men stood at the counter, one behind a cash register, the other
eating a candy bar and drinking a beer on the customer side, a
bored friend of the cashier, come to spend a lonely evening.

He counted off two twenties, walked back out to the car and
pumped the gas, his eyes and mind still focused on his sister. She
had talked all the way through Nevada, beginning with the story of
this weekend past, getting distracted, half intoxicated still and not
always making sense, but always making enough, coming around
slowly—and, it seemed to him, reluctantly—to the story of the surprise visit from their mother, during whose telling she had seemed
at intervals to attempt to make eye contact with him, gauging his

response. And so perhaps—he thought now, watching her sleep or pretend to while the old dials on the pump turned—he should have waited before attempting to bring her around to what he'd wanted to talk about, should have hesitated before bringing up the letters sent to the post office box he'd hoped would still belong to her and the message contained in them, the message she herself had addressed in her replies (though she seemed unwilling to acknowledge them now). Perhaps he should have waited, for it was when he'd pushed too far that she had drifted back into herself, had disengaged the instant his voice had become aggressive. And now he wanted those early moments back, wished she would just sit up and start talking again, so he could brush the dust off and retrieve from wherever she was hiding the girl she'd been and that he'd hoped to find, a lesson he would have to remember: that he had to be patient, that he had to allow her to come around to it at her own pace.

His change was resting on the glass countertop adorned with lottery advertisements when he went back inside to retrieve it, the two men having already forgotten him, engaged in distracted conversation. He paused at the chime of the door, looked out across the dark span of the lot toward the Buick, where it seemed he'd seen a shadow of movement, a shifting in the passenger seat. Was it Maddie? Turning in her seat to watch him, then ducking back against the window when he noticed? And what did it mean, this constraint of hers? Was it fear? Indecision? Or was it the beginning of something else— something like assent—that made her hide from him like this, stealing glimpses only when she thought they'd go undiscovered?

He wasn't back on the highway for more than thirty seconds when he saw a sign: WELCOME TO COLORADO. And then another: GRAND JUNCTION, 25 MILES. His sister was a silent form next to him again. She could sleep or fake it all she wanted. He knew it was in there, the anger he had felt in her letters and heard in her voice as she'd staggered off the path of the narrative he'd wanted her to pursue, had staggered into the delaying stories of all these years past, stories that had run her down and made her sleep, stories that he knew were a part of his letting her get there on her own. And if it meant having to listen to her recapitulate these twenty-four years in Vegas, if it meant having to suspend his own resentments in order to allow her to reconnect with hers, then that was what he had to do. The truth was that he had some difficult things to tell her, too. And that the telling could not come until he was certain— was completely certain—that she was with him. And so he watched her, waited, could feel the rightness of it all beginning to settle in with the comfort of the empty road after midnight, the blackened wall of night above the highway, just him and the wheel and the white and yellow lines leading them on through the harsh backdrop of the high plains. Grand Junction, 25 Miles. And then, Denver.

In Denver, it would begin.

Thursday

JAMIE DIDN'T READ ROAD SIGNS, could sit for an hour with the atlas in his lap and still not know what he was looking at, the road for him an unknowable commodity like fate. He was never the wiser when GB took the detour outside Toledo, exiting the Ohio Turnpike with daylight dissolving beyond the wide, fenced-in fields, mist spanning a gray river and night coming on as they crossed the Michigan border. It was less than an hour out of the way, the town named as their next stop, and though he had never been there, GB could already feel his anticipation building, his anxiety thickening like a stench. Three days with his brother had put him on edge, had made him desperate for another voice, another sound besides the blustery wind that blew insistently between them in the front seat of the Stingray, the dog dozing on his brother's lap, the sun lowering on another day that would have been breathtaking had it not been so dictated by road signs and traffic, so dimmed by aftermath.

They'd made it out of the city just in time, had been right on the other side of the George Washington Bridge when it happened, headed west when everyone else was headed east along crowded interstates through a vision of swamps and refineries, dead factories in the ashy valleys of steel. They'd pulled off at a mountain rest stop from six lanes devoid of traffic, had returned ten minutes later to find Interstate 80 a parking lot, the mass exodus of the largest city in the country having caught up with them. The following hours had been an apocalyptic period complete with cars abandoned on shoulders with hazard lights flashing and no one inside, on and off ramps clogged and backed up a hundred yards with otherwise-conservative-looking men straddling guardrails holding signs reading THE END IS HERE, nothing to do but squeeze along the breakdown lane toward another rest stop where Jamie had remained in the passenger seat, sweating, his hair wild from their driving with the top down, dressed still in his gray Columbia sweatshirt and sweatpants with the long trench coat on top while GB in his baseball uniform paced the lot and wooded embankments with the dog on his leash, tried to reconcile exactly what it was they were supposed to be doing.

Jamie was philosophical, deemed it all an appropriate metaphor, made GB pull into the drive-thru so he could order another orange soda. Lee Harvey Oswald had been seen in a bar the night before his big afternoon, talking unintelligibly of patricide. "Hey, why don't you show me your gun?" he said again to GB—who'd told him repeatedly that he didn't have one. "I can see it right there under your shirt. Don't you think for a minute I don't understand what you're up to. There are several extremely convenient coincidences taking place here." In the middle of the road, a man stood shouting into a cellphone; the siren of a police cruiser blared from somewhere behind them, stuck in the traffic and trying to push forward. "Only thing I haven't figured out yet," Jamie said, "is who you're working for."

He didn't actually sleep, GB had learned. When the daylight had at last crept behind the wild ridges that first night—headlights coming on in the shaded valleys along which they still moved at speeds below thirty—Jamie had closed his eyes sitting upright and drifted off for brief stretches, his arms changing positions, one leg crossing over the other, then lowering to the ground while the second leg came up to reverse the posture. He'd spend twenty minutes at a time in this state of limited consciousness, awake but not quite, and then speak out of nowhere the continuation of a conversation long since left behind—in some cases, a conversation GB did not recall at all. Throughout the following day, in the manic intervals between his restless slumbers as they'd crept across the Poconos, the narrow highway carved among the sheer hills with CAUTION: FALLING ROCK signs positioned at the base of steep cliffs, trekking then across the sparsely inhabited counties of north-central Pennsylvania, he'd received from his brother the long list of things they were not to come near—not in these troubled times when the Feds would be at their most guarded. Metal detectors and radios and microwaves, cell phones and anything that could be monitored, those big blue mailboxes on street corners, sewer grates. Anything that was in any way connected to some larger network or scheme was off limits for Jamie, had been—according to him—ever since he'd gotten out of the military. At the motel in a town called Clearfield, in a room with yellow wallpaper and green carpet and an old RCA with rabbit ears that received no cable, only the networks, GB had stared at the staticky images while Jamie stood at the far corner of the room, as far away as possible, the dog on the bed and looking back and forth between them. "You're scared of televisions, too?" asked GB.

"It's not that I'm scared of them," Jamie had said, his eyes taking on that narrowed look that seemed to foreshadow his sudden transitions in alertness. "It's not at all that I'm scared. I've merely learned over the years what their real purpose is. I've watched the agency and the federal government manipulate enough of my life already, thank you very much. I'll pass on letting them manipulate the rest."

Five minutes later he was motionless, cross-legged on the bed with his head tilted back against the wall, and GB had spent the next half hour watching him instead of the television. The Agency. The CIA. It seemed Jamie truly did believe that he was in their employ—or once had been. GB hadn't quite figured out the entire delusion, wasn't even sure Jamie had it worked out to a definitive timeline. All GB knew for sure about the last thirty years of his brother's life was what he'd been told by the man he'd hired back in 1983, in those months leading up to what he'd foreseen as his long-overdue retirement from baseball, when a decade of will and delusion had at last caught up with him and he'd begun to admit to himself just how empty his life might be if he ever up and quit this kid's game that had sustained him for so long. So he had hired this man to track down his little brother Jamie, only to have the response correspond precisely with his surprise call-up, thereby instigating the phone call he wished he could take back and the tickets to the ball games, the naïve dream of a brotherly reunion though the man he'd hired had been quick to point out that the place where Jamie was living was no ordinary apartment building, that GB's fears had come true and that the little brother who'd always seemed to him somehow incapable of adulthood, somehow not cut out for it, was living out his life in one of the countless formerly derelict tenements where they'd begun putting the wayward souls who'd previously inhabited the park benches and the railings along the walls of the Lincoln Tunnel. The mayor had initiated his new goals for cleaning up the city, said this man GB had hired back in the summer of '83.

Central Park had become a fairground of rape and drug abuse. A Beatle had been shot. A few years later the streets were devoid of beggars and madmen. Did anyone really think they'd all gotten jobs and moved out to the suburbs?

It had not changed much in the years that had passed. It operated under different management now, different funding categories, used different terminology to express the goals and long-term criteria by which it achieved its grants; yet he'd recognized its stale musty feel as soon as he'd entered, had recalled the confounding rigmarole of bureaucracy the instant he'd begun his attempts to explain who he was to the impatient receptionist in the ski jacket, her look of cool cynicism accentuated by the pierced eyebrow not abating until he'd presented her—after stepping back out to the Stingray to locate his wallet in the glove box (the bright dying gleam of the city and then the harsh silent darkness of the lobby again)— with identification that had matched certain records on file.

They'd fed him dinner: a bowl of tomato soup and a toasted cheese sandwich at a table of the sort found in middle-school cafeterias, a questionnaire on a clipboard placed in front of him, a few scraps in a plastic bowl for the dog, who'd inhaled the food and then settled down next to the old-fashioned heat register for a nap. In the lobby, he had paced tentatively while the receptionist had dug through file cabinets, pressed a button on her phone and carried on a low-voiced discussion. Ten minutes had passed. Then twenty. GB remembering that day all those years ago when his brother had come running across the floodlit field during the National Anthem, the first inning and then the second and then the third of the game that was supposed to be his debut spent instead in the bowels of Yankee Stadium, just him and a couple rent-a-cops restraining his brother and forcing him into a makeshift holding cell while he spewed wild tales of secret tunnels in the desert, red buttons in bottom shelves of ornate desks deep in the heart of the Kremlin. GB had been called sleepless into the manager's office the following morning and given the news he'd known was coming, a discursive speech to which he'd listened quietly—shirtless, dressed in baseball pants and socks and stirrups, no spikes, knowing that it was for real this time—then stood and walked out into the chill morning and took the train from 161st Street into Manhattan, got off at Columbus Circle and walked the seven blocks to this halfway house that was his brother's shoddy home.

He'd been almost ready to give up when the voice had at last arrived at his back. "Mr. Hill?" A woman, perhaps in her sixties, extending a hand to shake, leading him beyond the lobby with its marble flooring and wainscoting, its stained glass and exposed roof beams, a partitioned hallway leading past offices bearing heaps of paperwork on donated desks to the room at the back corner where the soup and the sandwich and the questionnaire had been waiting. She'd returned ten minutes later with coffee and a confession, had sat down across from him at the table, eying the untouched questionnaire before placing it on the antique built-in credenza behind her. The girl with the ski jacket had gone home for the night, the front door was locked now—admittance was closely monitored after hours, she explained, though his brother would be here soon. She had sat silently for a moment as if searching his expression, then surprised him with the admission that she had almost been there, that Jamie had invited her to come to the game and so she had almost witnessed it herself. Surprised him further with the confession that she still remembered GB from his last visit, still recalled his face from some fifteen years ago—though she supposed it had not been your run-of-the-mill visit from a relative. The baseball uniform might have had something to do with it as well. A cursory retelling of that long ago day had followed, details that made GB stare into his coffee. For he had marched right through those heavy doors that day, stirred with anger and sidestepping their attempts to calm him, exuding a measured urgency that was more about what had happened to him than what had happened to his brother. At the rear of the building had been a tiny courtyard, and it was here that GB had found his younger brother Jamie, barged out to find him leaning far forward on a bench situated beneath an ancient crabapple tree. A light shower had stirred up, a soft pattering that, combined with the embracing brick walls of this little apron of garden, had seemed to keep out the sounds of the city and lace their voices with an echoing quality, a crispness—so that he remembered even all these years later the words he'd spoken in his attempt to confront his brother, who'd crouched forward and remained silent until GB turned to go back in the building. Then his head rose and he had spoken what at first sounded like an apology, only to morph into more of his crazy talk, words GB had tried, over the years, to forget. "It was fixed," his brother had said, his head wet, rain dripping from his hair, a soiled image to accompany the impossible and yet nagging notion that had haunted him casually ever since—"Dad bought your way to the Majors. It was paid for by the kingdom of grease!"—the boy GB had sought out as a remedy still speaking as he'd turned to go back inside, stepped through the lobby and out the heavy front door toward the rest of his life. One last hesitation on the sidewalk, and then kill him in your mind.

But he hadn't. He had carried it with him like he'd carried all these other burdens—burdens he had struggled to explain while sipping his coffee without really explaining (for then he'd have to face them himself), burdens he had approached cautiously and then abandoned while the woman at the table confided in him how it had taken them some time to calm his brother down after GB had left. They had worried about him, had worried Jamie might one day leave and never return, were still worried about him. Leading him at last up the four flights of stairs, talking of his brother all the time, telling him how they could offer him a space but they couldn't make him stay here, couldn't make him take his meds, couldn't make him do anything, not with the laws the way they were and the lawmakers more worried about reelection than doing what was right. Unlocking the door at the far end of the fifth-floor hallway and following him into the room that had been his brother's home for who knew how many years now, its grimy linoleum floor ramped at the edges, its walls of gray paint over peeling wallpaper, a foam pallet on metal casters for a bed and a lone window loose in its casing, covered by a crimson sheet and looking down on an asphalt breezeway where that little garden had been, a single file cabinet pushed crookedly against the wall. GB stood in the empty center of his brother's room beneath the dangling cord and repulsive light of a half-burnt-out ceiling lamp, removing his cap, rubbing his hands through his hair and explaining to the woman how things hadn't exactly been easy for him either. How he'd been forced to give up on baseball after that summer of '83. How he'd settled down in Florida with a wife and a daughter and tried to make a life.

And how were *they* doing? the woman had asked, smiling and placing a hand on his shoulder—a polite, gentle, unremarkable woman trying to do good work in this hopeless place, offering him a diligent kindness he'd avoided then but longed for now, past midnight in the motel room in Pennsylvania, watching the news with the sound turned down on the old RCA, his brother cross-legged on the bed with his eyes closed, the dog curled up in his lap.

They were doing fine, he'd lied. Just fine.

———

OUTSIDE AKRON, THEY'D SEEN IT, rising above the trees beyond the exit ramp. It wasn't the first time. You couldn't go ten miles along any road in the US without seeing it—and of course GB had passed dozens during his trip up the Atlantic seaboard, lighting up the night from towers above the treetops and making him sometimes turn away and sometimes stare—but it was the first time either of them had seemed willing to admit it into the space between them, disregarding it on a principle broken now by necessity or just hunger.

It was the cheapest place and they were broke, feverish from the previous day's long haul and the unquiet night in the hard beds, the trip resumed in the early heat of the unseasonably warm morning with the country still reeling, that feeling of aftermath still hovering though they'd made good time through dreary river towns north of Pittsburgh, the dog curled up on Jamie's lap while he struggled against the wind to read a newspaper procured from the motel lobby. A strange bond had formed that night in Pennsylvania. The dog had never been one to sleep on beds; even in the house in Coral Gables he had slept on Emma's floor rather than in bed with her— yet the previous night the dog had remained with a head propped on Jamie's leg throughout his intervals of quiet and gabbiness, even into the early hours when restlessness had driven GB out to the parking lot to sit and stare at nothing in the front seat of the Stingray. It had continued the following morning when he'd stood at the checkout counter, watching his brother in his sweatpants and long trench coat step out to the car with the dog and the *Times* while he handed over his Mastercard and practiced what he'd say if it was declined, looked around at the newspaper racks bearing on their front pages the same bleary photos, another rehash of the president's speech two nights before on the television above the meager breakfast station, looking just as shocked as anyone else behind his podium.

Jamie had ordered a quarter pounder with cheese and taken it on a tray to a table in the corner of the dining room behind a little row of fake plants. GB had an instant of panic before he saw them, listened self-consciously to the sound of his baseball spikes crossing the floor, scanned the room for observing eyes as he sat down across from his brother and the dog. It was nothing to be proud of, this red-and-yellow erector set on a slab of blacktop outside the former tire capital. And yet even during this darkest of weeks the place was still busy with folks on the go, a quick stop for a burger and some fries procured from teenagers in weird caps saying *May I help you?*—a tasty unhealthy snack to keep the kids quiet for the next fifteen minutes and then back into the cramped car for more of the same.

Jamie had dissected his burger and begun inspecting the slop of melted cheese and mustard and ketchup, the dog perched up on the chair next to him and watching. "Look," he said, eyes earnest and darting between the burger and a point beyond GB's shoulder.

"What?" said GB. He had barely slept at all the night before, was going on something like six days without more than a dozen hours of sleep. "That's an onion."

"It's a tracking device," said Jamie, and lifted it from the burger, placed it on the paper tray liner, surveyed the room. "They've been following us since Scranton," he whispered. *"Don't turn around! Continue to act as if you're completely oblivious. Let me take care of them."* From the pocket of his trench coat, he retrieved a bag of spinach, selected a large leaf, wrapped it around his burger and, holding it all together with two hands, crouched low over the table and took a big bite, eyes up and searching as he chewed.

GB sat back in his chair. He didn't feel like eating his chicken sandwich. It had already made him sick just by its presence, the sight of his brother with filthy fingernails picking at his onions doing nothing to stir his appetite and the sight of the other patrons wandering like shock victims bringing back his own sullen discomfiture. He excused himself to the bathroom, went into the handicapped stall and sat with his pinstriped pants around his ankles, remembering the times he had used this same excuse as a way of getting away from *them*, a way of dodging his wife and daughter when the dearth of satisfying options on the long trips north from Miami to Orlando to visit his in-laws had made them settle for unceremonious meals in similar rest stops where he'd escape to the bathroom to gather himself, remaining seated on the toilet until he felt certain he had given them enough time to finish, until it was time to go back out to the car and resume the more comfortable conflict of what had become of their lives, their daughter distant beneath noisy headphones blaring expletive-laced rap music in the back while Tammy talked about work, talked about her father and about herself while GB watched the yellow and white lines recede before him and wondered what had happened to the woman he'd met.

She had gone into her father's business, was what had happened. She had become a real estate broker just like dear old dad and had lost in the process some of the charm that had made him love her. And because it had been the subject of perhaps every conversation she'd ever had with the old man, she'd felt the need to tell GB all about her monthly quotas and sales figures. Didn't care a lick about how GB's scouting job was going, in fact accused him of doing exactly what he'd promised he wouldn't back when they'd gotten together, the job a way of continuing to cling to baseball despite the lowly salary and the promise he'd made that he was giving it up for good. Why didn't he take the real estate exam? Because he couldn't fathom something worse than having to work with her and her old man, that was why. Of course he hadn't said this. Of course, because he was the one who had to keep a lid on things, the one who had to keep Emma always in mind, who had to keep these scenes in the car on these family outings from boiling over again into the arguments that could begin anywhere and deteriorate rapidly.

He had held his tongue, would allow his mind to trail back over their years together. How they'd met in South Beach—spring of '84—and Emma had come along just a year later. How he'd been all but emptied of hope in those drastic days, had felt after that night he'd stood on the green carpet of Yankee Stadium that his whole life had collided with a brick wall at eighty miles per hour and shattered, had been haunted by the thing his brother had said: that their father had been behind it all, an absurd statement that had nonetheless made him revise everything he'd thought he'd known about the last decade, about this desperate dream that had beguiled and betrayed him, about all the second chances and restarts that had seemed happenstance or lucky breaks at the time. He had come to question everything, was not sure anymore that he had *ever* been deserving of all that praise and promise. And so it had been with a resignation bordering on complete futility that he had accepted the offer the Yankees had dangled out for him, had become a low-grade scout in south Florida not because he liked it there or because it was what he wanted to do but because it was better than the pathetic options he could've imagined for himself outside of baseball. Thirty-four years old and on the verge of a crisis—but equipped with a low-grade salary and a furnished apartment compliments of the team (and also the Stingray that was always a great ice breaker)—he had embarked upon a winter of false reassurance, blazing a trail of credit card debt in seedy after-hours clubs in pursuit of the one thing he thought could make him feel better about himself: the easy consummations that had long been unanimously considered the most rewarding part of life in the minor leagues, an entire off-season of anonymous encounters at the ends of winding beach roads with women forgotten by the following evening, blondes and brunettes and redheads, bombshells one and all, names and features blending until one of them had called him out of the blue, asking for money. She needed a hundred bucks, she'd said. For an abortion.

Instead they'd gotten married. It had suddenly seemed right to him. As he'd explained it to her father the real estate developer while they'd double-teamed a twelve pack of Bud on a stone patio bordering a fairway the day before the wedding, Tammy was the surprise happy ending to his decades-long pursuit of the unattainable. And even if the flaws in this thinking had become apparent as quickly as their Caribbean-hopping honeymoon had devolved into arguments and boredom, it had all seemed trivial the instant she'd given him Emma, their personal incompatibilities becoming irrelevant the moment in the hospital when, trembling with apprehension, he'd first held his tiny daughter in his hands and felt all of his burning aspirations reduced by the miracle of her little fist wrapped around his finger to a simple understanding. She had completed him. It was an old threadbare phrase, but true—her birth the discovery of that nameless something he'd been searching for all his life, the feeling of wholeness he'd sought on a thousand baseball diamonds to no avail, her little face the inspiration for a whispered vow that he would never do to her what he'd had done to him, a promise by which he meant to rate his concerns from that moment on. How does this affect Emma? In doing what I am about to do, am I doing what is best for my daughter?

And though it had been an easy promise to make (and easy to keep, during those early years, when she'd been a toddler in pink onesies, a tomboy in pigtails), by the time he'd sat in those bathrooms waiting impatiently for them to finish lunch, it had become a process more endured than enjoyed. It had become more difficult as the endearing images captured in photographs depicting Emma grinning in pajamas beneath Christmas trees or curled up with her puppy in the backyard had been belied by that awkward phase called adolescence, a universe of depth and intellect he could not touch blooming beneath those headphones, a creature more complex and individual than either he or Tammy could ever have bargained for the night they'd sat together in his furnished apartment and come to the conclusion that they were ready for this, that they were ready to become parents together. A spontaneous decision they had never regretted, and yet one for which they'd each come to privately blame the other as the years had given rise to a casual hostility, a haughty levity—new aspects of a new Emma so incompatible with the old that it forced them to form unsettling allegiances, had made GB realize that in spite of the churning, almost painful love he felt for his daughter (for he really did simply adore her, attended her gymnastics meets with a fervor bordering on fanaticism) he felt something less for her mother, the woman with whom he'd made that hasty decision and ended up now, years later, with nothing in common but this precious thing they'd created by accident and had no idea how to deal with.

It had happened in an instant. His little girl had grown up. Or that was the way it had seemed, looked at from the perspective of the front seat on those long trips to Orlando, watching in the rearview mirror the languid movements of this young woman with her pierced lip and at least two tattoos she'd at first halfheartedly tried to hide from them. This changeling of a girl who'd gone to bed one night in the summer of her fifteenth year a polite and happy princess worthy of all their pride—a smiling, blessed girl obsessed with gymnastics and her pet dog—only to awake the following morning an unknowable presence, a brooding shadow beyond a closed door who wouldn't speak unless it was to scream at them, who'd up and quit gymnastics in favor of suspicious nightly outings with "friends from school" from which she would return well after midnight with a tarnished glaze to her eyes to find her mother waiting up in the kitchen, Tammy's arias of dissent fusing with Emma's rebuttals to form ear-shattering duets that brought GB out of the Southern Comfort-induced slumbers to watch messy-haired from the kitchen door, arms crossed and shoulder propped against the door frame while his daughter (at whom he still could not look without remembering her as the tiny miracle he could hold in his hands and bestow whispered unkeepable promises upon) marched past without so much as a glance, a final curse hurled from the banister beside the chandelier before slamming her bedroom door behind her, almost catching in it her poor pet dog who had come limping out to greet her.

This was what he'd tried to escape those days he went into the bathroom and sat on the toilet, these moments over cheap meals when Emma's resolute silence would make Tammy look at him under her eyebrows, would bring him back to all the nights spent staying up late in their bedroom, discussing her. What could be done? Four in the morning, voices low to keep her from hearing, though her room was down the hall and, as they had discovered later, over those months of stress and turmoil, she was often not there, having snuck out and crept three blocks down the street to be picked up by a noisy carful on its way to secluded beaches, their once treasured daughter congregating among crowds for night skinny dipping while they stayed up late and fought toward conclusions. Came to understand that while it was obvious that something had to be done, it was equally obvious that it could not be accomplished in this house of easy exits and slammed doors, that they needed to restrain her, to get her alone in some contained place from which she couldn't escape while they took whatever means necessary to crack that shell that had grown over her like a jagged chrysalis.

And so it had been early on the morning of one of their long semi-annual trips north to visit Tammy's father in Orlando that, somewhere around four, with the lamps on the nightstands long since switched on, with the sounds of Emma's and Tammy's shouts from another scene earlier that night still echoing, they had arrived at the determination that the long drive north might be perfect, the perfect opportunity to sit her down and really *talk* to her, to make her remove those omnipresent headphones and not let her get away with the I'm fines and the Nothing's wrongs for which she'd become notorious and against which they had become defenseless. To sit her down (for what choice would she have stuck in the backseat all the way from Miami to Orlando?) and ask the tough questions, tread the difficult territory and get to the bottom of what was eating their daughter once and for all. There in the strangely transformed light of four in the morning, they had promised they would

not back down, had shared a hopeful kiss and shut off the lamps—
seven o'clock would come early—and had awoken just three hours
later to see it all go wrong. She didn't want to go. There was a party.
A friend of hers was having a party and didn't they remember? She
had told them about it. Didn't *he* remember? (Her look of hatred
enough to wither whatever meager resolve still permeated his
exhaustion.) She knew for a fact she had told him about it, had even
told him the date. Or had he been too drunk to remember? Just like
always. And you wonder why I never talk to you! It wasn't fair. He
had told her she didn't have to go to her granddad's and so she had
made her own plans and now they were trying to make her change
her plans to go on some stupid trip with them when they'd already
promised she didn't have to go. Words spit at them as she'd stood in
the kitchen, dressed in jogging pants and a tank top, her hair a
tangled mess, the two of them all dressed up for the trip north on
which they'd meant to sit her down and rekindle the love she'd once
so openly given when she'd been a little girl, GB closing his eyes and
waiting for it to begin, the screaming and the slammed doors and
damaged feelings. He closed his eyes and waited and heard . . .
nothing. A heavy silence and then his wife's voice, collapsing all the
tense energy of the room and their lives to a pinprick.

Fine.

She didn't have to go. She could stay here if that was what she
wanted. Because the time had come—Tammy had explained to him
on their long drive north accompanied by the empty backseat—for
them to try a different approach. For she had seen the way the
neighbors looked at her and couldn't take it anymore, the way they
looked at her with pity and disapproval and their eyes saying I'll
tell you what I'd do if she were *my* daughter. The time had come for
tough love. And so they had driven in silence, had endured the

anxious holiday full of guilt trips and feeble excuses for Emma's absence and driven back the same evening, conversing in worn-out voices and coming through the doors at nine o'clock in desperate need of sleep only to find the house empty, had sat up in their customary places waiting for their daughter to reappear so they could have the conversation they'd already delayed too long, Tammy's rants regarding the need to put their foot down turning to concern and fear and then, by two o'clock that first night, to numb anguish at what she seemed to anticipate was not just another transgression, a call placed to the police at three in the morning resulting in their being told to call back when twenty-four hours had passed, the call placed when twenty-four hours had passed resulting in a team being sent out to the house, two detectives marching among the rooms looking for pictures and easy explanations, Tammy lashing out when Sunday had come and gone, swinging her fists at GB and absconding to the love seat where a little stack of Emma's school books rested and would continue to rest throughout the long torturous months to come.

In the bathroom, he lifted his head, pulled up his pants. He did not know how long he'd been sitting there, how long these meandering thoughts that had pursued him all the way north from Florida on Sunday had distracted him this time. He stood for a moment scanning the dining room, the silent families chewing with their heads down, a few looking up to make eye contact and then ducking away. His brother was gone. The booth beyond the fake plants was empty and cleared of trays, recently wiped down. He watched as a trio of college kids sat down with their meals. He closed his eyes and listened as if some voice might tell him where they had gone. A strange impulse led him to the registers, where he leaned far forward to check behind the counter while the teenagers in their weird caps and the patrons watched speechlessly. An outdoor playroom stood beyond the windows, colorful slides into vats of plastic balls, but it was empty even of children. He went back into the restroom, even knocked on the door of the ladies' room and, hearing no response, went in.

He stepped out to the parking lot and exhaled. There they were in the car, Jamie reading his paper with the white-faced dog smiling in his lap, looking askance as GB started up the engine and they pulled out of the lot, Jamie's leg nudging against GB's repeatedly in an attempt to get his attention, whispered *Pssst*s insisting GB turn his head to acknowledge him, at last beginning to speak in a lowered voice as they motored out onto the interstate and GB held up a palm to stifle it.

"Don't do that to me again."

Since then, his brother had been silent, rebuffed and taking it personally, involved in watching the side view mirror the rest of the way across Ohio while GB stared at the road atlas spread over the steering wheel, counting the exit numbers, the low skyline of Toledo rising out of the mist off Lake Erie while the dog looked back and forth between them as if remembering this tension, as if he'd been here before. They hadn't said more than two words to each other, and after he'd taken the exit north, traversing the last low miles of Ohio and crossing the Michigan border, GB had been glad for it, had been glad for the freedom to again let it wash over him, this silence that had been his only company and comfort, that had coated his loss and become a sedated sort of truth. For it was easier, he had found, to lie. Easier to respond to any casual interrogation with avoidance rather than to attempt to explain it, easier to evade the questions, like those he'd imagined the woman back in Hell's Kitchen would have asked had he told her the truth, than to see the looks of feigned sorrow, easier to tell an abridged version to the bar-keep on the Upper East Side than to hear the condolences that had grown so stale as to become insulting, that made him want to shout at people *Don't you dare apologize!*—that they didn't even have the right, that their apologies made a mockery of his true anguish and that no level of manufactured empathy could ever bring them closer to the reality of what it had been like. The endless waiting and ago-nizing over every ring of the phone, the slowly descending realiza-tion that this was really happening, that their daughter was really missing, the monumental weight lowering little by little as if to crush them as incrementally and painfully as it could, the brief necessary rekindling of their intimacy those first nights burning out and turning bitter, each of them lashing out with resentment and blame until there was nothing left to lash out at, until the word *separation* had begun to issue from their mouths in a resigned way they'd both known was for real, movers arriving one Saturday morning to find him floating alone like a trapped breeze in the house in Coral Gables—for he had quit his job, had simply not gone back to work after the day they'd reported Emma missing—three burly Cubans in tight-fitting white T-shirts huffing up and down the stairs while he hovered and watched them remove every last piece of his wife and his daughter, sitting cross-legged then at the threshold of her room staring in at the wide floorboards layered with dust bunnies while the sunlight through the window paraded across the floor to settle upon and then disappear from the far wall.

He had been unable to enter the room. And though for months following he had persisted in these painful vigils—had persisted through the autumn and winter in spite of the FOR SALE sign that had appeared in the yard, timing his sporadic visits from his motel rooms so they wouldn't correspond with the open houses and private showings conducted by Marc, the real estate agent—they had done nothing to soothe his loss. And though he had called Tammy at her new condo, had begged her to please just meet him for dinner, for coffee, she had refused, had found or was fighting to find some way to blame him for what had happened. If only *he* hadn't been so demanding of the girl. If only *he* hadn't insisted that it was time to give tough love a try. Their arguments over the phone had reached climactic crescendos, knocks on the walls and, on one occasion, on the door of his motel room—the owner, come to throw him out—and so he had taken to those long aimless drives in the Stingray, out into the Everglades or south along the Keys, only to find himself arriving always at the end back in Coral Gables, calling up Tammy to plead with her some more while he drove the streets of Emma's hometown whose every block was lined with buildings that reminded of her. The Montessori school. The gymnasium where she'd trained. Venues of a past life robbed of their significance and leading him along the memorized series of turns toward home, parking two blocks away and watching the shadow of the FOR SALE sign in the rearview while Tammy's sobbing escalated. She was crying now, bawling, she couldn't go on. And it was at this point that she'd handed the phone over to Marc, had put Marc on the phone to tell GB what was what, to tell him about *them*, about how *they* were coping.

Driving north now along the interstate in Michigan with his brother and his daughter's dog in the passenger seat, he remembered the desolate silence of that night, the moment he'd pressed a button on his cell phone to hang up on Marc, stepped through the shadows and moonlight of what had been their street looking over both shoulders, unlocked the front door with the key they did not know he still had and entered the silver pool of the vestibule on the

six-month anniversary of his daughter's disappearance to find—
there on the bare echoing tile beneath the chandelier—the letter
that had changed everything. The letter whose message had somehow given him the clarity to sleep—twelve hours of the deepest
sleep of his life, curled up on the hard floor of the vestibule. The
letter that had made him awake the following morning in that
empty house with a new certainty, had made him dig through draw-
ers for the pads of paper Marc kept there for jotting down numbers,
for quick mortgage calculations, had made him open up his heart
and pour out a reply that was like the loosening of four decades,
had made him drop this reply into a blue mail collection box and
return then every morning for three weeks, abiding breathlessly,
grateful for this new anticipation, for the way it so willingly and
conveniently replaced the other. And now, exiting at last at this
Michigan city he'd never visited, its streets silent on a Thursday
evening, he remembered the feeling when at last it was there, resting on the tile just like the first one had been. The second letter,
dropped through the mail slot at the end of its six-thousand-mile
journey. The second of what had since become an even dozen letters
now stored in the knapsack in the trunk next to the bat bag; an
even dozen letters from his half brother, Max, in Alaska, that had
picked him up from his sprawling grief and dragged him north to
New York City, across Pennsylvania and Ohio and now along these
empty small-city streets in search of a phone booth, hearing in the
rapture of this silence his brother's voice, or maybe Marc's, or maybe
Tammy's or Emma's, or maybe his own, asking himself just where
he thought he was going. Just what did he think he was doing here?
A reply whispered under his breath, inaudible in the windy hush of
the blanketing night.

I don't know. I don't know what we're doing here.

ANNABELLE SANCHEZ-NGUYEN WAS IN THE sixtieth hour of a couch-bound vigil next to the phone when she heard the doorbell.

It summoned her out of a half sleep populated by nightmarish visions and made her roll off the couch, tripping over the blankets. She had to navigate the narrow pathways, dodging the accumulation of almost twenty years spent within these four walls, too much furniture and junk, the whole house a tawdry museum of memories, photos on end tables and forgotten gifts and keepsakes. In the kitchen, she heard Dat rising, heard him rustling his newspapers, the ice in his martini clinking as he responded to both the doorbell and the sound of her stirring. "Let me get it!" Their daughter, Julia, had come in from Chicago two nights ago, and she too could be heard in the upstairs hallway, closing the door on the bedroom that still contained the decorations of her adolescence though she'd been gone for four years, trotting across the hallway and then down the stairs with a clamor recalled from bygone days. "Who is it, Mom?" Still half asleep, Annabelle stumbled toward the front hall, heard herself asking the same question, a random vocalization of her anxiety though Dat had not yet made it to the door and could not possibly know the answer. "*Who is it?*"

The place was a mess. It was not just the last three days. Over the years they'd become lax about keeping the house clean, had gone from proud homeowners to taking it for granted, so much clutter that Annabelle could not help but notice the look of not-quite disgust on Julia's face when she'd come through the door and given them both reluctant hugs. Six months ago they'd let go the cleaning woman they'd hired twelve years before, had determined that, with both the kids gone, they would combine to keep the place neat and swept and vacuumed and dusted themselves. Since then they'd already marveled at the accretion of half a year's worth of lint and debris in the corners of the hardwood floors, at the stale smell the place had taken on over the hot summer, windows shut and air conditioning cranking, an atmosphere of repose about which the last three days had made Annabelle hyperaware and scornful.

She had given up on watching the television some hours ago, though it still rambled on in the background like some overly talkative house guest. She'd determined that the mechanism that brought the whole world to every household was nothing but a torture device, could bring her nothing but more anxiety and reveal to her nothing so specific or important as what was happening with her only son, David, in his first week of his freshman year at NYU, able to see the entire terrible scene from his dorm room into which they'd helped him move only two weeks ago, lugging boxes up cramped staircases and dumping them on the floor, all three of them doing their best not to cry when he'd walked them to the subway that would take them to JFK. In the three days that had passed since the unimaginable had happened, they'd received only one brief phone call from him, full of static and with shouts and car horns in the background, and though they'd called his cell repeatedly and waited by their phone for a response, there had been nothing more. Julia had done her dutiful best at first to take her mother's mind off it, had made tea and tried to get her to do crosswords—their old standby—but Annabelle had resisted, had known she was being difficult but had remained catatonically planted in front of the television that showed only the same images over and over. When Julia had finished the crossword and inconspicuously made her way upstairs, Dat had come in for a few minutes, had sat on the recliner next to her, which was as close to each other as they ever got these days, had watched the footage with her and offered his running assurances. There was probably just a problem with the phone lines. David would call again as soon as he was capable. They would hear something any minute. He was doing it again. This thing he still did sometimes on the nights he'd awake to find her seated across the bedroom on the window seat, looking silently out at the street. He was trying to get her to explain, trying to reassure her, when all she wanted was to be left alone. Annabelle rested her head back against the couch pillow and closed her eyes. After a few minutes, she got what she wanted. She listened as he stood and made his way back out to the kitchen, where he had his own television. She heard him settle down into the hard chair and flip through the channels.

At one point she'd thought Dat was the perfect man for her: a quiet, hardworking, bookish type who never boasted but formed a solid soil in which she could thrive, a gentleman who held doors and brought her snacks and chocolate and flowers, a kind, protective type who always took her at her word and rarely sought anything deeper. She'd been amazed, and strangely pleased, that first night they'd met all those years ago, at how easy it had been to lie to him about herself, surprised at how self-preservation had made her a whiz at inventing narratives and passing them off as reality to anyone who bothered to ask. She had responded to a flyer on a telephone pole in the Somerville neighborhood where she'd been staying, twenty bucks and all she had to do was spend an afternoon at a lab looking at television screens and answering questions. She had not realized at first, when the unsmiling graduate student asked her if she wanted to go get a pizza, that he was asking her out. He'd seemed so diligent and single-minded that she'd thought at first it was merely a continuation of the experiment, and so as they'd stepped outside and walked down the street to the pizza parlor she had made up a story about being in art school, a silly lie conjured on the spot because who the hell was this kid scientist and what reason did she have to tell him anything resembling the truth? What reason did Annabelle have to disclose the information that she had ended up here because California had seemed not far enough away and because one of her old college friends had offered up a sublet spot, a place to crash in the slant-floored back bedroom of a triple decker on Winter Hill?

She had thought that would be the end of it. But he had surprised her with his persistence, and she had surprised herself with her willingness. So as things had progressed in their tame and nervous way Annabelle had slowly begun to consider words and phrases such as *fate* and *meant to be*. Perhaps it was impossible not to begin to associate any fleeting sense of happiness with a serendipitous forever when you were coming from a place like the one she was coming from. Or perhaps it was the story of Dat's own life, which he'd related to her on their second date: an adoption initiative in the aftermath of the Tet Offensive, five thousand Vietnamese children brought to the US and seven-year-old Dat Nguyen plopped down in a middle-class suburb of Syracuse. A story related with an unassuming honesty that made Annabelle cringe just to think of the lies she'd told him, a sense of shame filling her when she'd felt him move bashfully against her for the first time, his arm settling around her shoulders in a way that felt more friendly than romantic, yet also disarmingly endearing.

They'd been seeing each other for a month when she finally told him the truth, had brought him over to her sublet for the first time and sat him down on the twin bed in that creaking back room and confessed to him that the art student stuff was bullshit, Dat's face calm and unflinching while she'd spilled upon him the story of what she'd really been doing up in Alaska. And though she had thought while she was saying all of this that he could never possibly want to be with her after he'd heard what she'd done and had done to her, he had again surprised her with his impassiveness. "I can be your second chance," he'd said to her, and brought his arm around her again, more confidently this time.

Now, twenty-odd years later, here they were. Two recent empty nesters in a house turned dusty by neglect. A son away at college in a city that would now fill her with fear every moment he spent there. A daughter who lived two states away and grew irritated any time Annabelle asked her when she was coming home again. ("It's not *home* for me anymore, Mom. *Chicago* is my home now.") A ringing doorbell and all of them responding with shouts, impersonal and distracted, from separate rooms in the way that had become typical over the years. A strange race to the front door where Annabelle knew already they'd find a police officer, hat in hand. Or a neighbor, having gotten the story first in the strange way their neighbors sometimes did. But now that she'd arrived in the hallway, now that she stood at the bottom of the stairs with Julia pausing on the landing above her—"Mom? Who is it?"—Annabelle found that she could almost feel that baseball bat in her hands, could almost feel the constant cold of that cabin and the shadows that had moved through it.

It was Julia who helped her to her feet, saying, "Mom, what the hell?" with her typical mixture of frustration and concern. But the men were there quickly too, Dat with his hand on his forehead and his face painted with worry, the two men who'd been standing in the doorway when Annabelle had come out into the hall appearing above Dat's shoulders, faces mysterious but familiar, the sound of a dog barking behind them. She had not really fainted. It was not so much an act as it was the sort of automatic response that had begun in her childhood, way back in sun-blazed Simi Valley, a little girl's reaction that had progressed throughout college long after she'd known it was wrong—or not so much wrong as simply something a grownup shouldn't or wouldn't do. She wished now she could take it back, having realized that it was her momentary appearance of unsteadiness, leaning against the banister with one arm supporting her as she settled down gently on the staircase, that had mitigated whatever awkwardness might have prevented Dat from inviting the men inside. Because he couldn't just send them away while his wife was sitting in a heap at the foot of the stairs, could he? And they could hardly just leave without trying to make themselves appear useful, coming in to offer assistance as Julia guided Annabelle back to the blanket-strewn couch and made her lie down with her eyes closed. Nor could they refuse Dat's offer to head on into the living room and have a seat while he fixed his wife a glass of water. And could he get anything for them while he was at it? A beer? The glass of water with a bendy straw procured for Annabelle and a beer in a bottle for the one in the baseball uniform, who sat perched forward on the ancient broken glider in the corner while the other one with the glasses and the sweat suit and the trench coat refused Dat's offers for a chair to be brought in from the dining room and sat cross-legged on the floor with the chocolate lab asleep against his hip. Annabelle said they were old friends. Old friends from a past life. And she looked at them both for the first time, looked them directly in their eyes. Then she made a great effortful display of sitting up on the couch, Dat leaning forward from his recliner and Julia from the far couch cushion to ask if she needed help.

Of course, Annabelle knew who these two men were. It had taken a moment to convince herself, but she had known the instant she saw them that they were the adult versions of the two boys she'd once known as her stepsons, whom she'd once driven out into the desert east of LA to visit their mother, whose father she'd followed all the way to Alaska and with whom she'd spent those years she'd been running from when she'd met Dat, the characters who had populated that story she'd confessed to him (and only him, even all these years later) on that night in the back bedroom in Somerville. What a strange group they made, Annabelle thought, looking around the room. But the circumstances gave them enough to talk about, or at least things to say—the television mumbling on in the background providing the most awful icebreaker of all time. Dat broke the initial silence to inform their two guests at great length of the story of David while Julia interrupted to correct and corroborate, her gloominess having vanished the instant it was no longer just her and her parents.

"We were just there," the one in the baseball uniform said, and then explained how they'd come directly from New York, speaking with a tense vagueness about their last three days in the car, their crawl across Interstate 80 at fifteen yards an hour, his eyes on Annabelle as if waiting for her to interrupt, waiting for her to tell him he was saying too much. Dat was inquisitive as always, asking his pensive but benign questions about their routes, playing the role of the Midwesterner that he'd learned so well, Julia butting in to ask for details of the scene they'd left behind, digging for gory particulars as always, at which point the bespectacled man in the trench coat, rocking slightly, spoke up to tell them that it wasn't what anyone thought, that none of this was what anyone thought it was. The rest of them went silent for a moment, waiting to hear what might come next. But he lowered his eyes and returned his silent attention to the dog, gently patting its head, and Dat took up the conversation again with more of his polite questions, his courteous chitchat, reaching over to retrieve Annabelle's empty glass, to fill it at the sink and return with another beer for the baseball player, who seemed to Annabelle simultaneously desperate to speak and unwilling to divulge. Or maybe he'd simply understood what she had said earlier and was trying to remain under the safe heading she'd given him. A friend from a previous life.

The television droned on. The old grandfather clock she'd dug up a decade ago at some decrepit yard sale refused to divulge the correct time. When the man in the trench coat, still seated on the floor, seemed to have dozed off, Dat stood up and said he'd get some blankets. There was the couch and there was the air mattress. The two of them could decide. Julia stood and followed him upstairs to help, and for a moment Annabelle sat numb, realizing that it was just the three of them, she and her two former stepsons and a moment of avoided and then forced eye contact, GB leaning forward in the glider, elbows on knees and a nearly empty beer bottle held in both hands, the label torn and removed, Jamie alert and looking at her now through those thick glasses that distorted and magnified his black eyes, even the dog awake and watching her. For an instant they hovered there, all three of them poised, seemingly, on the verge of saying something, of trying to access their shared past, of trying to break this uncomfortable freeze of uncertainty in favor of a moment of recognition and acknowledgment. Jamie ran a hand through his wild hair. GB's eyes drifted up and off to the left, the sign of someone preparing to speak honestly and from memory. From the heart. His mouth opened, but all Annabelle heard was the phone ringing.

It was David. It was her son in New York City, wondering why in the hell they'd been so worried. He'd called and said he was fine, hadn't he? Yes, they said, but they'd lost him. The phone had just cut out. The tension that had built and then slowly alleviated and then built again was immediately relieved by the voice of Annabelle's son on the phone, though he was clearly dazed and exhausted, barely capable of answering their questions. There were three phones in the house, and listeners were dispatched to pick up the various lines. GB declined, sitting back in the recliner with what appeared to be relief. Jamie headed out to the kitchen with Dat though he didn't contribute much more than a cryptic question or two. When the phone call ended—when they'd finally finished expressing their thankfulness and when David had told them he had to go ("Seriously, Mom, I can't talk much longer.")—Dat set about inflating the air mattress and Julia set up the blankets on the couch and then they headed upstairs together with Annabelle while the guests remained in the living room in front of the television. In their bedroom, Dat placed a hand on Annabelle's shoulder—that same friendly, endearing touch from their second date—and then sat down on the bed to take off his shoes.

"You did fine, darling," he said. "You did just fine."

This was what life was like with Dat. This was what he provided. A blanket of protection that did not exactly keep you warm though it did keep you comfortable, or at least allowed you to feel hidden from the things you feared were still out to get you. He had proven a respectful man, attentive when he needed to be, and if their own relationship had gone through the loss of passion that was common enough at their ages, there had remained throughout a calm comfort between them. Annabelle could look around this house, with its keepsakes and corridors of memory, and feel something like contentment. "I can be your second chance," he'd said to her all those years ago. The sort of thing men said all the time but never meant. But Dat had meant it, had done what he could to help her transition between the life she'd left behind and the one he hoped to help her begin. It had been his idea that she contact Max and Maddie, and it had been Dat who had consoled her after she had received the full brunt of her son's fury, a fury that she had expected and knew she deserved, though it still leveled her. It had been Dat who had comforted her again after the trip to Vegas, after the shock and strain of seeing her daughter again had proven too much, after all the things she'd hoped to be able to say to Maddie had gone unsaid, her desire to make amends or at least speak of it in a way that might prove productive not strong enough to overcome the strange mix of resentment and postured acceptance she and her daughter seemed doomed to show each other. Then had come Julia and a series of phone calls to Maddie that had gone unanswered. Then had come Dat's full-time appointment at the university, nearly simultaneous with the news that Annabelle was pregnant again, David born just one month after they'd bought this house that over the eighteen years since had become a home. Then had come occasional phone calls from Maddie, her voice slurred, her intentions uncertain. When Julia had grown old enough to start answering the phone, to start asking Annabelle who Maddie was, and why she kept calling, Annabelle had struggled to decide what to do next. In the end, she had not had to do anything. The phone calls had stopped on their own. And though she had quickly gone from wishing they'd stop to wishing they'd start up again, Annabelle was never able to pick up the phone herself, could not face the daughter whose future and whose present she could not help but feel to blame for.

How do you leave behind a life? Annabelle had asked herself this question often in the years that had passed, had imagined the horrified looks neighbors and friends would give her if they knew about it, if they knew her secret history. But the answer was simple. The answer was you found a new one.

Still, beneath it all was a constant regret, a private compulsion that made her feel the need to look back on those years, a sorrow that returned to her, later that night, as she climbed out of bed—quietly, so as not to disturb Dat—and stepped over to her window seat. She had become, somewhere along the way, a keeper of things. She was a hoarder, as evidenced by the cluttered living room, the countless keepsakes and souvenirs that adorned all the rooms like a layer of memory. But she was also a keeper of secrets. There was a linen closet upstairs—the same closet that Dat and Julia had retrieved the blankets from earlier—and it was in this linen closet that Annabelle had discovered, one day not long after they'd moved in here, almost two decades ago now, that there was an additional drawer way in the back, a drawer that seemed invented for purposes of concealing things not to be accessed lightly. That day all those years ago, with Julia in her playroom and David across the hall in his crib, and Dat two miles away at office hours or crossing the quad to a classroom, Annabelle had known that this would be the place where she'd hide everything, the place where she would put every memento or detail she found about that old life: the collection that had begun with the little crayon-written note from his first wife and had grown to include newspaper and magazine articles about him, the rare letter from Maddie, a postcard of Alaska she'd seen once and felt compelled to cling to. She would take these little pieces of that old life and tuck them away in here, a compartmentalization of the heart. A cramped little space at the back of a closet to store the past in a world that forged inexorably forward. A quiet place to go back and stay for a bit while you fought to maintain the appearance that you were moving forward, that you had left it behind.

Sometimes, late at night, when she sat at this window seat look-ing down on the street where they'd lived for the last eighteen years and the side yard, she would see images from the past. She would see Julia and David diving in leaf piles in the yard, or bundled up in layers and trudging through the snow of a lost Christmas Eve, on their way downtown with her to last minute shop for Dat. She would see a giant field behind a tiny cabin in Alaska, a hospital waiting room where she sat looking up at a television positioned high on a wall, the view out a bus window on way her south to Anchorage with one child left behind and another departing for a parallel life. She would stare out this window and watch thirty years and more play out in an instant while her husband's deep breaths issued behind her. She would look out through saddening eyes until the details of the yard and the street blended into nothing more than a colorful pastiche, like something hanging on a wall in a museum, and only then would she be able to fall asleep, would come awake in the morning still twisted on the bench seat, her cheek cold where it rested against the glass, her neck stiff.

It was a shock, at first, to notice him out there. A form material-izing out of the shadows of this scene she knew so well, a figure standing next to one of the stately elms across the street while the dog sniffed at the fire hydrant. Reflexively, she backed away from the window, ducked behind one of the curtains though he was not looking up at her, though the lights in the room were off and from the street her little perch would appear as nothing more than another darkened window. He hesitated for another moment, then tugged gently on the leash and started off through the darkness, Annabelle's heart suddenly racing.

In that moment downstairs, when they'd been alone together, the first thing she'd felt was fear. A fear borne of guilt and shame but also that they might blame her or expose her, that their reasons for being here might not be benevolent. But as they'd sat there, the three of them, the tension like something hard and frozen between them, she had seen that they had no clear idea what had brought them here either. They seemed as lost in this moment as she was, not vengeful specters from her past at all but more like trapped ghosts wandering, looking for a way to escape, guided by some force they couldn't understand, no different from the forces that had once swept her to Boston and then to this little college town in Michigan where she'd helped Julia and David with homework and tended to them when they were sick and gone to their school plays, had cooked Thanksgiving dinners and made doctor appointments and watched the decades of her second chance spin by through the late-night transparency of this window seat.

She looked over her shoulder, saw Dat still fast asleep in the bed. Looked back out to the street, but the shadow of the man in the cloak was gone.

She had no idea what she was going to do with them tomorrow, but the strangest thing was she wasn't worried about it. Two decades of fretting and trying to conceal and justify this secret thing inside her had somehow been alleviated by these two men appearing on her doorstep and sitting awkwardly in her living room for a few hours. All these secrets and betrayals, these selfish acts produced in the simple engine of need—they were only what they were. They were nothing more. If anything, the years had dulled their edges, had made the space around them safe for something other than regret. Perhaps there was a value to the past, Annabelle thought to herself. Perhaps it was not always something to be feared, full of repercussions to be anticipated and dreaded, an artifact to be tucked in a hidden cabinet and forgotten. Perhaps you could learn to live with it instead of spending your life running. Seated there on the window seat, looking out over their suburban street, Annabelle Sanchez-Nguyen felt her body shudder and the tears well up, but what she felt this time was different. It was not sorrow or guilt. It came from the same place, but it was deeper and more complicated. It was something like courage. Something like love.

She knew she still had Maddie's number around here somewhere. In fact, she knew exactly where she'd kept it.

THE SNAKE WAS RESTLESS.

One hour before dawn, and he was prowling the streets of this small city, accompanied by a leashed dog he didn't remember acquiring. The houses looked so dark at this hour, tucked far back on shadowy lawns in a way that felt strange for someone so used to the claustrophobia of New York, neither taxi horn nor nighthawk shout to be heard. He was trying to piece it all together, the tangled webs of engagement and loyalty that had revealed themselves on this onerous and confounding mission. The debriefing held at the suburban home occupied by the three low-level operatives masquerading as husband and wife and daughter had introduced new avenues of tension and uncertainty, had made the Snake question where one lie ended and another began, where they overlapped and contradicted. And the meeting he'd had afterwards—the meeting from which he'd now fled along these streets in a fluster of confusion, trying to find his way back—had made him question everything he'd already begun to question.

He'd snuck away after midnight, just long enough after the phone call had come in from the senior investigator back in the city—or

rather, the teenage kid they'd commissioned to serve as his mouth-
piece. They'd led the Snake to a sequestered quiet room and forced
a cordless phone into his hand and there was the voice of the kid,
relaying the messages in a code the Snake recognized immediately,
telling him to locate the first guidepost that had been concealed in
the high grass of a fire hydrant across the street. Informing him
that he should be at the indicated location by half past one. To make
sure he wasn't followed. The Snake had waited another hour, ready
for any last-minute surprises, and then snuck out the backdoor with
the little clock on the microwave showing it was close to one in the
morning. Plenty of time to make it across the city.

The boy on the phone had been using an older code. But the direc-
tives, once he located them, had been clear enough, had led him
along residential streets until they began to give way to dark buildings of cinder block and concrete, weedy lots like glades with cracked
pavement and regions of shattered glass, disused roads pockmarked
by potholes and adjacent to the fetid river. Though it was night the
moon was high over the line of trees across the water and reflecting, illuminating the green rusted metal bridge that loomed up
ahead and then took shape beneath his feet, the Snake entering a
parkland by an unlocked gate and climbing a hill, then continuing
down a short, steep decline into a wet ravine cloistered by weeping
willows and sprawling oaks, a one-lane road of gravel and dirt lit
occasionally by the dull watery light of arc lamps, the asphalt undu-
lating at its edges with roots and age, a mist lowering into the
ravine so that the Snake heard the footsteps before he saw their
source. The click of firm, expensive shoes up ahead seeming to generate out of the silence, materializing in step with the sound of the
dog's leash as it jostled.

The Snake stopped in his tracks and stared straight ahead at the shadow that had formed fifty feet away in the fog. The shape of a man and, now, a voice cutting through the moist air.

"What's with the dog? That ain't one a them bitin' dogs, is it?"

The Snake didn't know whether to walk forward or wait. He didn't know whether to lie or run. The figure approached slowly through the mist, his expensive shoes echoing, a stride the Snake recalled though it had been decades, a posture somehow both confident and reluctant, as if trying too hard not to slouch. "I know that dog," he said. "That's GB's dog." And the leash slipped from the Snake's grasp, the dog rushing away as if drawn by some primal magnetism, crouching at the man's feet to be scratched behind the ears, smiling with snout held high. "Come on," the man said. A subtle nod of his head back toward the mist that had revealed him. "I want to show you something."

The Snake felt for the shank in his pocket but it was gone. Of course he had known this could be dangerous. Had known as soon as he'd stepped out into these unknown streets that he was on enemy territory, that the advantage he possessed always when these meetings took place in the city—the advantage of being able to duck away through the undergrowth and disappear toward the lesser-known exits—was gone here on this winding path that seemed to descend endlessly through this forgotten slice of parkland, leading down and down until the man paused up ahead, the dog stopping abruptly while he seemed to get his bearings, stepped over to the woods and peered through the trees. "Ah," he said, looking back at the Snake. "Here we are." He stepped up onto the embankment in his expensive shoes and suit and disappeared, the Snake hustling to follow so he wouldn't lose him, but there was no need. As soon as he'd climbed the rise of land he could see it, a clearing opening up perhaps thirty feet ahead, the man standing at the mouth of the dense overgrown woods and gesturing the Snake forward.

"Remember this place?"

The huge field behind the cabin was awash with wildflowers and they stepped out into it together, through the drift of an Alaskan breeze scented with snowmelt and isolation. Against a stool that rested where the yard gave way to the untamed field was the rifle, an old box of ammunition resting in the grass. "*Now* you remember." The man removed his suitcoat and tie and pegged them to the clothesline, retrieved a pack of smokes from the inside pocket of the coat and ignited one with his Zippo, the cigarette clenched between his lips as he crouched and reached into the ammo box.

The Snake was perplexed, the dog beside him panting and grinning. "Do you still live here?" he asked, and the man responded with a *pff* sound. Their voices seemed to echo unnaturally. "Heck no," the man said, finished laying the shells across the magazine and slid the bolt. "This bit in Alaska is long ago wrapped up. Finished up that pipeline and stood on the pier at Valdez and watched the first tanker cruising out into Prince William Sound with a ticker tape parade going on behind me, and you know what I felt? Not a moment of satisfaction. Well, maybe a moment. Took a sip of some cognac someone was passing around and said to myself, 'What the hell's next?'"

He raised the rifle and pulled the trigger. The shot sent a violent tremor echoing across the field, reverberating all the way to the distant mountains and back; then it was swallowed up by the deep silence. The man stood with the rifle still raised, watching. He lowered it and handed it to the Snake. "I guess you're probably wonderin' what I been up to, huh?" It wasn't really a question at all, though it carried the implications of one. The Snake stared at the rifle, glanced toward the cabin expecting to see little faces glaring out at them, but there were none. The cabin was decrepit, boarded up, clearly abandoned. The man had sat down on the stool now, arms resting on his knees, an old beer can in one hand. "I headed down to Texas for a while, but I ran into some trouble down there. Too smart for my own good, you might say. Dumped it all and headed up to Nebraska. Now I'm thinking about buying this place out in the country. You may have thought you were rid of me that day you marched off south from Fairbanks. Off to the military. Well, I let you go. Just like your brother, you were seventeen and had everything figured out and what was I supposed to do? Chain you to the furnace? I guess the military must not have worked out so hot, judging by you're wearing civvies and your hair's longer than a girl's."

The Snake had closed his eyes, but now he looked at him seated there on the stool. One last long sip from the beer can before he crushed it in one hand and chucked it toward the cabin, the Snake's finger on the trigger of the rifle. "Well?" the man said. "You gonna shoot that thing, or what?" Their eyes locking. He retrieved his suit coat from the clothesline, then reached forward and removed the rifle from the Snake's hands, placed it back against the stool. "Come on then," he said. "I got some more things to show you."

They stepped back through the woods, descended the embankment to the winding path, but it had transformed. It was no longer a dirt and gravel trail but a wide railroad bed with the sound of a train whistle approaching, the man in the suit coat crouching there waiting, asking the Snake if he was ready. The train came rumbling in and they hopped up onto the splintery wooden floor of one of the freight cars as it passed, the man grasping the Snake's hand to help pull him up. He lit another cigarette and rested on his haunches in the darkness of the dusty car while the Snake stared idly at the scenery that rushed by out the wide opening of the side of the train, a vista of high sweeping plains and distant mountains capped with snow.

"I brought you some pictures," the man said, speaking loudly over the rattling clamor, a stack of Polaroids appearing in the Snake's hands. "Beautiful, huh? The way the sun sets over those trees there? Well, those are all taken from this here horse ranch I been lookin' at buying. Been thinking you might even want to come live with me there. You could learn to ride, learn to help around the stables. In the evenings we'll play poker, just like in the old days. You see, I've stumbled onto something, my boy. I've stumbled onto that one thing I've been waiting to stumble on my whole life. Pretty soon you're gonna be hearing my name associated with the biggest money-making operation of the twentieth century, something that's gonna make that bit up in Alaska seem like a pittance, and I'm not above letting you kids have a piece of the pie."

The Snake looked up, and his father reached forward and seized him by the forearm. "This is our stop." And in the transitory moment that ensued the Snake realized this was not a freight train. This was the F Train, and they were coming above ground at 57th Street into the soot and splendor of an urban dusk, the shadows of Fifth Avenue rising around them in the grainy darkness. They were stepping along a familiar footpath that skirted the vocal bustle of the skating rink, past the chess and checkers pavilion, descending into the silence of the barren row of elms along the mall, last autumn's leaves sweeping across the pavement and surrounding them in a wind-blown rustle. His father spoke and the Snake listened while they made their way over to the Bethesda Terrace and stood beneath the Angel of the Waters, while they climbed up to the bandshell and sat together in the darkened space beneath the columns, the platform empty but for the grazing pigeons, his father looking at him now with an intensity that made the Snake turn away, that made the Snake look down at his feet. His father saying, "All you gotta do, kiddo, is look me in the eyes and say, 'All right, Dad,' and it'll be off to Nebraska." Saying, "Ah, look at you," with disgust when he did not receive the response he'd hoped for. And then standing and pacing across the moonlit bandshell saying, "I might've known. Got those stubborn eyes. Your mother's eyes. Haven't changed a bit, have you?" Saying, "Look, kid, what the hell else are you gonna do? For crying out loud, you're barely alive as it is. Living in some God-awful place I can't even imagine a son of mine living." Stepping over and staring down at the Snake with hands on hips. "Look at me, boy. You look at me when I'm talking to you. Can't you see I'm offering you a life where you don't have to sign a sheet to come and go?"

The Snake had understood. He had understood it as his father stepped away in frustration, then paused and returned again for one last try. "Now look. Here's the last thing I can do. Here's my business card. You keep it with you, okay? Now what I'm trying to tell you is that I've—what are you doing? What—what the hell do you think you're doing? Pick that up! I'm telling you, boy, to pick up that business card and—don't you dare walk away from me!" But the Snake had known that it was all he could do, hopped down from the bandshell and felt himself receding through the levels of this waking dream, back across the park and then in the cramped odorous flush of the F train. Back across the infinite stretch of the continent beneath the quiet night whistle of the freight train to the solemn field behind the deserted cabin and back through the mist-shrouded woods where his father's voice still filtered down from somewhere high up while the Snake kept his head down and tried not to listen: *"Fine!* If that's the way it's gonna be then the hell with you! I'll be sure to let your brothers and your sister know! When they all come wonderin' why I never contacted 'em, and when your brother GB comes running to me, wondering why the career I bought and paid for with my own connections is running out of steam, I'll be sure to tell him he's got you to thank! I'll send them all away and tell 'em it was the fault of their crazy brother living in a halfway house in Hell's Kitchen! I'll tell 'em to come and look you up! I'll tell 'em exactly where they can place the blame for their lonely, regret-filled, sorry excuses for lives!"

BY THE TIME THE SNAKE had stepped back across the green rusted metal bridge, traversed the neighborhood of vacant weedy lots to the residential streets with houses set far back from the roads, the first blue tinges of dawn had begun to light the eastern sky. But the Snake was still lost in what he'd seen, was still trying to situate that image of his father standing on the bandshell with the towers of Fifth Avenue in the background, a shadow in the moonlight berating the Snake for the mistake he'd just made. But at the time, it hadn't seemed like a mistake. And that was what made it so difficult to understand now. What had he been doing in Central Park, when he should've been in Russia? Or in that vast underground bunker deep beneath the desert? If this scene summoned up from the deepest part of his mind was in fact some disjointed fragment of memory, and if it truly was the last time he'd seen his father, then who was that man who'd been assassinated at the dacha outside Moskva?

The Snake's distraction had made him walk down the wrong street. He'd meant to walk one block further before turning left, but since the houses beyond the wide lawns were all so similar, he didn't realize he'd made a wrong turn until he saw the suspicious vehicle parked along the road beneath the elms. A black SUV where you'd least expect to see one, parked as it was in front of a row of houses with long driveways and two-car garages. The Snake put a hand over the dog's snout and ducked behind an old Volkswagen and watched. Crouched there in the street in the silent dawn, the moment of recognition that had almost grasped his mind vanished. Like a dream to the waking mind, it dissipated. Was not even a memory. He drew in his breath and darted across the street, commando-climbed a fence with the dog in one arm and then was racing across the backyards of this ordinary neighborhood, his resolve solidified.

He would not enter through the backdoor, which was no doubt being monitored, but through the bulkhead that led down into the basement. He wouldn't tell GB they had to go, wouldn't awaken him from his slumber on the couch. He would steal the girl's car—the keys, in fact, would turn out to be right on the kitchen table, right next to GB's, which he would use to get in the trunk for the knapsack and the bat bag. Of course the dog would have to come along with him now. He would leave nothing to give them any idea of his new understanding, would be on the road before his brother and their pursuers knew he was gone. Headed west with the sun. Ignoring the road signs. Who could trust them anyway?

Friday

FOUR IN THE AFTERNOON IN downtown Denver, and Maddie Hill was sitting on a bench outside Union Station, waiting for her brother. He'd driven them into town that morning from a hotel on the other side of the Rockies, traversing the Continental Divide at nine o'clock, emerging from the shady west to the bright world east of the mountains, had dropped her off and told her to get out while he located a place to park, told her he'd find her later, after he'd taken care of something. That was two hours ago, and she hadn't seen him since. "What do you have to take care of?" But he'd avoided her question in a way she'd already, in two days, become accustomed to. He'd been spastic, had put the car in gear the instant he'd dropped her at the curb, and she had stood on the sidewalk watching as the Buick disappeared down Wynkoop Street.

They'd spent the previous night in Grand Junction, a suburb without a city surrounded by mesas and high desert. If he'd been vociferous that first evening, something about the drive had changed her brother's demeanor, had removed that glimmer of the boy she'd once known, who was quiet but impassioned, reserved until given a reason for excitement, who'd sat in a rickety stool at her bedside all Tuesday afternoon and evening while she'd drifted in and out of sleep in her empty apartment, bringing her tea and soup and listening with his bright eyes peering out of his sparsely bearded face. The traffic out of Vegas had been at a standstill, a hundred thousand tourists trying to evacuate, Interstate 40 closed down and necessitating detours north along I-15 across Utah. He'd relented at last sometime after two in the morning, had been saying all day that he wanted to get as far away from Vegas as possible before nightfall, through Utah by midnight, hoping they could avoid stopping until they were safely in Colorado. He hadn't given any reason for this itinerary, hadn't told her anything specific about where they were going, though in her heart Maddie knew—she knew that this highway they were on would lead eventually to Nebraska. The long ride had left him exhausted, made him crash headfirst against the pillow after they'd finally crossed the Colorado border and pulled off at the first exit, asleep in moments with his arms flung out at his sides, lying flat on his stomach above the covers and fully dressed in his flannel shirt and rugged jeans. She, on the other hand, was wide awake, had at last slept off the lingering effects of her weekend in the desert with Prince Dexter. She waited in the dim halo of the motel room lamp until his breathing had become a soft wheeze that passed for snoring, then opened the door and snuck outside into the fragrant late evening.

She had nowhere to go, and it was cold. She started walking along the embankment beyond the line of motel rooms but got a chill from the breeze blowing over the ghostly mesa and, wrapping her arms around herself, made her way over to the car that had brought them. Teeth chattering, her own slightly jaundiced reflection visible in the side window, hair messy, eyes like pissholes in the snow (as Michaela would've said), she placed her hands on either

side of her face and peered into the backseat, saw the suitcase resting on the footboard, half tucked underneath the driver's seat. Imitation leather, two combination locks with bronze clasps adjacent to
the handle, three numbers each on a metal rolling dial. He'd told
her it was nothing she had to worry about, just something to do
with what he had to take care of in Denver before they continued
east, a brief detour before they could get going. He might as well
have told her the truth—might as well have told her it was enough
money for her to go back to Vegas and do the job properly, enough
money to make a relapse that would last until it killed her. Or
enough money to vanish from that city for good, just like Michaela.
But if he was evasive at times, he was abrasive at others, as if seeing her in person had fouled the plans he'd made, as if it had
destroyed one half of his conception of the situation, had tempered
the enthusiasm with which he'd come all the way from Alaska just
to find her and bring her along on this vague trip he'd devised to
save her from whatever it was he meant to save her from.

I didn't know I needed to be saved. The little resolute voice in her
head said this. She almost said it out loud. The real Maddie Hill—
the Maddie Hill she had grown to know over the past two decades—
certainly would not have hesitated. But in the presence of this adult
version of her brother she had already changed, had noticed herself
losing the edge that had always been a part of her and that she'd
thought this last quarter century had done nothing to soften. As a
sixteen-year-old girl in the lawless country, a pane of glass could
not have separated her from a mysterious suitcase whose contents
made her curious. She would have commandeered the handiest
heavy object and smashed right through, striking the window until
it yielded. She'd thought all this time had done nothing to soothe
her—saw now that all these years in Vegas lounges and casinos

and clubs had done a curious thing, had taken the young girl she'd thought she knew, the girl who never would have found herself in some motel in Grand Junction fucking Colorado (not unless it was her idea) and turned her, of all things, complacent. Had made her a wimp. Look at her: standing in the breeze in an empty parking lot at three in the morning, peering through the back window of a blue Buick.

Look at her: not even daring enough to break the glass.

IT WAS EARLY THE FOLLOWING morning, as they'd climbed the Interstate toward the Rockies, that he had told her he wanted to tell her a story. A story that he hoped would help her to understand. If she was willing to listen, that was.

She had understood this immediately as a sort of apology. He'd awoken her just after seven, had shaken the bed and urged her to get up, a shirtless form in the sunlight coming through the window, whose curtain he had flung open. It was when she resisted—when she'd rolled away from him toward the wall (she'd only had maybe two hours of sleep, had stayed out eyeing that suitcase for what felt like hours)—that he had picked up the alarm clock from the nightstand between the beds and hurled it against the wall, a crash and a rattling as it tumbled to the floor in pieces, then silence. "Max, what the fuck?" She'd lifted her head and watched him, wide awake now, the blanket pulled up around her chin, as he marched into the bathroom and turned on the shower.

Later, he'd been contrite. Issued an awkward apology as they navigated the twisting roads around Vail Pass, the sun ascending and throwing sharp points of light and shadow across the jagged scenery. "That anger you saw this morning," he said. "I hope you understand it wasn't meant for you. I want you to know that I don't blame you. I don't blame Mom, either. Not anymore. You two did what you had to do." For a time then his brooding had been disguised behind an array of strained smiles, but it had lasted only until she'd asked him again about the suitcase, and then things had returned to the way they'd been, Maddie turned away and looking only at his faint reflection, exhaling onto his image in the window until the condensation altered him, made him unreal, a construction of her own imagination that surprised her every time it spoke, every time his tense series of throat clearings emerged as a prelude. Then the voice: deeper than you expected from someone his size, a rasp at its edges as if from lack of use.

It was not his time at the university that he wanted to tell her about—though that was where the story began, where the series of circumstances and the styles of life he'd learned by the hand of their father and the words of Jed Winters had first begun to intertwine. The university in Fairbanks had provided him with room and board, a place to stay when he'd most needed it (the cabin had been no longer an option—not that he would've wanted it anyway—had been rented out by their father for an amount to be used in part by Max as a monthly allowance, but mostly for maintenance). The university at Fairbanks had provided him with a group of young people to be with (most of them from outside Alaska and therefore ignorant of the story of his father and the pipeline and his other secrets). Most of all, the university had provided him with an excuse to stay in Alaska, to stay in this place he'd come to think of, strangely, as his home. It had provided him with a way to start out a veteran of a world to which his peers were mostly newcomers. He'd found himself the subject, for the first time in his life, of an unusual sort of popularity. He was a boy who could make a good first impression. He'd seem lively, energetic, smart. Still, his college relationships came and went. Throughout those nearly four years, only two people had remained on a level of anything resembling his friends. But they were the reason why this story of his began at the university. Because that was where he'd met Beau Miller. And it was where he'd met Alice Bates.

They'd met as freshmen. Max and Beau lived down the hall from one another. Beau was from a place called Amherst, Massachusetts. The first week they'd met, Beau had asked Max to show him around the city. He wanted to see the place through the eyes of someone who'd grown up here. It was the only way you could really get to know a place, he'd claimed—and Max had not missed out on the New England accent, the ruddy smile, the looks that were handsome without being the slightest bit attractive. His nose was hard and bent, his teeth not entirely white, his hair coarse and wild. Yet he had a way about him. Max had arranged to meet him the following day at the foot of the hill down from the dorms and had not been at all surprised to find his friend lying in a bed of leaves, the heavy wind from the night before having thrown down a rug of color though it was barely September, bundled up in L.L.Bean gear with a girl, similarly bundled, the bright shimmer of her yellow hair standing out against the orange and red and brown leaves, the bare tree trunks, the rugged bushes, the mostly earth-toned clothing. The girl turned and Max saw her small pinched-up face for the first time, took it initially as an indication that she was angry for his interruption. Beau stood up, brushed his pants, and from the careless way he didn't reach forward to help up his companion, Max understood where he'd seen such facial features and mannerisms as belonged to his new friend before. The rough face and toothy smile, the arrogance. As Max met Beau's lopsided smile with a close-mouthed one of his own, he knew he was looking at a face that would from then on remind him of Lyle Greeley.

They'd spend Saturdays together, Max and Beau and sometimes Alice, who was a biology major, would take drives into the wilderness in the old pickup Max had bought off Sam Chainsaw, would bring along a case of Ruddy Hook, maybe some reefer, at most just the three of them, though Beau was always saying one of these days he'd get Alice to bring along a friend for Max. But she didn't seem to have any friends, only Beau, who demanded from everyone merely that he be the center of attention at all times. Alice Bates looked nothing like Jasmine. But there was something in her that reminded Max of Jasmine. And she had the *feel* of an Alaskan, though Max knew that she was from northern Vermont; she'd looked to him, that first day, like some fierce creature of the woods, her face pinched-up and marten-like, the features sharp and converging on her pointed nose. She barely spoke to him for nearly a year, though they saw each other several times a month. Their relationship existed exclusively through Beau Miller, so much so that Max had been surprised when they'd exchanged one day what seemed to him a telling glance. In previous encounters, she'd tended to remain silent, the three of them sitting on some bluff overlooking a hundred acres of Alaskan hills and valleys, a low sun or a speckled ceiling of stars, little voices lost in the landscape. Beau Miller was full of crazy ideas: buying a Cessna Caravan and spending the summer making runs from Fairbanks to Anchorage for students fed up with their remote setting; lining the Chena north of town with traps and using the proceeds to pay for a D9 Caterpillar. Alice was the girl-friend who would listen to his stories and smile and nod and roll her eyes. It was on one of these nights—twenty-one years old, and Beau

Miller explaining to them how he'd gotten all he could out of college, that he'd had enough of listening to old white guys talking about history and books and finance, that it was time for them to look for something bordering on true experience—that Max had noticed Alice looking beyond her boyfriend's eyes and directly into his. It had only lasted a second—she'd stood and walked languidly in bare feet over to the fireweed-draped ledge of the bluff only moments later—but Max had remained still for a moment, noticing how her eyes had seemed to forge a new bond between them, had advanced their relationship in some subtle way.

After college (after they'd dropped out; after they'd made and abandoned grand plans for the next stage of their lives) they'd gone their separate ways. Max had rented a cabin in Circle, a town of a hundred and fifty at the remote end of the last road leading north from Fairbanks, had trapped for three winters until he could afford the secondhand DHC Beaver with which he'd gotten himself into the mail-route business. He took off from a gravel runway north of Circle and flew a different course each day of the week, some of them north into the Brooks Range, some south and east along the towns in the foothills of the Alaska Range. He dropped off supplies in the wilderness for trappers, flew tourists across the savannas of the Yukon Flats for moose-watching excursions. It was an exhausting job, stressful, eighteen hours in the air some days, his routes taking him as far north as Kotzebue, as far south as Yakutat only two days later. But its benefits included a perch that let him see this grand land unfolding before him. On days he could avoid nasty weather, he'd fly four hundred miles without seeing a cloud, drove passengers and mail over tracts of wilderness so endless they were ethereal, the only human mark his own shadow on the treetops. And though he'd thought he'd found in this rusty cockpit and daily grind at fifteen thousand feet a place and a state of mind that could contain him and make him content, returning to his twelve-by-twelve cabin to make himself dinner and coffee and fall asleep before finishing them, waking for more long hours suspended in the atmosphere, looking down on the highest mountain range on the continent, he would later wonder if there hadn't been some ulterior motive for his doing it. He would wonder if he wasn't just delivering mail with the underlying hope that someday he'd notice in his cramped cargo hold a box, a bundle, a carton of materials, a giant crate commensurate to his old friend's ambitions and bearing his name on the label. Or if what he'd truly wanted all along was what he ended up getting some years later, long after he would've told himself he'd forgotten them: tucked under a pile, almost obscured, requiring the unstacking of a heap of parcels and then a moment spent staring, in disbelief, at the small package, smaller than a shoebox, bearing her name.

They lived even further out in the country than he'd expected, practically the bush, depending on your definitions, which were always hotly debated in local bars and post offices. Not far from the Canadian border, where a twenty-foot-wide swath of clear cut marked the north-south line of the 141st meridian for several hundred miles. Max had been flying since six o'clock on that late spring morning when he touched down in the remote makeshift landing strip tucked along a sandy bar high up on the Nation River, balloon tires jerking to a stop after a precipitous descent over dense spruce. Beau had his own plane, Max saw, though smaller—a Piper Super Cub crouched and hidden by brush and aspen at the far end of this shaded nook of the river at the base of a six-thousand-foot Alaskan hill, the sun this early in the year and the day having not yet climbed high enough in the southeastern sky to lend light to the clearing. Dawn came late to this silent ledge of land some fifty miles from Eagle, but evening would spread gorgeously over the glinting, crystal clear Nation. The mist was rising through the shade as he came up the mud path toward the cabin, a light on inside, a pair of shadows moving. Max saw a shotgun resting on the front porch— not a porch really, more like a warped ledge of wood—heard the door swing open, watched a shape emerge and paused his approach just before stepping up onto the stoop.

With the sun splashing on the low hill beyond the river, Beau Miller squinted his eyes; there was a moment, Max thought later, when he must have appeared to his old friend as nothing but a dark shape of a man without features or definition, backdropped by uncertain morning light. But it didn't take long for his eyes to adjust, and to Max's surprise he'd recognized him almost immediately. He'd stepped down from the cabin door and taken Max's hand and shook it. He'd known there would be someone new doing the mail route, had heard the news that their regular pilot had crashed into a mountain near Mount St. Elias, trying to find a route through the mist to Juneau. He'd known he'd be getting a new pilot one of these days, but he'd never expected the man to come right up onto his porch at eight o'clock in the morning. They were usually in a rush, the pilots, pressed for time, trying to beat some storm. They certainly never risked that dicey landing that required a controlled stall or close to it, usually just dropped the supplies from a couple hundred feet and off they went. But this one had not only dared the landing. He'd walked the two hundred yards along the rocky river bed from the airstrip to the front door, was now standing on the stoop.

"I'm your new mailman," Max had heard himself saying to his old college friend, the two of them sort of chuckling—two men in their late twenties now, no longer teenagers. When Max heard the footsteps inside the cabin, he looked over his friend's shoulder and saw the pinched-up face and the blonde hair, tied back and a few shades darker now. He saw Alice Bates smile a confusing smile. He saw the bundle she carried on her shoulder. A little baby boy that he learned over bitter coffee they'd named Lynk.

HE RETURNED JUST AFTER FOUR, a short burst of car horn startling her, making her turn to find him parked along the side of the road just thirty feet from the little bench in front of Union Station where she sat, his eyes trained on her through the windshield as he firmly nodded his head, once.

She didn't move. For the past hour, alone in an unfamiliar city, Maddie Hill had been forced into a rare introspective examination. She'd made up her mind to make up her mind. She hadn't quite figured out what solution she'd arrived at yet, but it had seemed she was leaning toward abandoning him, making her way west back across Utah to Vegas, returning to her unoccupied apartment, finding a way to set her life straight or to let it spiral toward oblivion. She'd been saying it to herself for the past hour as the warm day in Denver bloomed and settled toward evening: you have until he comes back here to make up your mind. She'd paced aimlessly, past the baseball field and then into Lower Downtown, which now advertised its trendy designation as LoDo on signs hanging from streetlamps. Years ago, when she'd visited this city as a teenager billowed on the winds of her own youth, this had been the part of the city the tourists avoided, the place where the murders and drug deals went down, where poverty stewed in dark alleys and shady tenements. Now it had been renovated, the abandoned buildings gutted and painted to house upscale restaurants and brew pubs, art galleries, and lofts in converted warehouse buildings. Still, she'd looked around at the bright facades on Market Street, the cool patios, full even now in the early afternoon on a weekday, and wondered at the fact that despite all they'd done to polish the grime from this newly thriving part of the city, they still had in their midst a killer.

A killer? Had she really come to think of her brother that way? And why had this realization not sent her racing back toward Vegas?

She'd traipsed down Blake Street and then right on 17th, waiting with the crowd that had grown as the day drifted toward quitting time. *Once he's back from wherever it is he's gone*, she'd thought to herself, *that's it. He's not going to leave you alone again.* Back in front of the station, she hesitated. Sat down on the bench with her face in her hands, and that was when she heard the soft bleat of the car horn, when she saw him looking at her through the sun-glazed windshield.

The leather was hot, sticking to her body. He refused to turn on the air conditioner. At first she thought he'd gotten lost. Mixed up by the complicated cloverleaves. Or perhaps she'd been distracted, trying to catch a glimpse of the backseat without his noticing. It was a few minutes before she realized she wasn't just imagining things, hadn't been deceived by city traffic and the road signs that often belied intent. They were off the beltway, back on I-70, headed back toward the Rockies.

"It starts tonight," he said, for it was turning toward late afternoon, the suburbs blazing gold, his posture in the driver's seat hurled forward, aggressive. "A place you've never seen before, I'm sure. A place he'd never let any of us be seen with him." She turned his words over and over in her head, knowing that he must be talking about their father, for though he'd not come out and said what this trip was about—not that she could recall, at least, and not in so many words—he'd implied it, had shown her his anger, had let her hold it in her hands like some untamed creature, scowling and feral.

"Have you ever been to Aspen?" he asked.

"No," Maddie Hill said. "Well, once. But it was—during college."

He looked at her, through her, watching her writhe with discomfort. "Neither has he. But that didn't stop him from buying a little part of the place for himself."

Maddie looked at her brother, who now looked straight ahead. "He has a home there?"

"It's not a home," said her brother. "None of his houses are homes. They're investments."

And while she had him facing forward, she took the chance to turn her head, to look at the floorboard behind the driver's seat.

The suitcase was gone.

———

HE HADN'T MEANT FOR IT to happen, Max Hill had told his sister as they descended the mountain roads that early afternoon. He hadn't sought them out, hadn't intentionally touched down his plane that day in the isolated clearing that would become his, hadn't planned or anticipated any of the events that had followed. But they had happened. *It* had happened. Out in the country, with not another soul for a hundred miles, not a town or hospital closer than Fort Yukon or Fairbanks. Not that it would have mattered.

They'd been trapping up at Beau's spring camp, deep in the desolate wilderness of the northern Yukon Flats, fishing for grayling and char along the Chandalar and the foot of the Brooks Range, poaching on Alaska Native land, they may have been. Beau couldn't say for sure because he never bothered to check. The federal government could go and bend itself over a fifty-five-gallon drum for all he was concerned. This was Alaska, he'd say, spreading his arms in the glazed morning with the fog dipping low over this swampy savanna devoid of anything but grass and low trees and rock, the sheer white face of the Brooks Range in the distance. This wasn't Amherst, Massachusetts. This wasn't Montpelier, Vermont, where Alice was from and where the same families had lived in the same colonial houses lining the town common since the days of Ethan Allen. If Beau wanted to set up camp and take some muskrat and beaver to fill his belly and his wallet, he was damn well going to. If someone else wanted to say it was their land, let them. If the federal government wanted to make a fuss, he'd introduce them to his associate. He patted his hip, from which dangled a Marlin 30-30 lever action.

Beau had become a recessionist, had joined the Alaskan Independence Party, would threaten to shoot anyone who called him an American, said Alaska was a colony, just like the Caribbean, just like all those countries in Africa. "I'm on their radar," he said. "They're just looking for a way to take me out and steal my land. That's why Alice and me are way up there by the border, so we can scootch right across when circumstances dictate. I want to watch them scramble to get the Canadians to do something about me. Ha! Then I'll just pull right back over the border into Alaska. You think it's hard for two counties or municipalities to cooperate? How about two countries?"

They were in the plane, Beau's Super Cub, following the procession of lakes and creeks along the flood plain toward the foot of the Brooks Range, where Beau had suggested they spend this last week of May at a nameless lake he called the Hundredmile for its approximate distance from the Yukon, the mighty river that bisected interior Alaska, two thousand miles long and spanned by only four bridges. Their month on the Fiftymile had been good to them, two coolers full of muskrat pelts in the bi-level baggage compartment retrofitted in the rear fuselage, a supplement to the real trapping Beau had done in the winter, loading up on marten and lynx in the traplines he ran along the Nation and the Kandik. At home, Alice would take over, was spending this month they were away treating the skins with the animal's brains, a process learned in the native village and which produced such high-quality hides that it had become their primary source of income. Beau would be hurled into rage if anyone suggested his woman was the one making the dough. He was the one who caught the animals, wasn't he? He was the one who got up off his ass and ran the traplines alone at fifty degrees below zero. Could you see Alice out there? Ha!

He was vitriolic today, even more boastful than usual on this cold spring morning, flying aggressively over the precipitous foothills and pointing out rivulets of land along the tributaries that spilled into the Hundredmile ("How 'bout there? You feel up for *that*?"), telling Max he felt the urge today to set this plane right down on a postage stamp, to dive in just above the treetops for a kamikaze landing that would bring your heart up to your throat, leave you gasping and *so alive*! For what was the use of living all the way up here if you weren't willing to stick your neck out every once in a while?

Above all else that he'd grown to despise about his friend, Max hated these landings. A month ago, they'd tucked themselves into a similar spot along the shores of the Fiftymile, touching down on a river bed speckled with sunlight and shade where they'd set up camp in a canvas tent and spent four weeks placing traps for the muskrats on the icy series of lakes, afternoons on snow machines making the rounds to clear the traps, late evenings boiling or roasting and devouring the delicious and hearty meat, drying the rest for later use and carefully stretching the pelts on wire wishbone stretchers. Up here, late April was the onset of spring, the days gradually growing toward the interminable lengths they'd take on in the summer, the air crisp and fresh with the smell of snowmelt but the lakes still vast white frozen fields, locked in shelf ice that would linger until late summer, the towering ridgelines to the north remaining snowcapped and impenetrable year-round.

Mornings on the Fiftymile dawned bright and frigid, the dime-sized sun creating enough glare to cause headaches by mid-morning. The two of them would be off early on snow machines or on foot, already laying siege to the muskrats when the first birdcalls colored the air and the blue light of dawn deepened the sky, Beau having already revved up his engine of protest, which could be triggered by nearly anything: a caribou stepping gingerly downhill over rocks toward a stream, a leave-behind from a previous adventurer, tire tracks. They didn't see each other often, Max and Beau, and though Max had been coming on these trips to the spring camp for three years now, the conversation never changed. It was always Beau going on with the same old chatter about the government and independence, how they'd cheated Alaskans out of the only thing they had, which was land, Max never contributing, just listening, wondering why he insisted on ranting over such things, why he didn't worry more about his own wife and son, wondering if he bored them with all this recycled banter, with the recitations regarding the

104 million acres of land the federal government had promised the state of Alaska in 1958, how they'd then taken 44 million of these acres off the table by giving them to the Indians in the Native Claims Settlement Act of 1971, how they'd appropriated another 240 million for their own purposes, thereby leaving less than 90 million acres from which the people of the state of Alaska were free to make their so-called choice. A good decision hadn't been made by the federal government in the state of Alaska since they'd voted to build the oil pipeline, and that had taken five years to get done, five years and a complaint from every group of tree huggers this side of the Rio Grande, each with some harebrained notion of protecting Alaska, protecting the land. As if Alaska were what needed protecting! Had these people ever been here? Had they ever actually-*witnessed* real wilderness?

Max wondered how many times Alice had heard these statistics and diatribes, how many times young Lynk had heard them. He wondered if his friend's bombastic tirades ever translated to a different sort of violence. He wondered how his friend had come to be this way, what combination of causes and influences had led from his being an idealistic boy from the East to a self-proclaimed crusader for the state of Alaska. And he wondered—if three days with his friend were enough to make him happy to return to his lonely cabin in Circle—what it must be like to live with him, to raise a child with him. He'd once asked Alice about it. An afternoon Beau had gone out to retrieve more wood for the fire. This had been the previous winter, after a trapping trip they'd made together up the Kandik River and Max had spent three days snowed in at the compound along the Nation—the "compound," as Beau referred to it, consisting of a tiny cabin and a pair of outbuildings tucked in a two-acre parcel of mostly wooded land only miles from the Canadian border. They had sat together at the table in the center of the main cabin drinking tea while Beau was outside with Lynk, the wind rattling the walls around them, the snow drifted in great dunes halfway up the window, the stove blazing hot and its glow reflecting on their faces, Alice telling him in a whisper what it was like. It was like walking around with a second head on your shoulder that never stopped shouting in your ear, never stopped telling you what to do, never stopped telling you everything you were doing wrong. You could ignore it but only for so long. You could look forward to the months it went away on trapping trips but then you spent those days in dread of its return. You could try to believe it every time it told you things would be different, but that just made you a fool. And you could pretend you didn't see that your son was turning into just another version of him, that you'd soon have two of them to contend with. Alice looked at the fire and said that it was just like this: it was like sitting in a little cramped cabin and feeling the constant temper of that wind outside, raging and never giving you peace. Max had sat back in his chair, looked around at the cabin filled with Beau's hunting and trapping equipment—the detritus of his half-finished schemes and distractions—and had realized then who his friend truly reminded him of.

Now on their final night in the isolated foothills of the Brooks Range they broiled and ate two whole trout apiece, evening bathing the mountain lake in a cloak of blue shadow. Beau was the cook, would not allow Max to get up, had placed himself firmly in charge of the cooking duties the way he thought he was in charge of every-thing, including Alice. People like Beau needed a tagalong to bear witness to their bravado and exaggeration. They needed a sidekick who would keep his mouth shut and nod his head and laugh at the right moments. They needed a good woman to handle the hard work for them, a woman to take for granted and disrespect, a woman to ignore while she slowly grew hard and resentful under the cold stare of indifference, a woman who deserved better. After dinner and a smoke, Max appreciating the gathering darkness, the way it concealed his expression behind the dim red glow of his cigarette, it was time for bed. They lay wrapped in sleeping bags at midnight and, after a few attempts by Beau to have a conversation, Max heard his friend's snores, and even those reminded him of his father.

He'd tried to convince Beau of an alternate landing. Still, his friend had insisted, had brought the plane in low, the air in this tiny hollow between the trees and the mountains high above the Hundredmile being whipped up and spun, the landing gear striking the ground and the brakes whining. And when he climbed out of Beau's plane and looked at the tiny strip of land on which his friend had set them down for no other reason than to give himself a shot of adrenaline, Max remembered the day he'd first arrived in Alaska, descending through icy mist to the runway at Fairbanks International, his father insistent despite his family's trepidation and shock. Looking at the isolated ledge of earth on which his fellow Alaskan had set them down—Beau already out of the plane and whooping with the excitement of it all, *Was that the shortest ground roll in history or what!*—Max knew exactly what he'd known that morning they set down in Fairbanks, knew that they'd arrived at a place from which they could not all expect to escape.

———

NEBRASKA WAS THE QUIETEST PLACE in the world. The high plains sang with loneliness. Friday night they spent in another dreary motel, two miles from the interstate, and Maddie felt so empty she locked herself in the bathroom. Max stood outside the door, asking what was wrong, what he could do, though when Maddie told him it seemed he didn't know what to do with the answer. In the end, he'd agreed reluctantly, a few final questions and then his heavy footsteps creaking the warped flooring, the door closing behind him. Maddie listened until she knew he was gone, then stood and stared at her own reflection in the mirror.

She wasn't dope sick. She wasn't sick at all. And yet that was what it felt like, this debilitating, soul-poisoning sensation she'd felt coming on that night they'd driven west from Denver into the Rockies, the night Max had shown her, without question, what was to be the substance of this trip of theirs. Earlier—at nightfall, parked in the otherwise vacant back lot of the motel, behind a dumpster and illuminated by an amber-hued sodium lamp—he'd shown her what they'd stopped in Denver for, had revealed what the money contained in the suitcase with the bronze clasps had purchased, had unzipped a duffel bag retrieved from the trunk of the car and held it out in front of her.

To Maddie, it had looked like a shoebox. It *was* a shoebox, oversized, the type cowboy boots would come in, its interior arranged in a spiral, walls lined with wrapped wire leading to a cluster of orange sausage-like tubes and a sack containing a slurry material with enough stored energy—once Max took the simple step of lighting the safety fuse—to blow an entire building sky high. It seemed Max's old friend and mentor, Jed Winters, had finally outgrown his grumbling, had learned what had happened to Max and scheduled a sit down, had informed her twin brother who'd once dug for gold with her in the backfield outside Fairbanks of a place in Denver where a man could procure such a shoebox as this one if he knew the right people.

So this is what they look like, Maddie Hill had thought, standing in the darkness of a motel parking lot: the hidden objects that had been exploding in parking garages and on city streets in Vegas for as long as she'd been there, the inconspicuous payloads that had been eliminating targets anywhere there was money and power to be gained or stolen, for as long as there'd been such things to argue over. It should have made her disappear, this man claiming to have once been her twin brother revealing this box that looked too small, or simple, to carry any weight, resting in the trunk of the blue Buick with the two of them looking in on it, a breeze blowing her loose hair across her face, unwilling to turn and look at him.

There was no questioning now what his plans were. Not after the previous evening, when their trip west from Denver had ended as promised in the dark environs of the ski towns and protected wilderness, roads rising up along stone walls and treacherous corners to hidden driveways leading to secluded high-priced estates. The acquisition of the shoebox had sparked something in him, an enthusiasm that made him tremble as he'd parked the car at the bottom of a steep driveway, went around to the back and flipped up the trunk, appeared for her again in moments, dressed all in black from head to toe, a stocking cap that he pulled down over his face, a six-gallon gasoline container in one hand. It was not the first time she'd been involved in spontaneous trips that had turned unexpectedly dangerous, morbid, illegal. It was something one risked when she ran in the sort of crowd with whom she'd willingly gotten herself involved. In Vegas, vandalism was an easy hobby, arson a cheap thrill. They'd gone out in great bands to beat on tourists, steal their money, and leave them with only their plane tickets. She'd thought she could never feel scared, could never be intimidated. And why would you, when fear was an emotion just as arbitrary as love, just as capable of being turned into excitement or hate if you knew how. If you were strong. It was this part of her—the part that had been raised up in the Flame Lounge and the French Quarter and then the midnight glimmer of the Vegas strip—that had made her sit in the passenger seat and watch as her brother walked up the driveway toward the shadow she knew to be a house among the pines. It was this anti-voice inside her that made her get out of the car and step up the path—arms crossed over her chest in the cold—and stand behind a copse of trees as the house began to light up. She'd covered her eyes, had turned back and marched down the hill toward the car, climbed into the passenger seat and leaned over until her face was between her knees, had waited and then heard him scampering down the driveway, climbing in the driver's side and urging her to look. She refused. It was not until he'd started the car and begun turning around that she raised her head and stared, the house ablaze in the clearing, the orange and red light conjuring her reflection on the window next to her.

She knew now what he meant to do, understood what she'd gotten herself into. Before the previous night's journey, before she'd witnessed what he was capable of with her own eyes, she hadn't been willing to look closely enough at what her brother had told her about Beau Miller, had been unable to scrutinize the accident that had taken place that had left Max marooned on the forested flanks of the Brooks Range, the Super Cub smashed up against a tree with its pilot impaled on the steering wheel. It was his bold landing that had cost him his life. As Max had predicted, there was not enough runway even for a Super Cub to take off, and when they'd attempted it, they'd gained a little altitude, had felt the engine buckle. Max's own survival of the crash had been little noted, spoken of vaguely though the other details were intricate, the eyes staring up through the windshield, a corpse that would remain until some starving creature braved the wreckage to dine. "I tried to tell him," Max had said to her in the Buick. And yet Maddie had been unable to look at him, unwilling to peek across the car to see his expression, to witness if it was the same she recalled from that night in the hospital bed when he'd tried to explain himself until she could take it no more and had told him to shush, those eyes of his so pleading and damaged. "I did it for you, Maddie."

He was alone, a hundred miles from Fort Yukon, but he had the snow machine. He still had all that muskrat meat stored in the coolers salvaged from the wreck. He had the vision of Alice, waiting three hundred miles away in the cabin on the Nation. Maddie could recall all of this now, staring down her own reflection in the bathroom mirror of a motel in Nowhere, Nebraska. She remembered how he'd told her of the long week's journey he'd spent alone on the Chandalar, making his way back through the wilderness by snow machine with the coolers on a makeshift sled behind him. She remembered the way he'd spoken of it like some weird saga that even then had seemed improbable, full of adventures involving abandoned cabins and grizzly bears whose roars echoed on the hillsides, Alaska Natives watching from the banks as he rode the half-frozen river in late spring, abandoning the snow machine when he ran out of fuel and continuing on foot until he came across a canoe overturned at the confluence of the Yukon and the Porcupine, removed the dead hunter and patched it up and continued.

She could recall all of this—though at the time of his telling it she'd still been caught up in her own story, still so briefly removed from the Sunday night effigy of the Burning Man celebration in Black Rock Desert, still trying to piece together what she remembered of that scene and what one thing had to do with the other.

Still recalling Prince Dexter next to her on a blanket in an empty moonscape, one side of their bodies scorching from the bonfire, the other side near frozen in the desert night, Maddie having come to the end of this weekend-long ritual having felt—despite his promises—no fast-arriving truth coming over the blackened mountains that encircled this dry valley. She had found, at the end, only a lack of resolution that had left her no recourse (in the backwards thinking of the addict) but to take the acid, to snort the dust, to swallow the pills and watch Prince Dexter do the same, though she had already seen through his game, had begun to see through it in his car—his ostentatious boat of a car with a trunk like coattails and a front end like a siege machine, rattling north over the grumblings of a failing air filter on Saturday morning, six hours on Route 95 to 447 north through Nixon and Empire and Gerlach, past the Nightingales and the dry Winnemucca Lake and into the northern barrens where the heat bleached the land beige—had perhaps even known as early as in his room two blocks off the Strip, the night before, Prince Dexter naked on the bed but for the briefs he'd slipped on.

Afterwards, he had lain above the covers, goose-pimpled from the air conditioning, and reminded her that it was this weekend, the famous or infamous desert festival where the photograph that had been the last taken of her friend Michelle Jones had placed her, the remote gathering of hippies and freaks and lovers in Black Rock Desert that Maddie had attended before though she never really remembered. He had been up on his elbows, his weight against her, ready to go again, prepared to convince her with what it seemed he imagined was a significant sexual prowess. But Maddie had already made up her mind that she would join him, had already determined that in a life such as hers there were few opportunities to come face-to-face with anything remotely resembling the truth, that it was crazy to deny even if it came packaged with a lousy lover who fashioned himself an investigative reporter when all he was—it had been clear to her, even then—was a gossipmonger. She didn't care if they reopened the case, had long since killed such romantic notions, had lost so much faith in the concept of justice that it was nothing more than a word anyway.

And so even when she'd seen his car—had heard the way that it, like his story, rattled along as if it might disintegrate at any moment—she'd been unwilling to revoke the benefit of the doubt she'd given him simply because she'd wanted to believe what he said, wanted to believe there might be an ending to the story of her friend Michaela. Even when they'd arrived at last at the desert city on the playa flat, lined with rows of RVs and hatchbacks and VW vans with psychedelic patterns painted on their sides, on their roofs, a camp of American refugees shirtless in the cooling evening, the setting sun throwing vanishing point shadows over the orange rocks where they danced like demons in firelight, she had fooled herself into believing it all. And though later—riding in the Buick with her brother, walking the streets of Denver deciding what role she was meant to play in all this—she would suspect Prince Dexter hadn't swallowed any of the pills she'd thought he had (had more likely spit them out the instant she'd turned her head, had pretended to take them simply to encourage her) at the time she had felt that old chemical kinship, the mental crutch that had been the basis for so many relationships in her past, her trip rolling off the mountains with a pace almost audible, a great ringing chord from the loudest organ in the universe, the world reduced to a stainless steel pole in an empty room that she'd just begun to wrap her contorted body around when Prince Dexter had spoken up from the

distant other side of the blanket and begun asking her the questions about her father.

The fucker had pulled one over on her. The photograph was a
fake, the story of Michaela and the body found in Lake Tahoe a lie,
a not-so-elaborate fib constructed in order to make her feel more
comfortable, to penetrate her considerable defenses, to get her to
comment on the vague "big story" of which he'd spoken earlier. The
"big story" that had nothing to do with a former stripper missing
twelve years from Las Vegas but was instead the story of her father,
George Benjamin Hill, whose rise from grease delivery man to fast
food millionaire to oil magnate to gas commodities trader and member of the board of directors of a Fortune 500 company was legendary. Legendary, too, were the tales of the marriages and children
he'd left behind. And though his contact with these peripheral
inhabitants of his life was known to be limited, it had happened on
several occasions over the years that individuals had shown up at
Maddie's place of employment, at the warehouse loft, asking for a
brief interview; and though in the past she had always refused
them—had thrown whatever was handy at them, had made ges-
tures and spit on them—Prince Dexter had managed to make it
past this first line of defense, had known, somehow, the correct way
to disarm her, to distract her with the cause of her last twelve years
of solitude and loss, to sidetrack her thinking enough to make the
story of her father worth revealing, worth opening her mouth and
letting whatever wished to come out come out while he—suddenly
alert, no longer feigning his own drug-induced stupor—retrieved
from somewhere his miniature tape recorder.

She'd awoke to find him gone, her body stretched out on the blanket at dawn, had hitched a ride as far as Tahoe with two young men
on their way back to Palo Alto, curled up in the backseat of their

hatchback beneath the gritty blanket to avoid the bright sun that burned the cool off the hard-crusted desert, five hundred miles along backroads and interstates on a Monday morning turning to afternoon, a two-hour layover outside Fallon at the largest trucker's paradise between Denver and San Francisco where she sat in the ladies' room and fought herself up from a meltdown. Watching the sun lower and then flatten against Mount Charleston from the passenger seat of an eighteen-wheeler, the night coming on and then brightening as they descended into the Las Vegas Valley, the ring of lights radiating out toward the mountains, feeling all of seventeen again in the cab of this truck with the driver she'd chosen for the way he'd seemed to avoid her at the truck stop when she'd at last emerged from the ladies' room, unlike the others who'd eyed her hungrily from the little hallways leading back to the rest stations. A friendly enough if somewhat self-righteous old geezer with a long white beard who told her again and again during their trip south on the interstate that he'd seen her type before, had driven hundreds of girls over thousands of miles in this part of the country, girls going to LA or Frisco or Vegas, all of them with the same stories give or take a few miserable experiences, all of them running from something as simple as their folks, from something so complex they couldn't put it into words, some of them illiterate, some just off scoring 1600 on their SATs, all of them in the passenger seat of his rig, listening to the pep talk he'd gotten damn tired of delivering because it never seemed to make any difference, never seemed to make any of them go home or call their folks or do anything that might actually help themselves. He'd held onto her wrist for just a moment, leaning across the cab as she climbed down into the parking lot of the gas station where she'd told him he could leave her, reluctant to let go, Maddie kissing her hand and blowing it toward him, stepping over to the phone booth and pretending to dig in her pockets for change long enough for him to direct his truck out of the lot and back along the access road toward the highway.

That was what his story reminded her of. The story of her brother paddling upstream on the Nation to the isolated two acres that had belonged until recently to his friend Beau Miller had made Maddie think of her own beaten-down odyssey along the debris-strewn streets beneath the overpass, crossing over into West Vegas, where she knew dozens of places where the party she'd abandoned—or tried to abandon, six months ago, twelve years ago—would still be going, even at three o'clock on a Tuesday morning, places where she could cop and pass out, where she could watch the dawn of a new day feeling nowhere close to forty-one years old, back in her famous twenties again, doing whatever the fuck she pleased with whomever the fuck she wanted, where she could suffer a poisonous breakfast from a garbage can and endure the verbal berating of a cabbie sick and tired of driving around smack heads, calling her all sorts of names and finally taking her directly to the Excalibur because she could not remember her home address, where she could at last come through the back doors after buzzing for ten minutes at the employee entrance, floundering at the rock bottom of her hardest relapse in her entire life, the hallways empty and labyrinthine, causing her to lose her way a dozen times before arriving at the main ball room to find a hundred-thousand people standing around on the floor, watching a movie, some in tears, some turning away from the crazy Hollywood spectacle of airplanes and explosions.

When he was only twenty yards away—having made the slow walk up the worn path in the long quiet grass from the airstrip toward the door of the cabin (for there was no canoe trip, Maddie knew, there was no month-long, three-hundred mile trek, there was no crash but rather a routine two-hour solo flight in the Super Cub, which would no doubt have been easy enough to sell)—when he had come close enough to see the faint shadows beyond the glass, the front door opened and there she was, alone now, Lynk off in the back woods, playing. She looked at him from the border of the front door with something less than guilt, watching him come up the steps carrying her husband's .30-30. And hadn't *she* looked at him in much the same way? Lightheaded in the medieval décor of the Excalibur? Hallucinating? She had to be! Because on top of it all— on top of the inexplicable weekend that had left her relapsed and defeated, on top of the entire staff of the Excalibur watching this crazy movie on the clock, the patrons being distracted from the gaming tables (the ultimate faux pas!), on top of the silence that rose over the usually raucous floor and the cell phones people were pulling out of their purses and pockets with nobody telling them to stop it right there!—on top of all that, there was this man stepping across the floor who looked just like her twin brother. His face was in hers, mumbling something she couldn't make out, the world turned mono, like an old recording played through a pillow.

Lying on the floor in the gaming room—having fallen against one of the slot machines, her mouth dry and bilious—she had not yet understood what it must have felt like to watch from a thick window his approach along the river from the landing strip. She had not yet known what it meant to see him coming and know you were not prepared for what you may have unknowingly gotten your- self into. Standing now in front of the mirror in the bathroom of the motel room in Nowhere, Nebraska, seeing and recalling the intense focus of those eyes of his, she wished she'd read all those droning letters he'd written her. She wished she'd memorized them, word for word.

KNEES UP, FEET RESTING ON the grimy silver bumper, Max Hill sat on the trunk of the Buick looking out over the swampy shallows of the Platte River, holding in his hands the shoebox that contained the instrument of his rage. He still couldn't believe that old Jed Winters, whom he'd once thought some old smokestack of a fellow who could talk a good game but not walk the walk, as they said, had actually put him in touch with the sort of individuals who could provide him—in return for all the savings he'd managed to summon from selling his pickup and his DHC Beaver—with the weapon he currently sat contemplating amidst the mid-American swamp grass, watching the sandhill cranes making their flight south overhead.

He leaned forward, placed the shoebox upon the earth, lid removed so he could study the progression from fuse to blasting cap, Tovex cast boosters to the ammonium nitrate and nitromethane mixture that was its heart. He reached into the front pocket of his light jacket and retrieved the package of dried-bark rolling papers and the little sandwich bag containing the sad excuse for medication he'd at last managed to obtain for his sister: an eighth of an ounce of low-grade marijuana being all the wife-beater-and-bandanna-clad boy at the apartment above the bar in the little college town along I-80 had been willing to part with. Even that much had taken some convincing, the kid a small-time upstart dealer who watched too much television, who'd told Max he'd start him off with an eighth for now and, if all went well, would remember him next time.

"Oh, you'll remember," Max had said, walking toward his car.

Out here in the black night of a foreign land—the only light what little reflected in the ghostly shallows of the meandering river—he was killing his doubt, smothering his remorse, wondering if he would've been better off leaving his sister in Vegas after all. He had understood for days now that she didn't feel the same way about things as he did, that she didn't blame their father exclusively for the messes of their lives. Though how could she fail or refuse to see the connections between the life he'd exposed them to all those years ago in Fairbanks and the creature she'd become? Max Hill was no shrink, but to him it was clear that Maddie was the one person, if there was any, who should have been most angry, most prepared to strike back—for if he'd ruined Max's life, he'd at least been able to enjoy a few years of something like happiness first, a few years of contentment out in the country, just the three of them, while Maddie's life had been ruined at sixteen, and everything after had been one futile attempt after another to get back what had been lost. These stories of this woman, Michaela, of her shameful career, of the last decade spent struggling to make ends meet in that cavernous vacant apartment, this trip out into the desert with the so-called investigative reporter: these stories of hers that she'd allowed him to learn over the last four days had baffled him as to how he'd made such a mistake. He'd expected her to be even more ready than he was, had recalled with pride the violent tone of the letters he'd received from her detailing the destruction they could wreak together, sloppily written letters that had at times been almost illegible, though back then he'd attributed it to the blind fury with which she must have scrawled them.

Now he understood. Having traveled across the dry basin and the high plains with her, he understood that the voice of those letters had been the voice of her addictions, all of them written in the deep fog of drug-induced mania and mailed off in the midst of multi-day benders. She didn't even seem to remember writing them. Certainly not sending them. It was this powerlessness of hers that got to him, the vulnerability she'd fought hard to conceal all those years ago in the alley between the Flame Lounge and the French Quarter, in the hospital bed where they'd embraced, this vulnerability she'd had no choice but to allow him to see now, that had threatened to weaken his resolve and had made him run from her, tonight, gather himself here on this sweaty riverbank some hundred miles from their destination, thinking she was the one thing he had not accounted for, that she could be more powerful than that shoebox if she tried.

For the last five minutes he had been sprinkling shake into the crease of the thin strip of bark, rolling it between his thumbs and forefingers. Now he lifted the joint to his lips and inhaled. Bunk. Couldn't hold a candle to the river people's rag. He moved to flip it toward the water but stopped, pinched out the cherry and placed it in his pocket, would offer it to her when he made it back to the motel.

As he replaced the shoebox in the backseat, he pictured her, wished he could summon the courage to say to her the things he wished he could say and to have her return that long-ago intimacy, the intimacy he'd felt in the hospital that morning he'd held her close though it made his bones press hard against his heart. Was that all he'd needed all along? Was that all it would have taken? For someone to tell him no? For his little sister to step in and say to him: Come here, Max. Come here. I know. *I know.* But we don't need to do this. We *don't need* to do this. Was that all it would have taken to return him to the person he'd been, before Jasmine and Lyle Greeley, before Beau Miller and Alice Bates, before any of the letters he'd mailed off to his brothers and sisters?

The Buick rumbled and started. Max adjusted the rearview mirror so that it showed him the shoebox in the back seat. The unnamed unpaved streets of Nowhere, Nebraska, stretched dust-parched before him, empty as sympathy, vacant as his heart on this Friday night spent murdering the yearning pulse of his doubt, the insistent murmur of a conscience.

Saturday

Nine o'clock. His eyes opened on a painfully blue sky, bright swaths of clouds spelling Iowa. He'd been dreaming of Emma: not of the last time he saw her—not the vision of pale walls and cold steel cabinets that had haunted his memory for the last seven days—but of another time long ago, a time he'd forgotten until it had resurfaced in the form of this restless dream. Now he'd come awake in a cornfield, his sprawled body forming a broken angel in the pressed-down stalks, a crop circle in miniature, an interstate rattling somewhere nearby.

This made well over twenty-four hours that had passed since he'd last seen Jamie, a full day gone by since he'd last laid eyes on the boy whose dilapidated room in the halfway house had shamed but not surprised him, whose silence as they'd sat in the surreal living room of the woman they'd once called their stepmother should have made him cautious, should have made him remember exactly what he was dealing with. The night before, in a hazy roadhouse bar he could now barely visualize, he'd let his failure loosen like old skin and slip to the floor, had regaled a dozen flannel-clad locals with the story of his life and the week gone by until each of them had

paid his tab and disappeared, leaving him at last with only a cra-
tered moon-like barkeep orbiting at a safe distance and never with
his back turned, who'd poured him a final drink whose golden surface in the frosted glass as he lifted it to his face was the last thing
he recalled.

In his ball playing days, GB Hill had never suffered from hang-
overs. Now he was being reimbursed for his luck all those years.

He'd risen from his itchy tomb and brought himself to his feet,
wishing he could temporarily remove his eyeballs to scoop out the
pain that lay behind them. A path led from the place where the corn
lay crushed in his outline to the mouth of the field, rose through
high September grass to the summit of a low hill topped by a single
sprawling oak tree, a swing fashioned from a plank and two cords
of rope hanging from one aged limb. He sat on the swing and held
his head, looked up and realized that in this low land west of Des
Moines the slightest rise could become a promontory from which
one could see for miles. Beneath him had spread the serene hamlet,
yet now that he'd arrived, having stepped down through thickets to
the main road, smelling his own repellent sweat, it was not at all as
he'd remembered it. He didn't recall any churches—only a concrete
building with no windows on a dead-end street with a few faded
fluorescent signs out front, a heavy door you had to push with all
your weight just to open. In his lonely state of mind it had been
exactly the kind of place he'd been looking for, the type of bar you
could find in these little towns of the Midwest, or occasionally in the
less-frequented neighborhoods of the cities back East, not much different from the one he'd found on the Upper East Side. He remembered coming in and sitting down, half returning the looks he'd
gotten, the quick once-over they no doubt gave every stranger. Then
another when they realized what he was wearing.

The man at the bar hadn't seemed too keen on talking to him. Not at first. Filled GB's glass and slid it along the bar toward him. They were all staring at the television, a bored, pessimistic bunch, the dearth of entertainment caused by the cancellation of all sporting events having left them with only stale analysis and highlights, and so their low-voiced conversations had strayed from performance to the crime of the players' salaries, the juice they were no doubt taking, how over half of them didn't speak a lick of English anyway. GB had tried hard to listen, smirked along with them, tried to join in though it was more difficult than he'd thought it would be. How did one engage one's self in a bar room bull session? He hadn't wanted to play the ex-player card, but eventually he did, and someone—a young fellow, brown eyes and freckles and a mop of hair—had recognized the name, had heard the half-legendary story of GB Hill, the can't-miss prospect turned head case, the fire-balling lefty who'd flamed out his first spring training, who'd disappeared for a while, had hung around the minors as an outfielder before being reincarnated just in time to receive his famously doomed cup of coffee with the Yanks in the mid-eighties. Most people who recognized GB's name were these sorts: card collectors, old Strat-o-Matic devotees, Bill James disciples. Baseball fanatics who computed batting averages while they sweated atop tractors.

"What else?" the kid had said, scratching his chin. "I know there's something else I remember about you . . ."

He'd faded into the background, had bought another drink for GB, and the remainder of the night was a blank corridor that now, seated at a window seat in the main street diner, sipping an iced tea with lemon that was already making him nauseous, a laminated menu that he couldn't bear to look at on the checkered tablecloth before him, watching the little movements of this town as the people spilled from the hardware store and the grocery into the streets, he couldn't bring himself to fathom. Had he really imagined it all? Then where was his car? There was no bar in this little farmland community. It was a dry town. So he'd been informed by a sparsely bearded man loading seed into the bed of a pickup truck next to the only stop sign at the only intersection, a man GB had thought was in his forties until he'd seen him up close, saw his bright eyes beneath the bill of his weather-worn ball cap that said he was no more than twenty-five.

"You'll search a long time for a bar in this town, fella," he'd said—gesturing up the single road with no sidewalks, pavement encroaching on yards and running past white houses with sloped dark-shingled rooftops, wide dormer windows looking in on cramped second floors beneath the eaves, a little business center with the hardware store and the diner. "Got a couple churches, though. Might wanna consider visiting one of them on your way out of town." And the hefty thump of the seed bag in the truck bed. The slammed door. The old engine starting up.

GB apologized to the waitress, laid down his last five dollar bill for the iced tea, and stepped back outside, thinking he'd just walk along this gravel-lined road until it ended, wondering if a church really might not be such a bad idea. It had been years since he'd attended one, and he wouldn't even have known where to begin— didn't even know if the doors would be open on a Saturday. Didn't want to face the guilt of a priest or pastor's countenance while, somewhere back a full day east, Julia Nguyen was no doubt still cursing his name, though she'd certainly made it home by now, would have had no trouble getting Dat or Annabelle or a friend to pick her up from the rest stop outside Michigan City, Indiana, where he'd left her, and take her back to her condo on the north side of

Chicago. It had been his mistake to bring her along, to expose her to this. It had been his mistake (and Max's) to think that a stop at Annabelle's house, which Max had located through means to which GB was not privy, would have any relevance to this thing they were doing. It had seemed to them, during the dark months of this wayward plan's formulation, that she could contribute something, that her presence would add fuel to the engine whose clattering din they'd mistaken for something significant. Instead they had found a woman irreconcilable with the one they'd known. Instead he had ended up driving across the upper Midwest with Annabelle's daughter, who had awoken him on the living room couch Friday morning with the story of her missing car—the story of how she'd come downstairs and stood on the front porch, had looked up and down the street, had come back in to find the keys no longer resting on the table where she'd left them. He was ashamed now to admit that he had encouraged it, was humiliated to acknowledge that he had told her he could use her help finding him and then had been pleased at the way it had made her seem to light up with enthusiasm. He was mortified now to confess that his first thought as he'd sat up on the couch had been not of his brother (missing now, with a car and, as he'd discovered later that morning, when they'd opened the trunk of the Stingray to throw Julia Nguyen's trendy purse inside, the knapsack and the bat bag) but of this young woman who had appeared to him as if out of a dream, already dressed in her jeans and tank top and ready to go, though her hair was pulled up messily, her face still lined from her pillow.

They'd gassed up on the way out of town, Julia Nguyen swiping her card and topping him off and becoming immediately inquisitive as they headed west along empty I-94 in the early morning hours, a trip she'd taken dozens of times and claimed to have once made to

Chicago in under four hours, urging him to kick it up to ninety on a certain straightaway west of Jackson. He had felt her excitement growing next to him, a strange reaction for a young woman who'd awoke that morning to find her car stolen. Instead of concerned or angry she seemed rejuvenated, as if they'd embarked on an adventure she'd been seeking, the combination of speed and mystery making her almost ecstatic. There was a hushed energy in even the questions she asked him—questions that sounded like dialogue from those movies GB had wasted away hours in the motel rooms watching, questions about what they were into, about what they were *really* doing on this cross-country drive to see the world, as GB had spontaneously called it the night before in response to her father's friendly but interminable questions. He had resisted and then begun to give her the same abridged version of the story he had given the barkeep back in Manhattan and the woman at the halfway house, finding himself enjoying her looks of excitement given in response to his retelling of the eighteen-hour blast up the East Coast at reckless speeds, GB allowing himself the opportunity to imagine the story as something far different than what it was, permitting himself to forget the details that had driven him and instead portraying it as some inevitable salvo against a moderate but largely overblown midlife crisis, telling her without further detail that they'd been on their way to Omaha to see their father, whom neither of them had seen in some thirty years and about whom—he could tell from her lack of response—Annabelle had told her nothing.

She had removed her sandals, rested her bare feet on the side-view mirror, and when GB's voice had grown strained from having to shout over the noise of the top-down Stingray, she had begun to talk about herself, had spoken, winningly at first, about her own life. How she'd gone to Northwestern, had turned her back on her parents' wishes that she attend the university where her father taught, their pleas and veiled guilt trips that she continue to live at home with them—as if that were an option that would have resulted in anything other than her killing herself in about two seconds. How she had fallen in love with Chicago, had gotten a job not in her field, which was art history ("Stupid, I know"), but at one of the high rises downtown. Whoring herself to corporate America. Not that she cared. It had paid for her Honda and the brownstone she rented on the North Side, near Wrigley, which she shared with her friends Renee and Chloe and Kate. But here her tone had begun to change; her voice had grown softer so that GB had to lean slightly toward her to properly hear. It seemed Renee's "issues," which were spoken of with air quotes and not expounded upon, were not as easy to put up with on a daily basis as they were when she only saw her on the weekends. And Chloe was a total slut and Kate was not much better. Or maybe it had nothing to do with them. Maybe it had more to do with her own life, what she had meant for it to become and what it actually *had* become, how it had gotten messed up somewhere along the line. Not drastically—she wasn't some drug addict or something—but that it had spun down to a speed at which she wasn't sure she could ever be happy.

GB listened from the driver's seat as she delivered circuitous and at times difficult-to-follow narratives concerning the foibles of a twenty-something living on the North Side of Chicago, working in one of the big office buildings downtown. The long gossipy lunches in airy chic ballrooms within walking distance, returning leisurely to her cubicle for two more hours of coffee and browsing the net before she rode an elevator ten stories down to the underground parking garage, scanned her card at an upright automated booth, and drove off into the urban afternoon, annoyed at the low-hanging sun, feeling parched and spent, as if she'd just spent the last eight hours as a corpse and awoken to find her real life somewhere far up ahead. It should've pleased her, she'd thought, having finally attained the freedom—both financial and physical—she'd always been missing. But she'd arrived to find it empty, her life still not satisfying, did he know what she meant? The days were long when they were spent always, without fail, in an office chair behind a computer screen, getting up to use the restroom and taking every detour you could think of to avoid the heavy plop of touching back down in your leather and vinyl tomb. It was like she couldn't find anybody that really understood her, the conversations during lunch and after work—at dive bars and bistros, guzzling microbrews— these conversations were clever, entertaining, but never resulted in her feeling anything deeper. The lonely rides home along Lake Shore Drive (half drunk, half asleep, sometimes with some barely known person in the passenger seat giving distracted directions to his or her apartment condo townhouse) were just the inadequate daily coup de grace of a perpetually mundane existence that left her craving something, like ice cream after a salty meal, comfort after all this chilled camaraderie. She was sick to death of the daily grind, bored out of her skull and starving for something *different*, something that lived far beyond the narrow parameters formed in that house where she'd grown up with its small rooms and the quiet street outside, the dreams and future they'd tried to train her to cling to, the timeline they'd thrown out before her when she was a little girl that had become bunched up like a long runner in a hall- way over the years, leaving her confused and capable of responding to that confusion in only one way—by imagining that something more glamorous and real was waiting for her in some parallel life if she could just find the means to arrive there, if she could just stumble upon the moment or the person who could help her break out.

He started, looked down to see that she'd reclined herself across the seat, was now lying on her back with bare feet still jutting from the passenger side window, the back of her head resting in his lap while she looked up at him, her slim body barely fitting in the narrow space between the seats, threatening to throw the shifter out of gear. He reached forward to protect it—and in his haste, his hand brushed one flattened breast, making her smile up at him. He tried to say he hadn't meant it, but she was already grinning wickedly, had already raised up to steal a kiss while he fought to keep his eyes on the road, was running her hands along his waist and thighs. Unconsciously, he let up on the gas. He'd been in the process of passing an eighteen wheeler when she'd rolled over in his lap and begun these movements that had filled him with something close to dread, his mind and libido worn thin after all the coffee and booze, after four nights with little to no sleep, four nights of spending every ounce of his energy keeping track of his brother and trying to avoid dwelling on where they were going, trying to forget the confrontation that rested at the far end of this journey and the wreckage he'd left behind. Now the eighteen-wheeler was several lengths ahead on the right, cars beginning to pass him in the right lane with drivers looking at him with exasperation, Julia having lowered her feet to the floor and still waiting for him to respond to her efforts. He wanted to ask them how they thought *their* driving performance might suffer if they had such a creature in their lap, wanted to ask her why she didn't just give up. Still, she'd fought against the obvious reality as if it constituted a challenge that would define her. With disbelief she wrestled with him, and he with something between shame and sorrow. Then she stopped moving, her head still in his lap, and lay there silently while they motored past the junction with I-96, past the eighteen-wheeler still puttering along in the right lane, GB accelerating as if it might return her to the enthusiasm she'd shown him earlier, as if it might bring back the woman he'd briefly been able to listen to as she spoke about her life and the girl it had allowed him to imagine. He wanted her to scream at him and throw punches so he could feel what she was feeling and respond to it, wanted to take her in his arms and comfort her, to take on the role of consoling father that he so dearly missed, to run his fingers through her hair but not in a dirty way, just as a continuous reminder of his presence, ready to provide what she needed to survive.

He touched her face and her husky, whispering voice strained up at him. "Don't." Then she rose primly and scrunched herself in the passenger seat. GB whispered, "I'm sorry," but she ignored him. He whispered it again, louder, but she ignored him still. He said it a third time, his hand creeping toward her, and this time she turned to face him.

"Don't."

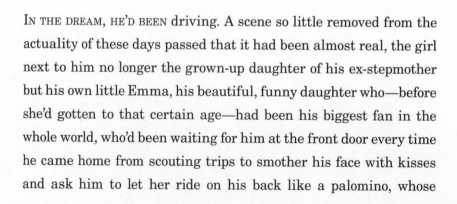

IN THE DREAM, HE'D BEEN driving. A scene so little removed from the actuality of these days passed that it had been almost real, the girl next to him no longer the grown-up daughter of his ex-stepmother but his own little Emma, his beautiful, funny daughter who—before she'd gotten to that certain age—had been his biggest fan in the whole world, who'd been waiting for him at the front door every time he came home from scouting trips to smother his face with kisses and ask him to let her ride on his back like a palomino, whose gymnastics meets he'd attended with a pride almost overpowering and in whose aftermath he'd climb down the bleachers to hug her in the glow of her perfection. His lovely daughter Emma who'd done everything with her father, who would've ridden to the ends of the Earth with him if only he'd asked, who'd been the one sympathetic person when—on a day he still remembered in her tenth year—she had returned home from gymnastics practice with her mother to find him sitting at the foot of the stairs, face in hands, unable to speak.

It had been Emma, on that occasion—not his once-beloved wife Tammy, who'd been running late for an appointment—who'd sat with him and hugged him and gotten him to tell what happened, who'd convinced him to give up the information that a phone call had come from someone calling himself the County Coroner of San Bernardino, California, who'd heard then for the first time—eyes wide, as was her way—the story of her grandmother, locked away in the remote desert for thirty years. It was his dear Emma, whom he'd that night elevated from the status of golden child to goddess, who'd encouraged him to fly out to California to take care of the body. Yes, of course, she'd come along. Oh, Daddy, of course! Yes, I have a meet this weekend. But so what? This is more important. I *want* to go along with you. I *want* to be there with you, Daddy, to help you say goodbye to your mommy. It was Emma who'd talked to Tammy upon her return, who'd kept GB's temperamental wife from flying off the handle when she imagined the expenses that would be incurred for plane tickets for two, who'd convinced her mother that it was a must that she, Emma, get to go along. GB, listening from the other room, heard his daughter's voice lower to a whisper as she attempted and ultimately succeeded in persuading her mother. The plane tickets had been secured by phone, and it was none other than his perfect daughter Emma who'd listened to him with bated breath as he'd gone on and on in the car on the way to the airport, checking the bags, reclining together in the darkened first class cab of the 747 at cruising altitude, stepping along the corridor at McCarran International Airport in Las Vegas and driving the rental car south from the city along the McCullough Range, he drinking coffee until his head spun, she being spoiled with milk-shake after milkshake from fast food restaurants along the inter-state, whatever she wanted. She was the one sitting with him, smiling at him, trying to keep him sane while the high sun glared off the windshield and made his head ache.

The body was in San Berdoo, at the county coroner's office, San Bernardino County stretching all the way from the outskirts of LA to the Nevada line, encompassing the entire Mojave and, though it was a four-hour drive from the city he barely remembered growing up in, the place where his mother had spent the last thirty years. Yet he'd determined, and had told Emma, who'd agreed as she always did (Whatever you say, Daddy) that their first stop must be there, at the Santa Jacinta Home for the Mentally Ill. I have some things I need to clear up with them, he'd told his daughter. Some things I need to resolve. It didn't add up. All the information he'd been given—right from the time when the phone had rung and the words of the county coroner had made him bolt awake (Am I speak-ing with Mr. George Benjamin Hill the Second? And are you in fact the oldest son of one Ms. Mary Hollister-Hill?) until the phone calls he'd made to the hospital—none of the information he'd been given made any sense. They said they'd found her in the same chair she spent all her mornings, coffee resting on the windowsill where it always rested while she looked out the window at the desert, a sixty-year-old woman, eyes still open, though glazed, who'd expired, seemingly without pain or fear, from natural causes.

Natural causes?

Then why, GB had asked his daughter, who shook her head obediently in response, ponytail swaying, was the county coroner involved? He'd never heard such phony horseshit—*pardon my French, sweetie*—as the line of bull they'd tried to give him, that all deaths of state hospital patients necessitated an autopsy, that the coroner's office had sent a deputy out into the desert to attend to the body and have it transported back to the office, that there was really no reason for him to be suspicious, that they had been through this before and truly appreciated his feelings but that it was natural causes and everything had been done by the book, and did he wish for them to ship to him any personal belongings of his mother's or simply throw them away?

Throw them away?

Even through his grief, it had moved him to see his daughter react to his storytelling, the way she half giggled as her daddy's voice grew more urgent in recounting the phone conversation to her in the car, any story he told first and foremost an entertainment for Emma. *Don't you dare throw them away! I'll be out to retrieve them on my way to the coroner's office!* He couldn't imagine what belongings his mother could possibly have, but he'd be damned if he was going to allow them to destroy them, these so-called doctors, these so-called public servants who'd been doing God knows what while his poor mother had been growing lonelier and lonelier out there in the desert. He'd be damned if he was going to let them dispose of the last remaining vestige of the mother he'd tried to visit—oh, he had *tried* to visit her several times, only to be insulted by smug voices on the phone telling him he had to make an appointment. An appointment to see his own mother! Telling him that after all this time they were worried it might "confuse" her, telling him that they just wanted to make sure she was ready for the "shock" of it. For he had to admit, they'd said, that several years had passed with nothing. He had to admit that this was something he maybe should've thought of a long time ago. And so he'd tried to come up with ways to move her east, to remove her from that sadistic hovel only to be foiled by stalwart insurance companies and fake doctors who said they knew best when really they knew nothing at all. Knew nothing about his mother and certainly knew nothing about *him*, about the various complications that had kept him away. And so now he'd be *goddamned* if he was going to let them hide the evidence of what he'd convinced himself was the truth, of what anybody with half a brain could see was true: that his mother, thirty years after dragging a knife across her throat right in front of her two sons, had finally gotten up the gumption to try again and, despite the people being paid to see otherwise, had succeeded in finishing the job.

And this—he said to his daughter, rotating the road map in his lap, trying to navigate while he drove this empty aisle through the desert, his daughter chewing on the straw of a long-empty milkshake, rubbing her fingers on the inside of the paper sleeve that had contained her fries, licking the salt from her fingertips—this screw job by those so-called fucking shrinks (*pardon my French, sweetie*) this was why they'd been forced to fly into Vegas rather than LA, this was why they'd been forced to spend a whole day trying to find their bearings in the desert, nearly running out of gas, filling up at a lonely pond of asphalt somewhere outside Needles—his daughter curled up in the passenger seat, asleep—asking directions of a toothless man wearing overalls in ninety-degree heat in

January who spit tobacco juice on his own asphalt and said he had no idea where such a place might be.

Nobody knew where it was. He wondered how in the world Annabelle had found it all those years ago. It was as if the place existed only in the voices of people on telephones, was part of some fourth dimension that the hot wind and sand swallowed up during the day and revealed only for five-minute intervals, like sunlight through pinholes in pagan monoliths. It was Emma, beloved Emma, picking at a cheeseburger—years before anyone could have predicted her aggressive vegetarian days, years before it seemed possible she'd one day have nothing to say to her father—who'd pointed out the tiny sign he otherwise would have driven right past at another perpendicular intersection of two desert roads among reservations, who'd unbuckled her seatbelt in anticipation of the serious energies required for them to successfully locate and arrive at their destination, to crack the riddle of the sands, both legs up on the passenger seat and pointing out the ancient building as it rose out of the horizon.

There it is, Daddy! Look! There it is!

A pastel fortress on the dunes, though it was not remotely that solemn place he recalled or imagined. It was no longer freezing inside; the employees no longer wore jackets and sweaters; there seemed to be more and better lighting; the people were nicer. The woman at the front desk did not tell him to log his name and have a seat like the receptionist at some overworked physician's office; she recognized his name immediately and told him to come with her, then led the way—introducing herself to Emma, talking enthusiastically about her own daughter's gymnastics career—to the top-floor hallway that didn't seem so dismal to GB, the bars removed from the door leading to the balcony off the hallway, improved security having made obsolete such precautions. Yes, the woman said as she scanned a card at the door, the Santa Jacinta Home had become not such a bad place over the years that had passed since GB had last had a chance to visit. Your mother, I'll go so far to say, was happy here. Content, at least. She even told me a few weeks ago that life had been okay to her.

The room was devoid of life. All that remained of her time here was a box full of little sculptures and a few paintings she'd done years ago, shiny desert scenes that seemed realistic enough. They'd destroyed it, he'd said to Emma in the car an hour later, the girl looking through the box at what remained of the grandma she'd never met. I can understand you being fooled by their lies, honey. I almost bought it, too. But it's all false. They're covering it up. Covering up the fact that my mother committed suicide in their hospital right under their smiling fake happy noses.

They ate hamburgers again, slept in a single-floor motel room outside Victorville, and were at the county coroner's office early the following morning, GB having drunk too much coffee again, having arrived with a twenty-four-ounce Styrofoam cup for his take-no-prisoners-I-want-the-truth-Goddamn-it conference with the coroner, whom he knew would take him aside and inform him—in a low voice, for these things always had to be handled gently—that it was not natural causes, that the death of his mother was not attributable to any of the things the people at the hospital might have tried to tell him, that it was not GB's fault, but theirs. And so he could stop feeling so guilty about it. He could stop feeling guilty because it had been their intention all along to keep him away, these evil miscreants who ran this miserable excuse for a hospital. Instead, the coroner had led him back to the office with a look of relief. They'd performed the routine autopsy, had found all in keeping with the report submitted by the physician at the hospital, and were ready to release the body immediately. In fact, if Mr. Hill could just provide him with the name of the funeral home that would be performing the viewing, he could have Mr. Hill's mother transported there by the end of the day, for a small fee of course.

GB had fought with him, had asked straight out what kind of a kickback he was getting for this, had begun ranting at the man while his daughter touched his shoulder and tried to calm him, the coroner looking downtrodden, telling GB that, believe it or not, Mr. Hill, your reaction is not an uncommon one. But I assure you with one-hundred-percent certainty that your mother did *not* commit suicide, but that she died of a heart attack, plain and simple, that she was an otherwise healthy sixty-year-old woman. Don't get me wrong, Mr. Hill, and don't think that I don't know what it's like to lose a mother and feel the guilt of maybe not having done all you could've while she was alive to let her know how you felt. But what you can do right now to make amends is take care of what's left to take care of, maybe stand at her gravesite and introduce her to her granddaughter. That's all you can do now, Mr. Hill. There, there, Mr. Hill, look at that. You've got a beautiful daughter who loves you, Mr. Hill. Yes you do. Now, Mr. Hill, if you don't mind, the name of that funeral home, please?

And because this was a dream—because he'd been dreaming all of this while sprawled in a cornfield and was remembering it now pressing onward past Des Moines and into the first waves of the great collective agricorps, signs rising from fields to declare OMAHA, 65 MILES while the perfect grid of crops on either side ran off in diagonal rows toward oblivion; because he had been in the wrong town that morning and had wandered up and down the lone street of the village he didn't recognize until it had suddenly occurred to him that there was more than one way out of a cornfield; because he had climbed again the low hill outside of town and seen in the distance the Stingray still parked in the lot of the bar of the night before, had trundled down the hill on the opposite side, across the fields and started up its engine; because of all these reasons and also because he was hungover and dry-mouthed and broke and disoriented and worn haggard by this week past, no longer with any clear notion of what he was doing aside from a deep burning need to arrive where he had set out to arrive—because of these confusing reasons and more, it had all become transposed, had become part of the same memory, the layout of the coroner's office not the same as the one in California but instead more similar to the one in Florida, the one he had arrived at just one week ago today, the morning he'd slung a bare arm across the bed in the Flamingo Motor Lodge and picked up the ringing phone and heard those words that had made him bolt awake again—("Am I speaking with Mr. George Benjamin Hill? And are you the father of a Ms. Emma Sinclair Hill?")—the day he'd raced across Miami on a Saturday morning to find Tammy already waiting outside in the parking lot with Marc the real estate agent, had thrown his arms around her and taken in her sobs as she took in his and they stood one final time together waiting to go inside and claim her, waiting to go inside and identify their daughter, who'd been found at last behind a dumpster in some lonely lot in Little Havana, the victim of an overdose, dumped by strangers or friends, his lovely daughter for whom he'd bought milkshakes and tried to lay out a soft-as-cashmere carpet of a life, now a shapeless lump on a silver slab as they stood behind a glass partition and watched the coroner lift the white shroud to reveal, unmistakably, the beautiful unmarked face of the daughter who, all those years ago, had helped convince him to have his mother cremated, who had held his head in her hands while he had cried with the urn in his lap and ridden along with him to find a place to dump the ashes, who'd rode along as he'd driven out to San Bernardino to find and show her one by one the places they'd lived when he was little, the ball fields he'd once dominated, winding up high in the hills above the city parked next to a picnic bench above a white lake looking out with his daughter across the skyline and the hazy blur where the land met the Pacific Ocean.

Because this was a dream, it seemed if he only hoped hard enough, he could have those days back: the days before Emma had returned with him on the plane and had seemed—in his mind at least—to have aged right there on the seat next to him, was not the same girl by the time they'd arrived back in Florida. Or perhaps it was simply that the changes had come so quickly on the heels of that trip which, despite its tragic components—or perhaps because of them—had remained his most nostalgic memory, the image of her sipping milkshakes in the rental car one he'd clung to and been unable to dispel during that Saturday afternoon into evening when he'd sequestered himself in the darkest corner of the darkest dive bar in Miami, trying to discern what it was he was supposed to do next, so drunk by the time he'd come to the decision that he could barely remember parts of it now, could barely remember returning to the motel room sometime toward dawn to slip on the replica internet-purchased Yankees uniform with his old number 54 that he'd ordered for himself one blacked-out night at four in the morning, to awaken the dog from his little doggie bed and lead him around to the back of the motel to secure his leash to a rusted metal spigot, to take the dog's head in his hands and promise someone would find him, that he'd end up with a sweet girl like Emma to take care of him, a final shake of his paw (a trick she had taught him one summer) before turning and making his way back out to the Stingray with his fingers in his ears so he wouldn't hear the barking. Driving the memorized streets then through the gloomy dawn to arrive at their neighborhood, to arrive at their street that dead ended at a cul-de-sac, stepping up the carpeted stairs and along the glass-lined breezeway to the threshold of her room, where he'd placed the bat bag and the knapsack on the carpet and sat down cross-legged and looked in at its emptiness, sat with his head in his hands saying, "I'm sorry, Emma. I'm so so sorry. I tried so hard." Reaching into the bat bag to retrieve from within the weapon he'd purchased when the first clues and leads to her whereabouts had run dry and the weeks had become months that had become unchanging seasons in that washed-out bright tropical world beyond the walls of filthy motel rooms, unzipping the knapsack and spreading the letters from his half brother Max around him as an excuse or an explanation, the cold barrel as it clicked between his teeth making him close his eyes and wait for the courage, the courage to pull the trigger and spread his brains all over the cream carpeting and the second-floor railing and the glass chandelier that was this home's finest feature, to end this gnawing and devouring suffering with a final twitch of a muscle in his thumb, waiting and wishing and hoping and hearing then the sound of the front door opening, footsteps in the lobby and Marc's voice echoing up, his wife's new boyfriend trying to sell a young couple on the lie that their future together belonged in this house with its built-ins and its breezeway and all this glass and light that had sold him and Tammy so many years ago, the whispers of the young awestruck prospective buyers as Marc stepped over to the light switch and flipped it on, illuminating the glass chandelier and the two-story entrance and, beyond—standing now at the railing of the second story with a baseball bat bag slung over one shoulder and a knapsack over the other, dressed from cap to spikes in a pinstriped New York Yankees baseball uniform in front of the room of his daughter who was on her way to becoming nothing more than another urn he wouldn't know what to do with—the silhouette of this house's former owner.

Of course there had been a scene. There had been a fainting husband and an ambulance siren bracing in the early morning. There had been nosy neighbors materializing at their windows and a conversation, or lecture, delivered by Marc in the shade of the fruit tree next to the FOR SALE sign, his wife's new lover telling him that he understood. He truly did. That he couldn't imagine what GB must be going through, but that his—Marc's—responsibility was to sell this house. And wasn't it really the first necessary step to their recovery when you thought about it—his and Tammy's—to get this place sold and move on with their lives and pick up the pieces? But how the devil was he supposed to help them do that? How was he supposed to help them sell this goddamn house when it was haunted by a real live ghost reluctant to leave its rooms? Words that had stuck with GB during the resulting drive back across town only to find that the overweight Cuban ladies who passed for housekeeping had already descended upon his room at the Flamingo Motor Lodge, a laundry cart with cleaning supplies dangling off its handles blocking the entrance and nothing to do now but retrieve the dog and go, gas up at the Mobil across from the Orange Bowl and climb the expressway over the river toward the interstate, set out with only the dog and the knapsack and the baseball bat bag in the Sunday morning glow of that city of pastel and palm trees and memories on this manic odyssey to Manhattan and Michigan and now the dark shadows of Council Bluffs, a cluster of bridges over the wide brown

Missouri, just hours from the conclusion of this journey that had shown him the world as he'd never seen it, that had made him think back to the girl Emma had been and the young woman she'd become and the adult she would never have a chance to be, the young girl whose up-beat gymnastics routine that last summer before she'd quit had been set to the tune of the old disco classic "I Will Survive" and had made him think there was nothing she could not accomplish, hours shackled to the interstates in the cramped leather of the Stingray that had made him review his own role in what had happened and understand what Tammy had meant, hours and days that had made him see now that even when he'd thought he had turned his life over to Emma, it had still been on his own terms, it had been only so long as she conformed to his idea of her, only so long as she agreed to remain nine years old. He had been ill-equipped to deal with an adolescent with her own problems, and so he had turned his back on her at the worst possible time: when it had first stopped being about him and had started being about her. He had driven her away, had provided with his own insecurities the motivation for her to turn on the father she'd thought would always be her biggest fan because she'd always been his. And so in his urgency to avoid becoming his father he had instead become something worse: a diluted form of him, less confrontational and demanding but just as distant, just as easily disrespected, just as ready a recipient of a conquering love turned to a brutal scorn.

It was in the car with Julia Nguyen, seeing again that arsenal of expressions of annoyance and disdain, that the bridge to these memories had begun to form in his mind. And it was in the bar of the night before that he had felt this new perspective pouring over him. After the sports shows had at last been replaced by a news broadcast that had made the kid who'd recognized him hours ago begin to stare with a new sort of scrutiny, after the ten minutes spent on the terrorist attack had given way to concerns that had seemed pressing beforehand, a whisper from the far end of the counter as the TV showed an aerial shot of a horse ranch, the voice somewhere between awe and disgust, rising and gaining the attention of the crowd of flannel-clad locals and even the bartender while the television image returned to the newsroom, where the beautiful anchor sat with the now infamous face in a box on her shoulder. "He's your *father!*" the kid was saying. "You're *George Benjamin Hill the Second*! Your father's that fella in the news! That fella who's goin' to prison for the rest of his Goddamn, miserable, horrible, lyin', cheatin', greedy-piece-of-shit life!"

And though GB had defended himself, had informed them of this plan of theirs, had told all these drunk, bewildered strangers that he was on his way out there as they spoke, had explained himself until he was doing so to an empty room but for the bartender trying to close up, something about this long drive on another Saturday afternoon into evening remembering the dream that had come that night in the cornfield had made GB see now that neither prison nor patricide were the answer. That if he'd learned anything from his own stint at the shaky reins of fatherhood, it was that forgiveness—even if it wasn't deserved (maybe most of all when it wasn't deserved)—was the only thing that could make life worth enduring. That if what he was truly interested in was salvation, and that if anything good was to come of these four decades of failure and eighteen months of anguish, then the only thing he could do now was to try and stop it.

When the dream had at last faded, and when the last sunlight of this Saturday evening had given way to the low skyline of Omaha, he was standing at the counter of yet another gas station, getting directions. No need for a map. It's easy enough to find. Follow River Road south of the city. Watch for the turn that says Billionaire Drive. You'll know you're going the right way from the television vans parked all up and down the road. You'll see the house soon as you come around the last bluff. You'll smell the horse shit a mile away.

3

"The Most Irresponsible Set of Actions by the Most Insidious Group of People the World Has Ever Known"

Saturday Night

THE OLD MAN WAS STRICKEN.

At four o'clock on the afternoon of the final attempt on his life, the seventy-year-old billionaire stood for the last time at the window of his office on the top floor of the tallest building in downtown Omaha, looking at the faded reflection of himself and his only grandson, trying to form words of wisdom and knowing that he would not be able to, knowing that he, George Benjamin Hill—grease-truck driver turned chairman of the board and (for the second time) acting CEO of the most successful company of the last decade of the twentieth century—would never again be able to communicate all he had meant to communicate.

The company was done, the whole building empty on this Saturday afternoon, the parking garage below vacant but for a single car, where in weeks past it would have been full, even on weekends. The sharks were in the water. His CEO (his son-in-law, until just weeks ago) had bailed. He'd recently engaged himself in a series of off-site meetings, with the managing directors, with the board, and later—after hours—with the CFO, all of whom had given him the same message. He didn't know what it all meant, these terms and figures

they'd thrown at him. He was no corporate finance expert. That
had been Jacob's job. He didn't know the accounting requirements
for an SPE or off-balance-sheet debt or the nitty-gritty of securitiza-
tion or even what a boomerang was. He hadn't been paid to know
these things. They'd paid him to take a tiny pipeline company in the
middle of nowhere and turn it into a national player. And that was
what he'd done. He had fought for a quarter century with the United
States government for the deregulation of gas delivery, had fought
on the side of the people for democracy, for capitalism, had tried to
earn the American populace the right to choose who would provide
them with their energy, had finally felt that taste of success and
now . . . Now it had come to this. His company bent over a board
with the whole New York Stock Exchange reaming them from
behind and every investment bank south of Canada lining up to
take its turn, his name finally known to everyone in the United
States of America but for all the wrong reasons.

Over the past week—a week that had offered him plenty of time
for reflection despite all that had taken place in board rooms and
conference rooms, in a plane thirty-thousand feet above the earth,
in a hospital room in Tulsa, Oklahoma—he'd tried to comb back
over the years in search of a turning point, some sign that the man
who'd stood at the port of Valdez on the day the first hot oil from the
frozen edge of the world had come pumping into a tanker at the end
of its eight-hundred-mile voyage would wind up in the place he had.
Those had been hard years—those years in Alaska. He'd escaped
from that isolated world a wealthy but uncertain man, nearly fifty
but still unsettled, another wife having left him and two children
having set off in their own directions. At an age when he might
have been thinking about retirement, he'd felt still in his apprentice
years, having at last logged a great personal victory—for in its first

year of activity the Alaska pipeline was said to have generated nearly a billion dollars in revenue—and now ready to do something even more unforgettable.

He'd put out feelers, knew his resume was impressive. He was not old; he was experienced. He practiced looking at himself in the mirror, memorizing ways of making his face look less like a grandfather's and more like an esteemed elder's. He stopped coloring his hair; instead he accentuated the gray until it was silver as stainless steel. He switched from cigarettes to cigars.

The first company to bite was a pipeline group out of Houston. He had not truly envisioned himself working for a company like Gulf-Corp, had thought himself done with the pipeline business until he'd met with the CEO in Houston, just off a plane from Alaska, a limo to pick him up at the airport, a car ride through the suburbs of a *real* city with no gray snow or muskeg to be seen. When he saw the skyscraper clustered among a dozen other skyscrapers—reflective glass windows and courtyards bordering busy city streets with restaurants and pubs and malls—he realized just how starved for civilization he'd been. When he saw the gilded lobby, the smartly dressed employees racing across a gleaming floor in thousand-dollar shoes, he understood he'd allowed his best years to drift away in a nowhere town two hundred miles from anywhere. When he rode the glass-lined express elevator from the courtyard to the top floor, when he came through a receiving room and into the office of the cowboy-hat-wearing CEO to whom he'd spoken twice on the phone, when he shook hands and exchanged pleasantries and realized that he was back among the difference makers, he realized also that it didn't matter what was said in this interview. He was sold. The CEO would hire him, would be impressed, of course— everyone was always impressed by Big Ben—and he would leave with a handshake and an impression of where he'd be in five years: in that very office, high above Houston. Running the show.

But the show was not so easily supervised as he'd imagined. They had the visual parts down. All outward appearances told a story of massive wealth and deals conducted in catered conference rooms. But the business itself was chugging along like an engine in Alaskan mid-winter, like a Cat in muskeg. It was the federal government, of course. The same monster that had gotten in his way so many times up north, that had done its best to interfere with every good idea every enterprising citizen ever had. With the limit they placed on the selling price, it was no surprise that honest, hard-working gas companies all over the Gulf Coast were going out of business, no wonder at all that they couldn't even generate enough profit to make it worthwhile to continue exploration. Even the half-assed attempts the government had made in recent years to keep the industry alive—the too little, too late motions they'd made when they finally realized they were taking solid American companies and making them insolvent (the hiking of regulated prices to producers and legislation restricting the use of natural gas, eleventh-hour answers to a long-term problem)—even these attempts had not worked. In fact they'd made matters worse. For now even coal and oil were cheaper than gas. The government had taken what was once the most cost-effective energy option on the planet and driven all of its producers and deliverers to the brink of bankruptcy.

It was into this quagmire that George Benjamin Hill had stepped in the late seventies when he'd signed on with GulfCorp—one of the largest pipeline companies in the country, with nearly two thousand miles stretching from New York to Florida. It was into this disaster of modern economics that he'd come directly from the

Alaska Pipeline job with only one thing expected of him: To save the company. To save the *industry*. To figure out a way to keep natural gas a viable energy source.

He was no economist. He hadn't gone to school for ten years and didn't have a half dozen letters attached to the back of his name. He hadn't authored dissertations on the wealth of nations, but he knew how to get to the bottom of problems. He knew how to ask the right people the right questions and how to track down the ones in charge of the decisions. He knew how to make deals, had been doing it ever since the day he'd met the milkshake machine man outside that restaurant in San Bernardino, had been thinking outside the box ever since that afternoon at Dodger Stadium.

He knew the first thing was to get the company out of its long-term deals with independent producers. He knew that in order to do it, he had to offer the producers something in return. *Tell ya what: I'm not above letting y'all sell directly to the customers, provided y'all use our pipelines exclusively.* He was no genius—except for when it came to compromise in a business setting, automatic with the idea of quid pro quo. *How can I get my way while still making everybody else think I made them happy?* With the money generated from this cost-cutting maneuver, he was more than happy to help out the competition by taking on their debt in return for a managing interest in their pipelines. His idea was to expand. Deregulation of gas prices was on the way—they'd been lobbying and negotiating and litigating for the last decade and a half—and when it did arrive, the company with the greatest pipeline system would win. He'd been presenting this idea to everyone at the company at every Monday morning meeting he'd attended since his arrival, had been pitching his plan to the CEO since his first week on the job, when he'd been told his mission with the company, had gone home and thought it over for an evening, and returned to work the following day with this plan already fully gestated.

He'd rented a place downtown, a condo in one of the high-rise buildings from whose balcony he could see the window of his office, whose light he liked to leave on when he left (often late at night, and only to return two hours early the next morning to the illusion that he'd never left). He lay one night in bed—not alone—and looked out the sliding glass door to the light in the far-off window. He'd been explaining to the woman his plan, wondering why the board was giving him such a hard time, why the CEO couldn't step in and assure them that he was right. "He can't do anything like that," the woman had said—her name was Beth, and she was with the company, was head of the development team and international exploration, had given a look to Big Ben as they'd eyed each other from across the board room that had told him he'd not lost his touch. Two weeks later, they'd run into each other in the parking lot beneath the building.

He couldn't remember how it had progressed from there; he only recalled that they'd been strangely without precaution as they'd marched out of the garage and into the hot afternoon, talking loudly, strangely devoid of remorse when they'd shoved their bodies against each other in his bedroom. She was a Texan, had learned to ride a horse before she could walk and played wide receiver on her high school football team after beating out the son of the head coach. She never told him her age, but he guessed her to be no more than thirty-five. A mature, noble face, a hard gaze that saw through the bullshit. She was married, of course—but then Big Ben had known this all along. Her husband was too wishy-washy, she'd said in bed that first night. Incapable of giving her either satisfaction or a child. Big Ben had enjoyed hearing her talk like this. He'd flipped her over on her belly and taken her again, her face jammed against the pillow. It was on a morning not long after they'd begun their affair—a Monday morning following a Sunday night in which she'd begged out of his requests that she join him—that he'd arrived at the office to find a memo on his desk from the CEO. He'd taken the elevator up, straightening his tie, had arrived to find him at his desk, his back turned: Albert Ventura Simonton, of the great Simonton Texas oil dynasty.

"Well?" Big Ben had said, out of breath and anxious for what he assumed would be good news. Instead Albert hemmed and hawed and eventually managed to communicate the fact that he was leaving. He'd been offered another position. A few things had come together and he was going to DC to become a policy maker. It nearly made Big Ben fall over. If Albert was gone, who would succeed him? Why else would the boss ask you to come up to his office first thing in the morning to tell you he was leaving unless he meant to tell you something else, something like "You are the new CEO."

He sat down in the chair on the other side of the desk and listened to the jumbled speech whose conclusion he already knew would be the finalization of his promotion. But halfway through he began hearing unexpected twists. The board was uncertain Big Ben was the best man for the job. They weren't sure he had the financial knowledge. He didn't even have a real college diploma. What kind of message would they be sending their shareholders if they hired him over any of the dozen Harvard MBAs on staff? Big Ben began descending down a long corridor, still hearing the voice of the boss, still listening to every word though not fully comprehending because he'd already comprehended all he needed to comprehend. He wasn't going to be promoted, and with one of the younger guys taking over, it would for all intents and purposes mean the exact opposite. For all intents and purposes, he was being *demoted*.

He heard the apologies, waved them away as he sulked out the door, stood waiting for the elevator to arrive, realizing that he had nowhere else to go. He couldn't face his office with its light that he'd kept burning for weeks, visible from his condominium window while he and Beth had planned a divorce and a life together. He had nowhere else to go, so he went to her office, came through the door to find her looking as business-like as always, her face already betraying something—some new expression that told him immediately he'd lost her, too. He tried to sit down, tried to explain why he needed to talk to her. Could they take a long lunch? But she shook her head. She turned away from him and said it. "I can't see you anymore."

"No," he whispered, stepping over to her and trying to force her to face him. "You can't do this."

"I'm moving," she said. "I'm moving to DC with him. My mind's made up. I'm moving to DC with my husband."

Albert had won her back, had convinced her to come along with him, that the life they'd shared in Texas was but a shadow of the existence they'd have in DC, where they'd have a place among the socialites of the world, where she could work as little or as much as she wished and they could finally focus entirely on having children.

For Big Ben, it was another moment when he could have given up, could have called his days among the cutthroat business world over and rested on his laurels, retired and traveled, maybe track down and spend some time with his kids, maybe rebuild burnt bridges. Yet his pride and intense hatred of failure—of feeling that someone else had gotten the sweeter end of the deal, any deal— would not allow it. Instead of disappearing, he'd found himself reborn again, had rubbed the right elbows and latched on with another company—GulfCorp's leading competitor, as a matter of fact, a company out of Omaha called E-Star, positioned on the cutting edge of exactly the kind of business he'd tried to get GulfCorp involved in. If twenty-five years previously he'd inhabited one persona when he'd met the ambitious milkshake machine salesman, now, the disheartening scene in the office of the man he'd thought he'd been groomed to replace sent him reeling up to be reshaped as another, galvanized and vengeful. Throughout his early incarnations of self, he'd had his family to tell and retell his stories to: the tale of the young Georgie Hill arriving in his grease truck at precisely the right instant. Alone, with not even a mistress save the nameless dozens who populated his evenings throughout the decade of the eighties, with no one to spill his resentments upon, he folded them up and carried them everywhere, wearing them like an extravagant suit, filling lulls at conventions and ribbon-cuttings with the story of how he'd latched on with E-Star, a second-rate company he'd transformed into the pride of Omaha, the corporate juggernaut smack dab in the center of the country.

He hadn't liked Nebraska at first. It had reminded him of Oklahoma, though it was colder and less dry than he recalled. He'd come here because this company was as dead set on the effects of deregulation as he was, agreed with his philosophy of growth, already controlled the major north-south pipelines connecting Texas to Iowa and most of the Midwest. But most of all was the fact that they still wanted an even larger share of the pie—were interested, in fact, in purchasing a certain pipeline company headquartered in Houston that was having severe financial difficulties. Big Ben had come to the decision that if he couldn't control GulfCorp from Albert's old seat in the top-floor office, then the next best thing would be to buy

them out, to make the men who'd voted against him in those meetings suffer. Less than six months after he'd moved north, he'd done
two things: he'd contacted a corporate raider he knew—a veteran of
the investing game he'd bashed heads with during the pipeline
years up north—and he'd developed a secret correspondence with
an old friend still inside GulfCorp. He'd tipped off the raider and his
group of investors; then he'd listened, through his insider, to the
grumblings that resulted. GulfCorp was an easy mark for such an
attack; with so many assets and so little debt, it was amazing they'd
stayed out of this game as long as they had. (Part of it, in fact, was
because of strings Big Ben, and Albert before him, had pulled.)
Through the eyes and ears of his insider, he'd sat back and listened
to the intensified staff meetings, had listened to the infighting and
indecision when other raiders joined the party, listened as finance
specialists went to the board with balance sheets that foretold
gloom. In order to avoid the unpleasant fate of payouts to half the
investing firms in the US—in order to make the company "shark-
proof"—there was nothing for them to do but grow rapidly and take
on huge amounts of debt.

For years afterward, Big Ben had relished in this victory, amazed
by nothing so much as how rapidly and effortlessly he'd managed to
conceive and implement his plan. He could still recall the frosty
early spring weather outside the office when he'd received the memo
that his old company, the great GulfCorp of Houston, Texas, wanted
to buy his new company. Even now, a full decade later, with all of it
crashing down around him, he refused to recall with anything
other than pride and pleasure the deal that had formed the mega-
company in charge of 40,000 miles of pipeline from coast to coast
and border to border with footholds in California, Texas, and Florida, a new reported debt of six billion dollars, a behemoth on the

verge of changing business forever, a vast juggernaut in need only of a single driven man to guide it toward its destiny, a position he had known without the slightest doubt would eventually fall to him, that after all these years of waiting, the stage of history was cleared for him to step out onto it, that the spotlight at last shone blindingly from the rafters upon him.

And he was right.

BY THE TIME HE'D SAID goodbye to the office on the top floor of the tallest building in downtown Omaha, had stepped through the double doors for the final time to find his daughter—the surprise daughter who had given him a grandson—seated still in the hard chair beneath the Renoir in the corridor, by the time he had taken the elevator to the lower parking levels with the two of them, his grandson immersed in his handheld videogame and his daughter offering a reluctant assistance that he shook off resolutely—by the time George Benjamin Hill had slouched into the passenger seat of Amelia's BMW (purchased by Jacob for their one and only anniversary) and risen from the garage into the street, it was evening, dusk having rolled in over the river, this part of the city abandoned.

She was quiet in the driver's seat, his daughter, having waited outside his corner office for the past hour—Two hours? Three? She'd become so quiet recently, a silence that had disturbed him, so accustomed was he to her previously fiery nature, solemn now behind the steering wheel as she drove them south along the surface streets, entered the on-ramp to the highway that would take them back to the horse ranch. So different from the manner in which she'd entered his life four years ago—the unexpected arrival of a daughter he never knew he had. Amelia June Simonton: an eighteen-year-old recent prep school graduate who was using what she called her gap year to travel the country, to track down her real father, about whom her mother had told her little until recently. It seemed Albert had died of a heart attack. So unsuccessful was his former boss's transition to DC that his passing hadn't even made headlines in the nation's capital, let alone Houston, though he'd once been the city's most generous philanthropist, and certainly not in Omaha, where Big Ben had just cashed in ten million shares of E-Star stock for a complete resodding of the three-hundred-acre horse ranch where he'd planned to retire like a cowboy, to conduct whatever consulting opportunities his reputation might bring him from the oval-shaped office in the white sandstone mansion he'd had built—because he could—based on the precise specifications of the most famous residence in the country, an immaculate modernized replica of the executive mansion, right down to the colonnade and portico, right down to the broad south lawn. The ultimate fantasy home in which he'd planned to awake alone each day, without the distractions of a family to deal with, without the obligations of his children—he'd tried to contact them, hadn't he?—and spend the rest of his life on a perpetual ride off into the sunset like the heroes in those old westerns he'd once adored.

Until *she'd* arrived at the office one morning, a strange whirlwind of a girl with pink hair. "*This* is Omaha? I was expecting more corn," she'd deadpanned. They were on the top floor of the downtown high-rise. Before the secretary had rung him to inform them of her presence, he'd been enjoying a nice dish of caviar with a couple of his top men, eating their lunches off silver platters, discussing not business schemes (they'd already done that) but which of the sample upholsteries laid out on the floor were preferable for the new company jet.

He'd nearly shot her, had nearly pulled the Browning Snub Nose he kept under his desk for just such a moment as this—an assassin barging through the doors. She was a hellion. Had more than a bit of her mother in her. When her hair wasn't pink it was purple or blue or black or green. He suspected she took drugs but had no idea how to approach her about it, was stuck instead with this mercurial mystery of a girl who spent hours killing time in the courtyard of the high-rise, bobbing under headphones and smoking cigarettes she'd rolled herself, who'd grown up in the shadow of Capitol Hill amidst senator's sons and punk rock coffee houses, who'd seen her father—her enabler—drop dead at the age of sixty-two and her mother wash her hands of her and move back to Texas with some oil baron (so she'd told Big Ben in one of her more lucid moments, in her grimy Audi on the way back to the horse ranch, where he'd said he supposed she could stay—though the next day when he woke and left for work with her still sleeping the sleep of teenagers, when he'd called everyone he knew in Texas, looking for Beth, she was nowhere to be found.)

He'd held another meeting that afternoon to inform them it wouldn't happen again, but they'd all laughed, old business men wishing they were young again, admirers of such youth and spunk, wishing in spite of themselves for the opportunity to revise the past that an unknown daughter of their own, crashing through the door, might have created. They laughed and slapped his back—all but one: the boy-genius Jacob Smart, twenty-six and already head of the trading department and new CFO. Jacob Smart was sharp as a tack but that day he'd been distracted, unable to concentrate, unconcerned with any of the decorative dilemmas regarding the air taxi. He'd waited until after the meeting and then approached Ben with the intense gaze typically trained toward financial figures.

"Who was she?" he asked.

She'd moved in at the horse ranch and established a certain corridor and set of rooms on the east wing as her domain, had commandeered and then shut them off, permitting Big Ben to come only close enough to hear the rhythms of the bass-driven music pumping at all times from her speakers, making the horses whine in their stables. For someone supposedly on a quest of self-exploration, she never seemed to go anywhere, unless it was to pester him at work, where she'd hang out on the concrete steps of the courthouse-style entrance, sunning herself, rubbing lotion on her tanned body, walking across the street for a pack of smokes or a candy bar or an energy drink, occasionally coming through the doors and taking the elevator directly to the top floor, where she'd recline on one of the couches, complaining about the heat or boredom. She'd interrupt him in the middle of important meetings, phone calls to his cell that he'd asked her please to avoid using except for emergencies, had called to get his credit card number to order pizza, to buy shoes.

It was the one time that he fought his urge to answer her call that it turned out to be a true emergency. A call came in to his secretary, who forwarded it on to Big Ben, who turned on the speaker phone to hear her, in tears, on the side of the interstate where she'd rolled the Audi Quattro in which she'd arrived and, miraculously— though the vehicle had been reduced to a twisted hunk of aluminum—escaped unscathed. It was on this day, after she'd gotten a taxi to his office, that she had come face-to-face for the first time with Jacob Smart, hers smudged with tears and a little scrape on one cheek, his captivated, intent, lost.

It was embarrassing. He was goofy around her. It was her mother's bored face and mischievous grin that did it, Big Ben knew, but that didn't make it any better, didn't make it any more acceptable to see his CFO in his silk shirts and ten-thousand-dollar cowboy boots sitting on the front steps with her eating burritos and ice cream cones and licking the drips off her chin.

He'd received phone calls from various high-ranking officials in the weeks that followed. "He's out there *again*! You need to *do* something! She's *your* daughter. Figure out a way to keep her away from here." But Big Ben simply couldn't. She could manipulate him in ways he'd never thought possible, especially from a daughter he'd just met—though in many ways that was the key. The fact that she'd lived without him for eighteen years, the guilt that he'd never have felt on his own had she not encouraged it with occasional uncorroborated stories of her childhood, unsupervised and out of control. Big Ben had known from the beginning that the whole sordid affair would not contribute positively to Jacob's performance, though he'd never guessed that it would go this far, the two of them taking two-hour breaks to sit on the steps of corporate HQ necking. At the same time, there was no denying the relief he'd felt at not having her constantly around, at her being no longer entirely *his* problem. It was while they were finishing their upholstery selections—another meeting Jacob had absconded from to join Amelia on the front steps, a day when they'd set off the smoke alarm by ducking into a back corridor to smoke "cigarettes"—that he'd come up with his idea to get them out of his hair. "Why don't the two of you go on a trip?" he'd suggested. "Take the new jet and go wherever you feel like going. Come back in a week with your heads screwed on straight."

They'd gone to Las Vegas, had come back with their heads screwed on no straighter but with rings on their fingers and tattoos on their ass cheeks that they'd insisted on showing everyone, the girl now calling herself Amelia June Simonton-Smart and waving around a little pregnancy test that said blue.

That was how he'd gotten a grandson to spoil. And it was amazing how quickly Amelia had been changed by her pregnancy. She became the role of mother-to-be as completely as she'd become the rebellious globe-trekking child of wanderlust, the two (and then three) of them living at that far end of the second floor of the mansion on the horse ranch, Jacob having given up his condominium in favor of staying with Amelia, who claimed to love horses though Big Ben had never seen her come within a hundred yards of one, had never even seen her so much as set foot in any of his three hundred acres other than the path leading from the front door to the garage where she kept her new BMW.

He'd seen the change in Jacob Smart as well, had witnessed the way the young man had turned the corner from promising to productive. They'd recruited him directly from Ansley and Surtain, the blue-chip consulting firm, which he'd joined directly out of Harvard Business School, which he'd attended directly after graduating from Princeton with highest honors. What Big Ben had liked about him was that he wasn't just smart. He had the other skills as well, the skills to make people believe what he had to say and take stock in the plans he came up with. He'd hired him first as a consultant, had worked out a contract with the boys at A&S to get him to work exclusively on E-Star matters, had been unconcerned with the cost—anything to get this young star at work for his company, for amidst all the bravado of the interview, all the banter between the two of them like generals sharing war stories, Jacob Smart had also given Big Ben some interesting things to consider during his interview.

"Question," the young genius had said. "What's the single most important interaction in the gas industry? Answer: It's the interaction between buyers and sellers. Everybody wants a deal. Everybody wants to save money. But what is it that prevents this from happening? *Risk*. Uncertainty. A change in the weather causes prices to fluctuate unpredictably. Even though there's plenty to go around, industrial customers can never be sure they can lock up enough. Meanwhile, the deliverers don't want to get stuck holding the bag. It's the excess that causes the uncertainty. Problem is: there's nowhere to put all the gas you don't want to take with you."

Big Ben had listened to this with his fingers steepled in front of his face. He lowered them and leaned back, crossed one leg over the other. "So you're suggesting . . ."

"I'm suggesting," said Jacob Smart, leaning forward—still months from the afternoon he would meet Amelia—"that the gas industry could become more profitable if it became more like the financial services industry. And I'm suggesting E-Star could become the richest company in history if it became the first bankers."

They'd lived like kings on this concept, had taken advantage of every new requirement that came along with deregulation, had stirred their fingers in the pot of every energy and commodities industry in the country. Big Ben had gloried in walking the floors of the company—his company—visiting with his employees, all of them with smiles on their faces because it truly was fun. They were the cream of the crop, had recognized an industry about to become tremendously lucrative and had been there at the right time to collect the royalties. At the same time, it hadn't been without effort—though it was difficult to call it work when you were rewriting all the rules. They were creative people with a culture built on making money no matter what. He'd talked to hundreds of young men like

himself and had seen the look in their eyes that told Big Ben just
what they thought of him, the look that said they had their eyes on
the prize and were willing to do anything to get there, that if getting ahead meant meeting whatever quotas the company gave
them—no matter what, every time—then they would do whatever
was necessary, not out of love for their boss or pride in their work—
those things, Alaska had taught him, were no longer viable motiva-
tional factors—but out of a sheer, unyielding desire to become the
next monthly bestseller, the next quarterly star, the next mid-year
high roller, the next CEO. Ben had encouraged it, had known what
it was like to be in their place, could still remember his own days
driving the grease truck, riding in unsafe planes over the Alaska
Range back and forth from Anchorage to Fairbanks, knew that
many of these men had families just like he'd had, people who might
have vied with the company for their attention, and any time he saw
somebody staying late, working on a weekend, sleeping at his desk,
he'd taken pride and a strange comfort at the sight of someone else
choosing the same path he'd stubbornly adhered to all these years.

It was for this reason that he'd been shocked to watch the change
in Jacob Smart. From the instant the young man had laid eyes on
Amelia, he'd been a different person: had stopped dominating every
meeting with intensely explained methods of surpassing quarterly
goals, of smashing annual plans. At home, at the horse ranch, Big
Ben's knocks on the doors of their separate wing went increasingly
unheeded. The Sunday dinners upon which he'd once insisted—the
table in the main dining room looking out on the south lawn heaped
with casseroles and meats and three kinds of potatoes, a full wait
staff filling their glasses and taking away plates—had become
lonely. Evenings he sat alone in front of the ten-foot projection
screen in his basement movie theater, watching old westerns and

wishing Jacob were around to hear him reciting the lines verbatim. By the time Big Ben's grandson was born, he'd begun to develop a rotten feeling about what was going on, about what exactly it was that Jacob did in his office two stories down from Big Ben's. They had less and less contact—no more did they sit together for long periods of time during the group vacations the company took after quarterly audits: skiing in Colorado, sailing in Palm Beach, week-ending in Hawai'i. In fact, Jacob had begun opting out of the vacations, citing the birth of their son, saying Amelia needed him around the house, saying that he was a father now—always looking askance at Big Ben when he did so. Ben had found the trips less enjoyable as well. He knew fewer and fewer of his employees. And he'd never realized until it was too late just how much he'd come to appreciate the presence of Jacob—the way they could speak so much with so few words, such was their connection and aligned viewpoint on the world. He should've seen it coming. Should've known all along that he was being hoodwinked. That a man who'd gotten to where he'd gotten by refusing to make his job secondary to his family had been turned into a schmoe by the son he'd never had.

It was so complicated. He still could not comprehend how it had all transpired. Even now—watching the bluffs above the river give way to the rolling countryside from the passenger seat of his daughter's BMW, having come off the highway and made their way to the dark two-lane road through trees that led to his three-hundred-acre horse ranch—even now he could not say where it had all begun, when the paper trail they'd constructed to hide all his company was up to behind the scenes had begun to reveal itself, when all the shady dealings and fabricated paperwork and phony audits and peculiar budgets forced through the accountants by means of a burgeoning portfolio of kickbacks had become too top-heavy to sustain.

By the end they'd had their hands in everything, had gamed the California energy market and built immense power plants in India and Nigeria, had sold securities and traded futures on livestock and freight contracts, on wealth derivatives and even wind and water. They had done things so outrageous and beyond the scope of monitored business that it had been like a videogame itself, just like the little handheld machine his three-year-old grandson was so entranced with, empty figures from nonexistent partners rolling into their accounts like scores on a pinball machine. How could he question it? What could he have done even if he had harbored suspicion? It was the result of a company so large it was without limits. Employees had cut personal deals with lenders that made everyone rich but the company; partners had sold stock options and cashed it out of the general pension fund; finance officials had created over a thousand special purpose entities in order to legally launder money, had used structured finance to create the illusion of growth, had used any accounting trick they knew to book profits that didn't exist, or wouldn't exist for thirty years, had done it all right under Big Ben's nose, had accomplished it all in the lower floors while he'd trusted them from the top.

Now it had all come crashing down, the polished walls collapsing to reveal the tarnished core of his company and his life. Just six months ago, he'd been handing the business over to his son-in-law, the young man whose genius it was that had gotten them started on this trajectory, the young man who'd fallen head over heels for his daughter Amelia June and brought him a grandson. Big Ben had not stopped coming to work—how could he, after having built this company into the juggernaut it had become?—but he'd entered into a sort of retirement, attending the meetings now only for fun, stopping by with the caterers to bring the boys filet mignon for lunch. He'd not even had time to see the numbers falling off the deep end, had been surprised one Friday morning just two weeks ago in his old office, kept furnished according to his standards so he could drop in whenever he wished, when an email turned up in his box telling him to take a look at their stock projections. It was a curiosity—that's what he'd felt that Friday morning. It was strange, but everyone seemed to be selling. They must've gotten some bad information.

But then he'd arrived early the following Monday to find the place like a tomb, people gathered in groups looking at New York Stock Exchange figures. Jacob's office was empty, stayed empty all day long—Big Ben hadn't seen him all weekend and, as it turned out, would never see him again, would sit waiting for the boy he trusted most in the world to return and put his mind at ease while the numbers out of New York continued to plummet. A news story broke on CNN that a scandal had been revealed within the nation's wealthiest company—a numbers game, a house of cards set to collapse, taking half the banks and financial institutions in America with it. A live report showed the front steps of corporate HQ, and Big Ben raced over to the window, looked down to find the tiny television trucks with camera crews in the street, reporters standing on the front steps so they could have it in the background of the shot.

No one was saying much. No one had too many details, which was a problem, because Big Ben still had no idea what was going on. Answers were not forthcoming. There were shrugs. There were grown men crying in their offices, cars laying tire out of the parking garage. By Friday afternoon of that worst week of his life, the late summer sun pouring through the glass walls and into the conference room where he sat with his COO, E-Star's stock had plummeted. Accountants and auditors were at the doors. The shred bins were full with boxes of documents piled up next to them, people doing all they could do and then hightailing it out of there. Phones were ringing off the hook with partners and clients and investors beginning to understand that their world was going up in flames.

What had caused it? There were a million reasons, but what it really boiled down to was that it had never been real to begin with. The company on which he'd built his reputation, the company that had finally made him feel successful, that had finally made him think he'd made it in this world, was nothing but a fake, hadn't turned an honest profit in over a decade, hadn't made a legit deal in as long as anyone could remember. Even one year ago, when they'd been featured in *Forbes* and *Fortune* and Big Ben himself had graced the cover of *People* magazine (beneath a heading reading "Why Is This Man Smiling?"), even when they'd been reporting profits in the billions, they'd actually been losing money. The debt was astronomical. Nobody even expected them to *try* to pay it back. It wasn't a matter of a company making amends for a mistake—it was a question of an entire country, an entire economy, trying to get back on its feet after what one analyst called "the most irresponsible set of actions by the most insidious group of people the world has ever known."

This was what it had come to, the seventy-year-old billionaire may or may not have been thinking that afternoon of the final attempt on his life, alone at the top of an empty building no longer his, confronting his own reflection and that of his only grandson, knowing there had to be something worth passing along, that in a life as eventful and influential as his there had to be something he could give the boy, who'd been a good sport and come all the way up to the top floor though his mother had seemed reluctant to wait in the hall. And what was the boy thinking as he stood attentively while his grandfather marched around the office, led the boy over to the glass wall behind his great ark of a desk, gesturing for him to look out over the city and the river? Did the boy think, as his grandfather may have, that there had to be some knowledge worth bestowing, an anecdote to arm the boy with some arsenal of the past? Was the boy surprised at all when, instead of sharing his wisdom, the old man looked around for something to throw? On the desk was a gold-inlayed globe, textured with topography, angled on the Earth's axis. He lifted it up and hurled it at the window, at their reflections, ready for it to crash through the glass, a change in air pressure and a chaos of wind. But the globe was light and the glass was reinforced. It bounced off and rolled hollowly toward the corner of the room, while the boy raised his handheld videogame and resumed his play.

THE HORSE RANCH WAS NAMED after his mother, her grandmother, though so distanced from that woman was Amelia June Simonton-Smart that she felt no sense of kinship, had felt none four days ago when she'd set out to pick up her father and her son from a hospital room three hundred miles away in Tulsa, Oklahoma, felt none as she returned late on this Saturday afternoon to find the road leading back to the ranch empty. Absent now were the media vans that had until recently been gathered on the dirt roads along the perimeter of the property, giant vans with the numbers of the local networks on the side and later the more recognizable acronyms of the corporate news conglomerates, trying to catch a glimpse of evil personified, trying to attach a human face to the scandal. Amelia June Simonton-Smart had tried not to give them the satisfaction, had eventually had her picture taken with middle finger extended as she drove past. It had taken them less than a week to discover that the electrical safety system on the twelve-foot-high brick fence was not functional. Then the vans were on their land, parked around the stables and on the south lawn, cameras trained through their windows twenty-four hours a day, knocks on the front door and the back doors and the patio doors, men appearing in the apple grove along the hillside with telephoto lenses, flashes flashing as she raced to sweep the curtains closed. An irate phone call to the security company had informed her that they hadn't paid the bill in over a year—that despite all the money her father and her husband were pulling in, despite the private jet and the vacations and the expensive lunches on silver platters, they had not even enough cash to pay the bills, not even enough to pay the mortgage on this outrageous piece of property and the massive empty statement of a home that rested on it, that the horses were starving and neglected, that half the staff had quit: had not been, as her father had told her—one of the final things he'd said to her—fired for suspected stealing.

The old man had had a stroke, and though the doctors at the hospital in Tulsa had spoken hopefully of his already startling recovery, Amelia June Simonton-Smart had known immediately that too large a part of him had perished. They'd never seen a stroke survivor who had retained such control of his motor skills, had found his bed empty the first night only to locate him marching obstinately along the halls, had found him in the bathroom in front of the mirror with IVs dangling from his arms, one side of his face twisted in a scowl. On the other hand, his cognitive skills had born the full brunt of the damage, and though anything was possible—so they said—it seemed likely he would remain in this stricken

cocoon for whatever interval remained of his life. He could still form
thoughts, the doctors had told her, could perhaps imagine the words
that would give them substance, but he could not speak and probably never would again. Which meant that the next-to-last memory
Amelia would possess of his voice would be the confrontation they'd
had the previous Monday evening, the day she'd spent pacing the
long halls of the mansion she'd called home for the past four years,
the evening she'd gathered the courage and stepped to the double
doors behind which his oval office overlooked the south lawn, had
entered to find him seated at his desk, the curtains behind him
pulled against the flanks of reporters who'd parked their vans right
there on the grass beyond the hedgerow, and had listened while he
attempted to win her back, while he wept and confessed to her that
it was all true, that everything she might have read in the papers
or seen on the television—all the monstrous tales of his company
run amok, of financial disaster like never seen before—was all true.
And that, yes (tears in his eyes and a catch in his voice), these were
dark times, but that he had a plan for the recovery of the company
and their lives, a plan that would bring Jacob back from wherever he'd disappeared to and restore their lives here on the three-
hundred-acre horse ranch, that he would not give in to these people
out in their yard, that he had never given in to anyone and didn't
plan to start now.

Looking back, she thought she could detect in his voice already
the slurs and inconsistencies that might have warned her of what
was to come, his voice not so precise and his movements herky-jerky,
his fist that struck the table quivering, as if some essential cir-
cuitry in his brain had corroded. The way he stood up, half stumbled to the window and threw the curtains open, revealing the lawn
bedecked with lights and movement, men sprinting up from the

shadows to stand beneath them and snap photos of this figure she
still couldn't believe was the man she'd briefly acknowledged as her
father. Arms spread as if basking in his own shameful publicity.
She'd fled the room, had searched for and eventually found Jake
alone in his closet, sitting on one of the shelves playing his videogame, had tried to hide in there with him, to take comfort from
their solidarity, only to have him shrug her off and march out into
his room and from there into the hallway, leaving her holed up in
her bunker away from the world, practicing the same angry distance he'd shown her since his father had vanished, since Jacob had
intimated to Amelia on a Friday night two weeks ago that something awful was coming, something that would take him away for a
while, the two of them talking in bed in a way Amelia had known
was bad. Jacob was one who fell asleep as soon as his head hit the
pillow, unless he wanted to have sex, in which case he fell asleep
immediately following his orgasm. He always slept on his side,
curled up. When Amelia had seen him lying on his back, hands
joined atop his chest in a false pose of comfort, she'd known he had
something bad to say.

The next day he'd been gone, their son downstairs on a Saturday
morning, sitting cross-legged on the rug in the middle of the living
room floor, playing his handheld videogame with his laptop singing
music in front of him, face-to-face with the dark mirror of the television that he hadn't turned on yet, waiting for his father to arrive
so they could watch Saturday morning cartoons together (their one
weekly activity), she having to come in and make the boy understand that it would not be happening today, that his father had to
go away for a while, but that *she* would watch cartoons with him, if
he wished, a conversation that had turned the boy to a venomous
little demon who wanted his daddy, who didn't want to watch TV

with his mommy, who punctuated each word with a punch to her chest as he screamed, *I . . . want . . . my . . . daddy!*

As Amelia June Simonton-Smart crouched in her son's closet, she thought that if it weren't for fathers, women could raise sons worth knowing, worth respecting. If it weren't for fathers, sons might grow up to be loving, secure, gentle, thoughtful, nonviolent people. If it weren't for fathers, mothers might get a chance, and if mothers got a chance, kids might not all be so wayward. Her own situation, for instance. Why had she driven all the way out here? Why had she spent so much time and energy? Why had she been so fixated—at a time when she should have been preparing to go to Swarthmore; she'd gotten in, after all—why had she been so intent on finding her *real* father? Was it because the one she'd known, the one she'd grown up calling *Dad*, had failed her? Had she thought that next to that imposter, her real father could not fail to appear striking, rich, good-looking, and successful? Instead, he'd been old, stiff, stodgy. He wore cowboy hats and looked ridiculous. His arms were too long, accentuated by the long-sleeve dress shirts whose cuffs he refused to unbutton and roll up. To other women he somehow came off as charming, had them laughing in seconds; to her, he could barely get out a sentence, was cautious, insecure, was terrified of her, as if he'd known the instant he'd met her that she bore some distorted understanding of him that—if discovered—could bring him down. Of course, this had not been her intention, had never been in her mind when she'd driven out here and surprised him at work in front of all his board members and fallen in love with his CFO, the young genius with the bluest eyes she'd ever seen. She'd meant to get to know him and, in the process, find out something about herself, had meant to blow into his life like a stray breeze—like a character in a Kerouac book—and blow out again before he knew it, leaving him wanting more. She had never imagined herself staying here for four years, settling down, getting married and pregnant (and even if these events had taken place in Vegas, they still had taken place, they hadn't *stayed* in Vegas as was generally promised). She hadn't planned to become a wife or a mother, hadn't meant to find herself four years later still living in the east wing of this immense mansion in a suite that—at eighteen, single, armed with a credit card and an empty summer—had seemed palatial; that now seemed overrun with Jake's toys and Jacob's dirty clothes, remnants of the man she wanted to forget, reminders of the life she couldn't.

She'd awoke, still in the closet, the following morning, her entire body stiff, and had stepped along the lush and columned hall beneath chandeliers to the sweeping staircase, had descended to find the house empty, the limo gone, the phone ringing and an unidentified voice on the other end telling her that her father—that toppling tower of a man she'd last seen only twelve hours ago standing with arms spread before a window and a dozen photographers scurrying on the lawn—was in a hospital room in Tulsa, in critical condition, recovering (so said the frazzled voice on the other end of the phone) from a massive stroke.

It had taken her half a day to put it all together, to figure out all that had happened while she'd slept, curled up in her son's cramped bedroom closet. He'd run away. Had stood in front of the window the night before promising he'd find a way to make things right, then had gathered his belongings while she slept, had taken her only son and absconded, leaving her to deal with the mess. Had somehow gotten the limo past the reporters and on the road to the airport, where he'd boarded a flight with the boy to God knows where, a flight that might be landing right now, halfway across the globe, the two of them vanished for good, had it not been for the *other* thing that had happened while she'd slept, the spectacle with which she'd been inundated the instant she'd turned on the television and that had resulted in the all-flights-grounded command that had foiled her father's attempts to flee.

She'd set out that same afternoon. While the rest of the country was glued to their televisions or out buying flags, she'd packed up her BMW for the four-hundred-mile trip south along the interstate between Omaha and Kansas City without even a road map until she'd picked one up for a buck seventy-five from a gas station fashioned from a trailer in a dusty used car lot. Four hundred miles across the empty plains of the heartland to pick up her son and the father she wished she'd never found, through the lengthy flats of western Missouri and the Ozarks to a place called Oklahoma, a place she'd never visited and hadn't planned to, though she'd heard him reference it several times as his birthplace, the place he'd fled decades ago to begin the life that had stretched from California to Alaska and now was ending here, in a hospital bed right back where he'd started. She'd noticed the difference as soon as she'd seen him, had been taken first to her blue-eyed son seated in a dim lounge down the hall from his grandfather, settled on a couch from which the nurses told her he'd not budged, had been sitting for the past twenty-four hours, barely eating, barely sleeping, reluctant to speak, fixated on his handheld videogame and staring at his laptop. A doctor had sat her down in an adjacent room, had explained to her all that she could expect from a victim of such a serious stroke, suffered just as his plane had been forced into an emergency landing in Tulsa, a situation that her son, sitting across the hall throughout this explanation, had witnessed in its entirety. The doctor had told her that she should be ready for an individual completely incapable of taking care of himself, should perhaps consider hiring professional assistance, to which she'd nodded as if intending to consider it. In fact, she'd determined immediately that this would be her course of action, for she had no intentions of staying in Omaha another month, another week, had felt while on the road— even on these rinky-dink interstates—that necessary pull of travel, had felt the urge to leave it all behind, an urge Jacob had suppressed in her for four long years. An urge that—with him gone, seemingly for good—she knew she stood no chance against. An urge she wasn't sure why she'd fought in the first place.

For three days she'd sat around the hospital, listening to the dismal words of doctors and waiting for them to set him free, for them to tell her it was okay to take him back to Omaha and the ranch, three days during which she'd watched fifty hours of television, the news coming in from the wreckage, search parties still digging for survivors, her father's name suddenly absent from the headlines, eradicated as if he'd never existed, his fifteen minutes of unwanted fame made irrelevant by a group of terrorists with box cutters, staying up late watching newscasters on endless loops, looking across an empty hospital waiting room at her son, who seemed not to have noticed a thing: not his grandfather in his stale blue bed, not the country turned upside down. Not a thing.

The return trip had been arduous, made on this Saturday in September, the late morning sun as they headed northeast on the Will Rogers Turnpike coming through the window of the car to land on her father's sallow face, the boy in the backseat as always immersed in his own world, Amelia June Simonton-Smart carrying on a conversation with a man the doctors had told her may or may not understand a word she was saying. And his reactions were no accurate gauge of his comprehension either. He seemed to grin constantly, this man of seventy who suddenly looked his age and then some, would smirk as she tried to explain to him her desire, her *need*, to get out, to do something with her life, her plan to remove herself from the domesticity she'd somehow found herself married to these last four years, though it had never been what she wanted. Her plan now was to travel, she told him, to take the boy and travel. It didn't matter where. As long as it was far from Omaha, far away from Washington, DC.

She'd spilled this out to him, unwilling to look at his reaction. Then when she'd finished—when she'd unloaded in her oblique way all the resentment she'd decided to heap upon him—she'd heard a chuckle escape his lips, had looked over to find the old man laughing. They'd warned her about this, had told her he might laugh at inappropriate times, might cry without provocation, had told her that it had nothing to do with emotions anymore, that it was just faulty mechanics, synapses gone haywire and firing randomly. She'd watched him laugh and had fought back the urge to laugh herself, had heard Jake in the backseat giggling and shot a glance in the rearview at the boy she hadn't heard laugh since his father had left, his face puckering up in mock seriousness when he noticed her watching.

Two hours later the old man's mindless laughter had been replaced by tears. It was afternoon by that point, the three of them having entered the southwest corner of Iowa, only an hour away, the sun having flipped sides and now shining through the windows on the driver's side, Jake lying down in the backseat, taking a nap when the noises began in the seat next to her. She'd feigned ignorance, had pretended that she didn't hear him, that she didn't notice the looks she'd at first thought were an attempt to get her attention, but that she soon realized were part of some search for an explanation. *Why am I crying?* he seemed to be asking her, a question for which she had a hundred answers and no response. It was out of these tears, out of this great purging of whatever synaptic patterns still lingered in his brain, that had come the words they'd told her would never come, the words that constituted his final attempt at communication, spoken as they crossed the Missouri at Council Bluffs and Omaha, the old man pointing up ahead at the cluster of high-rises in the downtown half a mile from the river, pointing unmistakably—though at first she denied it, imagined it impossible—gesturing persistently at the building that had been his, a grunt turning to a word: *Office!* And then the word becoming a sentence, a request: *I want to show the boy my office!*

That was how she'd come to spend the remainder of that late afternoon in the hallway on the top floor of the high-rise from which her father and her husband had conducted their vague business, restless and pacing, her uncertainty at just what was going on behind his closed office doors making her take time-killing mea-sures. Up and down the elevators for no good reason at all, stepping out onto random silent floors into an atmosphere of palpable guilt, the whole building an empty tower of apprehension, a sense of indel-ible filth that was still with her hours later as she drove them out of the parking garage and into the night, the man and the boy and the city gone quiet, exiting off the brightly lit interstate to the surface roads leading back to the horse ranch. Amelia June Simonton-Smart wanted to ask the two of them what they'd done, what sort of infor-mation had passed between them. The headlights sliced through the fog that had collected in these lowlands above the river. The gate was still unlocked and now ajar, though she didn't pay it any mind. She was too busy thinking about the man at her side and the boy behind her. She was so preoccupied with these thoughts that she didn't notice the blue Buick parked along the side of the road in front of the main stable until she saw a form emerging out of it, a form she at first took for Jacob before realizing it was a woman, a figure she then took for some crazed media person until she'd seen the disheveled clothes, the scraggly hair, the pale skin and dark eyes of a gaunt wraith, racing out in front of the headlights with both her palms held up to them, telling them to stop.

MADDIE HILL HAD BEEN SITTING in the driver's seat of the Buick with her forehead resting against the steering wheel when she'd seen the headlights approaching in the side-view mirror. She had put the keys in the ignition ten minutes ago, but she had not yet been able to turn them to start the car. She had not yet been able to do this thing she was going to do. *It has to be them*, she thought. *It has to be GB and Jamie.* Who else could it be? The whole place was deserted, the surrounding pastureland and fields so dark and featureless that she'd thought—at first, when they'd pulled off the main road an hour ago and drove along the narrow path between two fence lines—that they were in the wrong place. She had thought this until Max had directed the car on the wide turn around the copse of trees that shielded the property from the road and she had seen the expanse of it opening up before her.

It was huge. Too immense for description. Not just the house but the grounds that surrounded it, the twelve-foot brick wall with the single wrought-iron gate Max had been surprised to find unlocked, the narrow road extending between lampposts toward the far-off mansion. Of course she'd recognized the white-painted sandstone and the Georgian style, columned and centered by portico, a low row of hedges and fountains bracketing the lawn, large trees and a rose garden. And of course she had heard stories of this marvel her father had built, features on television programs about the households of the extravagantly wealthy, stories that had been passed along and reiterated by the journalists and gossip-mongers like Prince Dexter in whose faces she'd occasionally been forced to spit when they showed up on her doorstep in search of a story, in search of anything. She'd stared senselessly over the grounds as darkness fell, Max maneuvering the Buick along the arcing dirt road that led to the house, his eyes predatory over the flat landscape of fenced-in fields—empty, all of them, but for the rare gelding that raised its head to watch them—the windows in all the stables and outbuildings dark, the entire three hundred acres abandoned, though the white walls of the main residence reflected the growing harshness of the stars, the moon.

"Look at it," he said to her after they'd parked behind the largest stable, positioning the Buick between a ditch and a whitewashed fence, adjacent to the road but far enough so as not to be noticeable, the stable blocking the view of the car from the house. "If there was ever any doubt," he said, "if you ever had any reservations about what we're doing, all you have to do is look across that field. Look at it. He built himself a model of the White House on a three-hundred-acre horse ranch. Probably had the exact schematics shipped to the developer, right down to the furnishings in the Oval Office. This is what he built for himself while we wasted away with our ruined lives. Do you hear me, Maddie? Do you hear what I'm saying? If you had any doubt, if you wasted any time feeling like what we're doing is wrong, tell me those doubts are gone. Tell me you're ready now."

The night before, sitting on the toilet in Nebraska, she had heard the door of the motel room unlock and his hard steps across the floor, had heard him settling down right on the other side of the particle board. He'd spoken her name, the same voice and tone he'd used all those years ago in the cabin in Fairbanks when he couldn't sleep, the way he'd keep her awake all night with his bizarre banter. He had slid the plastic baggie containing the marijuana he'd brought under the door, and she had picked it up and looked at it. All shake. Next came a packet of Zigzags. She had already started rolling the joint, her fingers shaking, when he said, "Can I tell you what happened? Can I finish the story I started?"

The other day, he'd stopped with the journey down the Yukon, his arrival at Alice's door to find her standing on the steps. It was August, he was saying now, and she could hear him rising to his feet and pacing across the creaking floor of the motel room. August of '98, just three years ago. They'd been inside, he and Alice, the boy Lynk, now twelve, outside gathering firewood, when they heard something hovering and then descending over the compound. There was no mail delivery scheduled for today, and besides this was a helicopter, not a Cessna.

Maddie closed her eyes and tried to picture it while she finished rolling the joint. Her hands were trembling as she tried to imagine the helicopter touching down on the airstrip two hundred yards away, the two men approaching along the riverbed, one with a federal government patch on his sleeve, Max and Alice on the stoop and Lynk standing off in the field, at the mouth of the woods, looking on with a stack of lumber in his arms. She retrieved her lighter and heard the paper of the joint sizzle as she smoked.

"This your cabin?" said one of the men when they were within fifty feet, but Max didn't answer. Neither did Alice. The men came closer, gave their names and titles, asked again. "This your cabin?"

"It's *my* cabin," Alice said. "Belonged to me and my husband."

The two men looked back and forth between Alice and Max, turned to look at the boy, thirty yards off and still holding the lumber. "You got a deed of any kind?" said the government agent, and when his question received only silence, he went on. "Didn't think so. See, according to our maps, this land belongs to the United States government. Was claimed twenty years ago and set aside as national preserved acreage. So you folks, I'm sorry to say, are living on borrowed time."

And that—Max said, as Maddie leaned her head back against the sink basin and closed her eyes—was when he had stepped forward, uncertain what he was going to say until the instant it came out of his mouth. "I was so angry, Maddie. I could feel it all slipping away, so I said to them, 'Do you know who I am? Do you know who my father is? My father is George Benjamin Hill, the man who brought the pipeline to Alaska, the man who brought oil to Valdez, who ended unemployment and made millions for this state. I'm his son, and you're not going to throw me off this land. I deserve it. It's the least anyone can do for me.'"

Maddie had opened her eyes and was looking at the bathroom door as if she could see through it to her brother, but the two men standing at the foot of the stoop in Alaska were accustomed to such rants. They stuck around for a few more minutes, saying they'd be hearing from them, that they were sorry but this was not the seventeenth century. You couldn't lay claim to land anymore just because you happened to live there. "You'll be hearing from us," they said a final time to Max's parting words, and then the helicopter was up and away, disappearing beyond the trees.

"Is it true?" Alice had asked him later, and he'd sat her down in the cabin and tried to convince her, just as he tried to convince Maddie as she sat there in the bathroom, smoking the joint. But his words were confused. His words no longer made sense now that he'd told her he'd tried to capitalize on their father's name, now that she knew he had tried to take advantage of the status he said he was trying to destroy. They were the words he'd heard all those years ago from Jed Winters, words he'd internalized but that had unraveled and decayed in his mind. It wasn't about being owed, it wasn't about asking what your country could do for you. It was about freedom. It was about the American dream and each generation being better off than the last, each having more land to spread out in and more money and resources with which to enjoy it. It was about coming of age in a place where your dreams were always at least attainable; where you would always at least be left free to pursue what future you sought by a government attuned to your struggles but not greedy for your riches. It wasn't about having everything he wanted. But the government was supposed to never get in your way. If it did, and you knew a way to circumvent it, then it was your right to try. So Max had done just that. He wrote a letter to the Bureau of Land Management, told them who he was, told them who *his father* was, and did that change their opinion on these matters? Did that make them see that he had the right to remain on this land for as long as he damn well pleased?

Two months later the helicopter had touched down again. Max had stepped out of the cabin and along the mud path by the river to meet them, his whole body trembling, hoping against his skepticism for an apology. A reassessment has been made. Instead they'd given him the new updated timeline for his eviction.

"So that's how my story ends," Max had said to her, there in the motel room while Maddie stared at the joint and then dropped it half finished into the toilet. "They gave us one month to get off the land. Alice couldn't do it. She blamed me. Said it was my fault for trying to talk tough, for trying to strong-arm them into letting us stay. It would've taken them years to get around to throwing us off if we'd just laid low, she said. You just don't know when to quit, she said. Did I think they hadn't been out there before? And even Beau—*even Beau!*—who couldn't have a conversation about chicken feed without it becoming a rant against the federal government, even *he* had known when to keep his mouth shut and play along.

"She threw me out, Maddie," he said, his voice beginning to break for the first time. "And yeah," he continued then. "Maybe she was right. Maybe I don't know when to quit. Maybe I got greedy when I thought I deserved to not feel so alone. Maybe I should've spent the rest of my life by myself in that twelve-by-twelve cabin in Circle, Alaska, while he built a mansion modeled on the White House on a three-hundred-acre horse ranch. Maybe I shouldn't—" But here he stopped. His voice had grown gradually to almost a shout but now she heard him crossing the floor again and standing on the other side of the particle board. "Maybe then I could've forgiven myself."

Of course she had understood this for what it was. The thin door between them, his theatrics all bundled up and presented in an attempt to convince her that his resolution was the only one, that the only way they could ever hope to purge the past was to blow a hole in the present. In some part of herself, she knew they'd been headed toward this moment her entire life. For over twenty years her brother had been allowing his anger to build, and now he was ready to burst like a firecracker over the plains. And yet as they made their way across the rest of Nebraska today she had taken apart his story and tried to put it back together. She had tried to decide where her lines were drawn. She had known that she could not do what he wanted her to do, but she did not know what she was going to do about it.

Now she stood in the darkness in the dirt and gravel beneath the black wall of the stable on her father's three-hundred-acre horse ranch with her hands in the pockets of her jeans as he opened the trunk, waiting as he gathered the blankets he'd heaped upon his cargo, telling her that she would have to be the one to help him, that his impatience had won out and, since it was obvious GB and Jamie weren't coming, that they would have to do it themselves. Just like Aspen, he told her. And she stood there watching until she almost accepted it. Then she saw her brother reach into the trunk to remove the shoebox and the reality came washing over her again.

"Max," she said. But he kept digging in the trunk. "This is crazy, Max. It's crazy."

He turned and looked at her for a long moment, his eyes staring from the slot in the ski mask he'd pulled on. For days she had been trying to imagine what his reaction would be, how he would respond if she did this. Now he stared so long that she wanted to look away, but she didn't. When he spoke again his voice was low and harsh.

"Crazy? You're calling *me* crazy? Do you want to know what crazy is? Crazy is having a mistress and two children when you're already married to one woman with two other kids. Crazy is moving your family up to a wild west town on the edge of the tundra for seven years and thinking nothing could possibly go wrong. Crazy is leaving your seventeen-year-old son alone in Alaska and letting your daughter move to Las Vegas and your wife run off to God knows where just so you can get them out of your hair so you can go off chasing some new business venture." But Maddie had closed her eyes and felt it all building up inside her, felt everything that she'd ever wanted to say to her brother come out, and then they were shouting over each other about what crazy was. Crazy was bashing someone's brains out with a piece of rebar. Crazy was deserting your brother for something he'd done when all he was trying to do was save you. Crazy was killing your friend just because you liked his wife and wanted his land. Crazy was becoming a whore and a drug addict just because you were too proud to ask for help. Crazy was writing letters to your siblings to try to convince them that what they needed to do was kill their father. Crazy was being so strung out on junk that you wrote your own letters back saying it was a good idea and could you come along?

And at the end of it they both stood there, Maddie still in her jeans and tank top and coat and he in his black suit and ski mask. They stood furious, each waiting for the other to do something, but Maddie knew that she was done. She was done with him. She had to be. She didn't even have the strength to argue any more. He was her brother; he always would be. But she was not willing to die with him or for him. She was not willing to spend the rest of her life in prison or on the run in the name of an anger she did not feel. It was easy to say that family conquered all, but Maddie knew that it did not apply in this family. Not anymore. The man behind that ski mask—he was not the same person she'd dug for gold nuggets with in the back field of the house in Fairbanks. He was not the boy she'd played hide and seek with in the construction pit across the street from their house in San Bernardino. And he was not the brother who'd come to sit with her in that hospital bed on the worst night of her life, the night she'd stayed awake until dawn wondering how in the world she would ever recover from this, how she could ever look at Max or her mother or herself in the same way again. And yes, perhaps it was her fault for sending those letters to him, even if she didn't remember it. But that didn't mean she didn't have the right to change her mind. That didn't mean he had the right to tell her what she did or didn't want to do.

She tried one more time. "Max," she said. "We don't need to do this. We don't need—"

"No," he said to her. "*You* don't need to do this." He reached into his pocket and threw the car keys at her. They hit her in the chest and fell to the ground. She paused, then leaned forward and picked them up.

"I'm going in there," he said, "and I'm going to do exactly what I told you I was going to do. I don't care if there's anyone in there or not. I'm going to set this thing down on his desk in the Oval Office and set the fuse and get the hell out. That ski chalet was just the first, Maddie. The vacation home in Florida's next. Then the bungalow on the beach at Monterey. I've even heard there's a resort in France. I'm going to destroy them all, the way he destroyed the only thing I held dear in my worthless, shitty life. That little piece of land in the Alaskan wilderness where I wasn't bothering a soul."

"Max," she said again, but he held up his hand to stop her. He was holding the shoebox in one arm and backing slowly away from her.

"But what I want *you* to do is get in that Buick and drive away. And I want you to go anywhere in the world except for back to where you were. Promise me you'll do that, Maddie." He paused and stood for a moment, his body seeming to blend into the arriving darkness, and then he was gone, dressed all in black and barely visible, a living shadow sneaking toward the house by way of a ditch alongside the road, already fifty feet away by the time she understood what he'd said.

She turned and walked to the car, slammed the door and put the keys in the ignition, but then she just sat there. She was thinking of all the times she should have tried to stop this. What if she had smashed the window in the parking lot in Grand Junction and made off with the suitcase? What if she had stepped into the train station instead of back into his car in Denver? But in some way she had never thought it would get this far. She had never thought that he would actually go through with it. And so what was she supposed to do now? Was she supposed to try to be a hero? Was she supposed to run into the house and wrest the shoebox from his grasp? This was no movie, and she was no action star. She could call the police, but they would never arrive in time, and even if they did she knew she could eventually be identified as an accomplice in the Aspen fire and go to prison. She understood his anger, and she had once felt something similar, but she didn't feel it anymore, and she was not going to run into a house to argue with a man with a bomb in the name of a loyalty he had already betrayed.

With her forehead resting against the steering wheel, Maddie Hill reached forward and felt the keys in her right hand. And that was when she saw the headlights in the side-view mirror, saw the car pull off the road and to the right of Buick, as if the driver wanted to get a better look at who was inside. She was out of the door in time to see the man crawling awkwardly from the convertible. It was a Corvette, and he was dressed in a pinstriped baseball uniform. He looked drunk.

"Are you Maddie?" he said.

"Where's Max?" he said.

"I'm here to stop this," he said.

THE SNAKE WAS SEETHING. CLUTCHING a 30.06 bolt-action rifle. He was barefoot and standing next to a sawhorse in a shed on the Mother Mary Ranch, the dog asleep at his feet next to the empty bat bag and the knapsack whose contents had led him here. The weapon gave him strength, conviction. But his body seemed to have become lost, a figure with a firearm in his hands but no history. He had arrived here straight from the womb of his confusion, not lacking in memories but rather a means of interpreting them. He had stolen a car, but then he had not known how to drive it. He had ditched it at a truck stop and begun hitching west, had hitched all day and through the night, going where the drivers happened to be going in a disturbed zigzag across the country, never staying long with one driver because he made them uneasy with his silence, made them change their minds next chance they got. "Think I'm gonna leave you off here, buddy. Gonna have to call it quits on you and your dog 'less you're aimin' to see Lake Superior."

At the truck stops he had checked the maps hanging from push-pins in the lobbies of the service plazas, had perched himself atop picnic tables with the dog resting on the bench seat beneath him and opened up the knapsack, rooted through the stacks of papers and found a map. He'd skimmed through the letters but had grown distracted by the people coming and going. The Snake had lived his entire adult life in the city, a place where a man like him could manage not to stand out, could go about his business in the anonymity it demanded. At the truck stops, it was difficult to blend in. The Snake had watched the eyes on him as he sat on the table with his map and papers spread out around him. To the truck drivers, he hadn't said a word, had found that the best way to make tracks in this country was to keep your mouth shut, to let others think they were making the decisions. He'd take his place in the passenger seat next to the window, a view of the world to which he'd become accustomed, face pressed against the cold glass, the knapsack at his feet, the bat bag snug between his knees and the dog asleep against his leg, the engine of the rig firing up, the bearded driver letting it idle before steering his way out into the open pavement. The Snake pretended to be looking out the side window but would in fact watch the driver in the reflection of the windshield, keeping tabs on his movements, noticing the way they kept looking in his direction. When the truck drivers ducked their heads and tried to look him in the eyes, he turned away.

It had been late morning by the time he'd found the driver on his way to Council Bluffs, well past noon when he'd been dropped off at the gas station just off the interstate, the truck driver leaning out the window to wave at the figure standing in a Columbia sweat suit and a trench coat with a knapsack and a bat bag slung from his shoulders and a brown lab following along beside him. He had been amazed to find such a large settlement so different from New York, where city life surrounded you like a cold, steady rain—here it rose up like something hopeful out of the brown landscape, silver buildings in the far distance and getting smaller as they'd continued on foot, hours walking south along city streets that slowly gave way to suburbs and then very rapidly to corn fields, empty intersections with stop signs and dusty roads leading off in straight lines toward a perfectly perpendicular infinity. He'd worn out his shoes, had left them alongside the road, developed calluses on his feet as the sun lowered against the horizon. It had been no problem to locate the horse ranch, armed as he was with the items he'd discovered in the knapsack, barely decipherable letters on yellowed paper creased with folds and a large roadmap of the city and the lands south of it. There was a star in black marker at the bottom border of the map where a road labeled Billionaire Drive ran off the page, an arrow pointing south that the Snake had followed, two more miles in his bare feet as evening arrived and the world grew cool and vaporous and the Snake knew he'd reached his destination, knew it immediately upon seeing the words engraved across the granite archway over the entrance.

The Mother Mary Ranch

A one-lane driveway had led in from the road, the surrounding fence converging from both sides on the gate. He had stood in bare feet with the sun almost gone behind him and throwing immense shadows across the world, whispering the name he'd been whispering his entire life, the shape of the letters striking him with a new familiarity, making him linger on the word, holding it in his mouth like a stone. In anxious twilight he'd snuck through the unlocked gate and stepped around the turn where the trees ended, leaned against the stone pillars looking across the fields at the darkening mansion, crickets singing, the world otherwise silent. In the shed obscured by trees while the whimpering dog lay down and slept he had set out the bat bag on the dusty sawhorse, removed the rifle and inspected it, opened the bolt and laid three cartridges across the magazine, snapped it shut and sighted along the barrel.

He did not know why he was here exactly, but he knew it had something to do with the house. The grass was wet and cold against his bare feet as he stepped out across the fields. Then he ducked quickly to the ground. Two of the windows high up on the side of the mansion were suddenly illuminated, and the Snake watched as a figure opened one of the windows and looked out across the field toward something in the far-off darkness. The Snake lay flat on the

ground in the damp grass and brought the weapon to a ready position, but the man was gone. He had vanished back into the room,
but the light was still on.

It had begun gradually. Instances in which his eyes seemed to be
seeing two things at once, one reality layered over another and separating, a sensation that brought a feeling not quite like pain behind
his eyes, an agony not completely physical in nature. He'd spent his
early days in New York wandering up and down Broadway, looking
for hustles like he'd pulled off in Fairbanks, but this was a different
universe. He had arrived here largely by accident. At the recruiting
offices in Anchorage they'd told him his eyesight was too poor, and
so he'd gone and gotten arrested instead. Got drunk and got
arrested. When they let him out, he caught the ferry to Seattle. Still
had all that money from the fake IDs burning a hole in his pocket.
Someone in Seattle had told him that New York City was the place
to be. "If I were seventeen years old and without a tie to anybody in
the world"—this dusty, bearded man had said to him in the caboose
of a railroad car—"that's where I'd go. I'd catch a cross-country
train to the Big Apple." So that's what he'd done. And when he'd
gotten there . . . what? It simply wasn't what he'd expected. No one
to talk to. You'd think in a city of however many millions there'd be
plenty of people to talk to. But it seemed the bigger the city, the less
willingness to communicate. And this city was big. Big enough to
make him realize how small he was.

He had not thought he would miss them, but he did. He missed
the twins, and he missed GB. In a way he even missed those nights
in the backyard with his father, arguing over the pipeline. But these
were just emblems for the true nature of his missing. He'd see her
sometimes, would notice her on the opposite side of the street, her
face looking across the traffic and the sea of pedestrians to gaze

directly into his eyes. He'd turn and follow her, would think he saw her disappearing around a corner, but when he got there it was just an empty alley. He would remember the way she'd once run her hands through his hair. The sensations in his head grew stronger, more frequent. Sometimes, he would close his eyes and try to calm them, like walking through a giant house closing all the doors that seemed to have blown open in a raging wind and were now swinging back and forth on their hinges. If he was able to concentrate and slowly shut each of the doors, he could settle down for a moment in the resulting calmness. But then another would open, far off on the other side of this strange house with its endless corridors, and he would set out in search of it. People began to say odd things to him, people passing him in the street and looking him in the eyes and saying the most unusual things. That they knew what he was up to. That they had their eyes on him. He would find places to crash wherever he could, with people he met at bars. He had worked at a restaurant for a very short period of time, but then one of the waitresses started spreading rumors about him, and they had fired him. He had followed her home and she had called the cops.

It became harder to meet people. They all seemed to know things about him, though he didn't know them. One night he thought he saw her and had chased her into the park, asking her why she was running from him, but a jogger tackled him and someone called the cops. He'd begun waking up in police stations, in hospitals. No recollection of how he'd gotten there and no answers to the questions they were asking him. The holding cells with the noisy belligerent cops and frightening fellow inmates were bad. But the hospitals were worse. The pills had no taste until after he'd taken them, when a bitter dryness would crawl slowly up his throat and spread, would make his mouth feel like chalk and then spread across his sinuses and then to his eyes, clouding his vision with a veil of dry fog. His arms would begin to spasm and then they would itch. He would itch all over. Then came the rashes. But worst of all was what the medicine did to the house, went around closing all the doors and then sealing them up as if they'd never been there to begin with, the walls pulsing and becoming featureless and then closing in until his mind was not a house at all but just a room. A room with no windows and no exit, no floor and no ceiling and no walls either, just him. Just his body imprisoned in a world so constricted he couldn't move. He couldn't even think.

It was the missions that gave his life a sense of purpose. It was his secret that no else knew. The people who watched him walking along the streets and pointed and laughed could point and laugh all they wanted, because they did not know what he was really up to. They did not know that he was a soldier. They did not know that he had given his life over to the service of the United States government, that he was doing all of this to protect them. Those moments when he'd discover the discarded duffel on the marble wall behind the Maine Monument at Merchant's Gate, when he would descend to the pizza shop on 46th and Ninth for his slice of sausage, when he'd step along the puddled paths of the Dene with his contact in the suit coat, these were the moments that offered him a remedy to what he recognized, even when he was in the grip of it, as a sort of loneliness of the soul.

That was what this past week had been for the Snake. From the moment he'd seen the light in his window on the fifth floor, had climbed the steps and seen the man who looked like his brother and may well have been, had been whisked from the city and heard the tremendous sound and turned to see the tallest towers in flames, had been driven on roads crowded with vehicles in a postapocalyptic crawl across a landscape that moved from concrete and glass to swampland and suburb to mountain and pasture, had been sat down in the living room of a woman who looked like someone he remembered but spoke only with silence and handed him a phone on the other end of which was a boy whispering to him what he had to do and why . . . well, all of this had been leading somewhere, hadn't it? It had been leading here, to this moment. The moment the Snake had been waiting for all of his life.

The lights still pulsed high up on the side of the mansion. But now a dark shape moved across one of the windows. The figure was looking out again, dressed all in black, and for a moment the Snake's face calmed with the memory of her. For a moment, he could remember her coming to him in that cold room in the bunker beneath the heart of the country, could see her rappelling across the rooftops of a dacha in Russia. But this was not her. This was not the woman he'd hoped this mission would lead him to. This was not his mother at all. This was not what he'd been running toward; it was what he'd been running from. The Snake stood in the wet grass and raised the rifle. He sighted along the barrel and pulled the trigger.

GB HILL FELT LIKE A ghost.

He was lying on his back in the damp field, looking up at the slowly arriving stars, when he heard the rifle blast echo across the ranch.

He had barely been able to see the Buick parked along the side of the road in the shadow of the stable, but he had known it had to be them. The plates were Nevada; the car was a piece of shit. Not the sort of thing he could see his father driving. He had thought at first it was empty, but then as he'd pulled around to the right side of the car he had seen the door open and the woman get out, her face illuminated in the glow of the headlights that he had left on, the car still running. Where's Max, he had said to her. I'm here to stop this. And her answer had been so matter-of-fact ("He's in the house. With his bomb.") that it had taken a moment for GB to register the words. A bomb. There had never been any mention of a bomb. There had been endless dissections of anger, onslaughts of condemnation and fault-finding, lengthy commiserations and spewing of blame and fury. And yes, GB had gone along with it. He was as grief-stricken as Max was furious, or at least he'd thought he was. He blamed his father for all of his shortcomings and failures just like Max did, and he had known that there were perhaps violent intentions behind this. And yes, perhaps he had encouraged them. Perhaps he had even said he was willing to take part in them. But a bomb? And so although he had set off at a run across the fields and toward the house when the woman he would never have recognized told him what was happening, he had within moments slowed to a jog, and within moments of that was walking, and within moments of that he had paused in the middle of the field, looking up toward the mansion and knowing that somewhere in there was his half brother, that this man who had existed for him these past months merely as a voice in his head, as an endless barrage of words scrawled on a page, was now armed with a shoebox that was the unconscionable conclusion to this thing they'd created and pursued, this plan that GB knew he was partly to blame for, perhaps entirely to blame for, though he could not believe that he had played a role in it, could not believe now what his grief had led him to do. He had leaned forward with his hands on his knees, whispering, "I'm sorry . . . I'm so sorry . . ." Because he knew that he should step across that field and do what he'd intended to do ever since he'd felt his complicity pouring over him in the bar of the night before. But he knew also that he couldn't. He was too afraid.

When he'd seen the headlights, he had thought at first it might be the police. When he'd turned to see Maddie rushing out into the road next to stable, had seen the BMW slowing to a stop, the driver's door opening up, he had stepped forward and waited—had waited to witness his father emerging from the vehicle. But it was not his father. It was a young woman. He could see this in the splay of light that reflected off the back of the blue Buick. And then climbing out of the backseat was a boy no older than four or five, holding something in his hands and wearing a striped T-shirt. He did not know these people, and their presence here had sent him stumbling backwards, had made him fall over into the high grass looking straight up at the sky, and it was at that moment that he'd heard it: the sound he at first mistook for the shoebox, only to realize a moment later—after he had crawled to his feet, after he had scanned the field in the darkness that was like fine charcoal dust—that it was something even worse.

His brother was little more than a shadow, a tiny form he could have covered with one hand, a small figure seeming to tremble in the echo of the gunshot, looking down then at the weapon, which slipped from his grasp and disappeared into the shadows, and GB felt a great comprehending terror rising up inside him, knew even before his brother began to move what was going to happen next.

"*Jamie?*"

His brother turned, stood frozen for a moment, a hundred yards away and searching the darkness. Then he was gone, racing across the fields toward the mansion.

"*Jamie!*"

GB felt his baseball spikes dig into the grass, felt them propelling him across the uneven field in a diagonal path. He knew already there was no way he could catch his brother, even though he ran with a staggering gait, stumbling and hopping and off balance. When GB arrived at the door of the mansion it was wide open, flung aside by Jamie as he'd entered and raced along the polished corridors with wall-hung portraits, past the French doors looking in on period-decorated lounges, the hallway whose pine boards were illuminated by the vacant glow of the moon. GB's shouts echoed up the grand sweeping staircase that embraced the far end of the entrance hall in a sweeping half circle, his spikes chipping into the wood and making him stumble, crying out his brother's name as he raced along the upstairs hallway in search of the window he'd seen lit up on the side of building, its glass shattered by the bullet that had blown through it.

GB knew now that he really was a ghost. That something truly had been dead inside him all along. Not literally—he was still flesh and bone and could sense and hurt and cry. He could feel the ache in his limbs and the catch in his heart and the gasp of his breath. He could taste the phlegm that had risen in his throat from the running and could smell the perspiration on his body. Being a ghost was not about being of or not of this world. Not really. It was simply about being too scared to move on to whatever was next. It meant focusing too hard on the wrong thing. It meant haunting the rooms and realms to which you'd become devoted merely because to move beyond them took an act of courage, an act of faith.

He knew now that he'd been wrong when he'd stood that Sunday morning one week ago in front of the FOR SALE sign on the front lawn of his and Tammy's dream home thinking that these fragments of his life were all he had left. They were not all he had left.

He should have known and understood this countless times during the week that had passed: should have understood it when he slammed shut the trunk on that forgotten shelf of land above the Hudson River and climbed back up into the city; should have understood it when he heard his brother's approach in the room on the fifth floor of the halfway house in Hell's Kitchen and had turned to see him there; should have understood it in the hotel room in Pennsylvania, or when he'd rushed out of the restaurant in Ohio, thinking he'd lost Jamie once and for all, only to find him sitting in the passenger seat with his daughter's dog, ready to go wherever GB led him. He should have understood it at any one of these moments. A part of him had understood it. But in each of these instants of possibility he had seen also something that terrified him, the acceptance of a new life with new priorities and obligations that meant leaving others behind, the closing of a door when it was so much easier to linger there on the threshold, watching the sunlight play across the floor of any empty room, looking in at the replayed imaginings of something that was already gone.

That night at Yankee Stadium, when he'd seen his brother climbing up on the roof of the dugout, hopping down on to the warning track, and running across the infield, he had not been surprised. He had not been angry either. Not at first. The anger had come later, but what he had felt in that moment, initially, was a painful sadness. Not for him or his baseball career, but for Jamie and what the world had done to him. And now, as he turned the final corner in the chaos of his father's majestic, doomed mansion, as he saw his brother up ahead, standing at the open door looking in at the room with the light slanting to fall across his face, and as he ran those final twenty feet that separated them, he wished he could be back in that moment. He wished that he was back on that emerald field beneath floodlights in his one moment of triumph, his one moment of achievement, watching his brother run toward him. He wished that he could open his arms and let his brother run into them so that he could tell him it was fine. That everything would be fine.

When he arrived at the door, they stood there together for an instant, comprehending what they were facing, the thing that lay sprawled across the ornate rug in a crimson circle of blood spreading outward, the room strewn with broken glass and the debris from the ceiling where the bullet had lodged itself, the immense mahogany desk and, atop it, a shoebox. A duct-taped shoebox.

GB turned to Jamie, who looked back at him with confusion, something like fear flashing in his eyes behind the thick lenses of his glasses. For a moment, GB felt the thing he'd meant to do escaping, the way it always escaped. But there was no more time for misunderstandings. So he wrapped his arms as tightly as he could around his little brother.

4

Dust

RECENTLY, WE GATHERED: A SINGLE mother, a retired showgirl, a house-wife, and her adult daughter. We sat on the raised back deck of a bungalow-style home on a dead-end street in a college town with autumn falling all around. Just the four of us now, and a five-year-old boy diving among leaf piles in the yard. And Dat and David, home for the weekend, inside watching football. And a thirteen-year-old chocolate lab.

Two years had passed since that night the news vans returned, if briefly, to the Mother Mary Ranch outside Omaha. Two years since they'd lined up beyond the outer fence and the yellow police tape, spectral figures in the distance, cameramen with telephoto lenses and blonde reporters with microphones, sitting on folding chairs on the roof racks, peering through the fog and smoke and ash in search of one final news clip. Two years since the night fire trucks and ambulances descended upon those three hundred acres, lights and sirens blaring, dust storms along the narrow roads of the ranch and the horses in the stables in an uproar, two of them escaping and racing off before the rest could be led, snorting and bellow-ing, out into the adjacent fields. The thick hoses attached to the fire trucks were strewn along the gravel and draped over the white-washed fences; the rush of the heavy water jetting toward the flames drowned out the shouts while the EMTs, equipped with resuscitation equipment, dressed in bright orange field jackets, combed the premises. The first three survivors were found beneath the hay-loading window of the main stable, cowered by the radiating heat, two women and a three-year-old boy, his mother holding him in her arms while he fought to escape, fought for the chance to see the amazing vision of the mansion he called home burning to the ground. And yet the search had continued as the firefighters fought long into the night against the inevitable, rushing to safety when the portico on the south wall collapsed, releasing a cloud of hot wind that scorched the air and made the garage roof smolder (two hoses brought back to drench it before the fire could spread). Still the hunt for survivors continued through the dawn, when a gray sun rose beyond the black noxious atmosphere and turned the world eclipse colors; it continued even then because this little trio of survivors, this unremarkable group found in the shadow of a stable one hundred yards from what remained of the main house—which, in the revealing gloom of morning, was seen to be little more than frame and blackened post—was not at all what they'd come for, would be a fine story but not *the* story. For they'd arrived—all of them: the EMTs and the media still standing on the distant vans, drinking coffee and eating donuts now, even the fire fighters who crouched, exhausted, around their trucks in the breezy black morning—anticipating this to be the grand funeral pyre of one George Benjamin Hill, had expected to spend days digging through the rubble in search of, and eventually finding, the remains of the once-wealthiest man in the country—or to *never* find him, and what a mystery that might cause!—not knowing that instead of a dramatic conflagration to bring it all suddenly to the ground there would be grand jury indictments, instead of the quick hand of fate there would be the slow march of justice, there would be delays and appeals and jury selection and intricate details argued in

five-thousand-page briefs and—at last—when all these prelimi-
nary matters had been taken care of, when the entire country had
waited for the moment when he went on trial and then nearly forgotten his name, there would be a final headline eradicating it all,
one headline to remind everyone that he was just another old man.

That day at the Mother Mary Ranch—as the police and the fire
fighters and a team of volunteers combed the wreckage, finding
the bodies of what seemed to be three separate human beings—
the EMTs wrapped the survivors in blankets, gave the boy a lolly-
pop and the women Excedrin . . . and it was not until then, just
when they were getting ready to leave the scene, that one of them,
responding to something the little boy had said—something about
Grandpa—had turned toward the BMW (ignored, up until now, for
reasons no one could explain) and noticed that its windshield wipers were on, sweeping away the storm of soot still settling over the
ranch. It was not until that moment that one of them came over to
the vehicle with its tinted glass and black exterior and opened the
door. It was not until then that they found the man they'd expected
to discover at the heart of this tragedy, seated in the passenger
seat, a strange expression twisting his face. Crying.

No. He was laughing.

BY THE TIME WE—THE SURVIVORS—gathered on Annabelle's back porch
two years later, the story of that Saturday night into Sunday morning had become less like an ending than a beginning. We'd long since
put together the details of how it had come to take place, how the
plan (if it could be called such) had gone from confused conception to
haphazard execution. It had been Max's idea, initially. He had

followed his older brother's baseball career though this had meant a subscription to *Baseball America* that often arrived a full month late. When he'd heard, through a newspaper report he'd found, of all places, on the internet—through which he combed on a semi-annual basis in search of details about us by means of the donated desktops in the public library in Fairbanks, just a few blocks away from the hotel where he'd rented a room on a monthly basis, a dour residence where he'd stewed during the two years that had passed since the incident with the helicopter—when he'd learned through these most unlikely means about the disappearance of GB's daughter, he'd known it was time to reach out, to offer comfort and sympathy and an airing of grievances that, with any luck, would lead to a confession of feelings not so different from his own.

It had worked, though not at first. The pieces that survive of their correspondence—notebooks in the glove box of the Buick and a handful of letters, salvaged from a knapsack discovered in the high grass behind one of the retired sheds in a lost corner of the horse ranch, guarded only by the feeble old chocolate lab who came limping out of the darkness—show two men, one middle aged and one rapidly approaching it, reluctant to make a move toward closure. They tell each other their stories, try to convey something like warmth or wisdom, something like comfort for one another. And yet the tone is inconsistent. The record is incomplete. Some letters seem to be missing, pieces of their correspondence unaccounted for, seemingly important junctions in which thresholds were reached, assessed, and—somewhere in the lonely rooms of their lives—crossed. Maybe in these missing letters they fought and argued, maybe they agreed, for a time, to disagree. There must have been periods when even they recognized—through the mounting conviction of their anger and grief—the futility of what they were planning to do, the illogic of what they hoped to accomplish. And if they had been together—if they had sat in a room talking these things out rather than nurturing with solitude the vacant allure of these written words—could they have ever done it? Would they ever have achieved the initiative of turning these words into deeds?

We attended and helped plan their funerals, of course. We flew to Alaska and rented a ride from a bush pilot. We rode high above that endless stretch of wilderness, tried to imagine all the hours he had spent in that reclusive perch at fifteen thousand feet, the only signs of humanity his own shadow on the treetops. We went to Circle and tried to find the twelve-by-twelve cabin where he'd lived in a brief state of contentment before he'd found that package with Alice Bates's name on it. And we tried to find Alice Bates herself, but it could have taken months, and we weren't sure we wanted to hear what she might have to say. We stopped in Fairbanks, and we drove out to the old road that led to the narrow dirt driveway that led up a hill and around a copse of trees to the place where that giant field opened up and where that old cabin had once sat, but the road had been widened and the dirt driveway was now paved, and the house that looked down at us was no longer that ramshackle place some of us remembered but a pristine A-frame with one wall made all of glass.

We flew to Florida and met Tammy Pisarczek, who wore sunglasses but did not wear black at that funeral attended mostly by old ballplayers, former teammates and managers, a few of them now famous, all of them silent and reverent at the graveside where they set GB down next to his daughter. She invited us back to the condo where she lives with her fiancé, Marc, and we sat on the balcony above the water while she showed us pictures of Emma and we witnessed the fresh bloom of her grief. She had barely seen him in the year that passed between their separation and his death, and when she had he'd been unrecognizable and haggard. He was a mess, she told us, but then so was she. And for a short time they had lived in that mess together, had screamed and loved and fought and hoped, and in spite of himself he had been one of the reasons that she was still here, that she was still carrying on, was still picking up the pieces.

And we were there in New York, too. At the most heavily attended of the three because almost everyone from Rogers House was there. A woman named Clementina approached us afterwards, asked us if we'd come back with her. She led us up the four flights of stairs, down the long hallway to the room at the far end, the last door on the right. We stood in the room he'd called home for two decades, stood beneath the pull cord of the dull ceiling lamp looking at the single file cabinet filled with pages of nothing we could interpret, the narrow mattress and the single window and the rest of the room just emptiness, yet filled somehow with the answerless question of his predicament. Clementina walked over to the window, looked down. "There used to be a garden down there," she said, staring through the glass. And on her face we could see the optimism that they practiced as a way of life here.

Her eyes when they returned to us were damp and full. "He used to sit down in that garden for hours," she said. Then she shook her head. It seemed there was more she wanted to say, something about him that she needed us to hear, some anecdote or metaphor about that garden that would help us understand. But the words or the sentiment wouldn't come. She swallowed something heavy and significant. Shook her head again. Restored her face to that resilient smile and led us all back downstairs.

In the end, we found out about him the same way everyone else did. From the headlines.

Disgraced Billionaire George Benjamin Hill Posts Bond
Whereabouts Unknown

Annabelle has kept them, has maintained a history of the whole ordeal, though she can't say why. Her compulsion is inexplicable but irresistible, resulting in a drawer upstairs in a closet filled with messy folded stacks of news clippings, photos, the accumulated details of decades crammed into a small space as if in an attempt to compact it, to condense it and make it somehow easier to comprehend. From his wayward days in the aftermath of the pipeline's completion to his arrival at the top floor of the steel-and-glass structure that housed the company that briefly played the world like a parlor game, from the first inklings of a financial disaster all the way through to his final evening, even down to the lengthy exposé published in one of the less reputable tabloids under the byline of Prince Dexter, she has kept remnants of it all. That day we sat together on her back porch not long ago, she finally told us about it, waited until the football game had begun and Jake was down in the yard with the dog and distracted—then she leaned forward and took us all in confidence, told us she wanted to show us something. A short time later, she returned with an armful of stacked shoeboxes, spilled it all out on the patio table where it rested in disorganized piles for the remainder of the day, one or another of us periodically picking up a random article and leafing through it, not really reading but unable to deny our hands this tactile perusal of the past, though we all have different perspectives: some with guilt, some with anger, some ashamed, all to some degree ready to move on. Because how are you supposed to feel in the aftermath of such an event? Are you supposed to faint or flail about and carry on like women do in books and movies, or are you supposed to do what women have *actually* been doing for thousands of years?

An early Saturday afternoon. The shouts of the football game across town and a high battalion of clouds marching across the sky, the four of us sitting together and talking about whatever was left to talk about now that the various particulars and obligations had been worked out, now that the three hundred acres were officially gone, now that the company had been purchased in its entirety for seven million dollars by a British bank and divided into a dozen meaningless subsidiaries, now that all the assets and inheritance had been liquidated and his name and legacy that had meant so much to him had been left empty save the shame of being associated with the company now and forever emblematic of American greed run amok, the four of us sat together trying to decide what it all meant and instead found only that we each just wanted to be left alone to come to our own conclusions.

Annabelle, of all people, expressed an interest in going to see his grave some time—we know it is somewhere near Monterey, and could possibly find out more from the lawyers—suggesting an attempt at closure regarding the man whom she remembers from a few restless seasons in San Berdoo and near a decade in Fairbanks, Alaska. A trip to see him—or to come as close to it as is possible—for the first time since she escaped him over twenty years ago.

"That's still how I think of it," she says, looking at the rest of us one at a time. "An escape."

Dat stands behind her, having refilled the lemonade pitcher and brought it out to us. He places a hand on her shoulder, seems to be examining from a distance the collection of history arrayed on the table like a disassembled puzzle. She places her hand briefly upon his and pats it. Then he turns and walks back into the house.

Amelia tells Annabelle she should come visit. "After Julia and I are settled in California." A look of anticipation and excitement shared between the two of them. "Or wherever we end up," Julia says cryptically. Annabelle's eyes drift toward the sky. She still cannot believe that the two of them are going through with this, that Julia has quit her job in Chicago in favor of a destination-less drive west, headed for Los Angeles, San Francisco, wherever—headed toward a mysterious future with Amelia and her son, following whatever leads and plotlines they can unearth along the way.

"Oh, don't roll your eyes, Mother," says Julia. She's made very clear to her mother that this is not a spontaneous thing, that these thoughts of leaving it all behind and starting anew have been on her mind for years. They go off on a tangent, bickering the way mothers and daughters do, while the rest of us watch. Across town, we hear the football stadium rise up with a distant enthusiasm, and then seconds later we hear Dat and David reacting to the same event as it appears on their television screen, a sound that sends Jake rushing up the yard and through the clattering back screen door to see.

In some respects, we've come a long way in these two years. In some respects, we've become like a family, or maybe a new translation of that word, a new iteration more flexible and mutable. We've come a long way, but then how could you not when your lives together began with three funerals and then—just when the strangeness and sadness of it was beginning to dissipate—a fourth death. When joined by such circumstances, how could you not come a long way? We don't feel the same way about it. We have different perspectives. But we try our best to understand each other. We have to.

FORMER E-STAR HEAD, GEORGE BENJAMIN HILL, 71,
FOUND DEAD IN MONTEREY BEACH HOUSE

When Annabelle pulls out the lighter, we think it's to light the candles. The day is fading, the football game long over but merely replaced by another one, minus a rooting interest but still preferable, for the boys, to this endless outdoor conversation, this relentless rehashing and contextualizing. We think she's just lighting the citronella candles until she starts to fit everything back into the shoeboxes, the articles and the photos. When the shoeboxes are full, we each take one, carrying it in both hands like an offering. We each dump our share of the burden onto the seldom-used firepit at the rear of the yard, and then Annabelle leans forward with the lighter, while the rest of us step back and watch her do it.

———

MY ROOM IS AT THE back of the house, next to the room in which Julia Nguyen grew up, a small corner room with slanted eaves and one narrow window looking down on the yard and, beyond the pale wooden fence, the low suburban skyline of this college town, the rows of little houses running alongside the elms toward the brick rooflines of the academic buildings. It's above the kitchen, and so often during the late afternoons as the daylight fades and deep shades overtake the world, I can hear them down there. My mother and her second husband, their voices the low murmurs of old married couples, asking how come they're out of milk, have you talked to David or Julia lately?

I've always dreamed of a place like this, have always imagined a view such as this one, that encompasses such a spectrum of dream and possibility, of knowledge and learning, of careers full of success and pride, of such fine places for relaxing as on quads and in libraries and lunch halls, friendships formed and strengthened over four years and teary departures full of hope and nostalgia for a little town in the Midwest from which lives spiral out toward unknown second acts. I've always dreamed of a place and a view that inspired such memories and worldliness yet offered in its distance some seclusion and privacy. When the sun starts to set, throwing gold brilliance upon the top layer of all I see, I turn from the window, step out into the creaking hallway, pad along the weathered runner with my hand on the railing, the sounds and smells of the dinner that Annabelle, my mother, is preparing downstairs wafting up.

Some days, she's told me, it's like seeing a ghost. She sees me moving from bedroom to bathroom, hears me on the stairs and watches my body appearing out of the shadows, and it makes her heart stop, the aged specter of the young girl she once knew stalking her in ghostly form. But in the end it's just me. Her forty-three-year-old daughter who seems to have moved in. For good? Who can say? But she must understand that I seem to feel content here, something that I've been surprised by as well, surprised by the comfort I've found in this cluttered house with my mother and her second husband, surprised by my unwillingness to move back west and by the fact that I'm actually out looking for a job some days, to which Dat offers reassurance by telling me it can be tough this time of year when the students are in town. A man for whom I once wished nothing better than the loss of every cent on the gaming floors now offering me encouragement, not to mention a place to stay.

One of these days, I'll come home and tell them that I've found something, that someone has agreed to hire me. And then we'll have to face it for real. Then she'll know for sure that her forty-three-year-old daughter has moved in with her, and we'll be able to face together the fact of what we are: two women living calm, boring, redemptive lives in a college town in Michigan. We'll go out shopping and go to dinner together. We'll sort the mail on the kitchen table, provided I ever bother to get mine forwarded. We'll settle in and maybe watch some TV, maybe take trips together. Mom says she's always wanted to see Italy.

Sometimes, alone in the house, or taking little walks down toward the river, I think back to those five days I spent with my brother, five days immersed in his rage and the paralysis it created in me. I think about what I might've said and how a stronger person might have made a difference. I try to think of ways I might've stopped him or made him reconsider. But then I think about the person I was then and the person I am now. Two years clean and sober. I think about how other versions of myself—the girl I was in Alaska, the woman I became in Vegas—might have been in that house with him, with all of them. And then I think maybe that's why I was there. So I could see that car approaching along the driveway and run out in front of it before it could get any closer to that mansion and what was inside it. If I had followed my instinct in Denver and fled back to Vegas, if I had bought a train ticket instead of getting back in the Buick with him, would I still be here today? Would Amelia and Jake?

And then, inevitably, I think of *him*. I try to picture him as he moves about that beach house in Monterey, windows open to a breeze and the sound of the surf, his attendants with whom he has come here not around, having stepped out to buy them all some late dinner, or bottles of wine—for reports indicated that he was alone when his death took place, that they had returned at some time just after midnight to find him lying in the bed, on his back, calm and composed, hands joined on his chest. Standing on the riverbank, I try to imagine what might go through his muddled mind as he steps around that airy beach house; if he thinks at all about what he might say, if he could say anything, to any or all of us. I wonder, as I watch him turn out the light in the living room, carry his tumbler over to the kitchen and place it in the sink, step in his robe back along the hallway to the bedroom, to what extent, even now, he allows himself to realize all he has achieved and all he has ruined. As he lies back on the bed—hands joined over his chest as he looks out the French door leading to the deck and down a few wooden steps to the beach and the tide a hundred feet away—I wonder if he hears the front door opening, his handlers searching for him, if any of these things register. If, in his confused state, he thinks for a moment it might be one of us. I wonder if he lives to hear them coming through the door and into the bedroom, if he hears them saying his name. Or if he has by this point left his body, is watching now from afar, from the ceiling, or from the wind-tossed air above the ocean, watching not for their reaction, but to see how the whole ceremony is coming off. Whether or not the moment seems worthy.

I place my hand upon the blown glass doorknob of what is now my bedroom in my mother's home. It opens with a whine, though I try to do it softly. I step into the dark room. I sit on the bed and think about views and reality, the little lairs where children grow to become human beings. I think about lives and dreams, and what happens when you stop trying to live with a capital L. I try to decide if it's a blessing or just another compromise to settle for nothing more than existing.

———

"It BEGINS WITH A DREAM," Amelia says to her five-year-old son, their eyes meeting in the rear-view mirror. He's seated in the back seat, belt buckled, playing his handheld video game while the chocolate lab they call California rests its gray face in his lap.

"A dream and a tank of gas," says Julia from the passenger seat. They smirk at each other. It's their attitudes that will make them successful.

"I don't know what it is we're gonna find out here," Amelia continues, ostensibly speaking to her son, though he seems otherwise engrossed and Julia hangs on her every word. "But I promise it's gonna be something worth finding." They turn up the music, sing along with songs both current and old, sing with hope and with irony, with laughter and an irreverent sort of sincerity. Amelia turns down the radio and tells a story of her wayward youth while Julia rolls down the window to the let the wind toss her hair. It's a story perhaps unsuitable for a five-year-old, but Amelia has vowed that above all she will be communicative, will not visit upon her son the sins of her own parents, the quiet they leveled upon any act of individuality, the stern looks of disapproval. She will be friends with her son in the same honest and equal way that she is friends with Julia, will be able to talk with him about anything, will kill early on any sense of discomfort and awkwardness, will allow him to feel like he can come to her with any concern, problem—anything—and expect her to treat him not as a subordinate but as a human being, a beloved friend, a trusted confidante. She thinks it is the old silence of her parents' way that has caused all the trouble she's seen. She and Julia have spoken of it often: the outdated methods of child-rearing, left over from the days when your kids existed mostly to be your farmhands and only half of them survived anyway. She has vowed that this will not be the way with her Jakey. They'll go to the beach together, all three of them. She'll look so young that people will mistake her for his sister. They'll enjoy each other's company and also their private bond, the bond of a mother and a son uncomplicated by the existence of a father. When he's old enough to ask, she'll tell him he doesn't exist. That he never did. "You're an immaculate conception," she'll tell her Jakey. "You're the most perfect child in the world."

When the sun goes down they find a Day's Inn just off the interstate. It's not the most attractive place, but they lie down on the bed with a bottle of wine and turn on the television to watch their favorite shows; it's a Thursday night, must-see TV night, her blue-eyed boy next to her and Julia on the other bed, playing on her laptop and laughing loudly but distractedly at the shows. Around eleven, when Jake has dozed off, sleeping with his mouth open the way his father used to, they go outside for their only cigarettes of the day. They are quitting together, have almost managed it, have cut down to just one measly ciggy a day each.

How it calms her! It never fails to. Julia sits down in the grass while Amelia walks slowly out into the cool evening of the great plains, stands on the verge of somebody's corn field, listening. Opening up her senses. If someone saw her, no doubt she'd be in trouble. No doubt they'd give her some Smoky the Bear line. In America, you're always trespassing on somebody's shit. But she's not bothering anyone. She's a young girl—she's not even twenty-four yet! On her way across the country to a better life. The one she's seen on TV. She may not be a college graduate, she may not have made it to Swarthmore yet and may never end up going, but she's seen enough that she knows where she's headed. Knows what it takes. She's street smart. She may not have a diploma but she has ambition and a five-year-old son to keep her honest and a best friend to keep her smiling. Out West nobody will know her, and there'll be plenty of room for one more young girl yearning, burning to make it in the world. To fix however many generations of screw-ups by men. To begin again with a new emphasis. A woman's touch.

It's a start.

Acknowledgments

Thanks to my agent, Matthew DiGangi, my editors, Maxim Brown and Cal Barksdale, and the rest of the team at Arcade and Skyhorse for helping to bring this book into the world. Thanks also to my friends and fellow writers at Debut Authors '19 and Authors '18 for sharing the journey and providing advice and encouragement. Kathleen Rooney and Martin Seay offered early and enthusiastic support for this novel, and for that I owe them a tremendous debt of gratitude. My heartfelt thanks also to Chip Cheek, Laura van den Berg, James Scott, Kelly J. Ford, and Kaitlyn Andrews-Rice—and others I can't name yet at the time of this writing—for their kind words and generosity. For long friendships and help along the way, I'm grateful to Evan Speice, David Lubert, Pepe Abola, Shannon Derby, Katherine Covintree, Robert Arnold, and Melanie Ramsey. Most of all, thanks and lots of love to my family, all the Millers and Charlesworths et al., but especially my sister, who kept the faith when I was at my worst; my father, who bears no similarity to the eponymous patriarch of this novel; and my mother, whose nightly readings from *The Once and Future King* in my sister's bedroom a million years ago started all of this.